OBJECT OF DESIRE

Created in Rome under the Caesars, passing through the hands of saints and sinners, kings and courtesans, lovers of beauty and lovers of power, the famous Winchcombe Chalice had miraculously survived intact the turmoils and terrors of the centuries.

But never in its long history had this masterwork been surrounded by such intrigue and violence as in the amoral, avaricious 1980s . . . as an idealistic American archeologist, a mysterious Italian countess, a guilt-tortured English lord and a beautiful Manhattan career woman joined the cream of the art world and the scum of its underside in a whirlpool that threatened to fill the golden Chalice with sacrificial blood. . . .

AUCTION!

Big Bestsellers from SIGNET

AUCTION!

A Novel by

Tom Murphy

A SIGNET BOOK

NEW AMERICAN LIBRARY

TIMES MIRROR

Publisher's Note

This novel is a work of fiction. Names, characters, places, and incidents are either the product of the author's imagination or are used fictitiously, and any resemblance to actual persons, living or dead, events, or locales is entirely coincidental.

Copyright © 1980 by Tom Murphy

Ⓞ

SIGNET TRADEMARK REG. U.S. PAT. OFF. AND FOREIGN COUNTRIES
REGISTERED TRADEMARK—MARCA REGISTRADA
HECHO EN CHICAGO, U.S.A.

SIGNET, SIGNET CLASSICS, MENTOR, PLUME, MERIDIAN AND NAL BOOKS are published by The New American Library, Inc., 1633 Broadway, New York, New York 10019

First Printing, November, 1980

1 2 3 4 5 6 7 8 9

PRINTED IN THE UNITED STATES OF AMERICA

This book is for the Hartmanns:
Peter, Audrey, Karin, Christianne, and Anton,
with love.

I would like to thank Barbara Deisroth, vice-president of Sotheby Parke Bernet, for her witty, perceptive, and extremely well-informed advice in helping me research the background of this book.

Prologue

Felix Dupre walked down the white limestone front steps of his house, turned to the left, paused, looked up at the library window and waved at his wife. He smiled, wishing she could come with him.

Damned nuisance. Still, he had to go to the dinner party at the Bradys'. And Minnie had to go to her committee meeting: the Children's Relief Fund was largely Minnie Dupre's creation and she gave it priority over social pleasures. Well. It would be good to see Sam Brady and Edna. And their garden in Pound Ridge was famous. It should be at its peak just now.

Felix walked to the corner of Madison Avenue. The garage was just two blocks away, as close as you could get in this part of town.

The Jaguar was waiting.

It was a good thing, Felix reflected, that his life was a busy one, crammed with more invitations than he could accept, humming with plans and projects.

It was almost enough to make him forget the letter he had written to Jeff this morning, signed and sealed and hand carried to the safety-deposit box at the bank.

Felix turned the ignition key. Twelve cylinders pulsated into action.

The Jaguar emerged into the bright August sunshine, purring. Felix loved fine cars. The Jag was his special pet, resonant with a depth of luxury that had almost vanished from the cookie-cutter world of car building. The swirling grain of the walnut-burl veneers comforted Felix. The supple leather of the seats was an assurance that somewhere, at least, there were craftsmen who still cared enough to do a thing right.

Felix thought of his nephew and smiled. Only last week someone at the Harvard Club had mentioned one of Jeff's articles, hardly suspecting what pleasure the praise brought to Felix. Felix and Minnie had to rely on hearing about Jeff's success from other sources, because they rarely heard about it from him. Childless, Felix and Minnie had raised Jeff from the age of eleven, after both his parents had died, one after

1

the other, in the same terrible year. Felix was prouder of Jeff Dupre than of anything else in his life, even the House of Dupre, long considered the finest of New York's privately owned auction houses.

The Jaguar pulled onto the FDR Drive. Felix pressed on the accelerator. The car shot forward. There was a Purcell trumpet voluntary on the tape deck, all flourishes and clarion elegance.

It occurred to Felix that that same music might once have resounded off the massive stone walls of Berwick Castle. Felix had spent much of the day trying not to think of Berwick Castle, or its owner, Neville Fleet, Eighteenth Duke of Berwick.

Poor Neville.

That was Minnie's phrase. Poor Neville. Tragic Neville. It hardly seemed like yesterday evening that Neville had come to the Dupre house on East Sixty-Fourth Street to dine. To have that talk in the garden.

Felix had lived a long and observant life. He prided himself on his eye for objects of art and on a certain shrewdness about people. As the owner and principal auctioneer of the House of Dupre, Felix had seen many a drama unfold, small epics of greed and ambition, of the pure lust for possession. This was the animating force of the auction business and Felix thrived on it. But of all the dramas he had seen in nearly forty years at Dupre's there was nothing to equal the strange sad tale of Neville Fleet.

The car moved faster, sliding through the traffic toward the Triborough Bridge. If only Jeff could have been persuaded to join Dupre's, many things might be different now. But that was an old story: Jeff had never really been interested in the business, and while Felix wanted Dupre's to continue in Dupre hands, he also had the grace and the wisdom not to pressure the boy. Maybe, just maybe Jeff would tire of his digging and his academic life in Cambridge.

Purcell gave way to Vivaldi on the Jaguar's stereo.

Felix sped up the Major Deegan Expressway and onto the Saw Mill River Drive. The traffic was thinning now. He'd just eluded the rush-hour crowds. Felix loved driving, and the finer the car, the faster the pace, the more he enjoyed it. He hummed softly to the music on the tape deck. It was too fine a day to think about Neville Fleet.

But Neville seemed to be with him in the car.

Felix had weighed several possibilities in his dealings with the Duke of Berwick, but the conclusion was always the same.

The Berwick Castle auction must go on, and that would be the end of it. Of his long friendship with Neville. The sale had been announced. The prestige would be enormous. Every auction house in the world wanted the Winchcombe Chalice, not to mention more than a hundred other rare and irreplaceable objects. But the chalice! There was power in that gold cup, the power of myth, of legends. The chalice was touched with blood and magic, all through its long and lurid history. It was practically Sunday-supplement stuff: the publicity value alone would be worth a fortune, quite aside from the commission on the sale itself.

Felix pressed harder on the accelerator. The Drive was winding through country now. He opened the air vents to smell the fresh-cut grass. Even a few miles out of the city and the air itself was different.

The Jaguar was very quiet. Only the music punctuated the thoughts of Felix Dupre. He tried to make his mind wander to other, happier subjects than the unpleasantness with Neville Fleet. He thought of the motor trip he and Minnie would take next spring, after the auction season calmed down. From Paris through the wine country to Cap Ferrat. What fun it would be, tasting the new wines, seeing old freinds.

The Saw Mill River Drive swept into a wide curve. At the end of the curve was a big stone bridge, an overpass. Felix shifted down effortlessly, without thinking, and pressed the accelerator gently to pick up a bit of momentum. The car was moving at nearly seventy miles per hour. As ever, Felix had both hands resting lightly but firmly on the steering wheel.

Halfway through the curve there came a heavy metallic sound, one ominous thud. The car lurched to the left. Tensing but still calm, Felix maneuvered the wheel. *Never,* he told himself, *slam on the brakes in a skid.* The car seemed to be floating. The bridge was drifting toward him.

Felix looked at it calmly, knowing he was going to crash.

He touched the brake. The Jaguar slowed only a little, moved to the right a bit as if staggering, then to the left.

Felix thought of Minnie, of waving good-bye.

He thought of Jeff, of the letter in the vault.

Vivaldi was still playing when the car hit the rough-hewn stones of the overpass.

1

Rome in the reign of the Emperor Claudius, A.D. 43

The gold was alive now. Marcus watched it with a lover's eyes. He saw the first bubble swell the molten surface, rise, burst, and subside in soft ripples. It was followed by another slow bubble, and another. In a moment Marcus Helveticus could mold the chalice.

His client, Gaius Minicus, would be pleased. Having paid twelve hundred gold Aureii for the work, having provided the gold for the chalice and the rubies, Minicus deserved to be pleased.

The goldsmith still regretted the rubies.

They had been the only point of disagreement between client and craftsman. Helveticus would have preferred sapphires as being more like grapes. But no, his client was adamant. "Dark, richly polished, without faceting, my good Helveticus," he had said. "They must glow like old wine."

"Blood rubies, my lord?"

"Precisely. Rubies the color of blood."

Now those rubies lay waiting, perfectly matched for size, but varying somewhat, each in its own contour. They seemed alive, polished as though they had lain in the bed of some swift river since before the dawn of time.

Helveticus had earned his reputation as Rome's finest goldsmith. He had risen from slave to freedman on the wings of his skill. Now all of fashionable Rome came flocking to his shop. Even the emperor had come, the limping, stuttering Claudius. Helveticus was not impressed by emperors. He thought of the great golden phallus mad Caligula had ordered, ringed with spikes. He shuddered and reached for the mold.

This chalice would be a rare and special thing. Even the drawing had power. The conception was simple: a straightforward golden cup floating on a graceful stem, ringed with a band of rubies at the top and at the base. And overall, a golden grapevine would climb and twine, heavy with fruit.

The mold lay at hand, ready. Gently, with iron tongs, the goldsmith tilted the gold-filled caldron. The molten gold seemed to know where it was going. It crept along the crucible's pouring lip and fell into the welcoming orifice of the mold.

All of a sudden, pleasing and distracting, Helveticus felt a surge of longing for a woman—any woman. He had guessed for whom the cup had been ordered. Lydia Verus, the famous courtesan! He knew that Minicus was one of Lydia's patrons. And this chalice was surely not the sort of thing a man like Minicus would give his wife of long standing.

Helveticus smiled. His measure had been exact. The gold just filled the terra-cotta mold. The wax was running out of the tiny holes he had provided. Soon the gold would be cool, and he'd unmold the cup and begin brazing on the grapevine, leaf by leaf and grape by grape. Then he'd make a bezel frame to hold the rubies tightly. As he sat watching the cooling mold, an idea came into his imagination, dancing and teasing. The cup must have a texture on its stem, on its bowl, the better to show off the gleaming vine. He thought of his client's pleasure. He thought of Lydia Verus and the wine she would drink from it. He could almost feel her lips on his, and her warmth. It was as though she were somehow part of the cup. Part of him. The mold cooled. The rubies glowed with their own inner fire.

Rubies the color of blood.

2

Augustus 1978: an archaeological dig at Veii, north of Rome

The Tuscan night was cooler than the day, but not cool enough. Jeff Dupre lay naked on the rough sheet, alone and thinking of Carla.

He was always thinking of Carla.

Jeff lay there, very still. His eyes were closed and he was awake but dreaming, remembering her. He smiled.

Then he heard the sound: a dry hissing followed by a metallic clang, then silence. Then the hissing, scraping sound again. Jeff knew that sound well. It was the sound of dry Tuscan earth resisting a spade's thrust. That sound was a counterpoint to his work in the trenches that he had laid out systematically, making a grid of the hillside, probing.

It was not a sound that belonged to the night.

Jeff wondered how many of them there were out there and

if they were armed. The *tombaroli*. Grave robbers. Destroyers of irreplaceable evidence. Jeff took it personally. They were stealing Italy's past and Jeff's future. A lot depended on this dig, on every dig. The leap from assistant professor to full professor might depend on it. Surely his half-finished book on Etruscan funerary customs depended on it.

Sometimes Jeff thought about how much of his life was invested in the trenches of Veii, and it frightened him. He studied, back in Cambridge, until they threw him out of the stacks of Widener Library. In Veii, he was relentless, working longer, digging deeper than any of the hired workmen, worrying and calculating every detail.

This was the first dig that Jeff had run on his own. And it was going to be a productive dig, or he'd die trying. Maybe tonight. He felt every muscle tensing in the warm darkness.

He was completely alert now. His feet found the floor. Jeff moved fast and very quietly for a big man. This was his third season at Veii, and he knew the little rented farmhouse in darkness or daylight. The old cutoff jeans were on their peg behind the door. His two undergraduate assistants, Corky and Fred, would be asleep down the hall. There was no phone in the house, no way of calling the police. Not that the police cared about tomb robbers.

"*Tombaroli*," Jeff whispered to Corky Cabot, gesturing for silence.

Together, they woke Fred, got a flashlight, and slipped out the kitchen door.

There was no moon. The stars shone back from infinity, mocking the three young men who paused in the dense blackness by the door, listening.

The noise came again, a soft sound that was almost a roaring in contrast to the silence all around them. Each spade-thrust rang in Jeff's ears like an explosion.

He was getting a fix on the sounds now.

They came from the westernmost trench, in it or near it. Maybe two football fields away. Wordless, Jeff led his companions along a line of trees, past the primary ditch, through a field where vegetables still came straggling up through years of neglect. One lone olive tree stood between Jeff and the robbers. They were working by the faint light of one shaded lantern. The anger that Jeff had felt when first he heard the digging still burned in him. *These ignorant thugs are raping us.* Still, he paused, looking, listening, trying to get a feeling for how many there might be. Usually they worked in pairs, sometimes in groups of five or more. Always at night.

7

There seemed to be just two of them. They were digging on the bare earth to the left of Jeff's trench. He wondered why. Sometimes the *tombaroli* seemed to have incredibly good radar about where to dig. They were also very careless in how they dug: hit and run and hope for gold.

Jeff's eyes were accustomed to the dark now. He could see one of the men waist-deep in a hole, digging. The other stood nearby, peering intently into the hole. The sounds of digging continued. Suddenly there was a low exclamation from the man in the hole.

The anger was searing Jeff now, burning deeper because it was mixed with fear. They could have guns. Just last week, south of Pompeii, *tombaroli* had gunned down a pair of tourists who'd gotten too inquisitive late one moonlit night.

There was another muttered comment from the robbers' hole, and suddenly Jeff forgot to be afraid, forgot everything but the insult of this invasion, the damage it might do to his well-ordered dig.

He's found something, thought Jeff. And then Jeff's body began responding to this information. Instantly, without thinking, he was running, crouching low, trying for silence.

Jeff hit the first of them at full speed, diving in a low tackle, enjoying the crunch of the thief's flesh against the hard dirt. The man was gasping, breathless, when Jeff's fist connected with his jaw. He sank into silence.

The second man watched this for a moment, then began clambering out of his hole. He had the spade in one hand and something else in the other.

Jeff was still on the ground, breathing hard.

The man put down the thing he was carrying and raised the spade.

That was when Corky hit him from behind with a brisk karate chop to the side of the neck.

He fell like a tree.

No words had been spoken. The thieves' propane lantern burned brightly.

Jeff picked it up and looked into the hole. "The bastards," he said softly, "the fucking bastards."

The digger had stepped on a beautiful blackware urn. It lay in a dozen pieces, forlorn in the red earth.

Jeff cast the light on the thing the *tombarolo* had set down. It was a whole vase, a small redware oil jug patterned with cream-colored leaves and scrolls. Less valuable than blackware, but a treasure all the same.

Jeff couldn't resist turning the lovely little vase, looking at

8

it carefully. It was rare to find anything whole, unless the object were bronze or gold. He forgot the robbers for a moment. A find was a find, however you came by it. This vase would help. Tomorrow they'd mark this hole, maybe run a secondary trench in this direction.

Tomorrow. Jeff smiled, thinking about it. Then he snapped back to the violent night. The anger came back, and the outrage.

The man Jeff had knocked out began moaning. Jeff looked at him, disgusted.

"Nice work, Corky," said Jeff in answer to the boy's unasked question. "Now, let's find some rope and show these creeps they'd better dig someplace else the next time."

Fred was back in five minutes with a big coil of rope and a hunting knife.

One of the robbers opened his eyes then, and began wailing.

"Sure," said Corky, "the knife and the rope and maybe a few judiciously placed cigarette burns. And that's only the beginning."

Corky said this in flawless Italian, and the wailing intensified.

Jeff laughed.

They tied the men's arms firmly behind their backs and marched them to the farmhouse. There was an old root cellar under the kitchen, whose heavy door could be locked. Dark, musty, and filled with insects, it was Jeff's idea of an ideal resting place for the *tombaroli*.

The police could be called in the morning. They all needed whatever remained of their night's sleep. Convinced now that they were not going to be killed or tortured, the thieves began pleading and whining and invoking a regiment of saints. They were innocent. It was the first time. They didn't know it was private property. They'd never do it again.

Jeff felt sorry for them, but not sorry enough to let them go. They were probably out of work through no fault of their own. Even if they did have jobs, the Italian inflation was stratospheric. One stolen pot might put bread on their table for months. It could also wreck a dig like Jeff's.

When their wailing proved ineffectual, the men lapsed into a sullen silence. It was humiliating to be caught, and by three Americans at that. They climbed down into the root cellar like early Christian martyrs going to the stake. The heavy oak trapdoor closed over them with a satisfying thud. Jeff bolted it shut, sure that their prisoners were secure.

It was nearly three in the morning.

They stood in the kitchen for a moment, looking solemnly at the trapdoor.

It was a strangely quiet moment. Jeff looked at his two undergraduate helpers. Suddenly the little group felt like a family. This was not a feeling Jeff was used to, and he wasn't sure how to put his gratitude into words. "You guys were great," he said. "Above and beyond the call of duty. Thanks."

"You know what'll happen, most likely," said Corky, who had spent summers in Italy all his life. "A lot of paperwork and little action. And they'll be back out there in a few months, digging away."

"But after tonight, maybe not on our dig." Jeff grinned. It was a good feeling. Here was his own small corner of the world, and he was in full control of it. Give or take an occasional tomb robber. Give or take Carla di Cavolfiore. He said good night and went back to bed. And thought about Carla.

That was a situation definitely not in Jeff's control.

Well. He'd see Carla soon, maybe even tomorrow.

And with that happy prospect shining in his imagination, Jeff Dupre finally eased into a deep and healing sleep.

3

A Roman settlement on the Severn River in Britain, A.D. 46

All was ready. Gaius Minicus stood in the many-columned loggia that enclosed the inner garden of his villa. It was the finest villa in this outpost, which was not saying much. Britain was hardship duty, and Minicus had known that when he chose to come here as governor. He could not complain.

But sometimes he thought Roman thoughts. Sometimes he dreamed that he was back in his glittering marble palace on the Janiculan Hill, living life to the full and still loving Lydia Verus.

Minicus watched the sun creep slowly down behind the western roof. There went Apollo in his golden chariot, racing forever through a sky tinged with blood. *Yes, and his bright wagon will see Rome before I do.*

He thought of how Rome looked in the sunlight, of the sun fattening grapes at his holiday villa on the slopes of Vesuvius.

The shadows came sliding across the garden, British shadows, cool with the coming British night. Maybe this new contentment was only a dream. How could you give it a name, this strange and addictive new faith? Strange it might be, but with a power so strong it could not be ignored. There had to be more to it than just another slaves' cult, which was how his friends in Rome dismissed it. Rome was alive with cults. Isis, they worshiped this week, and Venus the next. Well, in the end it all came to one thing: belief. Faith. And Gaius Minicus had faith. He wondered how strong it would be, his faith, if put to the test.

The loggia was almost dark now. The new-turned flowerbeds lay ready for tomorrow's planting of the rosebushes he had ordered. Even the flowers were different here. Different flowers, dark and vengeful gods. Britain was a cold, cold place for one used to the Roman sun.

Something tugged at his arm. Distracted, Gaius turned, looked down, and smiled. Flavia! How lovely she was, his only daughter, she of the pale golden hair and grave sea-green eyes. And how often had he wondered if he was doing her an injustice to bring her so far from the pleasures of Rome. Well, the child was only eight now. Time would tell. And surely she seemed happy.

He reached for her little hand.

"Yes, my darling, I know. It is time, isn't it?"

Flavia nodded gravely and led him into the half-dark villa.

The chapel was necessarily very small. Small because it must be secret. Claudius had outlawed the faith, and to be caught in the new worship was to face death. And informers might be anywhere.

The altar was a rough wooden cupboard and on it two double-spouted bronze oil lamps glowed warmly. Six heads turned as Flavia led her father into the hidden room. There stood Arcadia, his wife these twenty-two years, and the younger boy, Germanicus. The older boy was being spoiled hopelessly by his grandmother in Rome. And here was Arcadia's maid and three other servants. The cook, Petrus, was also the priest. The blacksmith was a convert too, and it was he who had made the simple iron cross, ingeniously conjoined so that it could be snapped apart in an instant to become, apparently, two separate and harmless rods of iron. This cross now hung on a nail above the altar. On the altar was one of Arcadia's finest white linen table scarves.

And centered on the spotless linen was the chalice.

There it stood, burnished, gleaming. It was a fit vessel for

11

the wine that symbolized Christ's blood in the Mass. Minicus smiled as he thought of the goldsmith's leering insinuation that it was destined for Lydia. He looked at the cup, and it pleased him. And he thought how very far he had come from the overripe court of the Caesars.

The simple service began now. They prayed in silence and chanted in whispers. No one else in the great household could know their secret. The bread that the priest Petrus broke had been baked by his own skilled hands. The wine was Minicus' finest red, brought all the way from the villa at Pompeii.

The priest raised the chalice, and the little band of worshipers followed it with their eyes and with their hearts.

Gaius was the first to hear the trumpets of alarm.

Their shrill, bellowing notes sounded through the great villa on the hill. The noise, Gaius Minicus sensed, must be coming from the army encampment below on the riverbank. It sounded like some great beast dying.

For an instant they froze, the cup still raised, wondering. The chapel vibrated with menace. Then the trumpets sounded again, louder, unmistakable.

Minicus went into action.

"Hush!" he said, "and stay here while I see what is the trouble."

He was out of the room in an instant. Down the hall he went, and out the front door. He could see down to the camp now. And what he saw froze his blood.

Northmen, raiding and rampaging! He had heard of their sudden dreaded raids as they came up the rivers in their long-boats, dragon-prowed, many-oared, and swift. Pale, ruthless giants they were, howling in some unintelligible tongue while they pillaged, raped, burned, stole.

One look told Gaius the battle was lost. He ran back to the chapel. They must go to the nearby forest, and quickly. He pushed open the secret door, and his voice when he spoke was a commander's voice. "Quickly, run! Run, Lady Arcadia, take the children to the forest, and hurry. And don't look back."

Too frightened to question him, they scurried out of the chapel.

But Gaius Minicus stayed. He lifted the chalice and swiftly drank off what wine remained in it. Then he wrapped it in the altarcloth, grabbed the iron cross and the two sputtering lamps, and ran into the garden. There! A hole ready-dug and a young rosebush waiting next to it. He placed the chalice in the hole and laid the two lamps beside it. Then he placed the cross reverently over all and put the rosebush on top, kicking the fresh-turned earth into place as best he could.

Then Gaius Minicus walked deliberately back into the villa.

He was a Roman, and a commander, governor of this unforgiving province, and he would not run.

Gaius grabbed a sword and walked out onto the front patio. The night was black now, and there were men fighting in the outer court. He ran, and slipped. His sandaled feet went out from under him. Gaius was on his knees then, groping for the sword. He looked down and as quickly looked away.

He had slipped on blood. Roman blood. A severed arm lay on the pavement before him, its fist still clenched tightly around the hilt of a sword.

The next thing Gaius heard was a scream that might have come from ten tortured horses. He looked up to where the scream had come from. He was looking into the swiftly falling blade of a Northman's battleax.

And then Gaius Servius Minicus saw no more, and heard nothing.

4

Jeff Dupre's archaeological dig at Veii, north of Rome

Jeff knelt in the ditch. The blazing noontime sun burned out of a flat blue Tuscan sky. He sweated, shirtless, but the sun felt good on his back. He held a trowel, but his fingers sifted the dry red earth, searching for clues. Last night seemed a thousand years away.

Corky had been dead right about the local cops' reaction. They'd come, huffing and puffing, all ill-fitting uniforms and misplaced dignity, watching with amusement as the robbers came shuffling up from the root cellar. They were small men by daylight, small and cringing.

"One of them," said Corky as they drove off in the dusty police car, "is sure to be the judge's cousin's uncle. If it gets that far."

And now they were three hours behind schedule.

Maybe it was silly to worry about hours when you were dealing in thousands of years, but Jeff Dupre worried. The complete story of the old Etruscans was yet to be told, and

13

he wanted to be the man to tell it. There were fragments by the thousands. People had been digging near Veii, on and off, for more than two hundred years. And still the Etruscans kept their secrets. Why had they crumbled so easily under the influence of the brash and daring Romans? Just what were the mysterious powers of the great god Voltumna?

There was competion in scholarship, as in most other human endeavors, and Jeff felt it keenly. The surface cooperation barely masked urgent rivalries. Who would publish first? Who would rise most quickly in the rigidly stratified Department of Archaeology at Harvard? To Jeff, the search for knowledge was real and urgent. The quest for recognition was vital too, as detail piled up on detail, fact on fact, and still great mysteries remained unsolved. Jeff was determined he'd solve them. Before someone else did. Where, for instance, was the sacred grove of the god Voltumna, famed throughout the ancient world? In Etruria surely, and near Veii. Maybe on this very hillside. No one knew, yet the grove was out here someplace, maybe holding answers to any number of questions.

Veii was a focal point of the Etruscan world. When it was conquered by the Romans in 396 B.C., it had signaled the death knell of Etruscan influence.

No one knew just why the Etruscans had risen so high, then fallen so fast and completely.

Jeff was burning to find out.

He was sweating now. Streams ran down his bare chest, soaking the tops of the cutoff jeans. Sometimes sweat fell into his blue eyes, smarting. Still he dug. Jeff dug harder, studied longer, and revised his papers more often than anyone else he knew. Whatever Jeff had achieved he'd worked for, and worked hard. He'd sweated for all of it. Maybe the more so because he was a Dupre.

He thought of the *tombaroli*, and of where the vase they'd found might have ended. Maybe in the elegant auction rooms of the House of Dupre. It was an industry now, smuggling antiquities. Laundering them in Switzerland or wherever. Selling them with an aura of legitimacy. Who, in the last analysis, could really prove you hadn't found the damn thing in an attic in Old Westbury? Jeff was morally sure that the famous Calyx krater painted by the Greek master Euphronios had been stolen by just such *tombaroli* as the pair he'd caught last night. And the Metropolitan Museum had paid a million dollars for the lovely black urn. Could you therefore say the Met was an accomplice in crime? You could, and many

14

people had done so. But still the "hot pot" remained inviolate in the Greek collection at the museum, defying all attempts by the Italian government to trace its provenance to some robbed tomb.

Jeff thought of his uncle Felix Dupre, the kindest and most law-abiding of men. He wondered how many of the objects that passed through Dupre's every year were stolen.

Jeff was digging with a trowel in one hand, and his fingers probed the earth with the other. Now his diligence was rewarded with a fragment of an earthenware pot. Priceless! *Priceless?* He smiled, and probed further. It was the business of putting prices on artworks that had turned him off the auction business. Try as Felix had to persuade him.

Good old Felix. Jeff could think of him that way, now, four thousand miles away. Good old Felix and good old Aunt Minnie.

It couldn't have been easy for them, having an orphaned Jeff, age eleven, dropped into their glamorous lives.

It surely hadn't been easy for Jeff, for all their kindness, for all the comfort they provided so generously.

Jeff had been ten one carefree summer's day when his father had taken out the little yellow sloop and never come back.

No one knew what happened in the expensive ocean off Watch Hill.

Jeff had often imagined, telling no one, that Daddy was on a secret mission, not really dead at all. Or he'd been kidnapped by pirates. Or run away. Anything.

Then came a day, almost exactly one year later, when Jeff was called out of class to find a very subdued Minnie and Felix waiting for him.

He heard their words, barely, as if from a distance.

Mom couldn't be dead, not so quickly. A stroke, they said. She was too young to have strokes. Felix said that, too. None of it helped one bit. Something froze in Jeff's heart then.

He went to live with Minnie and Felix. They wanted him to call them that, none of this aunt-and-uncle business. He never saw the old house in Connecticut again. The Felix Dupres took Jeff to their big white stone house on East Sixty-fourth Street in New York. He went to a school where you had to wear neckties. Both Minnie and Felix took trouble with him. They were very kind. He could feel their kindness weighing on him. It was like this big rock you had to carry around and could never put down. Jeff liked his aunt and uncle. He even tried to love them.

But nothing could fill the empty place in his heart.

He dreamed about the empty yellow sloop bobbing in the blue sea.

Jeff had always been in awe of his uncle Felix, Dad's older brother. Felix was elegant, witty, told stories about famous people, laughed at things Jeff didn't know were funny. Felix was remote, moved easily in the highest circles of business and society, and had very high standards to match. When Jeff was drawn into his life, Felix made time for the boy now and then. But the simple fact was, he hadn't much time. There was always a distance, a touch of formality, a strangeness.

Jeff sensed that Felix expected things from him that he would never be able to deliver. This was unstated, for Felix was always kindly, tolerant. Too kind, perhaps, too tolerant. Jeff could see him turning it on sometimes, like a faucet. And once he'd overheard Felix saying to Minnie, "We mustn't blame the boy, darling, he simply hasn't had the advantages."

Jeff didn't know what his uncle meant. He'd had plenty of advantages. A happy home. Two parents who loved each other, and him. Barefoot summers and sledding-skiing-skating winters. Minnie and Felix loved him too—Jeff knew this in his eleven-year-old head. But in his heart it wasn't the same, and never would be.

The house on Sixty-fourth Street was almost never empty. People came and went, there were parties and laughter. Elegant ladies with blue hair pretended to be very interested in Jeff. They made him feel like a toy, like one of the rare paintings on the walls.

He quickly discovered the back stairs. He did much more than the required amount of homework. He read until Minnie feared for his eyesight. And soon it was time for him to go away to school, and everything got better.

At boarding school everyone else was alone too, at least for starters.

One summer, the summer of his junior year at Exeter, Jeff helped out at the House of Dupre, assisting a lady who was making catalogs for the upcoming autumn's sales. Jeff liked the work. You learned things, what things were, who made them. What they were worth, which he never entirely understood, estimating prices on paintings and statues that should have been beyond commerce. It was like putting a price on a smile. Jeff sensed that Felix would like it if he went into the business.

Felix entrusted him to the care of Morgan St. James, who at that time was the head of Dupre's silver department. Morgan was a tall, lanky man with prematurely silver hair and a humorous face.

Jeff liked him at once, and responded to Morgan's interest in everything old, in people, in Jeff Dupre especially.

Morgan could make Jeff laugh.

In all that summer, Jeff saw his uncle only occasionally at the auction house. But he was with Morgan much of the time, helping with catalogs, getting a glimpse of the strange inner workings of Dupre's. Jeff did not learn to love the auction business that summer, but his fondness for Morgan St. James stayed with him. Even today he made a point, when in New York, of seeing Morgan, sometimes having lunch or a drink.

When Jeff became interested in archaeology, it was Morgan, more than his uncle, who encouraged him, introduced him to curators at the Metropolitan Museum, lent him books.

Even now, more than ten years later, Morgan still wrote from time to time, and Jeff always answered.

It was that summer at the auction house that Jeff discovered a new love for old things. The older the better. Dupre's was doing a Roman sale, and Jeff found himself coming back to the storeroom again and again. Some of the Roman marbles might even be Greek in origin. There was a mystery to them. He imagined the old hands that had carved these marble gods and generals. Only, their hands weren't old then, of course, and that was the wonder of it for sixteen-year-old Jeff Dupre. That the work of those hands endured.

It was a kind of magic, and Jeff decided he would be a part of it. He would help solve the mysteries. He would be an archaeologist.

It was typical of Felix and Minnie that they helped him every way they could, even though this meant he'd be at home less often now. Sometimes Jeff sensed a kind of loneliness in them, underneath all the bustle and glitter of life on Sixty-fourth Street, beyond all the charm of their busy lives.

But the past called to Jeff with a deep and inescapable magnetism.

And maybe the best thing about the past was that it could never be taken away from him. The past could not die or drift out to sea. It was always right there, waiting, beckoning.

By the time he was in his second year at Harvard, Jeff began spending every summer on some archaeological dig or other, unpaid and learning, just as Corky and Fred were doing now on his own dig at Veii.

Senior year of college, Felix had asked him, quite formally, to come into Dupre's.

Turning him down had not been easy.

Felix, Jeff knew, would never press the issue, nor like him the less for choosing his own way in life. But his uncle's disappointment was palpable. Jeff could feel it. Still, he pressed on with his studies, with his digs, with graduate school and his research. Eventually he was granted a junior position teaching in Harvard's Department of Archaeology. He had a small apartment in Cambridge now and saw Felix and Minnie at Christmas and en route to and from his digs. Jeff worked hard, had a few close friends and love affairs that tended to be brief and casual. Ever since the deaths of his parents Jeff had viewed life as an emotional minefield, and had avoided commitment.

And then he met Carla di Cavolfiore. Carla! Just looking at her was a commitment.

He smiled now, thinking of her, and the thought brought him luck. His fingers touched a second fragment of pottery. He probed with a surgeon's delicacy, then lifted the thing up. The design of the underglaze revealed itself. Here was a near-relative of the oil vase the *tombaroli* had found. But this had been part of a good-sized workaday piece, a kitchen jug for milk or water or wine.

For grander occasions, if you were a rich Etruscan, you'd have imported blackware from Greece, or bronze, or even silver.

The fragment Jeff held was local. As he turned it in his hands, he thought of the *tombaroli* and where they'd dug. Corky had suggested running a little side ditch in that direction. You never knew. They'd start that experiment tomorrow. In the locked workroom at the farmhouse were hundreds of such fragments, all numbered, all cataloged and identified on a grid of the trenches. It was important to know precisely where they'd been found. Which was why the incursions of the grave robbers were so maddening.

"*Signor Jaaf, per favore?*"

Jeff looked up, squinting into the sun. Pepe, foreman of the diggers, stood at the edge of the trench, gesturing with some piece of paper.

There was always some damn bit of paperwork. Jeff put the potsherd back where he'd found it. He'd mark it on the master graph after lunch. He stood and stretched to his full height of six-two. It felt as though he'd been crouching in the ditch forever. It would be good to get out of the sun for a while, for lunch. A neighboring farmwoman came to cook for them, and her simple food was delicious. There'd be fruit, probably, and salad, and a glass of the rough red local wine. He'd hear what Corky and Fred had been up to this morning. They'd plan the new ditch. He'd put Corky in charge of that project. He was a good kid, Corky. Jeff climbed out of the ditch. He'd almost forgotten Pepe.

Now, remembering, Jeff smiled and reached for the paper. It was a cablegram.

Felix Dupre was dead.

Jeff stood frozen in the hot sunshine. He read the message over, then over again.

"FUNERAL DELAYED UNTIL YOUR ARRIVAL. COME AT ONCE." It couldn't be. People like Felix Dupre didn't die. They were institutions. They went on forever, like libraries.

Felix dead.

Jeff turned and looked at his ditch. His slow, slow highway to the past. Now it looked like a grave.

He thought of all the things Felix had wanted him to be that he hadn't been. Hadn't cared enough to be. You could fill a ditch with those things. Or a grave.

Jeff blinked the sweat out of his eyes. Only, it wasn't sweat. It was tears.

5

Berwick Castle, England, October 1938

Neville's heart leaped as his grandfather downshifted the sleek drophead Bentley and the supercharged engine responded with a satisfying growl.

They were rounding the last curve.

Now they could see Berwick castle itself, and Neville warmed to the familiar rush of pride he always felt coming back to Berwick.

It was more than just coming home. It was reentering the world where he belonged. It was gathering his destiny around him like magical armor, the past and the future all at once. For Neville Fleet was part of Berwick, and Berwick was part of him. So it always had been, for all the Fleets who extended in one glorious unbroken line back beyond the muddy splendor of Agincourt.

The boy looked at his grandfather and smiled. He wondered if every boy liked his grandfather better than his father. How could one not, when the grandfather in question was Duke of Berwick, confidant of kings, famed rakehell, and owner of this magnificent motorcar?

It was always an adventure being with Grandfather. To Neville at twenty-one the old gentleman seemed twice the man his father was. The duke cut a figure and didn't care who knew it. In his grandfather, Neville caught a glimpse of what the old Fleets must have been. All those hawk-nosed, dark-eyed adventurers who lined the portrait gallery for fifty yards on either side seemed to be alive in the present duke. There had been a time, Neville knew, when all England trembled should a Fleet of Berwick frown. Neville cared little for painting, but he often walked in the portrait gallery, just to be among them. There were Fleets by Holbein in cut velvet and cloth of gold, all ruffs and rubies. There were Vandyke Fleets of somber mein, and Fleets by Romney, improbably blushing. And every one of them had a story.

When other little English boys were story-told to sleep in company with the Mock Turtle or Peter Rabbit, Neville had heard about the lurid doings of his ancestors. These stories were laced with greed and glory. Swords flashed down the centuries. There were kings and queens and raging intrigues. Neville's boyhood echoed with the hoofbeats of all the ghostly Neville Fleets behind him.

It was a tradition to name the first son Neville, and this Neville was not only first but the sole child of his father's marriage. Thus Grandfather was named Neville, and father, too. It was confusing now that Neville was grown and they were all, sometimes, invited to the same parties.

Not that being a Fleet was all that easy.

There were definitely problems. Neville was facing one now, and he didn't like to think about it too much. He often refused to think about problems. Sometimes, if you did that, they went away. Or, if they didn't go away, then you could get angry. Neville knew he did that too often. But there you had it: the anger would come surging up in him. It had to come out somehow. It was like having to be sick.

Grandfather had been very upset when Neville shot the horse. That had been five years ago, but the boy would never forget the dressing-down the old man had given him.

"You have responsibilities, boy, you can't simply run about doing whatever damn-fool thing comes into your silly head.

You are a Fleet of Berwick, lad, and you must set an example. You have responsibilities."

"So did the horse, Grandfather. He did throw me, you know. I might have been killed."

"Then you should learn to ride better or choose your mounts better. And what's being thrown matter? I've been thrown dozens of times. One gets back on and rides the beast down."

"I'm sorry, Grandfather."

The old man looked at his grandson. He wondered where this oddly twisted offshoot on the family tree had come from. A gentle, fine-looking lad who was eager to please and capable of uncontrollable rages and cruelties at the same time.

"I think you are," said the duke. "It isn't enough."

"What must I do, then?"

"You must be better. Do better. Control yourself, boy. Learn that we simply can't do whatever we like in this world. Not when we are Fleets of Berwick."

"I'll try, sir."

"You damned well will try. And to help you try, you will clean out the stables this weekend. Alone."

Neville looked at the duke, appalled. The Berwick Castle stables held forty-some horses. Cleaning them kept four stable lads busy every day. He trembled, standing there, and looked down. "Yes, sir."

Now Neville was older. Just out of Oxford, by the skin of his teeth. There had been no more really bad incidents after the horse. None that Grandfather knew about. He smiled as the hedgerows rushed past the speeding car. There had been good times, many good times. And, more often than not, Grandfather had been part of them.

It was Grandfather who had taken him to see the man in the pit. Mortimer, the duke called him. He wasn't a man, really. He was a skeleton. An armored skeleton, lying just where he'd fallen three hundred years ago. Into one of the death pits in Berwick dungeon. Deep, square-cut, and all studded with sword blades sticking up from the bottom. Mortimer was kept intact to frighten children, for the dungeons were riddled with such pits. No one knew how many there might be. And no one, having seen Mortimer, wanted to find out.

But for young Neville the skeleton was better than just a warning.

The man in the pit was a talisman for Neville. For Mortimer had come to harm them. Mortimer had come sneaking

21

into the dungeons, sword in hand, maybe let in by some traitor. And Berwick had finished him. The castle itself had taken its vengeance, protecting the Fleets. As it had always protected them. As it always would.

The Bentley seemed to purr with satisfaction as the duke slowed it to pass through the tunnel. The car had been built specially narrow just for this tunnel. They passed through the barbican gate, under the iron-spiked portcullis and down the tunnel under the murder holes, under the second portcullis and into the great inner court.

The tunnel was forty feet long because the castle wall was that thick. Berwick had been a siege castle. Densely fortified, it sat high on its crag overlooking the Severn River in the heart of southern England.

The glittering dark green car seemed to pull daylight into the tunnel. With sun behind and more sun ahead, the car's brightwork and deeply lacquered paint flashed and sparkled as they flowed down the tunnel.

And then they were home.

It was a homecoming that Neville both feared and desired. He must make his decision this weekend. He must confront his father, and especially his grandfather. Already he'd written of his desire to enlist. Ominously, there had been no reply other than the suggestion they discuss it this weekend.

They were greeted by the butler, who mentioned that Neville's father was in the library. Neville's father was always in the library, buried in some damned book.

Dressing for dinner, Neville wondered what his life would have been like had his mother lived. Death at childbirth. He'd never known her. There were a few photographs, but no portrait. Aunt Eugenia, Mother's sister, had been imported to substitute. Aunt Eugenia had not been a success. She drank, which might not have been so bad had she not also giggled. Aunt Eugenia had gone back home. They saw her now only rarely, a sad old lady with henna in her hair and large wet eyes. The eyes, Neville had always thought, of a spaniel.

The three Neville Fleets sat down to dine in the splendid vastness of the James I dining room. Smallest of Berwick's dining rooms, it would seat sixty without strain.

The duke took the head of the enormous walnut table, flanked right and left by his son and grandson.

It should have been a happy meeting. It was not. The talk was strained. Behind each chair stood a footman in the herditary dark green livery of the Fleets. The times were growing liberal. Just a few years ago it had been decided, after some debate, to allow the footmen to leave off their white wigs, except on the most formal occasions. Young Neville thought they looked better with wigs on. He was going to reinstate the wigs when he inherited the title.

The food was overcooked, as Grandfather liked it. The wines, as ever, were impeccable. Dessert was young Neville's favorite: old-fashioned trifle.

With the trifle came a bottle of vintage Veuve Clicquot champagne. In silence Neville watched the bubbles create themselves at the bottom of a rock-crystal goblet that had been engraved with the arms of Fleet in Venice in 1732.

The duke coughed. "Well, lad, out with it, then. What is all this about joining up?"

As ever, the old gentleman could reduce his grandson to quivering submission with a glance. Which had the effect of making young Neville angry. He wanted not to get angry tonight. He knew himself when the anger came. He did things he wouldn't like the next day.

"It's just that all my friends are doing it. The Royal Air Force, Grandfather, will be to this war what the cavalry was in yours. In the Great War. And I just want to be part of it, don't you see? From the first."

The duke sighed and sipped his champagne. "Spoken, alas, like a true Fleet of Berwick. That is just why we must make another sort of arrangement, dear boy. The Fleets of Berwick are in short supply, Neville. We can't afford to lose you."

"Are you . . . are you suggesting I do something cowardly, sir?" Neville rose, his face livid. It had come so suddenly. There was no chance to plan. The anger was raging in him now. He shook with it. "Surely, Grandfather, we must teach this little rotter a lesson. This Hitler chap is not to be tolerated. Especially not by Fleets of Berwick."

"Sit down, Neville, you look like an ass." The duke's voice was cold now.

Neville sat down and seemed to shrink into the tall carved chair.

"You never asked," the duke continued, "what I was doing in town today."

"What were you doing in town today, Grandfather?"

"Not shopping for cheap sarcasm, lad, nor penny heroics either. I was up asking Winston if he'll let me do something—anything. It will be Winston, of course. It always is."

Neville wondered why life had so many more surprises than he was ever prepared for.

"But—"

His grandfather interrupted the boy's unformed response. "And I also asked about you, Neville. Winston understands. The trick seems to be making you understand."

"I understand the Nazis, sir. I understand England's position. And I understand what my friends will think if I do anything but join up."

"Friends! You talk of war as though it were a cricket match. What do you know of war? Of anything? This is going to be a long, dirty, rotten war, Neville. We may not even win it."

The old man paused, drank some wine. A footman refilled his glass. The duke's words hung in the quiet air, startling, heavy with doom.

Finally Neville spoke. "How can a Fleet say such things? It's traitorous!"

"Truth, boy, has no politics. It doesn't change sides. It's just there, like the weather. And these days we can't afford to choose our truths. That is a very expensive luxury, Neville, living off the capital of our expectations. I'd love for you to have a nice gallant little war. But you can't. And that's that."

"I will not," said young Neville very slowly, clinging to the last shreds of self-control as a drowning man might cling to a raft, "do anything discreditable."

"I bloody well hope not. I simply ask you this. What good will it do for your precious England, or for Berwick, if you go running like the damnable Light Brigade into the first burst of enemy gunfire, suicidally chanting battle songs?"

"Someone must."

"Indeed. They are known as cannon fodder. We did not raise you to be cannon fodder, Neville, and you won't be."

Then Neville's father spoke for the first time. "England needs you, Neville, and Berwick too. And your grandfather and I need you. Alive. I know that at your age, and being a Fleet, death may seem impossible. But it is possible. It is very possible. We didn't get to be Fleets by taking foolish chances."

Neville looked at his father, at his grandfather. He felt the anger seeping out of him, along with the pride. You could no more fight their will than you could fly to the moon. For the first time in his young life Neville felt trapped by Berwick, by being a Fleet.

He could feel the weight of these ancient walls pressing down on him. The silence was dense, the silence of a crypt.

"What," he asked, faltering, "shall I do, then?"

The duke laughed, a chuckling, crackling ripple of irony. "Do you actually imagine we'd let you do anything shabby, boy? How little you know us. You'll enlist, as soon as you like, and in your dear RAF, at that. And you'll do more good for all of us at headquarters in London as a strategic intelligence officer than you ever would at the controls of one of those damned contraptions. And it won't be without risk, or in any way a thing to . . . to be anything but proud of."

Neville sat and stared at his glass. It was nearly empty. Now, suddenly, in the silence that had filled the great dining room, he could feel Berwick closing around him. Protecting him. Whether he wanted to be protected or not.

He turned to his grandfather. "If you say so, Grandfather." Then he rose, stiff with the effort of controlling himself, and stalked out of the room.

In the dining room, the boy's father smiled. "Well done, sir."

The Duke of Berwick sat back in his chair. He permitted himself a smile. "There must always be a Fleet at Berwick, son. That's the important thing. That's what none of us can ever forget."

The footman appeared with a large silver box of Havana cigars.

Dinner was over.

"Shall we," asked the duke companionably, "have port in the blue drawing room?"

6

A hillside overlooking the Severn near Winchcombe, A.D. 832

Brother Paulus looked at the rosebush sadly, for he loved beauty, and surely it was God's will that the bush must go. The digging must begin, and here, for hadn't they waited long enough? The abbey must be built, and at last they were ready, and the site was well chosen, high on the hillside, near the river but not too near, facing south and east and with a lovely view that extended almost to the distant sea.

Other eyes had liked this site, for here where the rosebush had flourished for only God knew how long there were the stubby remains of old walls, good stonework too, perhaps Roman.

Well, the new Cistercian abbey would be of stone too, all the best, with cloisters and a fine church, not so great as to be called a cathedral but splendid nevertheless with its massive arches and carved saints and glass—yes, glass!—sparkling and glowing all jewellike, on fire with faith.

Brother Paulus signaled the workman and asked him to try moving the bush; surely God would forgive him this small delay. The workman must be made to dig carefully, to preserve the roots, and then, with luck, the ancient shrub could be replanted down the hillside, out of harm's way in the great digging and building to come. What wonderful profusion the bush put out, tiny pale pink blossoms that seemed to pour from the ground, and with a delicate scent, too. Surely a thing of such beauty should not suffer careless destruction, for didn't the Almighty create the little flowers, as well as all other living things both good and evil?

Brother Paulus left the workman to his task and walked slowly on to inspect the progress elsewhere on the site.

Scarcely as much time elapsed as would permit the saying of five paternosters when he felt a tugging at his sleeve. Brother Paulus turned, frowning. It was the digger of the rosebush, speechless with excitement, waving his arms like a madman, gesturing that the monk accompany him. What in the world could be bothering the poor fellow? Masking his irritation, Brother Paulus followed the man back to where he had been digging.

At least, thought the monk, he seems to have removed the rosebush without harm. The workman drew Brother Paulus close to the edge of the little hole where he had been digging, and pointed.

It was not necessary to point. Brother Paulus gasped, blinked, and for a moment could not credit what his sharp eyes plainly saw there. It can only be a miracle, and a true one, a sure sign from God that he wants his work carried forth, and by us, and here on this now sacred bit of earth!

There in the damp earth of late June lay a badly rusted but unmistakable cross!

For a moment the monk closed his eyes and prayed.

When he opened his eyes again, Brother Paulus fully expected that the cross would have vanished, that this was just some trick, that he had been working too hard of late, which surely was the truth. But still the cross lay in the earth just as the workman had discovered it, silent, older than old, radiating magic. His first instinct was to jump into the hole, to touch the thing and be quite sure it was real. He looked about him. Silently, other workmen had come gathering around the place, their simple eyes bugging with astonishment. Then Brother Paulus smiled, a fleeting smile, but a smile that rode on a wave crest of satisfaction.

He could feel conversions happening in the very air around him! There was a magic to the cross, and beyond doubt it would be a sacred relic of the new church. Then, pulling his scattered wits together, he sent for the abbot and proceeded to stand guard over the treasure himself.

The abbot was old and frail and weighed no more than a child. He was no burden at all for the muscular lads who all but ran down the muddy lanes with his sedan chair. Thus, with more haste than dignity, did the old man come rollicking up to the building site. The chair bearers knelt slowly and in unison, lowering the sedan chair gently to the ground. The abbot stepped out, walking with small, decisive steps to where Brother Paulus stood, transfixed, waiting.

The old man spoke first. "I hear of miracles, Brother Paulus, and wonderful things living in the earth, and signs from on high."

He was an old man, and he had seen much of the world, and in his experience, the "miracles" witnessed by well-meaning but highly imaginative serfs had a way of melting under the harsh light of reason.

Brother Paulus took the abbot's arm, said nothing, but only pointed.

Even as the peasant workman had first pointed.

The Cistercian abbot was a realist. He turned to Brother Paulus, and took the younger monk's arm, and walked a few paces from the hole, out of the hearing of the rest. "There may," said the abbot in a whisper, "be more. We must remove the cross to safety—rather, dear Paulus, you must remove it—and carefully, secretly, dig for more."

All afternoon and into the evening Brother Paulus and the abbot of Winchcombe stood watch by the hole where the rosebush had grown. The digger of the bush had transplanted it, and as the sun lowered, the workmen were sent home. And still the two monks stood by the excavation.

Finally, five trusted monks arrived, hastening on foot from Winchcombe, carrying food and lanterns. And spades. Hastily, like outlaws, they gobbled the food. Then, while the others stood in a half-circle with lanterns, Paulus stepped into the hole with a spade.

He knelt first, and gently lifted the rusted iron cross, fearing even as he touched it that the cross would crumble, or that God might strike him dead, might want the cross never to be moved from this spot. *And whose hand had placed it here, and why, and how had the rosebush come to make the cross's resting place more beautiful—and more conspicuous?*

The other monks had brought cloths from Winchcombe, and sacks too, for who knew what they might find?

Brother Paulus lifted the cross, and it held together, and God did not strike him dead. He raised the cross high over his head, then handed it reverently to the abbot.

Then in the flickering light of the oil lanterns, Paulus pushed the iron spade into the earth. He did not push hard, nor did he push far, for just inches beneath where the cross had lain, the point of his spade struck metal.

Paulus knelt again now, and scratched at the moist earth with his hands. "Come," he said, to no one in particular, "and bring the lamp closer."

The abbot himself stepped into the hole, carrying a lantern, and knelt next to Paulus as the younger monk dug with his hands. Even with the light closer, it was hard to see. His fingers seized on something hard, and round, and bumpy. He probed, scratched, scooped the earth away, and felt his fingers encircling . . . what? Paulus lifted the thing into the wavering light of the lamp. It was crusted with dirt, curiously shaped, and coated with deep blue-green patination, yet not rusted like the cross had been. Copper, then, or bronze. An oil lamp, by the look of it, and old as the hills! Eagerly, now and with new confidence, his fingers explored with all their strength. *What's this? Another, nearly identical lamp, green as the other, and just as odd. Who were these people, and why did they bury such a hoard? The cross and two tapers? Surely it must have been the setting for a Mass.*

Wordless, Paulus handed the bronze back over his shoulder, his fingers working frenziedly now, groping in the black earth made blacker by night.

Now, here's a new thing, round, surely, but bigger, with some rough design, and what soft greasy stuff clinging to it? The table linen of Gaius Minicus was of the finest, purest white, woven strong enough to last for generations, but not in the wet harsh earth of England. It was a black slimy ruin now, just barely clinging to the precious thing Minicus had wrapped in it.

The ruined cloth fell away as Brother Paulus eased the great chalice from its earthen prison. He lifted it high and heard a strange noise, the sort of noise the wind might make racing through trees. Then Paulus realized that he was contributing to that noise, that they had all gasped aloud, involuntarily, at the sight of the glittering thing he held in his upraised hand.

For here was no rust, no green patina of corroded bronze. Here, pure and unblemished and shining like some beacon through the ages, was a cup that might have been made for a king—or a god. The chalice seemed to gather what little light there was in this small circle of devout men, and amplify the light and bounce it back stronger and brighter and more glorious. And the rubies glowed too, glowed with dark fire, rubies the color of blood.

Surely it was a sign, and a miracle.

Surely it boded great good.

Surely it magnified every one of them in the eye of God and man, and their faith was confirmed in it, and now, beyond doubt, the Cistercian abbey of Winchcombe would have a force and a power that might even reach unto Rome itself!

These were the thoughts that danced in their minds, six monks and their abbot, as they stood awe-struck in the flickering lamplight on the hillside where soon—tomorrow!—the abbey would rise.

And glorious as their plans had been, they would be still greater now—what had been planned as a church for hundreds would be a cathedral for thousands! For surely the magic in this treasure would guide them, from this moment and forever until the end of time.

Once more Brother Paulus knelt in the damp earth, and once more his eager fingers groped, frantic now, for who knew what other glories might be sleeping in this miraculous place?

He probed and groped, and soon his fingers were scratched and bleeding, but he went on and on until the lamps began flickering and the abbot called to him to desist.

They all walked the five and some miles back to Winchcombe, reluctant to leave the sacred place, even to sleep.

Heavy as it was, the Winchcombe Chalice never left the steely grip of the abbot during the long walk back to Winchcombe that dark night. He smiled a secret smile, walking on the rough path, for the abbot could feel the strength in the chalice, feel it flowing into him, and into the men who had been with him this great day.

His mind raced with plans, bubbled with dreams, overflowed with delight. How, exactly, must he announce the miracle, and when? And how to contrive safekeeping for the precious chalice and its accompanying treasures? For there were men who roamed the land whose hearts were quite dark enough to covet even sacred treasures. Still, the chalice and the cross had magic, had caused themselves to be found again after who knew how long. The chalice, surely, would protect itself, now that it was up out of the earth again, seething with miraculous powers after its long, long sleep.

These were the thoughts of the abbot of Winchcombe as he walked through the blackest of nights, clutching his new treasure as a child clings to a new toy.

7

Jeff gripped the Jeep's steering wheel as the spunky little machine came flying over the plain, dragging its own trail of dust toward Cavolfiore.

The bag was packed. The phone calls had been made, miraculously, over the static-ridden pay phone in the local trattoria. Corky Cabot rode with Jeff. He'd take the Jeep back to the dig. Jeff would spend the night at Cavolfiore. Carla would take him to the Rome airport in the morning. The world's worst airport, but at least it was only an hour from the castle.

The *castello* di Cavolfiore squatted on its hilltop in the distance. Carla would be waiting. Jeff wondered, as he always did on this road, at his luck.

It had been on this road that he'd first met Carla.

Literally by accident.

Jeff had been speeding back from Rome and spotted an overturned Fiat van smoldering at the roadside.

And there stood a woman, dazed and bleeding from several cuts on her face. Jeff's Italian was rudimentary. She pointed toward the distant castle. He took her there, thinking she must be one of the farm workers.

She was, it quickly developed, the Countess di Cavolfiore, and very beautiful. The castle itself was old and ugly and in poor repair. The family finances, Jeff would learn, were in equal disrepair. There was just Carla and her brother Beppo. And Beppo was a classic ne're-do-well, all charm and chicanery. He'd charm the links out of your cuffs or the gold from your teeth. Luckily, Beppo was only intermittently at the castle. Even more luckily, Carla was there all the time.

She ran the castle's farms, supervised the making of cheese and of wine. She also supervised the selling of an occasional family treasure.

The day after her accident, Jeff left the dig early and drove to Cavolfiore, bringing her a basket of figs.

She loved figs. Her cuts were superficial. She invited Jeff to come back for supper in three days.

Three days later they were lovers, and had been all summer long. Two months.

There was only one problem with Carla. Jeff cared for her to a degree that scared him. Sometimes she seemed to care equally. Other times, Carla was elusive. She was almost alarmingly straightforward in words and deeds. But sometimes she would retreat into some inner world where Jeff could not follow. And in that inner world lurked demons.

She was, Jeff guessed, a few years older than his twenty-eight.

Her first marriage had ended tragically. After two happy years, her husband had come down with a debilitating nerve-wasting disease. It had taken five years for him to die. And Carla had nursed him all those years, right to the inevitable end. Then she had resumed her own name and come back to Cavolfiore.

Jeff had never considered marrying before Carla. Now he thought about it a lot. Carla was Catholic and very attached to Cavolfiore. Twelve generations of Cavolfiores had made it their home. It was not the kind of life he could expect her to leave readily. And Jeff definitely did not want to move full-time to Italy.

The castle loomed ever bigger.

As always when he approached the castle from its plain, Jeff imagined himself to be storming the grim old fortress. Sometimes he felt that way about Carla, too. Sometimes she seemed to be building walls around herself. Jeff understood that. He'd built many such walls himself.

What he didn't understand was the magic that would make those walls crumble and never come back again.

The Jeep was straining to climb the hill. Jeff shifted down. The Jeep groaned but responded. They hadn't said much on the drive: the wind made it impossible to talk. Jeff looked at his watch.

"New record," he said. "Fifty-seven minutes."

Then they were driving through the broken gate of the old

castle. Jeff stopped by the kitchen entrance. He looked at his assistant. Corky was bright, responsible, easygoing. Jeff hoped he wouldn't be too easygoing.

"Take care, Corky. You have my number in New York."

"If the Sacred Grove of Voltumna turns up," said Corky, grinning, "you'll be the first to know."

Jeff felt a twinge then. The damn thing could turn up anytime.

"Hang in there. You'll be fine."

Jeff hauled his small suitcase out of the Jeep. Corky roared off out of the castle's courtyard and down the hill.

Then she was there, touching him. Carla.

"Jiff," she said softly, "I am so sorry."

She never could quite say the e in "Jeff." He kissed her. For a moment he said nothing, thinking of Felix, taking warmth from her warmth.

"He was a good man and I loved him. I hope he knew that."

She led him inside, through vast empty rooms, out onto the terrace beyond. The finest thing about Cavolfiore was the view. You looked out over regiments of ancient olive trees, silver leaves dancing with a life of their own. Beyond lay the plain, and at its edge a distant ephemeral glitter that was Rome. Suddenly Jeff was very glad it was the height of the tourist season, that he couldn't get on a plane before morning. He took her hand, and together they watched the Harvard Jeep speeding back to Veii. It diminished, a bit of glitter and a plume of white dust, and then it was gone absolutely.

Just the touch of her made him feel better, eased the sadness. Maybe this was what love felt like. Maybe he'd better do something about that. He'd never thought about marriage except as a kind of abstraction. Marriage was something that happened to other people.

Like death.

He pulled her to him and kissed her.

Carla looked up at him with immense sad eyes, eyes the color of dark amber.

"You are sad too." He said this softly. It was a fact.

"I am thinking that you will not come back to Cavolfiore."

This was so unexpected that he laughed, and pulled her closer.

"Try keeping me away."

They stood like that, very close, his arms around her. Then suddenly he picked her up and carried her through the big cool reception rooms to the stairway and up it, and to her bedroom.

It was a path his feet knew well.

Jeff wanted her intensely, and the very urgency of his need for her frightened him. You weren't supposed to want anything that badly.

They made love in the soft shadows of late afternoon, with building pleasure made more poignant by the parting soon to come. Why, Jeff wondered, had she said he wouldn't be coming back? Then the question melted into his pleasure. It was always like this with the two of them: problems disappeared in the thrust and response of their bodies, in the closeness of their spirit.

"You," he whispered, "could make men jump through hoops."

She laughed, pinched his ear, kissed him. "But I do not want men, I want a man, and if he would jump through a hoop, I would hate him."

"I love you," said Jeff. The words shocked him. He had never said them before, not to any woman.

"Please," she said, "not to say that."

"It is true."

"You are very sweet, Jiff. But you know less than you think about love."

He held her closely, and silence fell down on them like a sudden snow.

Later, still naked and entwined, they lay on the silken coverlet. Jeff wanted to speak and was afraid to.

If there was an answer to her accusation, he didn't have it.

I know less than I think about love.

He closed his eyes for a moment, and still the answer did not come. Outside Carla's window grew an ancient vine, and on that vine perched one small and distinctly unmusical brown sparrow. It ought, Jeff thought, to be a nightingale, and the vine wisteria and in full bloom. The sparrow chirped in protest. Jeff laughed.

Carla, who had been tracing arabesques on his chest, looked up.

"We are so funny, then?"

There was anger in her eyes now. Anger and hurt. *She's touchy. God, is she touchy. She really doesn't want me to go.* He hoped that was a good sign.

Jeff bent a little and kissed her. "I had just been thinking, beautiful lady, that the little sparrow should be a nightingale, to make a perfect moment more perfect."

Carla's laughter floated up to join his somewhere in the shadows over the bed. "To me," she said, "he is a nightingale. Perfect is perfect, Jiff. We must not be greedy."

He cupped her breast in his hand and held it gently, gazing in wonder as though it might be some rare treasure from a dig. As though anything from the ground could be this perfect, this soft, this pleasing. He kissed it and drew her closer and felt the passion racing through him with the clear hot velocity of some shooting star.

"I," he said, "intend to be just as greedy as I can."

The sun was beginning to set when they finally arose.

Carla turned to him with a smile that would have defied da Vinci. It was that seductive. And that inscrutable.

"Tonight," she proclaimed, suddenly the Countess di Cavolfiore, "we feast. We shall dress. You must wear your dinner suit."

Jeff frowned. "I only have . . . what I'll wear to the funeral. It isn't a dinner suit."

"It will do."

She vanished, leaving Jeff to splash in her enormous Victorian bathtub. As he bathed he wondered what was up at the *castello* di Cavolfiore.

Something was disturbing Carla. Something more than just his going, although that seemed to be wrapped up in it too, somehow. Maybe she was waiting for him to make the move he hadn't dared to make. Maybe she really did want to become Mrs. Jeffrey Dupre. And maybe, tonight, he'd find out.

It was startling, to Jeff, how panic-stricken he became every time he thought seriously about marriage to Carla. Love her as he did.

The more you loved someone, the more completely you could get hurt when she left you.

As she inevitably would.

He thought of her and knew the fineness of her, the loyalty, and he knew she'd be every bit as loyal to her husband as she was to her rotten brother, or to this moldering old castle, or to the Roman Church.

This sure knowledge did not quench the fear in him.

Jeff knew women liked the way he looked. Getting women had never been a problem for him. Keeping them was something else: he had never wanted to keep one, not really, not for the long run.

Lost in the jungle without a compass.

He'd just have to tread softly. Maybe it was Felix's death that was throwing every emotion out of kilter. Maybe.

They ate in splendor from a round table on the terrace. The table was covered in antique lace over rose silk. The best crystal caught up the candlelight and played rainbow games with it. Old silver gleamed from a tea wagon nearby. A large crystal pitcher held Cavolfiore's own smooth red wine.

The ancient cook, Giuseppina, served them with great solemnity, all in black.

Carla, who was magnificent in blue jeans or nothing at all, had transformed herself into a creature of breathtaking splendor. Her chestnut-brown hair was swept up in the Edwardian manner, and she wore a garnet-red silk gown of the same period, square-necked, puff-sleeved, and trimmed with old lace. Around her long, graceful neck was a black velvet ribbon, and on the ribbon an old cameo: two Romans, a boy and a girl, one profile echoing the other. Jeff complimented her, and she laughed, pouring wine for both of them.

"It comes of having tall, greedy aunts. But you think I do not look too like a tea cozy, then?"

"You look fabulous. Is the cameo Roman?"

"So Beppo claims. But Beppo," she said with a small, fleeting frown, "would claim the moon is made of macaroni, if it suited him."

Jeff touched her hand. "Look, darling. The moon *is* made of macaroni. With butter sauce!"

The moon had risen, three-quarters full and golden, almost a butter-yellow in the fine windless night. Far away, a dusting of brightness on the horizon indicated Rome.

But Jeff didn't want to think about Rome or its airport, or the next time he'd be wearing this dark suit.

He wanted to think about now, and Carla. And a future that could be made with Carla.

The cook came with a wonderful pasta: fresh-made noodles with wild mushrooms in thick Tuscan cream from the castle's own cows, tossed with Parmesan cheese. Cavolfiore as a farm was almost entirely self-sufficient. Jeff wondered how self-sufficient its mistress was, what was troubling her. And could she possibly make a life in the world outside the castle's broken gates?

He lifted his glass. "Chin-chin," said Jeff. "Heaven is lined with pasta like this."

"And hell is getting the fair Giuseppina to serve it."

"Why?"

Carla frowned. "She likes you, as who would not. But she remembers the old days. The days when Cavolfiore did not have to pretend to be comfortable."

"But you love it?"

Her glance came over the top of the wineglass, level, darkening. "I love it. Someone must, and I do."

"Could you ever leave it?"

"I do not know, Jiff. I have made many promises. Even to myself."

She sipped the wine. Jeff tried to hide the doubt in his heart. What promises? And to whom? He could easily imagine some deathbed type of promise to take care of Beppo. Or some darker arrangement, maybe a betrothal to some rich old man. In that case, where was the rich old man? And wouldn't Carla have told him, warned him off? Maybe. Maybe not. Jeff smiled. It was not his most successful effort of the day.

The pasta was followed by tiny roasted game birds. After the game came small pillows of the whitest veal stuffed with cheese. Then a salad, then fresh peaches in a creamy sauce based on zabaglione, with espresso and tiny crisp macaroons.

She broke the silence. "You are sad. And I, too, Jiff. For you and for your uncle. And for us."

He thought about that. Maybe she was trying to say goodbye for real. Forever.

"You act," he said softly, "as though I'm going over the edge of the world."

"And so you are. It is there, you see"—she gestured with one sweep of her splendid arm, taking in all the darkness that obscured the plain. "There is the edge of my world, Jiff. Beyond is only darkness."

"It's only for a week or so."

"When you go on the airplane, a part of Cavolfiore goes with you."

"And will stay with me."

"We hope so."

Jeff bent quickly and kissed her hand. He couldn't think of a thing to say that would change her mood. Maybe it was more a time for deeds. She smiled at his gesture and stood up.

He followed her through the darkened castle and up the stairs. They undressed quickly, by the light of one candle. He found her looking at him gravely, the way a schoolchild might regard an ancient monument. Jeff didn't feel anything like an ancient monument.

She came to him. "A pleasing thing about you, Jeff, is that you have no idea how very beautiful a man you are."

He laughed. He was what he was, and never thought about it.

She reached up and touched his cheek. The brush of a feather. A dark bird passing in the night.

"I will miss you."

Jeff said nothing, but held her tight.

They made love with a quick fugitive urgency. Soon Jeff fell fast asleep. He dreamed of a sacrifice, with him as the victim.

In his dream he was tied to a great altar made from polished wood. He stared helplessly up as a giant fist raised an immense ivory-headed gavel for the death blow. It was Felix Dupre's famous antique gavel, used at every auction at the House of Dupre since anyone could remember.

The gavel rose higher and higher.

Then it came down, faster and faster.

Jeff had just opened his mouth to scream when Carla wakened him with a kiss.

8

The Claridge Grill, London, November 1941

The youngest of the three Neville Fleets would have died rather than admit it, but there was much to be said for the desk job his grandfather had arranged for him at RAF HQ.

For one thing, it meant he could be near Miranda.

And Miranda was the world now.

Even the damned war took second place, a thing Neville could not have imagined even six months before. Before he had rediscovered Miranda Loweswater.

Of course, the Fleets had always known the Loweswaters. It was inevitable. The estates practically adjoined, although Berwick was vastly larger. And Neville had known Johnny Loweswater quite well in college. Poor Johnny, crashed in the channel not six months ago. Of course, that sort of thing was so common now that one almost didn't mention it. Which suited Neville just fine.

The candlelight in Claridge's was a necessity, the product of electricity rationing and blackout. Miranda wore the flickering light like a crown. She was radiant, even in her dull brown WREN's uniform. Slim, blond, shining, and . . . well, Miranda. There didn't have to be anything more than that.

He swirled the last of Claridge's '29 claret in a big balloon of the thinnest crystal. "Confusion," said Neville, "to our enemies."

A flicker of a smile came to her lips. That was the best he'd done all night. He'd have to do better. Neville knew how she missed Johnny. Her only brother, after all, heir to Loweswater House. How right Grandfather had been. All the Loweswaters were completely shattered by John's death.

"You're sad tonight, darling," he said. "Can I help?"

Her smile came back again and stayed longer. "If anyone can, dear Neville, it's you. I was thinking how helpless we seem to be, here on our little island. I thought of Coventry Cathedral. I tried to imagine what it must feel like to be the man who bombed it. Or boy—they're just as young as ours . . . as Johnny. Six hundred years of faith and beauty gone because some German boy pushed a button. Could that actually make anyone happy?"

He reached for her hand and held it. "Shall I tell you what makes me happy? It's if you say you love me."

She actually laughed. It was the happiest sound he'd heard from her in days.

"I do love you, Neville. I love the fact that you are so very sure of things—of yourself. Of me. You're like Berwick itself: solid rock."

"No world that created Miranda Loweswater is going to end, darling, not while I'm here to stop it. Not just when I've found you again."

"You still think of me as a helpless kid."

"I still remember the day I fished you out of that damned moat."

"I was eight then. You must have been . . ."

"Fourteen or so."

"And very glamorous. I called you my knight in shining armor. And pestered the hell out of Johnny to bring you back."

"Well, I am back. Say I can come back and stay. Say you'll marry me."

Instantly she withdrew her hand as though he'd burned her. Maybe he had. Then, slowly, tentatively, her hand made its way across Claridge's gleaming white damask.

"I love you, Miranda."

It seemed that days had passed before she spoke. Months. "Yes."

"You mean . . ."

"Yes, Neville Fleet, I'll be happy to marry you."

He gaped. Fireworks began exploding in his head. Symphonies played. Miranda would marry him. There was a flatness in her voice, as though she were reciting lines in a play and hadn't gotten them quite right yet.

"Darling!"

She managed a laugh. "Fancy, dear: Miranda, Duchess of Berwick. Once again my knight in shining armor rides up and pulls me, dripping and muddy, from the moat of despair. Or was it the slough of despond? I do love you, Neville. And I am flattered and deeply moved that you'd want me."

"Shall we have champagne?"

"Let's!"

He signaled the waiter, who glided from nowhere as if glued to silent tracks, in the comforting manner of all Claridges' waiters from time immemorial.

But before the order could be given, the muted festive sounds in the Grill were shattered by the dread wailing of the air-raid sirens.

"Damn! We'll have to go to the shelter. Well, there's a good one hard by Fleet House, darling, so let's go there and then tell Grandfather. He'll be so pleased."

Neville signed for the check and they joined the hustling guests in a brisk but orderly exodus into the pitch-black street.

The first explosion seemed quite far away, perhaps across the Thames in Lambeth.

The second blast threw them both violently to the ground. Neville had his arm protectively around her, but Miranda cut her cheek anyway. He touched it with his handkerchief, thinking: This is the devil of a way to celebrate one's engagement. Then they hurried on.

The smoke grew thicker, more acrid. Things were surely burning, and not far away. Fleet House was just around the corner and across the square. An ambulance sped by, nearly clipping them, its headlamps taped half-shut.

When Neville's grip suddenly tightened around her, Miranda looked up at him, thinking he might have been hurt in the fall.

She saw that he was staring across the square. In the red glow reflected from the flames, his mouth gaped open and quickly closed.

Neville felt the pavement trembling under him. In his

stomach there was a pile of rocks, and his eyes kept blurring. Even Miranda's hand, clutching his, seemed unreal.

The impossible had happened.

Things like this simply could not happen to the Fleets of Berwick.

Fate would not dare.

But fate had dared.

All the splendor that had ever been Fleet House was a crumpled, blazing ruin.

Now they ran. Neville tried to remember whether his father and grandfather had been dining out tonight. He couldn't remember a thing. Their lives were so frantic these days.

It had been a direct hit.

A small crowd had gathered, some to gape, some to help. There were two air-wardens and a bobby. Neville made his way to the policeman. "Officer . . ."

"I'm sorry, Captain, but you'd best move on to the shelter."

"I am Neville Fleet."

The change in the man's face was immediate and gratifying. "Forgive me then, sir," he said, "but as you can see, there's nothing to be done until the cleanup chaps get here. I'm very sorry, Captain."

"Thank you."

Neville stood there, holding Miranda. The great marble house was broken, perhaps forever. The fine Roman Revival columns of its great portico were shattered, the pediment was in fragments, and all the glass had been blown out from hundreds of tall windows. The better to feed the flames that raged within. Flames! The house was filled with treasures. He thought of the silken carpets from Persia, his grandmother's beloved Táng porcelains, the furniture carved by Chippendale himself. Not to mention paintings by the score and, more to the point, probably the flesh and bones of his father and grandfather.

With an odd, strangled sound, Neville broke away from Miranda and ran up the blackened stairs. The wall of heat within prevented him from coming even close to the blown-out double doors. Maybe from the garden, he thought. If they'd gone to bed in the east wing, it might not have got to them. Yet. All the bedrooms were in the east wing, reaching out into the quiet of the garden, away from Fleet Square.

Blindly Neville ran down the stairs and past a frightened Miranda, wondering as he ran if he had a key for the little door in the garden wall.

His arm was gripped suddenly, in an iron vise. He looked up in outrage, wondering who would presume.

He found himself looking into the anguished eyes of his own grandfather.

"Stop, you idiot!"

The duke's voice could have stopped a regiment.

Neville gulped, ashamed of his panic. "Grandfather!" He embraced the old man. "You're alive."

"So they tell me. But I've got bad news for you, lad. Your father was in there."

Neville looked at his grandfather, and a rush of guilt came over him at the enormity of what he felt. Better father than you, sir, was the sum of it, the terrible lack of feeling for his own father that the young man had always felt but never quite admitted. Not to himself or to anyone.

The loss of his father was sad, but it was nothing to what Neville felt on seeing the wreckage of Fleet House.

Death was to be expected.

Wanton vengeance from on high was not.

He shuddered, passed his hand across his eyes as if that would clear his vision. He looked at Miranda then.

She was looking up at him with an expression of such compassion he could barely stand it. He thought of her dead brother, the enormity of her loss, and how pitiful his own feelings were by comparison.

"How bloody awful," he said at last, "to go like that."

The three of them walked slowly back to Claridge's. For a while they walked in silence, too crushed to speak. They paused in front of the darkened hotel. Claridge's would find room for all of them, Neville was sure of that. He took the duke's hand. "I think, Grandfather," he said stiffly, "that you should know Miranda has consented to marry me."

The duke looked at them, dusty, disheveled, a bit of blood dried on the girl's lovely cheek. The boy, given his propensities, could have done very much worse.

He smiled. "May you both be very happy, children," he said, "now and always. I think," he said, and impulsively bent to kiss Miranda, startling her, "that you shall grace Berwick in a most delightful way, my dear Miranda."

They could not find it in them to celebrate more than that.

They walked into the darkened front door of Claridge's, away from the horror that lay smoldering in the ruins of Fleet House.

The all-clear sounded then, mocking them.

41

9

Minnie Dupre opened the antique French doors that led to her clothes closet. The choice was large. She reached for an azalea-pink silk tweed walking suit. Damned if I'll wear black. He wouldn't want that. Hated me in black. The small act of defiance cheered her.

Not that she gave a damn what people thought if she went out in pink. If she went dancing nude in Central Park, it was her business.

It was so very hard to care about anything now.

She dressed quickly, looked at her reflection in the mirror, made a face of mock horror, and added a touch of pink lipstick. No point in frightening the servants; they were gloomy enough as it was.

Minnie walked down the curving staircase—how he had loved that staircase!—and into the library. Her favorite room, of all the twenty-some rooms in the house, and Felix's.

She had to keep reminding herself he was gone forever.

Somehow, if she'd thought about it at all, Minnie Dupre had always imagined them dying as they had lived—together. Or her going first.

At least he went out in some style. Felix, to whom style came as naturally as breathing. Felix, who could make a car move like the wind, effortlessly. Felix, who could break all speed records between Paris and Cap Ferrat without so much as grazing a chicken.

Minnie rang for the butler. Hastings quickly appeared, and she asked for coffee and a croissant.

"I'll be lunching in, Hastings, and alone. Tell Emmalee just something simple, an omelet or so."

"Yes, madam."

Hastings and Emmalee had been with them at Sixty-fourth Street forever. Well, more than twenty years. In New York that was forever. They held the household together. She silently blessed the impeccably tailored ramrod back of Hastings as he walked out of the room.

Felix's Rolodex was the only jarring note on the lovely old English yew-wood writing table. Neat as it was, the thing looked awkward next to Felix's gilt-bronze French candlestand that had been subtly electrified as a desk lamp.

The coffee came on its gleaming silver tray. She poured a cup and sipped it. Underlying her shock and her pain was one saving fact: Minnie had no regrets whatsoever about her life with Felix.

Her memories were happy ones, and luck had been with Felix and her all the days of their lives. Lucky, to have been born in comfort. Lucky, to have met each other at just the right time, and married. Lucky, maybe, even if it was luck born out of tragedy, to have inherited Jeff Dupre, who had become something like the child they couldn't have. Felix, she knew, had hoped and planned all those years to bring the boy even closer, to bring him into Dupre's. That was a regret for Felix. Still, Jeffy was Jeffy, and they loved him. And the boy loved them back in his own private way. Minnie knew that in her bones.

How good it would be to have the boy back. Well, hardly a boy: Jeff would be twenty-nine in a few months. But she thought of him as a boy. Minnie thought of her nephew as a painfully thin towheaded eleven-year-old trying very hard to be brave, and making it. A little boy with too much to be brave about. There were some things you could never replace in Jeffy's life, however hard you tried. How she had tried, and Felix too.

Well, now she'd have Jeffy back, at least for a little while. They'd be something like a family again. Minnie looked at the Rolodex. Intimidating. So many people to phone.

She worked steadily through the morning, taking some small pleasure in each flip of the Rolodex's cards. Friend after friend, and some business acquaintances too, who simply could not be ignored.

For the art world, this would be a state occasion. One of its great leaders had died and must be properly mourned.

Minnie hated the thought of it, the emptiness of it, but it must be done. Felix, she knew, would have wanted it done.

Felix had always exercised a great sense of style and form, a feeling for doing the right thing.

She sighed, thinking of him.

The phone rang.

Her first instinct was not to answer it. But she did answer. Life was going to go on, there was no point in pretending otherwise.

"Hello?"

"Minnie. How are you?"

It was Morgan St. James. Dear Morgan. If ever there was a rock in a stormy sea, it was him. He'd been wonderful, taking care of everything at Dupre's, helping any way he could. Felix had been right to make him managing director.

"I'm feeling better, thanks, Morgan. How are you?"

"That's why I called. I'm fine—it isn't really urgent—but I think you ought to know about any major moves we make here at Dupre's."

"Well," she said, "that's good of you, Morgan, but you do whatever you think is best, or ask Bunny Bartlett if it's about money."

"Thanks. I have talked to Mr. Bartlett. It's about Neville Fleet, you see."

"I'm afraid I don't."

"You know he's been selling things from Berwick?"

"Yes," she said. "Poor Neville. We knew him quite well, Felix and I. In fact we had supper with him just before . . ."

"I know. Well, he wants to clear out. To sell all the treasures of Berwick Castle. And he's asked for a rather large advance."

"How much?"

"One million dollars. Which is, I'd estimate, about one-fifth—very conservatively—of what the sale will realize."

"Well, if it will help, and it's all right with Bunny, why not?"

"He is selling the Winchcombe Chalice, Minnie. That's how bad it is."

She paused, caught her breath. It was like selling the Fleets' very birthright.

"The chalice too? It must break his heart."

"I'm afraid he is rather bitter. The death duties, you know."

"Well, I suppose it's flattering for Dupre's to have the sale. You do whatever you want, Morgan. About the money."

"Thank you. And if there's anything . . ."

"I thank you, dear Morgan. Really, there isn't. Poor, poor, Neville."

Minnie put down the receiver and thought of Berwick Castle. She thought of a ball there, just before the war, Neville's coming-of-age party. Pairs of bewigged footmen in full livery had flanked the great staircase every three steps, expressionless as statues, holding immense five-branched silver candlesticks, lighting the guests up to the great hall. And Neville—charming, eager to please, a little awed by it all. Poor Neville. It had seemed so permanent. The great bulk of

Berwick Castle itself and all that the castle implied: vast lands, dozens of villages, treasures, titles, all of that.

It hadn't taken Britain's Labor government long, once they came to power, to wreak revenge for two thousand years of being on the losing side of a class war.

At least dear Neville had something left to sell. There were plenty of his kind, Minnie knew, who were truly broke and defenseless. They had been bred to rule over the world that didn't exist anymore. And if that world had been unfair and cruel, there had also been a special glory to it. A glory that would not come again.

Felix's little Cartier desk clock merrily chimed twelve.

Once again Minnie reached for the Rolodex. Maybe she could get through the L's and M's before lunch.

10

Polly Kunimara looked at her tiny cubicle and grinned. Some quarters for the new head of the silver department at Dupre's! She had been promoted, but her rat's-nest office hadn't. For all the grandeur out front, the worker bees at Dupre's struggled anywhere some sadist with a slide rule could fit them.

One office joke was that they should be replaced with Munchkins.

There were days when Polly's dream of luxury was five feet more of workspace and one decent filing cabinet. Her desk was piled with manila folders and with papers.

An irreplaceable Hester Bateman ale mug that would bring at least thirty thousand dollars at auction lurched dangerously on top of a week's worth of uncompleted catalog reports. The Bateman mug, too, was waiting to be cataloged. And there, on the right, was a stack of photographs for Polly's evaluation. This was her least favorite chore. The pictures were usually amateur in quality, and it was almost impossible to tell much from any photograph, however distinct. Silver was all too easy to fake. It could fool your eye and your hand. So Polly's replies were always qualified: "If this is what it appears to be . . ." The final evaluation could only be made with the object right there in front of her.

Polly looked at her desk and shrugged.

The Bateman mug would have to wait. Ever since Felix's death, no one seemed to know which end was up. Not Morgan St. James. Surely not Polly herself. She was doubly saddened by Felix's accident. She had been fond of the old gentleman. And it had been Felix himself who had promoted her, just two weeks before he died. Who was to say what was in store for her now? Rumors were everywhere. They always were, in the art world. It was one part of the business Polly hated. The constant speculation: who was doing what to whom, and for how much?

She had heard the Dupre family intended to sell out.

She had heard the House of Dupre was in very bad shape financially.

Polly had heard so many rumors these last few weeks that she'd stopped listening to them.

This did not make them go away. They seethed in her subconscious like a nest of aggressive little serpents, coiled and poisonous and ready to strike.

One of the rumors was about the mystery heir, Jeff Dupre.

That he'd come marching in and sack them all. And if that happened, what could Polly do about it? She sighed. She'd worked hard all her life to get this far. To this dusty little cubicle in the House of Dupre.

Well, at the bottom line she did have good experience. She did have her doctorate in art history from Columbia, and she had worked her way up to being the head of Dupre's silver department, which was no mean feat for a lady of twenty-six, no matter if hell boiled over.

Which it seemed to be doing, hotter every hour.

Morgan St. James was the boss now. He'd always been scrupulously polite to Polly, no more, no less. She couldn't read Morgan.

He wasn't the kind of man you could go to and ask him just how things stood. Poor bastard, he probably doesn't know any more than I do, she thought, and reached out to touch the lovely old Bateman mug for luck.

It's you and me against the world, now, Hester, baby.

As she looked at the mug, Polly felt better.

There were compensations in her job that had nothing to do with titles or salaries. There was the pleasure of working with beautiful things. And there was the thrill of discovery, the chance now and then of truly helping someone.

Polly still got goose bumps when she thought of the old widower in Forest Hills in whose drab walk-up apartment she had recently discovered three silver bowls by Paul Revere. The man had sat silent in a threadbare chair: he'd recently had a stroke and was only partially recovered. And there, among the plastic dishes and early Grand Rapids furniture, were his aunt's sugar bowls, gleaming like beacons. The old gentleman had wept when Polly told him of his luck, and Polly had hugged him and wept too. The three bowls would bring no less than a hundred thousand dollars at auction. Enough to buy the man some extra care and comfort for his last years.

Sometimes there were disappointments, too. People who were sure they owned treasures but in fact had relatively worthless reproductions. Everyone in the business had some well-worn variation on the phrase "Yes, of course, it has some decorative value, but . . ."

Polly wondered about the young man who was rumored to have inherited Dupre's. There had been many a fantasy spun out around the unseen "Mr. Jeff."

To hell with Mr. Jeff, she thought. What about Miss Polly?

To have worked so hard, to have been rewarded at last, and now to see it all endangered just because a nice old man failed to control his Jaguar seemed a bit of irony Polly could have easily done without. Very easily.

When all else failed, Polly made tea. It was, she thought, her Japanese chromosomes trying to tell her something. She reached for her stoneware mug and the immersion coil that would make the water boil. That done, she found a tea bag and put it in the mug to steep. Betraying, she thought ruefully, all my thousands of Japanese ancestors. Well, the ancestors had been betrayed often enough now to be used to it. Surely, when Dad married his Irish girlfriend, there had been much spinning in graves. It was from this unlikely mixture that Polly and her three brothers had sprung: all of them tall and slim as reeds, with black hair and ivory skin and the faintest upward tilt of eye and cheekbone. People often thought the Kunimara kids were Vietnamese or Polynesian. Obviously a mixture. And a damn good one, she thought a little defiantly.

Polly had never felt beautiful. When a photographer stopped her on the street one day five years back and asked her to pose for a perfume advertisement, she recoiled. The man was obviously a pimp. His name meant nothing to her: Avedon. This had happened twice since then, with other photographers. Polly no longer suspected them of pimpdom, but she wasn't interested.

Whatever glory that kind of work might bring, it would be transitory.

What Polly was doing at Dupre's would build, and last.

And in the meantime there had been Christophe.

Speaking of beautiful, Christophe had lit out for California at almost exactly the time Felix Dupre had promoted Polly. Thank God for the promotion. For something to think about. Polly tried not to think about Christophe. It wasn't a very good try. She picked up the Bateman mug. Never fall for an actor, Hester old girl: somewhere behind those beautiful faces, they're always rehearsing an exit line.

Christophe had a series now. Any Thursday on prime time you could watch Christophe slug it out with the bad guys. Polly had turned the damn thing on by accident one night. And there he came, bare-chested, running right at the camera full tilt. That face. That body. Running, as he'd run from her.

Luckily, she'd been alone. It was not one of her happier moments. It was like turning over a rock and finding a black hole that went all the way to hell.

Not that they'd parted enemies. He just wasn't there one day. He'd taken all his clothes, one of the world's definitive blue-jean collections, his heavy little barbells, her two favorite Vivaldi records, and his vanity.

And he left a note.

He also left a gaping hole in Polly's life. When all his charm, energy, and sex were focused in her direction, Christophe was irresistible. What she never realized until he was gone was that the full blast of Christophe's charm would simply sweep away any one person: it was bigger than that, and it fed on bigger audiences. Ate them up, in fact. Well, he had a bigger audience now. He had all the world, and good luck to him.

Polly tried not to be bitter, and sometimes she succeeded.

It was something to remember.

It was also something to forget.

Polly frowned. Christophe. Ted Kavanaugh. She'd only really had two men in her life.

They couldn't have been more different, one from the other. Christophe was all flash and dazzle, pure raw electricity lighting up the night.

Ted . . . well, Ted was everything solid and steady and fun. Ted, who had given up the possibility of a downtown law career to join the New York City police force, of all things.

She had admired him for that.

She had learned to love him later.

But it hadn't worked out with Ted, either. She'd been so much younger then. Just four years ago, but it seemed like forever. Too young, too enchanted with New York, with the possibilities of her job to ever think about marrying.

It had ended badly.

It had ended with Ted wanting her more than she wanted him. Even though she did want him. Well, it was over now. And Christophe was gone. And what did she have to fill the long nights now?

Maybe, she thought, sipping the tea, which was still too hot, that's why you like it so much among the Reveres and the Batemans. Paul Revere would never run off with your Vivaldi records.

She unlocked her desk drawer and pulled out the little tape recorder. Polly always taped her catalogs and gave them to the secretarial pool for typing, then made any changes on the typed copy. It seemed to go faster that way. She clicked the machine on.

"Item four-twenty-six, Dupre Silver and Enamel sale of December 11. An exceptionally fine ale mug, capacity twenty-six ounces, silver weight 32.5 ounces. By Hester Bateman, London, circa 1780. This is a fine example of Mrs. Bateman's late period in the Adam style . . ."

Polly went on, cataloging the Bateman mug and several other pieces whose history and valuation she had recorded on notes during the past week. She recited her facts mechanically.

She was wondering what to wear to the funeral tomorrow.

11

Berwick Castle, September 1943

Neville and his bride stood in the courtyard, holding hands shyly, as though they were still teenagers. He could feel her hand trembling. He came closer, and folded his arms around her slender body.

Miranda looked up at him and smiled. "I still can't believe it, darling, that all this is ours."

He kissed her. That was what he most loved in Miranda,

the innocence, the childlike qualities. "For all the Fleets forever," he said, "and you are now a Fleet, Miss Loweswater, in case it hadn't occurred to you."

She laughed.

It was good to hear Miranda laugh.

"I always feel so safe here," she said softly. "Berwick is what England's all about."

"Berwick takes care of its own, as should England. Have you ever met old Mortimer?"

"I don't think so. Who's Mortimer?"

"One of my favorite residents in all the castle. Come."

He took her hand and led her inside. Down the great central hall they went, and into the oldest part of the castle, and through a small arched doorway and down winding stairs that had been cut into the living rock underneath the castle almost a thousand years past. The stairs were steep and crudely formed, their forward edges worn smooth by the feet of dukes and serfs and prisoners and by fifteen generations of Fleets.

Neville knew the dungeons by heart now. And aside from showing the skeleton called Mortimer to his bride, Neville had a plan for the dungeons. They would make a perfect bomb shelter. And they would shelter not only people, but the treasures of Berwick Castle, too.

The sight of Fleet House in flaming ruins was vividly burned into Neville's brain. He had had only the vaguest idea of the value of its contents.

The duke had educated him quickly and painfully. "More than two million pounds."

"And none of it insured?" Neville was not used to dealing with figures, or to thinking about money. There had always been plenty, and he had naturally assumed that there always would be plenty.

"A token, a token. A few hundred thousand pounds. We must get everything in Berwick appraised, and at once. This cannot happen again."

"You think they'd bomb Berwick?"

"Come, lad, what are you doing in that damned office at the RAF? Of course they'd bomb Berwick. Berwick's a symbol of everything they want to bomb. As was Coventry. They'd bomb Berwick and Windsor and Buck House and the lot, and never think twice about it."

Neville tried not to think about that conversation. He tried, and failed.

The dungeon steps wound down and down. There were six

50

levels to these dungeons, the lowest just a few feet above the riverbed of the Severn.

Miranda clung to him. They reached the second level, and he led her down a corridor to the right. A powerful electric torch made a yellow carpet before them on the rough-hewn stone floor.

And here was the death pit. Neville took Miranda's arm, anticipating her reaction. She screamed at the sight of old Mortimer, and grabbed at his arm and held him very tight.

Neville laughed.

She twisted in his arms and slapped him, hard, on the face. Still he held her.

"Why did you do that, Neville?" she asked, her eyes wide with panic. "Why?"

He pulled her close. "Darling, I am sorry. I'm so used to him . . . well, I just didn't expect you'd be so upset."

A tear formed at the corner of her left eye. "I get upset easily, darling. But this . . ." She pointed to the pit and would not look in it.

"This is only Berwick, protecting its own, my darling," he said gently. "I only wanted to share all of Berwick with you. I want you to be a part of it all, the past and the future too."

"Dear Neville. I am silly, aren't I?"

She wiped the tear away and managed to smile.

"You are the loveliest woman in England . . . in the world. Ten Berwick Castles would not be good enough for you, my darling."

Gently, his arm still around her, Neville led her back from the pit. And all of the way he spoke to her of Berwick, of his love for the castle and for her and how his two great loves were bound together, inextricably and forever.

"Dear Neville," she said again, squeezing his hand in hers.

They had reached the main floor of the castle now. He led her down the hallway, past the little chapel and into the blue drawing room. It was empty. Neville and Miranda were alone in the castle for their honeymoon. The duke had tactfully left them quite by themselves, rightly guessing how much of a luxury that would be in the midst of the frantic wartime hub-bub that was London in 1943.

They sat on an old French divan and held hands.

For the tenth time that day Neville blessed his grandfather. It still felt like playacting, but here he was, the future Duke of Berwick, with his bride, alone and in command. And what loveliness was his to command! Neville looked at her with a hunger that was more than sexual. He wanted to possess her entirely and in every part of his mind, his heart, his soul.

They did indeed have happier things to remember, even now, just three days married, than the destruction of Fleet House and the death of Neville's father almost two years before.

To Neville, their wedding still seemed like a dream.

An impossibly beautiful dream.

He had wangled a whole week away from the RAF. They were married quietly, in the Loweswater family church at Spurge-upon-Thames. Miranda had chosen a short white afternoon dress. Over it she had worn her grandmother's point-de-Venise lace veil. She had carried a small bouquet of lilies of the valley from the garden at Loweswater House. The reception, for just fifty close friends and family, was at home.

Still, the event made headlines. His ancient title. The romance of Berwick Castle's heir. Miranda's distinguished family and her startling beauty. Britain at war needed to be reminded what she was fighting for.

Neville and his bride seemed to personify everything that Britain held most sacred: family, honor, youth, tradition.

They brightened breakfast tables from Edinburgh to the Isle of Man.

Neville and Miranda had driven the short distance from Loweswater House to Berwick right after the reception. He could smell the sweet fragrance of her bridal bouquet even now.

The duke had a surprise waiting for them: the suite that had belonged to Neville's parents had been especially redecorated for the young couple. It filled the third level of the great round tower: three rooms, roughly wedge-shaped to accommodate the curve of the outer wall. There was a large bedroom with many windows, a sitting room, a dressing room, and a bath. The room had been freshly painted in a soft blue trimmed with ivory. A small painting by Stubbs of a palomino being walked on Hampstead Heath hung over the white marble fireplace. There was a dazzling Persian hunting carpet Neville had never seen before. Fresh chintz on the bed and in the curtains. There were flowers everywhere, and champagne cooling an antique silver-gilt bucket. A note from the duke gave them his blessings and a large check.

"Listen, darling," Neville said, reading: " 'To Neville and Miranda, who are the future. With all my love and fond expectations on this very happy day. Neville, Duke of Berwick.' "

"He's a dear."

"Yes. He's a rare specimen. A lot to live up to."

Her reply was a kiss.

In the silence of twilight, inside these thick stone walls, surrounded by Berwick Castle and a thousand years of legends, it was almost possible to imagine that there was no war. Almost. Even here in the heart of the castle, every window was heavily shaded to observe the blackout regulations.

But there love needed no light other than its own radiance, its own unquiet fire.

Neville was every bridegroom, eager, urgent, scarcely able to believe in his good luck.

Miranda was emphatically not every bride. "I'm so afraid," she whispered. "I only want to be good for you. I want us to be as happy as this always."

His fingers found the buttons of her dress. "We will be, my darling," he whispered. "I promise."

12

Minnie Dupre stood aside from the crowd and watched her nephew as he came through the door from customs. There was a moment before Jeff saw her. Minnie was grateful for that moment.

She hadn't expected the wave of emotion that hit her then. He looked so young, so vulnerable. Jeff was Felix's blood relative, not hers. Yet it seemed to Minnie that a part of her life was coming down the hallway at her, smiling. It must be like this to be a mother, she thought: he looks too thin, even with the suntan, even with his hair streaked almost white by the sun.

Then he saw her. "Minnie! You didn't have to come fetch me."

He kissed her and lifted her right off her feet, laughing. Jeffy's arms might be thin, but they'd logged many an hour on the business end of a shovel. He looks like a schoolboy still, she thought, in his blue jeans and the alligator shirt. Time seemed suspended. For a moment it was almost as though Jeff was a schoolboy, coming back from some sun-drenched holiday. It was almost as though their hopes for the boy still rang true. As though Felix would be at home waiting.

Jeff had one small suitcase and a clothes bag. The limousine was waiting. They settled down in the cool, spacious rear compartment.

"I'm terribly sorry, Minnie," Jeff said at once, blurting it out. "He might not have known it, but I loved Felix."

"He knew, my darling, be sure of it."

"How are you?"

He looked at her: she was obviously tired, strained. Unusually quiet.

Now, for the first time, the impact of Felix's death hit him head-on. It was one thing to get an unexpected message in a trench in Veii. It was quite another thing to see what the event had done to his aunt. To his only living relative.

Minnie was not what Jeff would ever call beautiful, but she had always been elegant, laughing, radiating happiness. She was not and never would be the kind of woman who takes her wrinkles to the surgeon.

You never noticed what lines age had made on her face. Too many other things were always happening there. But now Jeff noticed, and he worried.

Now, for the first time, Jeff was aware of the effort Minnie invested in her charm, her thoughtfulness. Coming out like this to meet him.

And what had he done to deserve it? To deserve her love, or Felix's? He'd been born a Dupre by chance and orphaned by chance, and they'd taken him in like their own.

And he'd paid them back by building walls around himself just as fast as he could.

He took her hand then, and pressed it. Her hand was cold.

Finally she answered his question. "Rotten, if you want the truth. Something like this happens, Jeffy, and nothing seems to make sense anymore. I never thought of myself as living for Felix. But of course I did. You always do, when you love someone. And it's all nonsense, what people say—about at least we were happy, at least there aren't any regrets. The happier we were—and we were happy, weren't we?—the sadder I am now. I'm not going to be a hypocrite and deny it. That much, I can do for his memory."

"What can I do?"

She smiled. It was a quick little smile, a catch-it-while-you-can smile.

"You've already done it, Jeffy. You are here. That means everything to me. I was so wrapped up in my life with Felix,

54

and you always seem so self-sufficient, that it hadn't really dawned on me that we're all there is. You and me. The entire family is riding in this car."

The rented limousine slipped quietly through the blistering August afternoon: cool, sleek funereal. Jeff and his aunt talked of many things. But mostly of Felix. She told Jeff about tomorrow's memorial service, how his uncle had asked to be cremated and buried in the old family plot in Westchester.

The car moved briskly down the Long Island Expressway. In silence now, the first rush of questions and answers having subsided, they glided past the shabby remnants of the last World's Fair. The immense hollow sphere that had been the fair's symbol, the bare bones of a terrestrial globe, gleamed dully now through layers of grime. The skeleton of hope. They passed the overpopulated graveyards that ring New York's airports like a sadistic joke. They plunged into the dark heart of the Midtown Tunnel and resurfaced on the other side into the insistent glare. The heat outside was relentless. There seemed to be no breeze at all. The trees looked dusty. They wore their leaves with a sluggish air. It wasn't anything like the crisp dry heat of Veii.

Jeff thought of his trenches, of the potsherd he'd left where he found it, of Corky directing the dig. Well, it's a good break for Corky, and the kid deserves it. And the Etruscans have been waiting for more than two thousand years. They can wait a little longer. If the *tombaroli* don't get there first.

"It'll be good to get home."

Minnie smiled, and her smile carried a sharp pang of guilt right to Jeff's heart. He meant what he'd said. It was good to be home. He did want to help. But there was another, unstated emotion in him, impossible to deny: It'll be even better to get back to Veii, where I belong. Veii and Cavolfiore.

The Dupre house looked to Jeff's eyes exactly as it always had looked: splendid. Built of white limestone in a time when craftsmen were plentiful and cost was no object, the house had a French lightness that belied its size. There were classical pilasters and pediments framing the tall windows. Iron spun like lace made elegant balconies on the parlor floor. Fifty feet wide and four stories tall, the Dupre house reflected the easy grace of its owners. Jeff wondered what it would be like without Felix. Maybe Minnie wouldn't want such a huge place now, just for herself.

He wondered what it cost to run a place like this, the taxes, the servants, heating, all that. Jeff had hardly thought about such things before. In his little apartment at Cambridge, on his digs, he was always more or less camping out. He walked up the six limestone steps, carrying his luggage. The door opened as if by magic. Hastings had been waiting for them. "Welcome home, Mr. Jeff."

Jeff shook the butler's hand. "It's good to see you, Hastings."

It was. Jeff felt the house all around him: cool and elegant and protective. Felix's house. Felix's creation. The lightness of the place, the easy rightness with which the furniture and rugs and paintings fit together, made it a work of art. Jeff had always taken the Dupre house for granted: it was where he'd lived more of his life than any other place. But now, at twenty-eight. Jeff had seen many houses in many parts of the world. The impact of Felix Dupre's house was the greater now. Jeff knew, merely standing in the front hallway, that Minnie would never leave Sixty-fourth Street. And it was easy to understand why.

It was not easy to understand why he had never really felt at home here. God knew Felix and Minnie had done everything to make it seem like home. *It's because I'm really a turtle, and my home is wherever I happen to be. I carry my little hard shell around with me, and I spend a lot of time keeping strangers out.* Still, standing in the elegant foyer of Minnie's house, Jeff felt like a guest.

A very welcome guest, but a guest all the same.

"Let me say hello to Emmalee," he said, "and shower. I'll be down in ten minutes."

Emmalee Jefferson was a monument to her own good cooking. Solid but not fat, the black woman was nearly six feet tall and imposing. Her solemn features broke into an enormous grin when Jeff came into her kitchen. "Mr. Jeff, you are too skinny," she said, laughing as he kissed her. "Those Eyetalians must be putting the evil eye on you."

"If anyone can save me, it's you, Emmalee: what's for supper?"

"That," she said momentously, "is for me to know and you to find out. But you wouldn't be all wrong if you guessed there's an egg on it."

"Schnitzel?"

"You got it."

"I love you. Emmalee, how's my aunt? She looks tired."

Emmalee frowned. "That's a sad, sad lady, Mr. Jeff. Don't eat right. I mean, we're all sad, but she's the saddest. It will pass. Mrs. Dupre has what it takes, never fear. That lady has moxie."

He smiled. "Moxie. It's been a long time since I've heard anyone say that. She does have moxie."

The cook cracked an egg deftly and cupped the two halves of the shell one inside the other. "It's good for you to be here, Mr. Jeff. She missed you. We all missed you."

"Thanks. I missed you, too."

He went up the back stairs three flights to his old room.

Minnie and Felix never changed it. There was his autographed football, signed by the entire Yale team, his most treasured possession at age twelve. Trophies for swimming sparkled from the bookshelves. There was a picture of his parents that he'd forgotten about. They were sitting in the cockpit of a big sailboat, looking impossibly young in party clothes: she dark and elegant, he tall and blond and laughing. I must get that copied, he thought. They look so happy in it.

Jeff thought of the yellow sailboat, empty, drifting.

Hastings had unpacked. Jeff had forgotten about houses where they unpacked for you. He'd brought very little: his one dark summer suit for the funeral, some blue jeans, a few shirts. There would be clothes here, he knew. Jeff hadn't grown an inch taller or an ounce heavier since he was eighteen. His schoolboy clothes would still fit.

He showered and changed into clean jeans and went down to find Minnie.

Minnie had changed, too, into something yellow and flowery. It was easy to understand the gesture. All of Minnie's mourning would be done on the inside.

Automatically, without asking, Jeff made their favorite aperitif: white Lillet on the rocks with a wedge of lime. He handed her the big cut-crystal glass.

"It seems dumb to say cheers," he said quietly, "but, anyway, cheers."

"Not dumb at all, my darling," she said, smiling. "Cheers, indeed. The last thing, the very last thing he'd want would be for us to moon about like old dishrags."

"It's odd," said Jeff after the first small sip of the icy drink. "This is even his drink. I mean, it was Felix who gave me my first Lillet. My first drink of any kind, whenever that was."

"He was a born teacher. He had that magic in him: to make everything fun."

Jeff hesitated, then sat down in Felix's old wing chair. "I wish I could have been more what he wanted me to be."

"Jeffy, he was terribly proud of you, of what you've done. And what you're doing. It was understandable, he always wanted a son and Felix loved Dupre's: it was natural he'd want you to have it."

"Will you sell out?"

She hesitated. Jeff wondered if he'd been too blunt.

"We'll talk to Bunny about that tomorrow. I've invited him for supper after it's all over. I think I'll sell, Jeffy, unless you want the place. It isn't really very profitable, you know, and I'm surely not interested in running it. If we can get a good price, well, that money will do you more good, in the long run, if it's well invested now, in something else."

"Don't, for heaven's sake, worry about me, Minnie. It's you we've got to think about."

She smiled. "I'm fine, darling. As fine as you can be when your heart's just been ripped out. But, truly, I'll be all right. With or without Dupre's. What I need at the moment," she said, sipping the drink, "is you."

"And you'll have me, just as long as you want."

They walked down to dinner then, and Jeff wondered, disloyally, how long his aunt would want him around. His own timetable allowed for a week. If it had to be more, then it would be more.

Emmalee's schnitzel was even better than Jeff remembered. And there was homemade peach ice cream for dessert.

"The way to my heart," said Jeff, "is paved with Emmalee's cooking."

"Have you met anyone?"

He laughed at her quaint way of putting it. "The other night we met a pair of tomb robbers. But that's not what you mean, is it?"

"No, darling, I am being a coy old lady. Of course it isn't. My generation thinks that marriage is the natural order of things, all evidence notwithstanding. We imagine that it magically confers happiness, that everyone who isn't married wants to be."

"I'm romantic enough to go along with that. But only with someone very special. And to answer your question, I'm not sure."

"Then there is someone?"

"There could be."

"Well, Jeffy, she's a lucky girl."

"I'm not sure she'd agree."

"If she doesn't, maybe she doesn't deserve you."

Again he laughed. "You make me sound like the prize in some cosmic raffle."

"You are, my darling. I know you're too shy to admit it to yourself, Jeffy, but that's exactly what you are. And I don't know what I'd do without you."

Jeff looked at her. He felt torn, and he felt helpless. Torn by guilt and by the impossibility of doing anything, really, that would help her.

The only way to help Minnie was to bring Felix back from the dead.

All the things Jeff might have done and hadn't came back to haunt him now.

Suddenly his life seemed selfish, uncaring.

It took something as big as death to make him see that.

His aunt smiled, and he smiled back. But the air was filled with questions, and Jeff didn't have any of the answers.

He couldn't live her life, not now, not ever.

It was all he could do to live his own.

And still she needed him, just needed him to be here. Well, then, here he'd be. For a while, anyway. Until the worst of it was over.

And even as he sat there struggling with his guilt, Jeff found himself hoping it would all be over soon.

13

The Royal Palace of Hampton Court, April 1531

The diamond-paned window was half-open to the bright morning. Outside, tulips danced in a breeze merry as the king's heart. Yellow they were, and red, his favorite colors. Merry they were, and proud. King Henry paused for a moment in a shaft of sunlight so yellow it might have been spread on the air with a butter knife. He smiled, and reached for his lute. It was a day for singing.

Henry's voice was clear and surprisingly light for a man of his age and girth. Henry Tudor felt the music gladdening him. This very day she'd be here! The Lady Anne was coming down from Hever Castle. He stopped singing and laid down the polished, inlaid lute. The promise of the freshening year was mostly the promise of Anne Boleyn.

So much had happened, and so much more was about to

happen, and all for the love of Anne. Wolsey down in disgrace, dead now, but doomed in any case, and Henry in his palace. The cardinal had aimed too high. Henry had coveted the palace from the first. As he had coveted the Lady Anne from the first. Now the greatest palace in all England was his. Just as all the treasures of the popish monasteries, abbeys, and cathedrals were his, glittering mounds of gold and silver, silks and velvets, lands and villages too! Rome had challenged him, to its eternal sorrow, and now all that had been Rome's in England was Henry Tudor's.

Soon Anne would be his too, for all her proud resistance.

Henry looked down at the hundreds of tulips, fresh, proud, and merry. He thought of girls' skin, smooth as tulip petals. Henry thought of all the merry ones, the ladies fine and frisking, serving maids and countesses. He thought of Bessie Blount, who gave him much pleasure and a son. The son his Spanish wife could never bear him. God's judgment, that was, for taking his brother's wife. Henry thought of Anne's elder sister, Mary, eager and fragrant. Too eager, perhaps. The Boleyns were all rather eager. All but the Lady Anne. Anne was a risk-taker. To withhold her favors from her king, lord, and liege! That was risking all. And Anne's gamble was working. Henry, bred in the chance game of kingship, was the first to acknowledge that. And he loved her the more for having wit enough and spirit enough to bring the thing off.

For bring it off Anne most surely would. She would have his hand before he had her body. He, who could have any woman's body for the asking. And—yes!—her head too, for that matter.

They accused her of sorcery, cited the odd little sixth finger that was trying to sprout from her left hand. Maybe she was a witch. Surely she had bewitched her king good and proper. But Henry knew this witchcraft had nothing to do with dark powers.

Lightly, seductively, Anne played upon the strings of his fickle heart. He danced to her tune now, and knew it, and reveled in the dance.

The Lady Anne Boleyn not only attempted to rule the king's heart, she carried it off with the same easy grace with which she wore the latest styles from the French king's court.

Had she learned this sorcery at the court of Paris?

Henry tried to recall their very first meeting, and could not. It had been during the enormous celebration at the Field of the Cloth of Gold. She had been just thirteen then, little more than a child. What magic had been wrought in the eleven years since!

Henry, who could have any woman in his bed with the crook of a finger, quivered with longing for her. This slender, quick, dark wraith of a girl who'd kiss and laugh and elude him as if she were made of smoke and moonlight. Henry felt his flesh glowing with the proud urgency of lust, and he knew Anne was much more than moonlight.

A girl who could make kings tremble thus was a creature to be reckoned with.

And Henry felt the day of reckoning coming ever closer, warming him. Damn Catherine! Damn Rome! It was Anne he wanted, and a son, and Anne he would have. And fine lusty boys, Tudors to fill this palace, and the great hall a-building, and all the other palaces royal, now and for all time. His sons, and Anne's. What sons they would be, all fire and wit, clever sons, strong and quick with the gift of laughter, loving life and all its pleasures. Especially one pleasure. The Tudor grasp on England's throne had been too hardwon, and too lately, to let it slip away for want of an heir.

Henry strode from the room, the great golden chain around his neck clinking merrily. Automatically his hand reached up to the chain. He fondled the great jewel that hung there, an immense ruby that had once belonged to Wolsey. Fitting that he should wear Wolsey's jewel in Wolsey's palace. Henry smiled at the thought. And at the thought of the vast, uncounted, uncountable riches of all the monastic orders in the realm, flowing into his treasury through the Court of Augmentation. Well-named court!

As Henry walked, his mood lightened. He brushed all thoughts of the Tudor succession from his head. He tried to recapture the buoyant feeling with which he had taken up his lute earlier on. She was coming! It was April. Green tendrils were shooting up to dance in the embrace of the sun. And his Anne, Lady Anne, Anne of the haunting eyes and quicksilver laugh, Anne would be here at Hampton Court. And she would have a very special present.

Henry Tudor, the eighth king of England to bear that name, entered the antechamber of his bedroom suite. Through the open doors he strode, smiling, nodding, giving away nothing of his innermost thoughts.

The king's own bedchamber was empty. Henry quickened his pace as he approached the big room. After all, wasn't he a man on an urgent mission? The mission was nothing less than altering the very destiny of England. And alter it he would, in the most delightful way!

Henry entered his bedchamber and closed the carved oak door behind him. He crossed to the wainscoted wall next to his bed. The paneling was carved in a pattern contrived to resemble the folds in an altarcloth. Wolsey's conceit; little had the vainglorious cardinal imagined to what frolics his sacred panels would bear witness. Henry laughed, and the walls rang with the king's glee.

He pressed a corner of the wainscoting. A hidden door swung open, subtle as the cardinal's mind. There was a deep recess within.

Something gleamed there. Henry reached in, crouching, grasped the shining object, and withdrew it.

The Court of Augmentation had done its work well.

Henry held the big goblet on high, letting it catch the sunlight. For a moment he wondered if this was too splendid a gift for a country squire's daughter. But no! Nothing was too much for the Lady Anne.

He tried to imagine the expression on her dear face when first she saw the thing, and could not. That, too, was part of Anne's appeal: her moods were as unpredictable as the very clouds in the sky. Would she think it vulgar? But who could think the Winchcombe Chalice anything but a masterpiece of the jeweler's art?

It twinkled. It beckoned. The cunningly wrought grapevines seemed to tremble in the fresh spring air, to drink in the light. The rubies glowed with a warm, mysterious light of their own. Red as pleasure. Softly polished, they had a fine liquid promise. Like the lips of his lady love. His Lady Anne.

Henry imagined Anne's lips touching the rim of the chalice, the chalice filled with his rarest wine. She loved her wine, did the Lady Anne. They all did, at the court of the French king. Henry would just as soon quaff his ale, or mead, or malmsey. But for Anne it was the red vintage of Burgundy, no less.

Well, she would have it, and from the rarest goblet in the land. And tonight. And soon, soon . . . He closed his eyes to imagine the having of her. Soon. Very soon.

His hand tightened around the vine-crusted stem of the great chalice. Henry caught himself praying, then threw his head back and roared with surprise and laughter. *For I am the church now, and shall I pray to myself?* His eyes sparkled with delight at the realization.

Lucky chalice, to press those lips. Lucky king, to be so

close to paradise on earth! Henry Tudor blinked his shrewd blue eyes open and regarded the Winchcombe Chalice with respect.

Yes, beyond any doubt, it was a fitting present for the lady. A great rarity, as was she. A work of the most consummate beauty, as was she. A magical fusion of brightness and sensuality, as, by all the gods that ever were, was his Lady Anne Boleyn!

Henry gently replaced the chalice in its secret hiding place and closed the door. Again he tried to imagine her face when he made his gift. Again he failed. He sighed. A heavy, balding man who, before very long, would be forty. And still no son on the right side of the blanket. *Just wait! Just wait. The game isn't over yet, not by a longbow's flight.*

14

Jeff woke unrested. He hadn't slept much.

His room was haunted by the ghosts of all the things he hadn't done for his uncle in his lifetime. The service was scheduled for ten o'clock, in old St. Thomas' on Madison Avenue, just up the street from the House of Dupre.

At half-past nine Minnie and Jeff were standing side by side in the church's foyer, waiting to receive the mourners of Felix Dupre.

Minnie still resisted wearing black. "Black isn't a color, darling, it's a state of mind."

Jeff remembered her saying that one time long ago. Today she wore a plain silk dress of navy blue, and pearls. Jeff, too, was in his one good dark blue summer suit, feeling stiff and formal and sad. He wouldn't know most of the mourners, and they wouldn't know him. The whole damn service was a gesture, a symbol, something Minnie felt had to be done. One more milestone on the road to where?

Minnie stood closest to the entrance and greeted people first.

Thank God.

It was an impressive-looking crowd. Jeff recognized about one face in ten. They would be rich, most of them, collectors and curators and gallery owners. And, of course, friends. The entire staff of Dupre's was coming, Minnie had said, but for a few security guards. Jeff shook hands with elegant old men, Felix's contemporaries, and with sleek jet-set women, young men with restless eyes who made Jeff think of the ghosts of gigolos. He thanked them for coming. It seemed the simplest thing to say.

He said it again and again.

Morgan appeared, one friendly face in a sea of strangers.

He bent to kiss Minnie on the cheek, said something to her, softly, that Jeff didn't catch. Then he took Jeff's hand and touched his shoulder with the other. Not quite a hug. More than a handshake.

The good old face looked sad today. But Morgan managed a smile. "Jeff. I am so very sorry. How are you?"

"Very happy to see you, Morgan. Thanks for coming."

"You'll come by the store while you're here?"

"Sure. How about tomorrow?"

"I'd like that. Look forward to it."

Then St. James seemed to realize he was causing a bit of a traffic jam in the receiving line, smiled, and made his way into the church.

A cab came screeching up to the curb and a girl got out. She unfolded herself from the backseat: tall, slender, dark, and very beautiful. Slightly Oriental. Jeff stared, forgot the name of the old lady in front of him, blushed, shook the lady's hand, and stared again.

The girl was walking purposefully up the stairs now. She wore a dress so simple it was almost a cartoon: a sleeveless sheath of sapphire blue with a modestly scooped neck. No jewelry at all but for one thin gold chain around her long graceful neck. Her glossy black hair was simply coiled in a kind of bun. She came up to his aunt and extended her hand and murmured something Jeff couldn't catch.

Jeff had an urgent impulse to see what all that hair would look like uncoiled.

"Jeff, this is Miss Kunimara, who's the head of Dupre's silver department."

"How do you do," said Polly. "I'm very sorry about your uncle."

"Thank you for coming," was all Jeff could manage. "We'll miss him a lot."

"So will I," said Polly, and vanished into the church.

If Jeff had been hit on the head with a two-by-four it could hardly have been more startling. *Of all of the damn impossible emotions to have in the receiving line of a funeral, you turkey, lust has to rank as number one.* Then he composed himself and turned to the next person to pass through the line.

"Thanks for coming," Jeff said solemnly, wishing he were anyplace else in the world but here.

The service was mercifully brief. Felix Dupre's oldest friend gave a moving eulogy. Bunny Bartlett had been Felix's roommate at Yale, and they had been best friends ever since.

Bunny spoke with the force of the board chairman he was, and with warmth and skill and undisguised affection. He told a humorous anecdote that dated back to New Haven in the 1930s, then wound up his tribute thus: "Felix Dupre left many legacies, and we are all the richer for having known him. For Felix was that rarest of beings, a truly gentle man. A man of honor. A man of goodwill. I loved him. I think we all loved him. And no man can leave a finer legacy than that."

There was organ music, and a prayer, and it was over.

Jeff had known Bunny Bartlett for years. Bunny now headed up one of New York's finest investment-banking houses. He managed the Dupre money and knew more. Felix had often said about the financial workings of Dupre's, and of the Dupre family, than Felix himself. It was Bunny Bartlett who advised Felix on all things monetary. It was Bunny's bank that acted as trustee of Jeff's inheritance from his parents. Bunny was all pink-cheeked energy, hearty, a man who loved to laugh. He looked as though he rode to the hounds. He radiated a fine sense of being forever in charge, and liking it.

Jeff looked at his uncle's friend now in wonderment. *How in the world do they do it? Where do they learn to put it all together like that? If anyone asked me to make a speech, I'd be mumbling and muttering and swallowing my tongue.* Felix's generation amazed Jeff. They all had it to one degree or another: a special confidence Jeff was sure he'd never feel. It came, not from money or power or high birth, but rather out of some deep inner conviction that they were right. It encompassed the gallantry that won wars and stretched empires. What a blessing it must be to feel like that, Jeff thought, never to question yourself, never to see all six sides of an issue.

This elusive quality was going. It was almost gone now. The death of Felix Dupre brought that home with chilling clarity: one day it would all be gone, all the courage, all the style, all the chivalry that seemed to be as natural to men like Felix as breathing. Jeff wondered, from the depths of his sadness, what in the world would replace it.

Jeff had many a doubt about himself, about his own generation.

It was a generation that knew too much, a generation numbed by its own options. A generation capable of fighting for the eighteen-year-old vote, and then not voting. Being young in the late 1960s was like racing along in some brash new car with a hundred redundant gadgets, and suddenly a classic old Rolls-Royce glides by, instantly making everything else seem cheap and temporary, nonchalantly erasing forty years of so-called progress.

There was a special grace in the Felix Dupres of the world.

Jeff regretted, and bitterly, that he had been so absorbed in his own feelings and ambitions that he'd never taken the time or trouble to know his uncle better. *I could have learned a lot.*

Bunny rode with them in the hired limousine that took Minnie and Jeff up to the old family burial ground in North White Plains.

Jeff dreaded the trip. His mother was buried there, and there was a marker, too, for his father, whose body had never been found.

The ashes of Felix Dupre rode with the driver. They were sealed into a tacky neoclassic bronze urn. How Felix would have hated that urn, Jeff thought as they pulled onto the FDR Drive: Felix, for whom the curve of a T'ang vase was music; Felix, who could spot the one authentic Queen Anne chair in a room filled with copies. How preposterous, really, to be burying Felix at all.

The family graveyard occupied a far corner of an old village burial ground half-surrounded by woods. The last time Jeff had been there, he was eleven years old, burying his mother. He had never been back. He recalled the day, the pain, the blessed numbness. But the place itself seemed new to him.

Some of the markers went back to the Revolution, but the Dupre monument was circa 1878 and very ugly. A black granite monolith, tall and forbidding, it was simply engraved with the name "DVPRE." Roman. The *v* for a *u*. At each corner of the mournful obelisk, four urns were placed, carved from the same black stone. Small markers were set flush with the grass to mark the individual graves. Jeff's parents shared one such marker. It gave Jeff a start, because his father's name was the same as his. "JEFFREY DYPRE, 1920–1969." The three of them paused at this marker and stood for a moment, saying nothing.

There would be no burial ceremony for Felix.

They simply delivered the urn to the sexton of the local Episcopal church and moved on. The marker would be carved and the urn buried in front of it later in the week. Felix hadn't wanted a graveside ceremony of any kind.

The big Cadillac poured itself down the winding lanes of North White Plains and onto the highway.

"Well," said Minnie with a little sigh, "that's that."

For a moment her words just hung in the silence of the limousine. There seemed to be nothing more to say.

Bunny Bartlett sat on the far-right side of the backseat. Minnie was in the middle and Jeff on the left. Bunny leaned forward a little, a big, ruddy, white-maned yachtsman with intensely blue eyes. "Tell me, then, Jeff, what are your plans?"

I'm going to take over some small South American country and get large loans from the United States government. Jeff squirmed. It was the kind of question to which no answer seemed adequate. *My plans are to get the hell back to my Etruscans. To feel Carla's arms around me in the soft Tuscan night. To finish my book. To taste an Italian peach warm with sunshine. And what are your plans, Bunny?* But Bunny had every right to ask that question.

Jeff squirmed on his seat, trying to think of a plausible answer, a reply that wouldn't upset Minnie.

Jeff cleared his throat, unnecessarily, buying time.

"Well," he said, "naturally I'll stay right here and help Minnie for as long as she needs me. To settle . . . whatever needs to be settled. Then, I'll go back to Veii. I have a pretty important dig waiting out there. Important to me, anyway."

"There's no interest in the firm, then?"

"I'm afraid not," said Jeff. "Felix surely tried his best to bring me into Dupre's but it never took."

"He told me that," said Bunny. "It seems a shame, after three generations, to see it go out of the family altogether."

Jeff sat there. He hoped he didn't look the way he felt: hunted.

Bunny's voice was smooth, warm, persuasive. It was very like Felix's voice. Well, they'd been together at Yale, their backgrounds were similar: northeastern-fancy, traditions, old money. *I've been through all this, years ago, it's all settled, don't drag it up again now,* thought Jeff.

It was as though Felix had come out of the grave to have one last try. *Rest in peace, Felix, please?*

Minnie broke in then. "Well, you know, Bunny, the way it was with Felix. The way some people cultivate their gardens, he cultivated Dupre's. He liked the objects themselves, the sense of discovery, of educating a broader and broader public. It was really Felix Dupre who made the auction business something like democratic."

"Yes," said Bunny, "broadening the base, he called it. Maybe, these last few years, he broadened the base too much. Dupre's hasn't been making the kind of money lately that you'd expect. Considering how the auction business is booming."

"I know it sounds stupid of me," said Minnie, "but I have no idea what Dupre's might be worth. I mean, one doesn't hear of these firms being sold very often."

"Hardly ever. The takeover of Parke Bernet by Sotheby's was a stock deal, a merger, really. But you can be sure of this: Dupre's is worth a lot. Just start with the building: you own that outright. Corner lot on Madison Avenue. The air rights alone are worth at least a few million. And the good name of the firm—regardless of the profit picture—that's worth plenty, too. I'll be surprised, Minnie, if you come out of it with under eight million. And that's conservative."

Jeff sat back, astounded. Bunny was used to huge sums. He tossed them off with the casual air of a man feeding popcorn to the pigeons. To Jeff, eight million dollars was an alarmingly large chunk of money. He looked at Minnie. She was examining her fingernails as though she expected to discover some invisible flaw in them.

"Felix," she said quietly, "wasn't really a manager."

"That," said Bunny, "was just the problem. He was too gentle. He kept people on who were . . . well, 'deadwood' would be the kindest word. People took advantage of him all the time. If he knew it, he wouldn't do anything about it. Felix ran Dupre's like a private club. It must have been a most pleasant place to work, but that isn't what makes money."

"This is a dumb question," said Jeff, "but how does one go about selling an auction house?"

Bunny laughed. "Discreetly, my boy, discreetly. One lets it be known—naming no names—that a certain type of property might be available. Undoubtedly, there will be nibbles. In fact, sad as it makes me to say it, I've had a few phone calls already, just as a result of Felix's death. But my feeling is that we should bide our time awhile. Not seem too eager."

"We aren't too eager," said Minnie. "I keep hoping Jeff will have a change of heart."

"Don't count on it, Minnie." Jeff's heart sank as he said it. Maybe she had been counting on his staying, despite her brave words. He looked at his aunt. She was smiling a little distractedly. "I'm sorry, Minnie," he said, "if I was rude. But you really mustn't count on my doing anything with Dupre's. Maybe we shouldn't be talking business anyway, so soon."

"I don't mind, Jeffy, thank you: it's like going to the dentist. The sooner you get it over with, the better you feel. Bunny knows I have no head for business, Dupre's or any other. I—we—did hope you'd come into the firm. That's no secret, and it's no secret that you'd rather do your archaeology. So we'll sell, whenever Bunny thinks the time is right."

Amen, thought Jeff. And for all that he loved his aunt, she managed to make "do your archaeology" sound like making something out of Lego toys. Probably that was how it seemed to her, a rather elegant game, a sort of cosmic crossword puzzle.

"I've heard," said Bunny, "from St. James, about this big sale of the Duke of Berwick's things. Now, that is going to make headlines. The Winchcombe Chalice, after all. I say let's hold off any serious negotiating until after the sale of the Duke of Berwick's things. Now, that is going to be when?"

"Three weeks," said Minnie. "Morgan's rushing to get the catalog out."

"That's not much time, is it, Minnie?" Jeff remembered the summer when he'd helped assemble auction catalogs at Dupre's.

"No, especially not for a sale like this one. Neville, poor man, seems to be in a tearing hurry."

They were heading into the city now. The car moved in stately silence over the Triborough Bridge and onto the FDR Drive once again.

Bunny told Jeff about the state of the auction business, how competition was increasing: more dealers after fewer great estates.

"Then there are the unions. They're always with us. Every expense is soaring. All those guards, the heat and electricity. And, while sale prices are up, we tend to remember the record-breaking prices, the million-dollar Renoirs and so forth. In actual fact the average price at Dupre's last year was in the neighborhood of three hundred dollars. Million-dollar paintings included."

"So there must be plenty of things that go for very little."

"You bet. And the meter, so to speak, is ticking away no matter what the price." Bunny smiled. "It's a fascinating game, though. I think Felix infected me with it. I sometimes go now just for the drama, even if I'm not bidding."

The car pulled up in front of the Dupre house.

They went into the library and had a drink. Bunny made two Lillets and, for himself, a generous bourbon on the rocks. He lifted his glass. "To Felix."

"To Felix."

They drank. It felt strange to Jeff. It was as though he had barely known his uncle at all, and now it was too late. He hadn't noticed the sunset, but suddenly it was dark outside. Jeff's mind was filled with all the images of the day: Bunny's eulogy. The ugly bronze urn. His parents' grave, one-half of it forever empty. The wonderful-looking girl from Dupre's. He stood up, restless, and walked to one of the tall windows that looked out on Sixty-fourth Street. Across the street was a lamppost that gave off a blistering cadmium-white glare. Next to the lamp was a tree, a fat-trunked old sycamore that had been there ever since Jeff could remember. He thought of what it must take for a tree—or anything else—to survive in New York. He studied the mottled patterns of the tree's trunk, with the peeling bark revealing sudden unexpected patches of beige under the brown suface.

The brightness of the streetlamp made the shadows under the tree darker than normal by contrast.

Jeff stood idly at the window for a moment.

Then something—someone—moved.

Now, for the first time, Jeff could make out the shape of a man standing motionless under the tree. Staring at the lighted windows of the Dupre house.

Why?

Was he one last mourner, come to pay some silent respects to the dead, too shy to ring the bell? Some unknown neighbor walking a dog? But there was no dog.

Minnie said his name. Jeff turned to her, smiled, replied.

When he returned to the window a moment later, the dark shape was gone. Or maybe he had imagined the whole thing.

Maybe he was seeing ghosts.

He smiled at his own foolishness. Something about this day made it easy to imagine all kinds of sinister things. He stayed at the window. When Hastings came to announce dinner, Jeff didn't hear him at all.

Suddenly Minnie was touching his elbow. "Are you," she said with a little laugh, "back with your dreary old Etruscans already, my darling?"

He forced a smile. "I was someplace else, Minnie," he said, and bent to kiss her cheek. "You can be sure of that."

And the three mourners of Felix Dupre walked down the polished hall to their dinner.

15

Berwick Castle, England, 1950

The duke was dying. There could be no doubt about that now. The doctor had said it, the look on the nurse's face said it, and the duke himself said it. Cheerfully.

Neville sat by the old duke's bed, watching his grandfather's face. It was parchment-pale, pale as the petals of the sweet double-headed narcissus that sprung up in Berwick forest every spring. The duke would not see another spring at Berwick.

He seemed to be sleeping. The sheets were crisp Edwardian linen embroidered with the Berwick crest. The duke's pajamas were white. The centers of the daisies Miranda had brought from the meadow that morning added a spot of color to the deeply shadowed room. There were a water glass and several bottles of medicine on the dark oak bedside table. And, incongruous in the clinical surroundings of a sickroom, a glittering swirl of gold and rubies: the chalice.

Neville wondered why the duke had asked for it, of all the treasures at Berwick.

It was midafternoon on a bright July day. But the duke's bedroom looked like midnight. The old blackout shades were drawn, and the heavy silk brocade draperies had been drawn over the shades. Only the little bedside lamp gleamed, weakly. Darkness seemed to be gathering in the room, crouching, ready to strike. Neville wore an open shirt and a thin linen jacket, and he was cold.

His grandfather's breathing was regular, barely detectable. The white woolen blanket rose and fell, rose and fell. The old man's hands were resting on top of the crisply folded sheet that masked the blanket's edge. So pale they were that it seemed to Neville he could see right through them. The heavy gold ring carved with the ducal crest was too big for the duke's finger now, but he insisted on wearing it all the same. Neville thought of those hands on the wheel of the Bentley drophead, squeezing off a few rounds of his Purdy shotgun, stroking a horse's flank, pouring brandy, snipping off the end of a Havana cigar. He thought of the duke's face, laughing or scornful or even angry at his grandson. But always, the face and those hands had been vibrantly alive, fearless, always in motion.

It seemed impossible that the old man was ninety-one.

The death of Neville's own father in the bombing of Fleet House had been so sudden, so entirely unexpected, that it had sometimes seemed like a bad dream. Nine years had passed since that black night. The duke had been an old man then. No he was ancient, legendary.

And he was going to leave Neville all alone with the ghosts of Berwick, and Berwick's debts, and Berwick's honor to maintain.

At least the old man had the joy of seeing his great-grandson.

At least the duke knew there was an heir for Berwick now, a fine lusty child going onto four years old.

Neville felt suddenly restless. Where was the damned nurse with his tea? He turned in his chair, as if turning toward the door might make her walk through it.

When he turned back, the duke's eyes were open, unblinking, staring at him.

"Grandfather!" Neville's whisper echoed loudly in the silent room.

"Hush." The duke's voice was not the voice that Neville recalled so clearly, having heard it all his life. It was a strange sound now, a sound like wind in the leaves. It was a ghostly sound, an echo from the crypt.

"Did you . . . ?" the voice went on slowly. The duke's dark eyes seemed darker in the weak light. He strained on his pillow, turned his head a little. "I see you've brought it. The chalice. Give it here."

Neville handed the chalice to his grandfather. The old man smiled. His right hand reached for the cup. The pale fingers twined around the golden grapevine that decorated the stem. The chalice wavered. The duke used his other hand to steady the first.

He had never been a religious man. Now he looked strangely sacramental. He looked, thought Neville, like some ancient priest.

The duke stared at the chalice with hypnotic intensity, as though he might be trying to conjure up some spell or spirit. He was still staring at the cup when he spoke again.

"It's all here, lad. All in this old cup. Everything that was Berwick. All we were." The duke paused, but not because he was finished. He breathed a little faster now. Neville saw one bead of sweat forming on the old man's brow, and wondered what he ought to do about it. Where in hell was the nurse? Slowly, slowly, the duke brought the golden cup closer to his face. Gently, still clutching it with both hands, he lowered the chalice and let it rest on its side on the blanket. He turned to Neville, straining for the words. His grandson leaned closer, wishing there were a way to help him.

". . . all we were," the duke went on, "and all we could be again." He gasped, like a man sinking in water. He paused, and his lips trembled. The doctor called it pleurisy, but went on to say that at the duke's age, in his frail condition, almost anything could take him. When the old man spoke again, it was all Neville could do to make it out.

"They'll be after you, lad. For the taxes. Damned socialists! They'll try to take . . . everything. Don't let them take this." The duke's eyes fell to the chalice.

Neville spoke more loudly than he'd intended. "I won't, Grandfather! I promise. No matter what."

The duke smiled. "Not so loud, boy. It's only me . . . and them."

He looked past Neville into the shadows that filled the room.

"Who, Grandfather?"

"The Fleets, boy. They're always here, always watching. Waiting. They know we'll be joining them one day . . . and . . . and . . ."

The words escaped him. His lips moved, seeking.

"And what, Grandfather?"

Cords in the old man's neck tightened. He dug his emaciated arms into the mattress and lifted himself up a little, and leaned toward Neville. "And we must be ready to answer to them, boy! Not to God or to the damned government, but to them . . . the Fleets . . . to ourselves. Remember this. Remem . . ."

He collapsed all at once and subsided onto the pillow. It was like watching the air escape from a toy balloon.

73

There was no sound at all in the darkened room now, but for the pounding of Neville Fleet's own heart. The chalice rolled unseen to the edge of the bed and fell to the richly carpeted floor.

The sound of its impact brought Neville to his feet.

"Grandfather!"

Neville touched the old man's wrist, as he'd been taught to in the RAF.

The Duke of Berwick was dead. Neville leaned across the bed and kissed his grandfather's pale cheek. Then he knelt and picked up the Winchcombe Chalice. He held it in one hand, and with the other reached out and closed the old man's eyes.

"I'll remember, Grandfather," he said to the stillness. "I shan't ever forget."

Then the brand-new Duke of Berwick walked out of his grandfather's room to find the damned nurse.

16

Jeff got up early the next morning. Rising time at Veii was seven, and he had carried his internal Etruscan time clock with him on the jet. It was just a little past seven now. He showered and shaved and checked the drawers and closets of his boyhood room. Finally he chose a faded blue button-down shirt, crisply pressed khaki trousers, and a dark blue tie. Over this went a madras jacket in shades of blue and green. He surveyed the result in a mirror and smiled.

Sixties nostalgia, he'd read in *Time* on the airplane, was making a comeback. Then he'd be right in style. It had always seemed to Jeff that the real American nostalgia was for the future.

His aunt wasn't up yet.

Jeff thought of her as he wrote a note. The note said he was going to spend the day at Dupre's, as Bunny had asked him to. But what Jeff thought about now was Minnie herself, and how she'd spend the rest of her life.

Surely not at Dupre's.

There had been something in Bunny Bartlett's manner last night—all day, in fact—that had made Jeff think that maybe, just maybe, something might develop between them. Bunny had been widowed for some time now. It would fit. Maybe too neatly. And who the hell was he, Jeff, to contemplate arranging someone else's love life, when he couldn't even organize his own?

He smiled at that, left the note where she'd be sure to find it, and went down to breakfast.

Emmalee bustled around the kitchen and gave him the requested toast and orange juice and coffee. Reminding him he was too thin. He resisted her offer of waffles and ham, or strawberries and cream, or a steak and homefries. He breakfasted alone with the *New York Times*.

The paper was filled with news that meant nothing to Jeff. Summer in New York: crime was up and employment was down. The world was only superficially at peace. Nations whose names he'd never heard seemed to be emerging with the persistence of mushrooms after a long rain. Politicians sniped at each other: an election was not far off. There were coups in Latin America, hunger in the Far East, devastating rains in India. It was all new and all the same. The paper reminded Jeff how very removed he was from the daily give-and-take of life in America, in the rest of the world. And it reminded him of how very little he could do about any of the world's troubles. He, or anyone else.

When he finished the paper and his third cup of Emmalee's superb coffee, it was a little past nine. He got up, stretched, told Emmalee he wouldn't be back for lunch, and walked out of the kitchen door onto Sixty-fourth Street.

After just two days away from his trenches, Jeff felt physically restless. He wanted to run in the park, play four sets of tennis, swim, climb a tree. Instead, he'd promised Bunny to spend the day making himself familiar with Dupre's.

Not, as God and Bunny and Minnie Dupre well knew, that he wanted any part of the place. Yet Bunny was right: it would be his one day if they didn't sell immediately. He ought to have at least a working knowledge of the place. Bunny, as Felix's financial adviser, was familiar with his will. He was, in fact, executor. The will was simple. All Felix had went to Minnie, and after Minnie, to Jeff.

"And, dear Jeffy," his aunt had been quick to remind him, "we have to take Felix's death as a lesson, to all of us, of just how suddenly it can happen."

So Jeff would spend however much time it took getting familiar with Dupre's. He knew he could do it in less than a week. He'd make himself do it that fast. And Jeff knew he could count on Morgan St. James to help. He'd just stick around long enough to appease Minnie.

Dinner last night had been educational.

Without going into details, Bunny had made it apparent that Minnie was going to be very well taken care of. Felix had not been wealthy: his main asset was the firm. But he had been thoughtfully insured, and Minnie had money of her own. There would be no question of altering the style of her life. She could sustain the Sixty-fourth Street house indefinitely. She had friends, charities, an adequate income. And the prospect of selling Dupre's at a substantial profit. Jeff need feel no regrets in resuming his old life. He promised himself he'd see more of her, invite her out to Veii. If she'd come.

It was very good to know Minnie would never have to worry about money. For himself, Jeff was curiously indifferent. He knew that he wasn't rich. There was a trust fund from his parents' estate, which paid him about ten-thousand dollars every year, on top of his small assistant professor's salary. He lived conservatively. In Cambridge, he rode a bicycle. Most material things left him untouched by desire, unless they were very old. His apartment was furnished with good old things, mostly from the storage warehouse where his parents' furniture had been sent when his mother died. He seldom shopped for anything other than groceries.

Jeff had all he wanted. He liked his life, his work.

If he should inherit money one day, well and good. If that money came from Minnie, Jeff hoped the day would be a long time coming.

Minnie should be happy. She always had been.

Maybe happiness was a habit, something that would go on regardless. Jeff hoped so. Because he was fresh out of ideas on what he could do, personally, to make her happy. Now that Felix was gone.

He opened the front door. It was a good day. Jeff headed toward Madison Avenue.

Toward the House of Dupre.

Madison Avenue glittered on the bright summer morning.

Here were the boutiques and art galleries and antique dealers' shops where, within ten or fifteen blocks on the upper avenue, it seemed that half the world's treasures had been gathered, beautifully displayed, priced to the hilt, and offered for sale.

Here in half an hour you could buy a T'ang horse, an

Hermès scarf, an African tribal fetish, a Mogul's carpet, or Marie Antoinette's chamber pot.

Here, some of the most elegantly dressed people in the world wafted along the immaculate pavement in search of new playthings: gifts, ornaments, something to wear.

And here, too, on or near Madison Avenue, were the world's great auction houses: Sotheby's, Christie's, Dupre's.

Bunny had summed it up at dinner.

"It's all coming here now, Jeff. This is New York's time, just as a hundred years ago it was London's time, and after that, the time for Paris. Ten years ago there were about a dozen foreign banks here. Today there are one hundred and twenty-eight. Half the fancy co-ops on Fifth Avenue are owned by foreign people whose names you've never heard, who command big money. Why? Because they're fleeing, Jeff. We are the last safe place."

That had been news to Jeff. He was used to things being news to him. Sometimes he thought he liked it. The element of surprise was a kind of benchmark. It measured the success with which he'd constructed his own world, ruled by his own tastes, his own priorities. It was a measure of his control of his own life, that so much else in the world seemed out of control.

Jeff walked slowly, tasting the atmosphere of the street.

No one but Morgan was expecting him at Dupre's, and when he got there he'd probably upset them, make them nervous or more unsure of their future than they were right now.

As he walked up the avenue, it seemed to Jeff that he might have recently landed from some other planet. He looked in windows at next year's clothes—never this year's, although one little shop displayed a Victorian lace camisole to be worn as a sort of an evening gown, at twenty-five hundred dollars. He wondered who would buy it, and how many other, similar dresses she'd have, and where she'd wear them.

He saw the tragic, empty faces of young girls who believed in fashion magazines, all alike. This year they were sulky, pouting. A few had manic, frizzed-out bride-of-Frankenstein hairdos. Jeff saw older women of incomparable chic, so painstakingly put together that it must be for some occasion, for some special role. What occasion? What role?

The women came in every shape but fat. They had wise, observant eyes, survivor's eyes. And they were always alone. Women in this rarefied atmosphere outnumbered the men six to one.

What men there were ran in two types.

Some were young and sleek and theatrically good-looking, gliding among the women like eels through sea grass. And there were a few older men of diplomatic mein, each gray hair disciplined, shoes ablaze with flawless shine, often with a small conspicuous rosette or ribbon in the left lapel of their fluently tailored suits.

Where are they going, Jeff wondered, and what will they do when they get there?

For the last two blocks of his five-block walk, Jeff could see the House of Dupre gleaming on its corner across the street.

Dupre's had started life as a storefront antique shop on Nineteenth Street just west of Gramercy Park. That store was a discotheque now. Jeff's grandfather had built the present structure in 1932, at the depth of the Great Depression, defying all economic advice. And he had been right. Dupre's blossomed in its new location. It was within walking distance of the very rich. Shopping the Dupre auction exhibits became the chic way to spend one's afternoon. It filled the time between luncheon and the hairdressing appointment. And it very often resulted in sales.

The House of Dupre was five stories of white limestone in the art-deco manner, all rounded corners and rippling moldings. The main entrance was deeply set into a wide bronze framework. Around this frame a notably silly frieze depicted naked women chasing attenuated bronze gazelles. Jeff smiled. All that must have seemed very sophisticated in 1932.

He stood for a moment looking up at the doorway like any tourist.

"DVPRE, LTD." was carved deeply into the white stone above the door.

It reminded Jeff of the carving on the family tomb.

It also reminded him of all the work, all the hopes that had come together in that name, this building. How it would all end now, unless he did something about carrying on.

It was too much to ask.

They had no right to ask it.

Jeff tried to remember the last time he'd seen Felix, and what they'd said. Christmas last year. And what they'd said, in the end, was simply good-bye. Never knowing it really was good-bye.

He looked up at the crisply-carved letters.

"DVPRE"

Jeff wanted it to mean more to him. But it was just a name

on a building. If it had been the Acme Wrench Company, he would have felt just the same. Indifferent.

Bunny had told them that the good name of Dupre was worth a lot, no matter what condition the business itself might be in. It was hard to imagine, standing here in the morning sunlight, looking up at the sparkling limestone facade, that conditions within could be anything but fine.

Then Jeff took a deep breath and walked through the big bronze-edged glass doors.

The reception lobby was spacious, paved in marble and usually displaying paintings from an upcoming auction on its walls. There was an information desk that sold current and back copies of the famous Dupre catalogs, and a few selected art books on subjects of interest to collectors. Three elevators were framed in bronze, but without the naked women or gazelles.

Jeff pressed the button. It took a few minutes for a car to descend. As they ever had been, the Dupre elevators were manned by uniformed guards: black men, more often than not, in the handsome uniforms Felix had designed for them. Fawn-colored jackets over chocolate-brown trousers. Jeff knew that each one of them carried a handgun in a shoulder holster. The jackets were individually tailored so that the guns remained inconspicuous. Jeff had never heard of a gun being used at Dupre's.

"Four, please," he said. The guard didn't recognize him. Why should he?

Four was the executive floor of Dupre's. Three was storage, cataloging, small offices for some of the staff, and the photographic studio where the catalogs were shot. The top floor was clerical. On the second floor were exhibition rooms, four in all, including one very large hall, and the auction gallery itself, a miniature theater seating two hundred. For the great, famous auctions, there was a closed-circuit TV system to the exhibition galleries, where folding chairs would be set up to handle the overflow.

The lobby of the fourth floor was designed, successfully, to impress. There was a large, subtly colored Persian carpet on the floor. An eighteenth-century camelback sofa invited clients to wait comfortably. A pair of antique mirrors reflected each other from opposite sides of the lobby. And a very well-groomed white-haired woman receptionist sat behind an old French writing table that held one discreet black telephone, a handsome lamp, and a bowl of fresh anemones.

She smiled at Jeff, professionally.

I'm a stranger here, he thought, and I deserve to be. He wondered if she'd been at the funeral. He couldn't remember her, and it was obvious that she didn't remember him.

"I have an appointment with Mr. St. James," he said, smiling. "My name is Jeff Dupre."

Her briskly organized face changed at once, softened, became more human. "I'm Dilys Winn," she said, "and I am—we all are—very sorry about your uncle."

"Thank you. So am I."

"I'll ring Mr. St. James."

Morgan came out himself, coatless, sleeves rolled up, smiling. He took Jeff's hand. "I'm so glad you came. I've made your uncle's office ready for you."

Jeff managed a smile. Good old Morgan.

Morgan can't know how very little I want Felix's office, or any of the rest of it. I'll have to tell him, reassure him the carpet isn't going to be yanked out from under him.

They went down the hall to Felix's office.

Jeff had grown up visiting the place.

It was big, handsome, elegant. It filled the southwest corner of Dupre's with two large windows facing the avenue and another looking out over the side street. There was a working fireplace faced with salmon-colored marble, antique English paneling of pickled oak, dark parquet floors, worn but lovely old Persian carpets, a pair of deep comfortably modern settees flanking the fireplace, bookshelves, nicely framed Hogarth engravings, a big old partner's desk.

Jeff walked around the room while Morgan ordered coffee. The regret came back now, stronger than ever in Felix's private office. Why didn't I try harder, Jeff thought, why wasn't I more what he wanted me to be?

He was standing looking at a framed print, number one of Hogarth's comic series *The Harlot's Progress*. He felt Morgan's hand on his shoulder.

"Look in the upper-right desk drawer," said Morgan.

Puzzled, Jeff walked across the room and opened the drawer, feeling like an intruder.

Then he laughed. Morgan had remembered. There was a small box of English licorice toffees, Jeff's favorite candy. He'd been addicted to the stuff as a kid and all that sixteen-year-old summer Morgan had teased him about it, told him his teeth would rot. Felix Jeff was sure hadn't noticed. Or, at any rate, hadn't mentioned it. Which would be typical of Felix. Remembering was typical of Morgan St. James.

Jeff looked up and grinned. "You remembered."

"I remembered."

"Thanks, Morgan. I haven't even thought of this damned stuff for years."

"For old times' sake."

Morgan sat on one of the settees. Jeff picked up the candy box and sat down on the other settee. He opened the candy and offered it to Morgan.

"Ick. Disgusting stuff. Help yourself."

"Some things don't change."

Jeff smiled and put a toffee into his mouth. It was magical, exactly as good as he remembered. He'd lay in a huge supply to bring back to Veii.

Morgan made a small throat-clearing kind of noise. "Whatever happens, Jeff, and I say this knowing you'll probably want to sell the old store, losing Felix Dupre has been just a tremendous sorrow to everyone here. The man was beloved, a legend, really."

"Yes," said Jeff slowly, "I guess he was."

"He wanted so much for you to be a part of it."

"I wish I could have been."

"But it's going well for you, the teaching and all that?"

Jeff smiled. It was typical of Morgan, when his world was likely to fall apart at any minute, to be thinking of other people.

"It's fine. It's what I want to do more than anything. Sometimes, like anything, it can be a pain in the ass, but basically, I like it a lot."

"Good. That's fine."

Jeff paused reaching for exactly the right words. "Morgan, we—Minnie and I—want you to know that if we do sell, nothing need change. You'll continue in charge and all."

The secretary knocked softly and walked in with a tray containing an old silver coffeepot and two cups and a plate of cookies.

"Well," said Morgan, "I do appreciate that. One never knows, does one? Yet, I have a feeling I'd find work, even if a new owner should find me not satisfactory."

"Impossible."

Morgan laughed. It was not a happy laugh.

"Let's cross that rather fragile bridge when we come to it, dear boy. In the meantime, Mr. Bartlett phoned and asked me to help you with your education. I don't think he remembers I have already helped you with your education that summer . . ."

"When I was sixteen. I'll never forget it. Weirdly enough, that summer got me interested in archaeology."

"Not weird at all. Half of what we do is a sort of archaeology. Think of, say, the duke's chalice."

"Minnie mentioned that. Some item. But she didn't tell me all about it."

"Well, Jeff, it isn't signed. Which already tells us something, because the chalice is the work of a master, the sort of man who, even in Rome, probably would sign an object of this stature. So, without really knowing, we infer that he was asked not to sign the thing."

"But why?"

"Likelier than not, because it was commissioned by a rich, secret Christian. Who wanted it to be untraceable. In any event, it got to Roman Britain—to Winchcombe—and was buried along with two bronze lamps and a crude iron cross. Dug up by the very monks who were building the Winchcombe Abbey on the old Roman site. They, of course, took it as a sign from on high. Made it their chief relic, used it in the Mass, attributed to it powers of healing, all that sort of stuff. Then when Henry Tudor—Henry the Eighth—took over all the Papal properties in Britain, he gave the cup to Anne Boleyn as part of the marriage settlement. Well, of course, Henry later took Anne's head, and got the chalice back, too. Mary Tudor, Bloody Mary, inherited it in time and gave it to her husband, Philip of Spain. It's certainly had a restless, bloodstained career. Well, old Philip sent it sailing right back to England again—on the Armada. It was thought to have been lost that way. Disappeared without a trace for nearly two hundred years. Then, in Venice in the eighteenth century, one of the Fleets found it in some obscure antique shop. And it has been on the altar of the private chapel in Berwick Castle ever since."

"I wonder," said Jeff quietly, "if it will find a really permanent resting place at last. In some museum, maybe."

"We'll see—and that's the fun of this business."

Morgan's eyes sparkled as he contemplated the several fates that might befall the legendary cup.

"I guess it's something of a coup for us to sell it."

"To say the least. My estimate is two to three million, Jeff, but I know it's conservative. For the Winchcombe Chalice is unique. There is simply no other object of Roman gold known to us that is of this quality. Not to mention the rest of its history."

"Bunny told me Dupre's has been having a rough time, Morgan. Why is that?"

"The economists call it a profit squeeze. It was a conscious decision of Felix's to stay small. He wanted Dupre's personal, manageable. Which is all very well, but we still have to provide services comparable to the giants. To Sotheby's, for instance. We must have fancy catalogs, do appraisals, send our people everywhere soliciting. We are not really in bad shape, but we don't always get the really big, plummy sales these days. And, of course, not having branch operations hurts us. We just don't have the flexibility of the big boys."

"What would you do, if it were yours?"

The kindly face regarded Jeff wisely. Morgan sipped his coffee.

"Expand. Felix and I had many a discussion about that. He actually agreed that we should do it, but he could never quite bring himself to make the move. I think it was a question, perhaps not of his ego, but of wanting to supervise every detail in person. He was a perfectionist, you know."

"I know."

"But now," said Morgan, rising, "let me give you a little tour. See what mischief we're up to these days."

"I'd like that."

Morgan led Jeff into the exhibition rooms on the second floor.

"Now, you see a typical setup. Exhibitions for three auctions in three different rooms. Over there"—he pointed to a room perhaps thirty feet long by twenty feet wide, filled with desk-height glass-topped exhibition cases flanked by many folding chairs—"we have a rare-stamp exhibit. That's a growing category, a European craze that's fast spreading here. They're more valuable per ounce and per square inch than anything else. So very easy to flee with, should the need arise."

The room contained several gray-haired men, each with tweezers and a loupe, scrutinizing stamps.

Morgan led the way past the stamp room into the biggest exhibition hall.

To Jeff's eyes it looked like everybody's attic, multiplied by a hundred. There was furniture, most of it Victorian and opulent, intricately carved dark wood vying with lush satin brocades and fringes. There were at least three Frederick Remington bronze sculptures, all Western motifs, including the famous bucking bronco and rider. There was jewelry in a glass case, several hunting trophies dominated by the head of a ram with immense curling horns, rifles of all descriptions and several handguns, Indian artifacts, pots, baskets, and some ceremonial clothing. There was a fabulous old saddle in black leather, heavily decorated with engraved silver. There was a vast bronze-and-crystal chandelier that looked French, and more. More items than Jeff could see at a glance, much less understand. He was disappointed. Except for the Remington bronzes, it looked like a rummage sale.

"What in the world," he asked Morgan, "is all this?"

St. James laughed. "It looks like a jumble, and it is. It's our annual fall sale of Western memorabilia. A very hot area of the auction business, if I do say so. We've only been doing it for five years, and every year it gets better. You'll recognize the Remingtons, of course. But it's the other items that are really fascinating, not so much for their aesthetic value as for their historical or even sentimental associations. That saddle belonged to Bat Masterson. This chandelier, which is handsome in its own right, French, from the eighteenth century, will double in value because it once belonged to the famous San Francisco madam Lily Cigar. And the American Indian items are soaring. There are so few, and they are just really coming into their own."

"Amazing. It's really amazing."

"That's the thrill of it. The sense of discovery. For instance, this winter we're having our first major sale of antique clothing. Everything from Renaissance pointy-toed slippers to a 1935 shimmy dress hand-sewn with fourteen pounds of bugle beads. If you fell into the lake wearing that one, you'd sink like a stone."

"And I thought it was all paintings, furniture, and antiquities."

"Well, to be fair, most of it still is. But the definitions of what is art are broadening by the minute. Maybe I shouldn't be talking about what is art so much as what is auctionable. And that's getting to be damn near everything. If someone came to me today and proposed a sale of manhole covers, I wouldn't throw him out. There are serious collectors of antique barbed wire."

They walked through the Western exhibition and into another, smaller room. Here on tables were dozens of old Japanese swords and daggers. In glass cases were many small pierced disks of bronze or iron, often decorated with miniature relief sculptures in gold or silver.

"Japanese armor and sword furniture. That's another booming field now. Some people hang the blades alone, others collect only the little blade guards you see in that case, the tsuba."

Jeff went to the glass case and studied the sword guards. Most were round, although a few were square with rounded corners. They were about three inches in diameter. Pierced through the center to receive the blade, most also had a pair of smaller oval holes flanking the blade. Each tsuba was decorated thematically. Some were engraved, others had applied sculptures in half-relief. The one Jeff liked best was a perfect and perfectly complete little landscape in which a buck deer and a doe drank from a stream. The buck was rendered in gold, the doe in bronze. The stream was incised into the steel that formed the tsuba itself. Behind the deer, a branch of blossoming plum grew, decked with silver blooms. All in less than one square inch at the lower left of the sword guard.

"It's incredible," said Jeff. "What do you estimate it'll go for?"

Morgan checked the catalog. "It's eighteenth-century and not signed. Between twelve hundred and two thousand. Signed, it'd be worth much more. You have a good eye: that's a fine example."

"They're all fine examples."

"Shall I leave a bid?"

Jeff smiled. "No, thanks. But it's a discovery. I never knew about tsuba before."

"They were the great all-time miniaturist sculptors, beyond question. They breathe, the best ones. They transcend scale."

The last stop on the tour was the third-floor storage, photographic, and appraisal area. Here the department heads and their assistants were crammed into any space available. Here unsolicited objects were brought for appraisal. Morgan led Jeff down hallways and around corners. Jeff knew he'd never be able to find his way on this floor without a guide. They poked their heads into a photographic studio, there a silver catalog was being shot. It was a blaze of lights, wine-velvet backdrops, and glittering silver. The photographer and his two young assistants seemed to be engaged in some sort of avant-garde ballet. They never looked up from their task.

Morgan and Jeff moved on. The halls were cluttered with every sort of art object, all tagged and waiting to be removed to the storage areas or to the auction gallery itself. A severe Gandharan Buddha smiled thinly at a French nineteenth-century oil painting of a coquettish milkmaid. A pair of immense bronze urns, taller than Jeff, nearly blocked the passage. I wonder what the fire department has to say about all this clutter, he thought, and decided not to ask.

"What," Jeff asked, "do you do to protect diamonds and gold and things like that?"

"There's a very secure strong room on the basement level, a vault, really, all lined with steel. And the security is better than it probably looks. No one can get out of the building after five without an escort guard, or an alarm goes off. And all these floors are both locked and continually patrolled. We've never had a major theft, although small items have been known to vanish from time to time. And in the exhibition rooms, it's terrible: they'd swipe the varnish off the floors if they could. We remove everything that's easily stealable: finials from valuable lamps, for example. But still, things vanish, and that, of course, diminishes their sale value."

"But we're insured?"

"Of course—to the hilt. But there's no sense making a claim unless it's a substantial one: the rates only go up. So pilferage is another way we bleed, fiscally, although, luckily, not a major cause for alarm. Last year we sold more than fifty thousand individual items. Something like a dozen turned up missing, and none of those was especially valuable."

They wound around another corner and Jeff got a glimpse of the beautiful part-Oriental girl he had met at the funeral, tucked into a tiny cubicle of an office, talking earnestly into a tape recorder and leafing through papers as she spoke. She looked up. He waved and smiled. She smiled back, and kept talking into the small black microphone.

Soon they were back in Felix's office. Jeff was amazed to find that two hours had passed: it was nearly noon.

Jeff didn't even sit down. He was restless, had felt hemmed in almost since he'd gotten off the jet. He turned to Morgan. "It's good to know you're here, Morgan. Especially for Minnie. She's never been interested in managing Dupre's, hardly ever comes here, I gather."

"Not often. Dear lady."

"Yes. It'll be hard for her."

"Anything I can do, Jeff . . . well, you know you can count on me."

"Thanks. And thanks for the licorice."

Morgan grinned. "Rot your teeth."

They shook hands rather formally, and Morgan went back to his own office, which was just down the hall.

Jeff stood where he was for a moment, wondering what the next move should be. Then he reached for the telephone.

Polly Kunimara sat in her cubicle, speaking quickly into the machine. The phone rang. And rang again. Damn! She clicked the recorder and picked up the receiver.

"Polly Kunimara speaking," she said in an even voice.

"Miss Kunimara, this is Jeff Dupre. I have an important question for you."

"Of course, anything I can do."

"Do you happen to be free for lunch today?"

Polly frowned. Her first reaction was to refuse. But, the fact was, she had no plans for lunch. And Jeff's interest was flattering. Whatever he might want. *Keep that chip off your shoulder, Polly: all good-looking men aren't inevitably creeps.*

"Why, thank you," she said after the briefest of pauses. "I'd love to."

"Twelve-thirty?"

"Twelve-thirty."

Jeff put the receiver down very slowly, as though it might explode. And for the first time that day, he felt a kind of exhilaration, a sense of something positive happening.

Polly.

He'd never seen a girl who looked like Polly. Maybe the special grace, the sense of mystery, were just some trick of heredity. He doubted this very much.

Polly.

Suddenly Jeff grinned.

The afternoon was looking very promising. And, after all, Bunny Bartlett had asked him to find out all he could about the House of Dupre.

17

Berwick Castle, England, 1950

Neville Fleet shuddered.

It was so typical of his majesty's damnable Inland Revenue Service that they couldn't wait even a day for this interview.

The day of his grandfather's funeral.

The day he officially became Duke of Berwick, whatever that might be worth.

Neville thought of almost everything in terms of worth these days. He had to. The death duties from his father's estate were still unpaid. The compounding effect of his grandfather's duties had built up into a debt of monstrous proportions.

He braced himself and walked down the hallway.

The old family solicitor, Henry Clifford, had come down from London for the interview.

The horrid truths of the Fleet-family finances were slowly sinking into Neville's astonished brain. What right had Grandfather to shield him from all this?

Neville had loved his grandfather.

But the old man had left him a pauper. Worse than a pauper, a massive debtor.

Never in his thirty-three years had he felt so utterly alone. There had always been someone: Grandfather, Father, Berwick itself. Well, there was still Berwick. Just barely.

The Inland Revenue man was not unknown to Neville, but they had never met. The little bounder, Smythe-Davies. He must be a bounder, to write as he had written. The subtle threats. The barbed insinuations.

Neville opened the door to the small library, where his guests were waiting. *Guests!* Gladly he could have thrust the pair of them into Mortimer's pit!

Neville went in smiling. That smile was the triumph of a thousand years of breeding. A small, pale triumph it was.

Smythe-Davies was young, under thirty. He was plump, thin-skinned, with a small goldfish mouth pursed in eternal disapproval. The world was a wicked place, and Smythe-Davies was bound to correct its many failings. Beginning with the feckless Fleets of Berwick.

"How do you do?" asked Neville, wishing him dead.

"It is a pleasure, your Grace," murmured Smythe-Davies, a touch of mockery riding on his obsequious tone. His voice fairly oozed. God save us, thought Neville, from the revenge of the lower classes.

He ordered tea.

It came. Small sandwiches were passed. Neville couldn't eat.

Smythe-Davies discreetly heaped his little plate.

"Well, then," said old Clifford, rubbing his bony hands together like some insect in a cruel mating dance, "shall we commence?"

There was no avoiding it.

Smythe-Davies knew more about Neville's finances than Neville did.

His majesty's Inland Revenue Service was prepared to be accommodating, most accommodating.

What this amounted to was that Neville would pay off the debt, in quarterly installments, forever. Beyond forever. Neville would pay, and his heir would pay, and the heir's heirs, to infinity.

Paying and paying.

It was intolerable. More than that, it was impossible.

"It seems, Mr. Smythe-Davies, that my income will be almost nonexistent, after the expenses of maintaining Berwick. The revenues from the farms—as you know—don't begin to do it."

Smythe-Davies frowned. It was a small, practiced frown, the frown of a nanny who imagines her small charge is contemplating mischief.

"There is," he said smoothly, "always the National Trust."

"Never!"

There was thunder in the duke's reply.

"They do take excellent care . . . you could continue to live here . . ."

"To make a circus of it, to have strangers trooping about at all hours, to turn my family home into some sort of public freak show? I'd sooner sell onions from a barrow in the street!"

"I hope," said Smythe-Davies gently, "that will not be necessary."

There was a stiff and indignant silence.

Smythe-Davies stood up. He gestured to a small old painting on the wall. "If I may presume to say so, your Grace, you are far from lacking in resources."

Neville felt his blood boiling. He hoped he could endure the interview without working himself into some sort of apoplectic fit. He knew paintings and things like that were valuable. The loss of Fleet House and all its treasures had been education enough in that arena.

"The facts are," continued Smythe-Davies with the maddening air of a man who had better things to do, "that you presently owe the government a quarter of a million pounds immediately, with—if we stick to the schedule Mr. Clifford and I have worked out—substantial amounts every quarter until the basic sum has been eradicated. Not counting, need I add, interest and penalties."

It might as well have been a death sentence. By slow bleeding.

"Berwick itself," continued Smythe-Davies, "is entailed. But its contents are your own, in fact they make up a great portion of the estate we are taxing. Yet you are free to dispose of them as you will. And such things are most valuable. You might consider them your working capital, your Grace."

Neville felt his stomach drop. He thought of his old friend Felix Dupre, of the famous auction-house. And he shuddered.

He envisioned himself pacing the empty halls, and Berwick denuded of its heritage. He gulped, caught his breath, stammered. "I need time," said the brand-new eighteenth Duke of Berwick. "You must give me time."

They left. Neville couldn't face Miranda just now, or the boy Neville.

Instead, he went to the chapel, and from the chapel down the stairway that led to the family crypt.

The Berwick crypt was directly underneath the chapel, but far bigger. While other dukes of the realm were often buried in England's great cathedrals, Berwick had always gathered its dead home to Berwick.

A fat candle still guttered near the place where they had interred his grandfather this same morning. The mortar wasn't dry yet. Neville could smell it, wet and earthy.

Now Neville stood alone in the great vaulted crypt, alone with all the ghosts of Berwick. Grandfather's dying words were carved on Neville's memory, as if memory itself were stone. The Fleets were here—everywhere in Berwick— watching. Waiting.

The candle flickered. There was only one other light, a bare bulb, back at the crypt's entrance.

The shadows were long and dark, the deepest black. There was no noise at all but for Neville's own deep breathing. As the flame of the solitary mourning candle darted and danced, some of the shadows moved with it. Or seemed to move.

Neville could see flashes of ancient brass that marked the medieval tombs of the very first Fleets: stiff knights in their brazen effigies, rigid in their armor as they must have been implacable in their conquest of this very rock and all the lands around it.

The first Fleets had all been soldiers.

Then had come the courtier Fleets, who fought only when fighting served them or their king.

Here lay the famous sixth duke, who had ridden out with Coeur de Lion.

Here, Sly Nevil, eleventh Duke of Berwick, who had charmed and schemed his way through all the tricky currents of the Tudor court. The family name had ever been plain

"Nevil" until some dandy in the reign of Queen Anne began to embellish it with the second *l* and the final *e*.

They were all here, the heroes and the scoundrels, and most of their women too. And many a Fleet baby was in this crypt, often unnamed, for the old days one didn't name an infant until its third or fourth year—so few survived that long.

But they were here.

He could feel them, feel their power.

The air was thick with it, almost suffocating.

Today his grandfather had joined this endless line. His father too—or at any rate, the charred unidentifiable bones that were thought to be his father's, exhumed from the ruin of Fleet House—were here. And one day he too would be here forever.

Neville could feel them. He felt all the weight of Berwick pressing down on him.

What should he do now?

Where would he get the money for the death duties?

How could he keep Berwick from becoming a public trust?

The silence was intense, thick, palpable.

"Help me!"

Neville's anguished shout sounded and echoed in the vaulted crypt.

"Help me!"

The scream became a wail, and the wailing echoed off into silence that seemed even deeper than before.

18

Jeff asked Polly to suggest a restaurant. It had been years since he'd had more than a hamburger in New York. When he was with the Dupres they almost always ate at home or at some friend's house.

"I'll take you to the company store, as we call it," she said. "It's right around the corner, maybe a bit chicer-than-thou, but with good food, and they know me."

They certainly did.

Les Piquets was a transplanted Paris bistro with dark wood walls and real gaslights flickering persuasively in Art Nouveau frosted-glass globes shaped like lilies. The headwaiter smiled and joked with Polly and immediately led them to a spacious round table in a secluded corner.

"I usually take clients here," she said when he complimented her on the special treatment, "and sometimes we come here ourselves. Between the Dupre's gang and Parke Bernet, we pretty much support the place. At lunch, anyway."

"What shall I have?"

"Everything's good, but the quiche is spectacular. And the endive vinaigrette, if they have it."

"Sold. Tell me, Polly—"

"What's a nice girl like me doing in a place like Dupre's?" She contemplated him for a moment. "Well, *Jeff*," she began, emphasizing his name ironically, making him wonder if it had been presumptuous to use her first name before she invited him to, "that's a long story. Why don't we order first?"

He hadn't noticed the waiter hovering at his elbow. They both ordered quiche and endive, with mineral water for Polly and a glass of red wine for Jeff.

"Did you mind me calling you Polly?"

She looked at him, appraising. She liked what she saw. *Smart, with good manners, in good shape, and not at all bad to look on. Tanned and lean and older than the preppie clothes would indicate—late twenties, maybe. Maybe more. Definitely, most assuredly, not an actor. Not a Christophe. Not a sayer of soliloquies, nor a gazer into mirrors. He looks quietly confident, as he has every right to be, being a Dupre. He makes it look so easy*, she thought, *but then, it probably has been easy.*

"No," she said, smiling, "I didn't mind."

Jeff looked at her and thought of Carla. Their drinks came. Carla's image faded. Polly was here. In many ways, she was the opposite of Carla, or seemed to be. Polly was very crisp and defined. Girls like Polly always knew just where they were going, and went there fast. He wondered where Polly wanted to go, and with whom.

"You were making fun of me," Jeff said, smiling, "but I really do want to know about your work at Dupre's. I spent the morning with Morgan, getting a quick tour. I'm trying to learn at least a little about the business, starting from scratch. Less than scratch."

She lifted her Perrier. "Here's to education."

Jeff only smiled, and raised his glass.

"You are, of course, the object of every kind of rumor and speculation, Jeff. Prodigal heir returns, all that. It's very natural, in a family firm like Dupre's. It's also very nervous-making. Is he going to be this year's edition of Caligula? Are we going to be sold out to the Acme Shoe Conglomerate because the boss's wife wants to redo her living room in Peoria? It's weird and scary at the same time. There are people at Dupre's who really care intensely about the old firm. Who have given a big part of their lives to Dupre's. And while we try to be modern, it's really a very traditional kind of place. I'd hate to see it turn into some kind of computerized operation with a drip-dry soul."

He heard her words, but he looked at her eyes. Her eyes were a shade of brown so dark that the iris merged with the pupil into a single dark and impenetrable disk. Beautiful. You could dive into those eyes and never want to come up for air.

"I'd hate that too."

"What are you going to do about it, if that isn't out of line?"

Feisty girl. He liked that.

Jeff laughed. "I wish I knew. I really came back to be with my aunt—she's all alone now, but for me. I've never had much to do with Dupre's. Nor has she. She's a good lady, Polly. She'd never do anything . . . unbecoming to Dupre's. And there's no immediate reason to sell at all."

"I guess," she said, "it's a little hard for me to understand your not wanting Dupre's: that place has been my whole life, pretty much, for three years now."

He grinned. "If I'd inherited the Acme Widget Company, I wouldn't want that, either."

"What do you want?"

Feisty indeed.

"The usual things. To like my job. To do a few things well. Love. To like getting up in the morning. Not to do anybody any harm, if I can help it. I always have had a problem with the commercial side of Dupre's."

"You think it's tacky to be 'in trade'?"

"Not at all, but—for instance—the fact that I like wine doesn't mean I have to squash grapes, or does it?"

She laughed. "Hardly. I thought I detected a little element of put-down there."

"You did."

Jeff smiled, but he wasn't giving any ground.

"A girl likes to think she does an honest day's work, Jeff."

"I'm sure you do. It isn't a question of honesty. To each his own, okay?"

"Okay."

The quiche came, not a moment too soon. Jeff tasted it. It was delicious. "Fabulous," he said. "There isn't anything like this on my dig in Veii."

"What are you digging?"

"Etruscans."

"Grave robbery?"

Jeff got the message. "That's part of it. We've learned a lot from their graves. But it's more than that, of course. It's every part of their lives. Which are still mostly a mystery."

"At what point," she asked, sipping the bubbly water, "does it become okay to rob a grave? I mean, if we got our spades and started excavating one of those cemeteries on Long Island, we'd end up in the can, right?"

He looked at her. "Such big chips," he said, "for such beautiful shoulders. It's like everything else in the world, Polly. If the government says it's okay, it's okay. Until you get a new government, which, in Italy, happens about once a month. Morally? That's another question. In most of Europe, modern-day graves are turned over every ten or so years. To make room for the new customers."

Polly smiled a gentle smile. She reached out and touched his hand "I'm sorry, Jeff. I do have a big collection of chips on my shoulders. More chips, in fact, than shoulders. And there's no reason at all for me to take any of it out on you. The fact is, Dupre's has been . . . well, not too good lately. And when your uncle died, that just made everything worse. We all miss Felix. He was unique, and a damn nice guy. I miss him especially. Just about the last thing he did before the accident was to promote me. And now, everything's sort of drifting and here you are trying to make sense out of it and I'm giving you a hard time. Forgive me."

"There's nothing to forgive. The last thing in the world I'm looking for is a yes-woman." He laughed. "I guess today, it'd be a yes-person."

"Something like that."

"Tell me about Dupre's."

"First, the bad news. Has anyone told you about the deLamerie fake?"

"No. What's a deLamerie?"

"Paul deLamerie, a very famous silversmith who worked in London in the eighteenth century. Died in 1751. Rather French in his influences, and most elegant. Some of the silversmiths of the time had workshops so big they were really factories. Not deLamerie. He had two apprentices, and a very

94

extensive output. Today, his things get enormous prices, when they're available. Well, this lady no one had ever seen before dropped off a sensational teapot one day. I saw it and loved it. So did Morgan, and Felix, and two outside people we called in. We sold the teapot for eighty-two thousand dollars to a British collector we've known for years. We—meaning the firm: I didn't know the man. But he had three other examples of deLamerie at home, all of unquestioned provenance. Two of the three had been bought by this man's family from deLamerie himself. He took our teapot home. Side by side, it didn't measure up. Felix was alarmed. He flew over there, and agreed. Really, there was nothing else he could do, considering who the customer is, and our long relationship with him. So Felix, as they say, cheerfully refunded the man's money. You can bet he wasn't so cheerful when he got back. Because the woman had already collected her money. And when we went looking for her, guess what, there was no one by that name at the address she gave. So Dupre's was well and truly fleeced."

"What did the police say?"

"They never heard about it. At least, not from us. We did everything we could to keep it quiet. In the art world, though, that's about like trying to keep the Hiroshima bombing quiet. Word seeps out. We can't muzzle the buyer, for instance. Dark hints are hinted. The only salvation is that it happens to everyone. Not very often, but it happens."

"Only in silver?"

"Silver's probably the easiest to fake. But it happens in painting and in furniture, and sometimes in pottery. Anything metal can be cast or molded, patinated, if the faker's clever enough, and given signs of wear. Hallmarks are easy to fake. If our customer didn't have the real thing at home, the chances are millions to one his teapot would now be the star of his collection. Of course, nobody knows—or wants to guess—how many fakes simply slip through out net. Ours, or Parke Bernet's, or anyone's."

Jeff looked at her. It was disconcerting to have to ask hard questions of a face attractive enough to melt rocks. The idea of a deliberate forgery being expert enough to pass inspection by Felix Dupre, and Morgan and Polly too, was boggling. Jeff knew that there were fakers in every line of the art-and-antiquities trade. Sometimes fakes were even planted where archaeologists would find them.

But Polly's story brought it all sickeningly home.

"Has anything else like that happened lately at Dupre's?"

"Not that I know of. Morgan would be the guy to ask."

The waiter came and took away their plates. Hers was as clean as his. They asked for filtre.

"My ignorance," he said "is a pure and beautiful thing. Thanks for the information Polly. How would you say morale is— was— before Felix died?"

"Not bad. There's always grumbling. We tend to feel oppressed I guess maybe all salaried people do. You know, who ever has a big enough office who's ever paid an adequate salary, who's ever loved enough by management?"

"I'm salaried and I know the feeling very well. Overworked and underpaid. If I didn't really love what I'm doing, I guess I'd grumble a lot more than I do."

She stirred her coffee, smiling. "I feel that way too, Jeff. And I'll never stop being grateful to your uncle. He gave me my big chance."

Jeff was silent for a moment. His head was swimming with a disconcerting mixture of desires. His response to Polly was quick and immediate. He wanted her, wanted to know her better, wanted to touch her, to make love to her. And always there was an image of Carla di Cavolfiore, gentle, loving, somehow elusive. *Hell, for all I know Polly's married.* He looked at her hands: long, slender, elegant. And ringless. *I ought to feel guilty.* Finally Jeff spoke.

"Felix," he said, "was famous for his good taste."

She laughed, a big, unselfconscious laugh.

"Tell me something else," said Jeff quietly.

"I'm at your service."

"Tell me you'll have dinner with me tomorrow night."

Her eyes were unreadable. "I'll be delighted," she said. "I think that would be just fine."

19

The Queen's Chamber, Palace of Whitehall, March 1536

The wind's cold fingers seemed to be clutching at her throat. Anne shivered, and drew the soft fur cloak more closely about her. And in her heart, too, she shivered.

It was all ending, and she could no more stop it ending than she could turn back the wind.

Anne, Queen of England, Ireland, and Wales, lawful wife

of him who made the law, sat quietly in the window of her private sitting room. Drafty as it was. She sat in the window because it was too cold to go out and she could feel the great palace of Whitehall closing in on her The largest palace in all Europe it had been enlarged, rebuilt gilded and polished, and draped in rare tapestries and rich silks. All for the love of the king for the queen.

Henry could and would take from her all he had given: the jewels this palace, her infant Elizabeth, even her life.

What he could not take was what Anne Boleyn had never possessed: illusions. How clearly she had seen the gameboard from the start. How deftly she had played the game. the highest, swiftest game in the world, and for the highest stakes. And now, dark and inevitable as night, was the endgame.

She stroked the rich fur of her cloak. The wide-set eyes that so delighted Master Holbein slowly lowered. and a smile formed upon her pale. full lips It had been a fine game, well played and she had won. At least for a while.

From the next chamber there came a soft and tinkling sound. Someone was gently strumming a lute. Anne's smile deepened She knew whose hands caressed the strings. She knew the voice before it came gliding to her ears on the bright wings of a love song.

Anne stood up, and as she stood, one teardrop fell on the soft brown fur. Good Mark Smeaton, trying to cheer her! Fair Mark, young. strong, clear of eye and straight of limb, his hair more gold than the king's had ever been. Mark. who lived for love. lost in some courtly dream. Yet fires burned in young Mark Smeaton whose heat, if he were to be believed, was all for her, for the queen of his heart, Queen Anne. A pretty conceit, from a pretty lad.

Anne walked into the chamber where Mark sat playing, smiled her most gracious smile, and bade him continue.

Henry the King, it was said, had once been young and slim and fair.

Anne sat on a low stool close to where Mark played. His long, deft fingers seemed to be coaxing the lute. As his eyes coaxed her, and his clear, gentle voice.

Anne looked into Mark's soft brown eyes, flecked with gold. She thought of her king, her husband, her lover. Henry Tudor, forty-five and obese, who had once looked like this. Like a god. Anne looked at Mark's smooth skin: how old could he be? Twenty? A little more, or less. Hardly more than a boy. How fine and strong he was. And filled with love. Mark's would be a simple, natural, unquestioning love.

Anne the Queen looked at her lutanist and smiled. The king was accusing her of adulteries on a scale that would make a Messalina blush. That the accusations were entirely false mattered not one whit. If Henry the King decided that his wife was a harlot, a harlot she would surely be, and with many a fawning courtier primed to reassure Henry of the correctness of his views.

As they had reassured him when he wanted to rid himself of the Spanish queen for love of Anne. As they would reassure him when he wanted the moon to be made of marzipan, or toads to fly.

In that moment something changed in Anne's mind. She had been too cautious for too long, calculating every move from the cut of a gown to the cut of a smile. Anne rose and walked to the lute player. His song continued. She gently rested a hand on the top of his golden head. "Good Mark, who so cheers his queen, you must be thirsting from your song. Would you taste some wine?"

His response was strong and unspoken. The lute answered for him. Mark quickly, fluently, built the languid chords of the love song to a thrumming climax.

Then he stopped the song entirely, laying his strong hand flat across the strings. His eyes leaped to her face in the sudden silence. "There is no wine so rare as humble spring water, were it poured by my lady the queen."

His words were light. His tone was grave, for it compressed all of his vast longing into a courtly trifle.

Anne walked to a cabinet. He sat as he had been sitting, transfixed. She opened the cabinet, a huge carved and gilded edifice with many doors. Inside were bottles and decanters and a flash of gold and silver. Anne reached for a decanter. She placed it on the table, hesitated a moment, then stretched her slender arm back to the deepest recess of the cabinet. Her fingers knew the shape they sought, even where her eyes could not quite penetrate the darkness. Her back was to him now. He could not see the object she withdrew.

All at once, the queen turned, smiling mischievously. As she had smiled at the king. Smeaton's mouth opened in astonishment, then closed. He said nothing.

The Winchcombe Chalice glowed in the half-dark chamber, vibrating with the force of a thousand legends. Mark Smeaton knew them well, but he had never, before this moment, set eyes on the cup itself.

Anne Boleyn lifted the chalice in a fine mocking toast. " 'Tis only fitting, good Mark, that a cup given in love be used in the offices of love. We will drink, and be merry, and the devil take tomorrow!"

She drank, sipping at first, then fully, tilting back her famous swan's throat. A thin trickle of wine escaped the corner of her mouth. The golden cup gleamed, gathering in the light. The rubies smoldered.

Mark Smeaton watched, hypnotized. He rose, and walked to her, and encircled her slim body with his eager arms.

"Then you would share a simple loving cup with a lady, good lutanist Smeaton?" There was a ripple of merriment in her voice, a fine soft mockery of all that had been, of all that might be.

He held her tight. The words came slowly to his fluent tongue "I would, my lady."

Mark kissed her then, buried his face in the delicate, beckoning arc where her neck met her shoulders. Anne could feel the warmth of him, the urgency. She smiled, and still holding the chalice, reached both of her arms around his strong, broad back, returning the pressure, fitting her body to his, tremor for tremor, pulse for throbbing pulse.

They stood thus for a long moment's yearning.

Then Mark lifted her in his arms as though she weighed no more than a flower, and carried the queen to the room he had so often entered in his dreaming, but never, yet, in this life.

As the handsome lutanist bore Anne Boleyn out of the chamber to her bedroom, there was a very soft, whispering sort of sound. It might have been the wind, but was not. At the far end of the room, deep in shadow, a small, well-oiled section of the wainscot paneling slid shut. The thin, rabbit-faced woman who crouched behind the spy hole could scarcely contain her glee.

The wanton bitch. The flaming hussy. She, who laughed, and mocked, and trod down God's own laws as though they were unclean rushes underfoot! Bewitching the king, poor man. And playing the queen, so high, so proud. Well, that would end now. And Lord Cranmer would pay well for the evidence. The spy waited, still crouching like some forest creature, well-practiced in all the arts of sneaking. One of the queen's own serving maids she was, not that that haughty bitch ever took proper notice. Holding in her breath, aching in every joint from her long, cramped vigil, the woman was at last satisfied that the queen and her paramour could never hear her. Only then did she ease herself backward down the narrow passage squeezed behind the panelling.

It ended at the back of a linen closet. Soon thereafter, the maid let herself out of the closet, carrying a stack of freshly laundered bed linen. She smiled as she walked, thinking of one bed that was going to need new linen shortly, thinking of the reward that would be hers. And she thought, too, of the rightful punishment of sinners. Surely, God in his wisdom must be smiling down on her in this hour, instrument as she undoubtedly would be of his divine will.

In the bedroom of Queen Anne, the Winchcombe Chalice stood neglected on the queen's dressing table, its rare contents barely touched. For there were other, sweeter pleasures to be tasted on the bed nearby, as Mark Smeaton lived his love song to the fullest and Henry Tudor's queen drowned her fears in rapture.

20

Polly thought about him all day long. Had she accepted his invitation too quickly? Shouldn't she have waited, found out more about him, been a bit harder to get?

She stood in her studio apartment looking in the mirror, trying on dress after dress, holding them up in front of her, appraising the result. Too fancy. Not fancy enough. Too sexy. Was it possible to be too sexy? It definitely was.

Jeff seemed open and earnest, yet there was something, some barrier she hadn't overcome. The question was, did she want to? Maybe she'd find out the answer tonight.

It had been nearly three months since Christophe left her.

In all that time, Polly had had two dates, both arranged by kindly friends. Both flops. Her failure, not the gentlemen's. She had gone through a period of numbness, of an inability to respond. It must have showed on those dates. Poor guys.

But Jeff Dupre was something else.

Polly was interested in Jeff, and not because he was a Dupre.

Although being a Dupre couldn't hurt.

Especially a maverick Dupre, a Dupre who wasn't playing

the game. A Dupre who had made his own terms with life, where and when he wanted to.

Part of the reason she liked him almost at once was that Jeff was so obviously reluctant. He wanted to get back to his own turf, and Polly could hardly blame him for that.

She thought of Jeff, rummaging in her tiny closet. Thought of the restaurant, too, which she'd passed but never visited. Understatement. That wasn't much of a problem, because most of her clothes were on the simple side. To match her budget. She settled on a shirtwaist in a cream-colored material that looked like silk but had come out of a test tube. That and a dark-green-and-violet scarf, and the neck unbuttoned not too deeply. Navy-blue shoes. Period.

She was five minutes late, sensing that Jeff would get there a few minutes early.

Polly walked into the pretty little Italian restaurant, through the small bar, and was greeted by the headwaiter. Jeff sat at a corner table sipping something white. He saw her, grinned, stood up to help her with her chair.

"Hi," he said.

"Hi, yourself." Polly looked around. "Very nice. I've heard the food's terrific, but I've never been here."

"My aunt suggested it, so it has to be."

She looked at him. The preppie clothes. The tan. The toothpaste-advertisement smile. The impenetrable blue eyes.

"She's a remarkable lady, your aunt."

He only smiled. "I looked for you today."

"I was in Boston," she said, "soliciting."

Jeff looked at her, questioningly.

She laughed. "Calling on the executors of three estates. Got two of 'em."

"Do you call them, or do they call you?"

"Sometimes a bit of both. Usually, they call us. And maybe a few competitors, and compare estimates and bids. It's only fair. It is also, sometimes, a little cutthroat and vampirish. Sometimes we're the next crew after the undertakers. Today it was mostly silver, so I was alone. If there were a lot of furniture or paintings, I would have brought someone for them. Sometimes Morgan comes, if it's really fancy."

"Tell me about Morgan."

She looked at him, speculating. "Morgan is Morgan. He knows his stuff, both as a scholar and on the platform. He's very good: you should watch him sometime. Other than that, I don't know a whole lot about him."

"Felix apparently was very big on him."

"He was."

"You sound as if maybe you aren't."

"It shows? I don't hate him or anything, Jeff, he's been very kind to me. Seeing as how Felix promoted me, and Morgan could . . . well, sack me in a minute if he wanted to. I guess I don't feel the rapport with him that I did with your uncle. But your uncle was special. Very special."

"He was. I feel like the grand inquisitor. Stop me if it gets too heavy. That isn't why I asked you out."

She smiled and ordered white wine. "It also isn't why I accepted."

He looked at her for a quiet moment, wanting her. "Good," was all he said.

Divino's food lived up to Jeff's expectations of it. They both ordered veal, hers scallopini sautéed with lemon, his a broiled chop stuffed with cheese and Parma ham.

Polly was an education: her love of the auction business in general and of Dupre's in particular was apparent, and contagious. He asked her advice and she responded generously.

"What I don't understand," said Jeff, "is how Dupre's can be what it is, and have so many good sales, and still not really make money."

"Well," she said, "naturally I don't know about the accounting parts of it. You can bet it isn't a question of the staff's being overpaid. Anyone in a comparable position in an ordinary business would probably make twice what I do—and that's true across the board. There's profit-sharing, but there don't seem to be that many profits to share. Not lately, anyway."

"How does Dupre's attract such good people?"

"Easily. We're whacko. Everyone in the arts is a little bit crazy. Museum people too. You have to love it or you wouldn't put up with it. And it is possible to make money, eventually, by going into business, having a shop, or even starting an auction gallery. New ones do open up, and some of them do well. Bill Doyle, for instance."

Jeff had never heard of Doyle, and said so.

"Bill's a good guy. He had a rather small shop for years, one of the few on the Upper East Side that wasn't a ripoff, and then he just branched into the auction business about five years ago. He's doing very well, by the look of it. Hot competition for a place like Dupre's—for everybody."

"How do you get things to sell?"

"By soliciting, as I was today. Executors and heirs come to us, and sometimes we go to them. Felix invented Discovery

Days, and we were the first to advertise, you know, bring in Grandmother's chamber pot and we'll see if it's worth anything. Those days are very popular, and they generate an amazing number of sales for us. And, of course, the whole institution of auctions is spreading. It used to be very neatly divided. Either really tiny country auctions or big fancy, million-dollar Rembrandt-type auctions. And Mr. and Mrs. Middle Class were scared of places like Dupre's or Parke Bernet. That isn't true anymore. Everyone comes. The conventional department stores are so damned expensive, anyone who likes old things—or old-looking things—is much better off at an auction. But you know all that."

He laughed. "What I don't know about the auction business would fill a whole encyclopedia."

Jeff looked at her, close enough to touch her, wanting to touch her, and afraid to.

Afraid of how she might react.

Afraid of why he felt like this, only a few days after leaving Carla.

And maybe you could think a feeling to death. Especially when it was such a fine warm feeling as he was having right now.

Cavolfiore seemed very far away.

Being with Polly tonight was the first good time he'd known since coming back to New York. A good time, and maybe it would get better. Maybe it would get a lot better.

She replied to his comment, quite serious, working girl out with the boss and not forgetting it. Jeff wondered if he could make her forget it.

"Well," she said, smiling, trying to help: "We really just go along, doing our best. It isn't a line of work that lends itself to innovation. There were auctions in Rome and Greece, and essentially the process is exactly the same. To the highest bidder go the spoils. It's very simple."

"Morgan tells me you're getting into a broader range of categories, Western stuff and so forth."

"That's happening. In a perfect world, there'd be a sale going on every day. We try for that, everyone does. And no one makes it. Summer, for instance, used to be a total loss except for an occasional country-estate sale, on the premises, that sort of thing. But Felix was thinking of trying a few summer sales next year. Maybe we'll still do that. And we are widening the range. Ten or so years ago, no first-rate house would do a thing like auction cars, for instance. A few months ago someone's 1935 Duesenberg brought almost half a million dollars."

"Imagine the day you scratched the fender."

"I bet they almost never drive them."

The waiter came. Neither of them wanted dessert. They ordered espresso.

"Profits," said Polly: "it sounds grim."

"It is if you own an auction house. At least, this auction house. The ledgers didn't look too terrific today."

"More and more auction houses are competing for a finite body of stuff. It recycles. We see items coming back for the second, third time. So does everybody. I sold a punch bowl last fall that your grandfather had first sold in 1933, and your uncle in 1960."

"It could go on forever."

"Maybe. The quality, though, is not getting better. With a very few exceptions, we're seeing a process of mediocritizing, as Felix called it. The great objects are not being recirculated. They end up in museums, and the game stops. Try to buy yourself a Vermeer, for example. There simply aren't any, for any price. When the Rothschilds sold their estate at Mentmore with all its contents—it was fabulous, Jeff—well, no one is accumulating on that scale anymore. When Berwick Castle goes, it's gone. Dispersed. Rich people are simplifying their lives. If you can't get good servants to polish the silver, you probably aren't going to have a whole lot of silver."

"You can bet I'm not."

"Insurance is a problem, too. Ruinous."

"Not to mention forgeries."

She looked at him, then at her coffeecup. "A lady could take that personally, especially if she was in charge of the deLamerie-fake sale."

"I'm sorry, Polly, really: that wasn't what I meant. I meant, you'd be careful, if you were starting to collect just about anything."

"*Caveat emptor,* as they say. You bet. Any good house, naturally, will refund your money if you can prove a fake. It isn't a major problem. Not yet. But, the higher prices go, the more tempting it becomes for the fakers. The deLamerie teapot earned somebody over eighty thousand dollars. If it was made from scratch, it might have taken a couple of weeks. That's damn good pay for a few weeks. You could take the rest of the year off."

"Could you not. What do you mean, Polly, when you say if it was made from scratch?"

"Often they take a genuine old piece and add hallmarks. The teapot was really most convincing. It might have been old. An eighteenth-century French chair, for instance, is valuable. Signed by one of the great cabinetmakers, it's priceless. So that's tempting, too, not to mention simpler."

"I get the impression," Jeff said, "that all attribution is a fairly dicey business."

"It sure is. Museums—the smarter ones anyway—are in a frenzy of reattribution. The nineteenth century, in particular, was cavalier as hell about who did what. And, of course, fraud was hardly unknown even then."

"The Etruscans, some of them, did a fairly lively trade in fake Greek artifacts."

Polly grinned. "And the Romans faked, too. There's a quite famous Egyptian bronze falcon in the National Museum that isn't really Egyptian. It's a two-thousand-year-old fake. The Chinese, of course, practically made a religion of it. Not intentional forgery for money—although they did that too—but it was a mark of your skill to be able to recreate things in the style of some old master. So we continually find, say, five-hundred-year-old copies of a thousand-year-old scroll. By the time a thing's that old, no one can really tell."

"Thermoluminescence will tell, if it's organic."

"Oh, sure, but it takes a while, and it isn't cheap. We just couldn't afford it on a regular basis. But if I were buying anything serious, and had doubts about it, that would be a good investment."

"I bet you don't have very many doubts about anything."

She had been in the act of lifting the little espresso cup. Her hand froze in midair. "I guess," she said softly, "you intended that as a compliment. I have to tell you, Jeff, the wrath of my samurai ancestors is never far from the surface."

"Would you rather I thought of you as all fluttery and given to attacks of the *vapeurs?*"

She saved it with a laugh. "Not bloody likely. I'm touchy tonight. I have been, ever since Felix died. It's known, clinically, as insecurity. Maybe being out with a Dupre makes it worse."

"I'm a Dupre in name only. Think of me as a simple, underpaid archaeologist from Cambridge, Massachusetts."

"I'll try," she said, "but it won't be easy."

The check came, and Jeff paid it. They walked out into the dark and balmy night. Jeff was interested to discover that dining well in New York seemed to be cheaper than in Rome. And a lot cheaper than Paris or London.

Polly lived just a few blocks away, on Seventy-third Street between Third Avenue and Lexington. It was an old brownstone town house that had been converted into chic little apartments.

Jeff had one thought as they walked, a thought he could hardly express. How to prolong the evening? He couldn't really invite her to Minnie's house, not thinking the way he was thinking. Not wanting her the way he wanted her. He'd never had a girl overnight at the Dupre house, although Felix and Minnie had always made a point of encouraging him to bring his girls for dinner, to parties, before or after the theater. But in the last analysis, it was someone else's house and he didn't feel comfortable using it as a hotel.

They paused at her doorstep. Jeff struggled with banalities, feeling uncomfortable.

Polly seemed to sense this. She paused, turned to him, smiled. "Can I make you some green tea? Or a drink? I don't really keep much booze, but there's some. Basically I only drink wine."

Jeff looked at her. He couldn't tell what she was thinking. Maybe it was better that way.

Her apartment was on the second floor. The house had been remodeled handsomely, still retaining the late-Victorian flavor of its darkly wainscoted staircase. Above the wood was a rich wallpaper that looked like the marbleized endpaper of old books: all mauves and wine reds and ivory. The lamps were brass and cut glass.

Polly's apartment was a complete contrast to the opulent stair-hall. One big room with an ell, it was completely white: white walls and ceiling, white canvas draperies at the two tall windows, white marble fireplace. Even the rug was white, wall-to-wall, punctuated by a few small, fine-looking old Oriental carpets. The furniture was simple, clean-lined, and mostly modern.

"It's beautiful, Polly."

"Such as it is. I like it. It's a quick walk to work. Is tea okay?"

"Tea is fantastic."

She set the water to boiling, and rinsed a big white teapot in hot water.

While the tea was steeping, he kissed her. It was a very good kiss.

"Goddammit," she said when they stopped. "I was afraid this would happen."

He kissed her again.

"What," Jeff asked, "is there to be afraid of?"

She laughed. "Believe it or not, I am a lady of some scruples. I'm afraid of a lot of things. Like being thought easy. Like running the risk of someone's thinking I am after the heir to Dupre's. All kinds of things."

"Isn't it enough that I'm . . . that I want you very much?"

Her eyes told him nothing. Her arms were around his neck. They tightened, and Polly buried her face in his chest. "Let's pretend that it is. Enough."

For a moment he was unable to believe his luck. He kissed her again, gently. Then less gently. She said something softly. His name.

Her bed was in the little ell. To Jeff it was a refuge, a solace, a place of discovery and joy. Polly was elegant in everything she did. Sometimes it was the elegance of a wild thing, sometimes a tender glory, soft and yielding, delicate as petals, shimmering as pearls.

She was not at all like Carla, but Jeff didn't think about Carla, then or for a long time afterward.

After a time they lay silent.

"I'm almost always afraid," she said softly.

"You said that. You have no reason to be afraid of me Polly."

"It isn't you. It's will the guy like me enough, will I be good enough, and I'm especially scared when someone's very good-looking. Like you."

"No one ever mentioned to you that you're a knockout?"

"That's different."

He laughed, and kissed her. "It sure is."

They made love again. After a time he got up and dressed. Polly was dozing. She stirred at the sound of him, opened her eyes, sat up in bed.

"You're going?"

"I know it's silly, but my aunt will worry. Don't get up, Polly. I can let myself out."

She got up anyway, found a robe, and slipped it on. "I guess," she said with a funny off-center grin, "that our tea is a little cold."

"Only the tea."

He kissed her and stepped toward the door. "Will you be in the office tomorrow?" Jeff planned to have lunch with her, and supper and breakfast, too, if that were possible.

"Only in the morning. Then I'm off for Palm Beach and Dallas for two days, more soliciting."

He laughed. "That's what I get for falling for a solicitress. But I'll see you in two days."

"If you like."

"I like. I like very much."

"Good night, Jeff. Thanks for supper."

"Thanks for being Polly."

He kissed her again and walked down the carpeted stairs to the front door.

Jeff walked west on Seventy-third Street to Park, and down Park to Sixty-fourth. The night was cooler now. It was just after midnight. He had no way of weighing what had just happened. It had happened, like a sudden glorious rainbow, all glowing and unexpected, shimmering, transient and unforgettable.

Maybe it wouldn't be so transient. Jeff wondered if he could sustain the magic. She was a funny, prickly girl, for one so sleek to look at. There were many sharp edges in Polly's character. It wasn't the comforting softness and womanly mystery of Carla.

But whatever it was, was fine.

No one walked on Park Avenue at midnight. The double-lane avenue stretched glittering toward midtown. There was a rush of cars, a sparkle of traffic lights rhythmically changing from red to green to yellow. An occasional doorman came out into the street whistling for a taxi. Park Avenue was calm and nearly silent now, snug behind its walls of money.

Jeff turned right on Sixty-fourth Street. He felt better now than he felt since hearing about Felix's death. There was a sense of expectation in the August night, maybe a first hint of autumn.

Quiet as Park Avenue had been, Sixty-fourth Street was quieter.

Jeff's mind was soaring. It leaped and darted: Veii, Felix's funeral, Cavolfiore, tonight's restaurant, Polly's apartment, Polly. He thought of Minnie and wondered if she'd be home yet and waiting up for him. Bunny had taken her to the ballet tonight.

He was walking slowly, ambling. He stepped out into the street about fifty yards from the Dupre house.

The car was black and very quiet. It had no headlights on.

Jeff didn't hear it until just before it struck him. And by then it was too late.

There was just the impression of something huge rushing at him, something big and dark and deadly. He saw it and tensed and leaped to the right.

The car swerved toward him.

The impact was sudden and brutal. The car caught Jeff on his left thigh, threw him high in the air, and sped on into the darkness.

Instinctively, Jeff tucked his head into his arms to cushion his fall.

It wasn't enough.

The impact seared, throbbed, numbed. He landed in a tuck, taking the brunt of it on his upper left arm and shoulder. All the breath went out of him, and for one blinding moment it seemed like he'd never breathe again. He was glued to the gritty pavement by his own blood.

All there was was pain. And then came darkness.

21

Berwick Castle, November 1960

Neville Fleet walked with the doctor in the bleak winter woods. Even with company, it was a lonely walk. It was almost as if the barren trees mocked the emptiness of the duke's life now that the boy was away at Eton, now that he was alone with Miranda, and Miranda's madness.

For madness it was, clear and plain.

It had not come suddenly. For years now, Neville had noticed her drifting, always gently, in and out of reality. At first he had taken it for a charming vagueness. Miranda was charming, had always been a little vague. But the gulf between absentmindedness and her present condition was a wide one, and deep, and it had taken Neville some time to force himself to face the fact that she had crossed it. Perhaps never to return.

It would have been easier, in a way, if her sickness had been accompanied by raving and violence. That, at least, might be readily seen, handily dealt with.

But the form of Miranda's madness was a gossamer thing. She held sanity like water in her hands. It kept slipping away as though it had never been there at all. More and more she lived in the past.

He would come upon his wife to find her deep in conversation with her brother, who had died in the Battle of Britain. She called the dogs of her childhood, asked advice of her dead parents, spoke of the new plantings at Loweswater House her ancestral home, which had been deeded to the National Trust years since. The tone of these ramblings was always soft polite. eager to please She included Neville in her chatter and became upset when he failed to answer the question of for example, her dead brother, questions that only Miranda could hear.

Luckily little Neville seemed unaware of her sickness.

Miranda was fine with the child, always had been. She seemed more alive when the boy was home But he was home so seldom now. It was hard for his father to believe his son had just turned fourteen Full of himself happy with school, always visiting some pal, or bringing friends to Berwick. Well and good: the duke wanted his son to be free from cares. The cares would come to him soon enough. As they had come tumbling down on his father, with the inescapable violence of an avalanche.

Miranda's insanity was only the latest blow.

The other problems were all financial. Debt loomed over the duke surrounded him engulfed his every waking hour, disturbed his fitful sleep. There seemed to be no end to it. Even thinking of Miranda's illness made him think of money: he knew what good psychiatric advice cost these days, and it made him cringe Even with the discreet help of Felix Dupre. covertly selling off the Berwick paintings one by one, the duke was hardly able to keep pace with the schedule of payments imposed by her majesty's Inland Revenue Service in the hated person of Smythe-Davies.

The psychiatrist kept talking and talking. The textbook terms echoed in the silent wood. Some sort of schizophrenia, the man called it. There were, of course, chemical means of controlling it, of numbing her mind. Thorazine was mentioned Treatments abroad, perhaps. The duke reminded his guest that Miranda refused even to leave the courtyard of Berwick Castle.

"I feel safe here." she kept saying. pleading.

How safe would the poor creature feel, Neville wondered, if she knew the true state of his affairs? He determined she would never know. He could do that for her, at least. For the memory of what she had been to him It had been three years now since Neville had thought of her as a woman.

Three years. And the consolations in between had been few and far from satisfactory.

They walked and walked It felt good, at least, to be out-of-doors. Their walk was aimless, but it imparted a sense of purpose. The doctor was at Berwick incognito. Neville had asked him for the weekend, to observe, to diagnose Miranda, to make suggestions.

That they would be costly suggestions, Neville had no doubt. He wondered how much therapy he could buy with a Holbein. If there were any Holbeins left at Berwick, which there might not be. How much Thorazine could be exchanged for his great-grandmother's Georgian silver?

Neville found himself relieved that his grandfather hadn't lived to see Miranda in her present state, or the present state of the family finances. Even though the old gentleman had been largely responsible for their grief. With his extravagance. With his mortgaging all that could be mortgaged. With his fine disdain for any kind of financial planning. And, in the end, with his cursed death duties. Ninety-seven-percent death duties on an estate that was overborrowed to start with.

They walked up a hill and paused at its top.

In the distance the towers of Berwick Castle were silhouetted against a gray and blustery sky.

Berwick still had the power to stir deep responses in Neville's heart. These responses were touched with sadness now, edged with despair. The castle looked so strong: there it stood, as it had stood for nearly a thousand years, impregnable, defiant, assured.

The rot was all on the inside, and Neville knew that unless he did something to reverse the tide of events, Berwick might fall. What siege tower and battering ram and arquebus and cannon had ever failed to do, a plump, arrogant little man named Smythe-Davies could achieve with a stroke of his intimidating pen.

The duke sighed. There had been some measure of gallantry in the old days. Even if you were beaten, it would be by some worthy foe. To be defeated by the likes of Smythe-Davies was worse than shameful.

He turned to the psychiatrist. "Do you see any hope at all, then?"

The man smiled benevolently. Neville decided his guest thought him a fool. "There is always hope, your Grace," said the most fashionable psychiatrist in London. "Wonders are happening all around us, every day."

Neville looked around and could see no wonders. Even Berwick on its crag had lost some of the old magic.

"What," Neville asked bluntly, "do you suggest, specifically?"

"Maintenance. We can do that chemically. I shall prescribe

Thorazine, and perhaps some supplementary tranquilizers. You can report on her condition at regular intervals. And from time to time I'll just happen by. As if by accident. If you were to plan any extensive trip with the duchess . . ."

"You can be very sure we won't do that."

"It might be wise," said the doctor pausing to fill his pipe, "were you to employ a psychiatric nurse for the lady. In mufti of course."

"She already has a perfectly good maid. Do you think there's any danger? I mean to say, why a special nurse? Wouldn't that be very costly?"

The doctor looked quickly at Neville and as quickly averted his gaze as though what he had seen on Neville's face had frightened him.

"More costly than a ladies' maid, I'm sure. A good nurse might be worth say four thousand pounds a year."

"Out of the question."

Neville though of Smythe-Davies. In the old days Miranda would have been surrounded by nurses round the clock, if she needed them.

Once again the doctor gave Neville a rather fishy look.

He thinks I'm a miser thought Neville. He thinks I'm out to deprive poor old Miranda of the proper care. He finds it impossible to conceive that the Duke of Berwick might actually be flat broke that he has to scratch for the fees at Eton, that the roof of the west tower leaks like a sieve and will keep right on leaking because the Duke of Berwick owes her majesty's damnable Inland Revenue Service the better part of a quarter-million pounds.

He cleared his throat.

"Of course if you consider that it's vital, well, we'll look into it. But that does seem rather steep, if it isn't an emergency."

"From all you tell me, and from what I see, it is far from being an emergency. The illness seems to have come on her slowly. It is possible—a great deal of work is being done on the subject—that these things are caused by chemical imbalances. Or by some glandular deficiency. That certain chemicals check the symptoms is already most hopeful. It may be possible, one day, to bring them completely around. One never knows."

The two men walked down the hill into the forest of Berwick.

Neville caught one last glimpse of the castle. He thought how Miranda had always told him she felt safer at Berwick than anywhere else. And how little either of them had ever guessed that Berwick would one day become her prison.

"Yes," said Neville quietly, "one never knows."

22

Jeff felt the throbbing distantly as though his battered left leg was half a mile away but still part of him. The throbbing had a heavy percussive quality to it: angry gnomes were hitting him with hot sledgehammers.

He heard voices. Minnie's. Two others.

It seemed like the biggest effort in the world just to open his eyes. He did that slowly, unsure of the result.

They had put him in his own room. The lights were mercifully low. There was a uniformed policeman and Minnie, and a man Jeff didn't recognize, probably a doctor.

"Hi," he said weakly, feeling the inadequacy of it.

Minnie came to him and took his hand. That felt as distant as the pain in his leg. They had given him something, some drug to make him float.

"Jeffy," she said softly, "my poor Jeffy. What happened?"

There was an eager audience for his reply: the cop came closer and the doctor too.

Jeff looked at his aunt. She'd had all the trouble one woman needed. And he wasn't sure not really. The car had seemed to be swerving at him—deliberately. But maybe it hadn't. Maybe it was a mistake, a drunk, some joyriding kid who simply couldn't drive.

And maybe it was deliberate.

Maybe someone was trying to kill Jeff Dupre. Maybe someone had known he was going out maybe someone had been waiting. Why were the car's lights off?

"I didn't see him," said Jeff slowly from inside his chemical haze, "and I didn't hear him. His lights weren't even on. It was a black car, or very dark anyway."

The policeman spoke up then. "And he never stopped, Mr. Dupre?"

"I don't think so. I guess I must have been knocked out."

"You were," said the policeman. "I found you in the gut-

113

ter. Thought you were a drunk. Luckily, no one else had seen you. Your wallet was still there, with this address."

Jeff opened his eyes wider. "Thank you very much, officer."

"Could you eat anything, Jeffy?" Minnie hovered nearby.

"No, we ate. It was very good, your restaurant." He winced. The throbbing was less distant now. Jeff blinked, swallowed some air, fought to keep his eyes open.

"What did you give me? I feel . . . far away."

"Codeine. It'll help you sleep."

The guy in that car wanted me to sleep for a long, long time, Jeff thought. Maybe forever.

He closed his eyes. The last thing he remembered before sinking into a heavy slumber was an image. Jeff saw a yellow sailboat bobbing on a clear blue sea. It was a pretty picture. Only, there was no one in the sailboat, no hand on the tiller, where his father's hand should have been.

For just a moment, when he awoke, Jeff forgot where he was, and what had happened. The room was bright with sunshine. His old room. He could have been any age. He felt both very young and frightened, and very old and weary. Then the throbbing, searing pain in his leg came burning its way into his brain, and he remembered it all. He remembered Polly, and the speeding car, the impact, the drug.

He tried to move the leg. It felt like someone was grilling it over live coals. Every inch of it ached. It was amazing to Jeff that the damn thing wasn't broken. He assumed it wasn't. There was no cast, just a big bandage encasing his thigh, with bruises spilling out from behind it, blurry and mottled blue with brown under the tan. He wondered who had undressed him, who had done the bandaging, what kind of shape his clothes were in.

There was a knock. Hastings poked his gray head in and asked if Jeff would like breakfast on a tray. Jeff decided he would, very much. Ten minutes later the butler was back with grapefruit juice, coffee, and a steaming plate of Emmalee's famous buckwheat pancakes and sausage.

"Emmalee," said Hastings, smiling, "says you are to eat every bite, or there'll be hell to pay. How are you feeling, Mr. Jeff?"

Jeff struggled to sit up in bed. Hastings set the tray down on its wicker legs, which bridged Jeff's lap, and helped with the pillows.

"I have felt better. But I guess I'm lucky to be here at all. And please thank Emmalee."

"I will do that."

Hastings left Jeff to his pancakes and the morning *Times*. The pancakes were far more appetizing than the contents of the paper He ate more than he thought he could eat, and tried to make some sense of last night's accident. *If it was an accident.*

A few minutes after he'd finished the last of the pancakes, there was another knock on his door and Minnie popped in. She saw his tray and smiled. "Well, that's a good sign. How do you feel Jeffy?"

"All things considered, pretty good. It was a fairly narrow escape, though."

"You gave Bunny and me a terrible turn, Jeff. We'd had a drink with the Atkinsons after the ballet, and we must have gotten back just after it happened. There you were, all messed up, and the policeman, and Hastings in his bathrobe—he'd already called the doctor. Luckily, there don't seem to be any fractures, no permanent damage."

"Only to my ego. It was pretty damned stupid. I mean, I am old enough to cross the street by myself."

She laughed then. It was good to see her laughing, even if it was from relief. "Yes," said Minnie, "indeed you are."

"What did the cop say?"

"Very little. Lucky he came by when he did. He'll be back this morning, later on, to take a statement. You weren't up to it last night."

"No," he said, "I sure wasn't."

It would be a simple statement. *I was hit by a speeding car, by Jeff Dupre.* With no evidence of any malevolent intentions. With, probably, no hope of finding the car or its driver. Jeff had no memory of the license number All big American cars looked alike to him now. This had been—he guessed—a big American car of the Mercedes-Benz-design-ripoff variety. Of which there were probably a dozen look-alikes on the market. He smiled at his aunt with cheer he did not feel, and sipped his coffee. "I'll get up soon. It really feels better today."

"Take it easy, darling. There's no hurry."

But there is. There's a great big hurry. To get back to Veii. To figure out where I am with Carla . . . with Polly. Something about the near-miss of last night made Jeff very eager to get on with his life, wherever it might take him. He had come so close to not having a life to get on with.

Minnie left him, taking the breakfast tray. Jeff forced himself to get out of bed.

Once he was standing, strangely enough, he felt much better. He made it to the bathroom and took a long hot shower, dangling the bandaged left leg outside the shower curtain to keep the bandage dry. He shaved slowly and dressed in faded khaki trousers and an old alligator shirt. He would not be going out today. Not if he could help it. Jeff was glad, for the moment, that Polly was out of town. One less explanation to make.

The doctor, Minnie told him, had said to take it very easy, to keep the leg elevated, not to walk on it any more than he could help. Slowly, gingerly, he limped down the curving staircase.

Minnie was in the library. "Would you like more coffee, darling?"

"Thanks, yes, I would."

She brought back a pot and two cups on a silver tray. They sat in the sun-filled room, surrounded by books and memories. They always had had tea there, and cocktails, and usually, coffee after dinner. The house was quiet. The library was the quietest room in it, insulated by the thick oak bookshelves and their heavy cargo of wisdom.

They sat there quietly for a moment. Then Jeff asked the question he had been waiting to ask of Minnie for years, and never dared to. Never dared because he was afraid of what she might say. Of what the truth might be.

Somehow Felix's death, and the narrow escape last night, made Jeff care very urgently now. So urgently that he was willing to face the consequences, whatever they were.

If Minnie loved him, she'd be straight.

Jeff knew she loved him. And he'd never known her to be anything but very straight indeed.

"Tell me," Jeff asked his aunt, "how it was with my father."

She looked at him over the coffee cup, her fine dark eyes very alert. They had never talked about the accident.

"You are very like him in some ways, Jeffy. Quiet and deep. And more than a bit of a rebel. And of course, you look quite like your father. He was a Viking too. No one knows where that comes from—all the other Dupres were dark as dark. Well, the two brothers were always very close. Closer, I think, for being separated. Your father had his architecture, and it was going well for him, he was beginning to get very interesting commissions. And for all we could see, he

116

was happy in his marriage. I don't recall ever seeing even a hint of disagreement between them."

"You were there that day, in Watch Hill?"

"I was there. So was Felix. You were there, too, but off with a friend someplace."

"I don't even remember saying good-bye."

"Probably you wouldn't have. No one was going anyplace special. Or at least, we didn't think so."

"He wasn't ill, or anything like that?"

"No, darling, not that any of us knew. Of course, it did occur to us, what you're building up to."

"But you don't think so?"

"No. I definitely don't think so, and neither did your mother, or Felix. Inexplicable things do happen. The amazing thing is that they don't happen more often. I've heard of people who had—as they say—everything to live for, who killed themselves. But somehow I just can't believe that of Jeff, of your father. He was too good on the water, for one thing. He had great respect for the sea. I think, if he were going to . . . do something, it wouldn't have been in that way."

"I'm sorry to be so damn gloomy, Minnie, especially now, after the accident and all."

"You haven't asked me about that."

He looked at her, then quickly looked away. "Minnie, I didn't mean to suggest . . ."

"Darling, I know you didn't. These dark thoughts do creep up on us—all of us—from time to time, and the only thing to do is . . . well, deal with them as best we can. Chase 'em back to wherever they come from. When the state police called me that night, Jeffy, I guess you can imagine the pure shock of it. Shock is a real, physical thing, and there's a good reason for it. Shock makes you numb. Well, I was numb all right. I simply could not credit the fact that Felix was gone."

"I couldn't, either, Minnie. I still can't."

She smiled, and sipped the coffee.

"Well, of course, a time came when the numbness wore off. Luckily I am not given to things like tranquilizers. The temptation must be a strong one. Just to defuse the pain, with chemicals. Well, I didn't do that, for his sake as much as mine. I wouldn't. And sooner or later I got to thinking the same kind of thoughts you must have been thinking about your own father's death."

"If he's dead." Jeff paused, rubbed his eyes. The yellow sailboat had just sailed back into his consciousness. He wanted it to go away. Forever.

"Sometimes," he went on quietly, "when I was little, I used to think he wasn't really dead at all, that he had gone away on some secret mission, that one day he'd come back, smiling, a hero. But he never did."

Minnie reached across the small distance between them and touched his hand.

"No one will ever know that for sure, will they, Jeffy? But I think it's beautiful that you wanted him back."

He looked at her. "I still do."

For a moment she said nothing. Then she smiled a strange, secret smile. "Yes," she said, "I know that feeling. There hasn't been one minute since . . . he went, that I haven't expected him to walk through the door of any room I'm in. I think I always will."

"I hope so. It would be too bad to forget something as good as what you had with Felix."

Later, the patrolman came by with forms to be filled out, with more questions. To which Jeff had none of the answers.

23

The next day Jeff's leg felt so much better that he stopped taking codeine. The throbbing continued and there was still a lot of soreness, but the leg was functional. He could walk on it without wincing. And walking, he felt, was probably a very good idea.

Being cooped up in the house had made him restless. There was a new exhibit at Dupre's, for a painting auction. He wanted to see that, and the auction too. He decided to walk up to the Metropolitan Museum and visit the Etruscan rooms, grab a sandwich, and take in the painting show later on.

As he left the house, Jeff stood for a moment looking down on Sixty-fourth Street. It was almost shockingly normal, considering he had nearly died there the night before last. Cars were parked dutifully on one side of the street. A black woman in a maid's uniform walked a dog no bigger than a rat. Jeff looked closer. Maybe it was a rat. He smiled. No assassins were lurking. He stepped out onto the sidewalk and turned toward Fifth Avenue.

Central Park was a bright monument to normalcy.

Kids played Frisbee, matrons wheeled baby carriages, an ice-cream vendor stood, crisply uniformed, next to his bright white truck. Jeff found an empty bench and sat, stretching his long legs out in front of him. The sun felt good on his legs.

A glossy and sophisticated-looking squirrel came walking daintily down the path. She looked at Jeff with mild disapproval, nodded her head, and moved on. Obviously, a squirrel with better offers than any Jeff might make her. He laughed out loud, then stopped and quickly looked about him, left and right.

If anyone had seen him, they might think he was crazy.

And they might well be right.

Still smiling, he got up and walked back to the avenue and up to the Metropolitan Museum.

The Etruscans never failed to calm him.

Here were the rows of urns and vases he'd known since childhood, the bronzes green and pocked with age, terra-cotta heads and marble busts, smiling the mysterious Etruscan smile. Leonardo might have first seen the Mona Lisa's enigmatic smile on some Etruscan tomb sculpture. The Etruscans had that same sense of gently beckoning you, of inviting you to share their secrets.

And they did know secrets, of this Jeff had no doubt. Just what those secrets were, no one knew. Jeff intended to find out. The Met's Etruscan collection had changed very little since the last time Jeff had seen it. Compared to the vast collections at the Villa Giulia in Rome, and in Florence and other, smaller museums scattered throughout Tuscany, the Met's collection was only adequate. Jeff found a limestone fragment mislabeled. It was probably the side of a sarcophagus, and the Met had it coming from Chiusi. If it did, thought Jeff, then somebody moved it in the old days. Which might be possible. Barely possible.

Jeff stayed with the Etruscans for nearly an hour, then left without seeing anything else. He considered going up to see the famous Calyx krater in the Greek vase collection, but he knew it would only remind him of the *tombaroli,* so he skipped it.

The sun was bright on the broad steps of the museum.

He walked to Madison Avenue and found a coffee shop. One dry hamburger and two iced coffees later, Jeff walked slowly down the street to Dupre's.

Polly, he knew, would still be in Texas. Until tomorrow. Tomorrow he'd feel better than today, just as today he felt better than yesterday. Thank God there was no fracture, no cast. He tried to imagine making love in a leg cast.

He was managing the leg quite well now. Somehow it seemed important to hide the limp. Jeff walked slowly, practicing. Moving that way, with many a pause, he could probably carry it off. *For whose benefit?* He frowned at this unexpected interest in deception. Maybe it was no more than respect for Felix. Things one did or did not do because one was a Dupre. One did not complain. One did not show weakness.

Jeff couldn't remember Felix ever putting that philosophy into words, but it was a constant presence in his life, as physical as his house, as well-remembered as his laughter.

And Jeff thought that it might have been this unstated, deeply felt obligation that had driven him into the ditches of Veii. Driven him to create his own world, with its own standards.

If his life had depended upon making a list of those standards, Jeff wondered if he could do it. Well, he thought, I do no harm, I tell no lies, I try to give pleasure where I can, I lead no one astray with false promises.

What promises had he made to Carla? To Polly? To the House of Dupre?

It had all seemed so simple until Felix died.

Suddenly Jeff, who had never wanted a permanent relationship with any woman, found himself deeply attracted to two women.

Suddenly he was forced to examine the world of his aunt and uncle, which he had always taken for granted, with the frightening detachment of a scientist.

He was near Dupre's now. The leg was feeling better. The day had grown much warmer since Jeff left the house. He walked into the tall, shaded lobby of the auction house and welcomed the cool. The elevator was cool, too, and there were no other passengers when Jeff rode it up to the second-floor exhibition rooms.

He was more at home in Dupre's now, even without Morgan or Polly to guide him. He knew what the exhibition was about, because Polly had told him the other night at supper. Which seemed like months ago. It was for the first auction of the fall season, traditionally a big painting sale in the increasingly flexible category called "Old Masters."

"Old" meant essentially pre-nineteenth-century.

The exhibition galleries consisted of three rooms, one huge, one medium-sized, and one quite small. These spaces could be further divided by the placement of tall folding screens covered in taupe carpeting, as were the walls of the galleries.

These screens were deployed throughout the two larger galleries now, densely hung with paintings. As were all the walls. The permanent glass-shelved vitrines that were built in against the far walls held miniatures.

There were hundreds of paintings—four hundred and sixty-five, Jeff saw from the catalog—all sizes, all ages, of every quality and condition. Here were somber Madonnas from fourteenth-century Sienna, fat Dutch children about to burst their starchy ruffs. Jeff saw the staid family groupings of de Vos, the ripe still lifes beloved by the materialistic Flemish, bloodless North German saints, brooding peasants from nineteenth-century France, merry Louis XVI shepherdesses. English ladies with improbably pink cheeks, often holding their epic hats against the perpetual breeze. There were sleek horses, fat generals, minor aristocrats, and princes of the church. Nobles from the court of Versailles looked scornfully at Jeff from beneath their towering wigs. There were Venetian scenes that looked almost—but not quite—like Guardi, grim Spanish cardinals more than half in love with death, frolicking urchins, pet dogs, sailing ships, a world full of landscapes, and one vast, unappetizing study of a plate heaped with all-too-realistic dead fish.

In all the collection there was really only one drop-dead masterpiece. Jeff found it at once, and he kept coming back to it, refreshing his eyes and readjusting his judgment after plowing through acres of mediocrity.

It sat alone, in a square vitrine in the middle of the biggest gallery.

The painting was no more than fifteen inches high by perhaps twelve inches wide. It was a still life of mixed flowers against a dark background. It had been painted by Pieter Brueghel the Elder, and it made everything else in the huge room look cheap. There were tulips, cabbage roses, irises and lilies, a completely improbable collection, since half of the bouquet would be out of season if the other half were in bloom.

It hardly mattered. Jeff could almost smell the flowers. They had been arranged in a simple green glass vase placed on an unpretentious wooden tabletop. The painting sang with life.

On his third visit to the little Brueghel, Jeff stayed for about ten minutes, transfixed. He wanted to digest the picture, to make it a part of his soul forever, to know it as you know a lover. Here was the power of art that went beyond money. Jeff thought as he stood there that he would pay almost any amount for the picture, if he could.

"Well," said a familiar voice at his elbow, "I've been looking for you, Jeff. How's it going? Are you discovering all our little secrets?"

Morgan St. James stood there, smiling. He had a well-thumbed copy of the painting-sale catalog, and he was making notes in the margins.

"I'm fine, thanks. Are you planning on bidding?"

Morgan laughed. "Would that I could, especially on that. I'm actually making notes to myself, sort of actor's cues, if you will, trying to think of clever things to say when I'm on the spot. If I have to be clever, which, thank God, I usually don't. When it's all in motion, you see, everything goes so fast I don't really see the object as an object. So I sometimes have to rather feign scholarship."

"I'm looking forward to seeing you in action."

"I," said Morgan with an expression of mock horror, "am definitely not. I get butterflies every time. And this"—he lowered his voice and leaned closer to Jeff's ear—"is, but for the flower piece, definitely not one of our best offerings."

"The Berwick sale really will help, won't it?"

Morgan looked at him for a few seconds before answering. "It could help get us back in the running, Jeff. In the real running, I mean. In the big leagues."

"What do you estimate on the Brueghel?"

Morgan had the figures in his head. "I say three hundred and fifty thousand, but I'll be surprised if we get less than four. It is an extraordinary little thing, most appealing, very accessible, which many great paintings are not."

"I wish," said Jeff, smiling, "that it were accessible to me. To my budget, that is."

He went back to the fourth floor with Morgan, checked Felix's desk for messages. There were none. Jeff sat down at the desk, looked at the telephone, and was a little surprised to discover he had no one to call. His best friends from school and college were scattered, and he wasn't in the mood for acquaintances. Or for the kinds of girls whose mothers had Jeff's name on a little blue list somewhere. Suddenly he felt the leg again, throbbing.

Jeff took the elevator down and walked out onto Madison Avenue. His head was a jumble of images. Everything about Felix had always seemed entirely first-class.

It was a shock, and a shock that seeing this exhibition of

paintings had brought home vividly, to realize that Felix's auction house was in danger of becoming something less than first-rate. Maybe a lot less. Jeff didn't know enough about the New York auction scene to measure this accurately. He'd have to find out more.

Not that there was anything especially wrong with Dupre's. It was just that Dupre's had been surpassed.

Jeff wondered if that had been depressing enough to Felix to make him crash the Jaguar deliberately.

It was a complicated question.

When Jeff thought about Polly, and about Carla, life became more complicated still. There was a fine-looking flower shop three stores ahead. He stopped there and bought a big bunch of white daisies for Minnie.

Jeff felt better after that.

There was nothing complicated about daisies. Nothing at all.

24

Berwick Castle, September 1966

The Duke of Berwick looked out from his study window at the two boys in white. He smiled. What a fine sight they made, the pair of them, just turned twenty and bursting with health, young Neville so fair and his friend so dark.

The duke paused at the window, savoring the moment, reluctant to go back to the depressing task that awaited him on the desk. It was no day to be going over the household accounts. The sun was shining, the air fairly shimmered, and each leaf on the thousand trees of Berwick Forest seemed to stand out with a special clarity in the crisp blue air.

There might never have been such a thing as an overdraft or a dunning letter from one's tailor.

The duke watched his son and young Eversley as they walked out of the forest and across the great lawn. They must have been playing tennis. Or were about to play. The boys paused as he watched them, and young Neville made a great sweeping gesture with both arms and roared with laughter clapping his pal on the back.

Not a care in the world. Well, and why should he have? Hadn't the duke done everything conceivable to shield the boy from the sad truth about the Fleet-family finances? The day would come, of course, when the boy must be told, when the reality of their situation must be dealt with. But not yet. Not on a day like today. Later, perhaps when the boy turned twenty-one. The duke grimaced at the thought of his son's coming-of-age celebration, at what it must cost.

There were times, now, when the duke was almost grateful that Fleet House had been destroyed in the war. At least he had an excuse for not giving the party in town, where everything cost the earth.

Here at Berwick, things were different, more manageable. The castle itself was so impressive that anything happening here took on an extra dimension of grandeur. If the champagne weren't vintage, if the footmen were hired for the occasion to supplement the sadly depleted household staff, it might go unnoticed. Except by the duke himself. And by Miranda, although it was little enough she noticed these days, poor creature, drugged as she was around the clock.

The duke was seized with a sudden and almost overwhelming urge to share in the boy's fine careless pleasure. He raised his hand as if to wave, knowing they could never see him behind the glass. He wanted to cheer them on in their heedless merriment, to say, "Yes! Laugh, dance, love, and all the rest of it, and to the hilt. And do it now, while you can, for the cares come crushing down on you soon enough." He stood at the window for a moment longer, then slowly lowered his hand.

The boys were out of his sight now. The duke tried to remember what it had felt like to be twenty years old, and could not. He sighed, and turned, and walked slowly back to the heap of unpaid bills on his desk.

The hinges on young Neville's bedroom door were large and brass and had been wrought locally sometime in the eighteenth century, during one of the many interior restorations of the castle. The hinges were expertly oiled. Neville had done this himself. He loved things that were smooth, and sleek, and moved easily. Like this door. Like Eversley's body.

Neville opened the door silently, and closed it, and slid the bolt home. Eversley, naked as a fish, stood at the far end of the big room, studying his reflection in a tall looking glass.

"Coo!" said Neville, chuckling. "If it h'ain't Black Narcissus."

That was part of the game, their special code, aping the talk of cockneys. Without taking his dark eyes from the reflection in the mirror, Eversley replied, "Garn, yer onny loves me fer me body. Did you cop the champers, then?"

Neville set down a silver bucket containing ice and a magnum of his father's best Veuve Clicquot 1959. Then he went to a tallboy and opened a secret drawer concealed in the molding at the top. He took out a small box and set it beside the champagne. Quickly, neatly, Neville stripped and hung his tennis clothes in a closet. From a shelf in the top of the closet he took the Winchcombe Chalice and set it on the table near the ice bucket. Then he opened the little box and extracted two sugar cubes. He walked to his friend and handed him one of the sugar cubes. "A trip to the moon," whispered Neville, "on gossamer wings."

Eversley managed to tear his eyes away from the mirror. He regarded the heir of Berwick Castle evenly. "Me muvver sez never accept sweets from strange men. Is it acid, then?"

"Of the best California."

He winked a comical wink and swallowed the cube. .

Neville did the same, then walked to the ice bucket and expertly twisted off the wire that held the cork. Slowly, making a ceremony of it, he rotated the magnum, holding tight to the cork until it slid free with only the slightest hissing sound. Then he filled the glittering chalice and held it high. "Kings," he said softly, dropping the cockney accent, "have drunk from this chalice."

He handed the cup to Eversley. Eversley drank, keeping his eyes on Neville, sensing the solemnity of the moment, wondering how long it would take for the LSD to start working, and how strong a dose it had been. With Neville you never knew. That was one of the fascinating things about Neville. He always operated right on the edge of real danger. Sometimes he operated beyond the edge.

Eversley smiled, and handed back the chalice. He had never seen the famous cup before: this was his first visit to the castle. Eversley was a little awed by the casual manner with which Neville treated the chalice, but it wouldn't do to show that. Not here, not in Berwick Castle.

Neville drank deeply, never taking his eyes off the young man who stood so close. He licked his lips and set down the goblet. And smiled. "Now," said Neville, "we both are kings." He reached out his hand and took Eversley's hand, and led him across the richly carpeted chamber to the bed.

An hour later they were soaring.

The LSD suffused their bloodstreams and the champagne sparkled in their brains. Neville saw rainbows within rainbows, heard celestial music, traveled in a magical kingdom where everything glittered with the wild, free promise of new sensations.

He looked at Eversley and giggled. Eversley was staring deeply into one of the polished rubies that rimmed the neck of the chalice. "There is," said Eversley solemnly, "a whole bleeding universe in there."

Neville laughed and staggered to the window. The sun was setting in a flourish of pink and lavender clouds, in a blaze of tangerine-red glory. "The sun," said Neville in wonder, "is setting. And it's got my name on it. Must go say bye-bye to the sun, mate, old Phoebus in all 'is fucking glory."

"There is," said Eversley, who obviously hadn't heard one word, "a whole bleeding universe in there."

"And up yours, then," said his host, feeling slighted. "I'll go say bye-bye meself, so there."

Neville gathered himself together and walked steadily to the door. Doing this took an enormous effort of will. He forgot entirely the fact that he was stark naked.

The stairway to the east tower was right outside Neville's door. In the days when Berwick Castle had its full complement of servants, one of them might well have seen the young master on his climb. As it was, Neville encountered no one.

The door to the top of the tower was open. It swung out with a groan. Must oil the bastard, thought Neville. Things are going to hell around this mucking place.

Then he looked up and saw the sunset.

The sun was half down now, sinking fast. The clouds were turning from lavender to deep purple. The LSD fragmented this image into a wild kaleidoscope of reds and purples and black. The shapes in Neville's vision kept changing, too, now hard-edged, now a mad impressionist blur, now a billion tiny dancing dots, now a cosmic explosion.

His whole life surged up in him. He was a king. King of the world, the sky, and the planets too! Of the universe! He saw the bird then. It was not like any bird the boy had ever seen. This bird was huge, and dark green, and had immense eyes of a fiery yellow. It circled the towers of Berwick like some prehistoric nightmare.

Yet it was not at all threatening. It seemed to have a message for Neville Fleet. *I am the king of the universe and this is my steed. On his back I shall soar through the dark skies of midnight to . . . what new adventures?* The bird circled closer, silent, flapping its huge green wings.

Yes! To ride through the night, to have adventure, what larks! Neville watched the bird, which came closer and closer.

His bird, his steed, chariot of the night. What a thing to tell Eversley. Mabye, if Eversley was very, very good, he'd even give him a ride. On . . . what was the creature's name? It must have a name. Well, that would come in time. The bird would surely tell Neville its name.

"Come here, bird, great green bird."

The bird came closer and closer. Neville felt the power of it. His power. All he had to do was seize the moment. Which was a very Fleet sort of thing to do. He thought of his father, how proud he'd be. To have his only son king of the universe, soaring triumphant on that spectacular steed.

The top of the east tower was deeply crenellated; its walls were four feet thick.

Neville stepped up onto the crenellation. The bird was close enough to touch now, circling just this tower.

It was only a matter of stepping onto the bird's broad green back.

The duke had gone for his usual twilight stroll. It was good to get out in the air, alone, away from all the worries that seemed to lie in wait for him around every corner of the castle.

There was Miranda to worry about. Her condition shifted from nearly normal to the extremes of madness, and the best psychiatric minds in England could do nothing but send huge, unpayable bills. And always there was the Inland Revenue. Smythe-Davies lay in wait, too, baiting another kind of trap with another kind of worry.

Smythe-Davies, so patient, so bland. So ready to spring the trap, to sell him up, literally, if he didn't meet the unappeasable payments. How cheerfully would Neville have killed the man, if killing would have stopped the demands. But there would be others where Smythe-Davies came from; Neville never doubted that. England bred them like maggots.

He sighed.

There was a certain low rise in Berwick Forest where the duke liked to pause on his walks.

It afforded a superb view of the castle.

Sometimes, standing alone upon this little hill, with Berwick's towers gilded by the setting sun, it was possible for Neville to forget his troubles for a while, all the cares of the present and all the bleak prospects that undermined the future.

He stood there now, and breathed deeply.

The air was clear, pure, lightly scented with leafy smells.

Berwick Castle looked eternal. And at least, tonight, there would be supper with the boys to look forward to.

He gazed, transfixed, at the nine great towers of Berwick.

Then, suddenly, a demon from a dream, a naked figure appeared at the very top of the east tower. A man. A boy. Dancing, gesticulating, in a frenzy.

The duke gasped, looked closer. The distance was more than a quarter-mile. But the form, the coloring, slender, fair-haired: it could only be Neville.

He watched and as he watched, the naked figure stepped gracefully to the top of the highest crenellation of the tower, waved both young arms in a kind of benediction, and stepped calmly off the tower in screaming fall to the rocks on the riverbank below.

The duke screamed too. "No!"

The futile yelling echoed in the forest and was lost.

The duke was running now, a man not young and not in training. Still he ran, ran all the way to the base of the tower, clambered down the rocks.

And he forced himself to look at the bloody pulp that had been Neville Fleet, heir to Berwick.

The boy's father stood there, quite alone.

He had never felt so entirely alone before.

It was beyond sadness.

He knelt and touched the boy's hand. It was still warm in the late-summer-afternoon sun.

And that was how they found him, kneeling, silent, holding the dead boy's hand as the shadow of the great east tower moved down upon the pair of them with the swift finality of a theater curtain.

25

Jeff decided to come late to the painting sale. He hadn't gotten over his uncomfortable feeling of being an intruder in the House of Dupre. People here watched him. They were friendly, they helped him, but in their eyes Jeff saw unanswerable questions. He embodied their fears and their expectations and they endowed him with magical powers. It was magic, he told himself, to have been born a Dupre. However reluctantly he played the role that Felix's death had cast him in, Jeff was the determining force in Dupre's future now.

It was as much fun as walking around with a large sack filled with rocks. After a certain point, all you wanted to do was put the damn thing down, whatever the consequences.

Jeff was thinking about those consequences as he slipped into one of the few empty seats near the back of the auction gallery at Dupre's.

He had spent part of the morning with Bunny Bartlett.

It wouldn't be necessary for Bunny to send an accountant to look at Dupre's books. Bunny did that regularly, in the course of handling Felix's financial affairs, which were naturally deeply involved with the affairs of Dupre's.

Jeff had raised the question of Dupre's being second-rate. He'd asked if this might not be at the root of the firm's unhealthy profit picture.

A question Jeff had not raised with Bunny was whether someone might have reason to try to kill him. Jeff had thought about the accident and decided to call it that. Until who-knew-what proved him wrong. As the policeman had been maybe too eager to remind him, there was no evidence at all: hit-and-run, stolen car most likely, and they didn't even know the make for sure, much less the license number.

Jeff was eager to hear Bunny's opinion of Dupre's.

" 'Second-rate' is a hard term for what Dupre's is, Jeff." Bunny stroked a bronze panther that was the sole ornament on his enormous desk. "Felix decided many years ago not to expand overseas, or to the West Coast. That decision has kept Dupre's small. Dupre's will never be a Sotheby's. Felix didn't want a Sotheby's. He was never interested in being the biggest. He liked to compare Dupre's and Sotheby's as being analogous to Jaguar versus GM, the small, perfectionist operation versus the multinational giant. Of course, in the end, it didn't work out quite like that."

"I'm not sure I understand, Bunny."

"Felix wanted Dupre's to be personal. To be a size he could manage easily. But he found, as competition from Sotheby's and some of the other big houses got more intense, that he had to expand in spite of himself. To offer the same services, even though the kind of sales Dupre's was doing might not really justify such frills. He was caught in a classic squeeze—damned if he did, damned if he didn't. Morgan—Morgan was Felix's attempt to delegate the management of Dupre's. He hoped Morgan would help Dupre's expand but keep that personal touch that was so important to Felix. And I think it was beginning to work."

"Morgan seems to know his stuff."

"Oh, yes," said Bunny with just the hint of a frown on his open face, "that he does."

Now Jeff watched the managing director of Dupre's on the platform, thinking about Bunny's words.

There was a sense of theater in the big room. Felix had always declared there was no drama like a hotly contested auction, but Jeff had never felt it before. In fact, he'd been to only two or three auctions in his entire life.

The room was, of course, a kind of theater. It seated three hundred people in twenty rows of chairs with a wide central aisle and narrower aisles on both sides. The auditorium was raked slightly to give even the last rows a good view. The stage was shallow and raised only three feet from the auditorium floor. The auctioneer's lectern was an ancient black-oak pulpit rescued from some Jacobean English church. In it, Felix had looked positively evangelical. Morgan looked like what he was, a charming master of ceremonies.

It was twenty minutes after the scheduled start of the bidding, and Jeff knew that auctions at Dupre's always began on time. He also knew that the average selling time per item was one minute.

They were bringing up lot number twenty-three now. Morgan was a bit ahead of schedule.

In the center of the stage was a large vertical easel mounted on a stout round steel column. The easel itself began at tabletop height and rose six feet above that. It was a Janus easel, two-faced, with a well-oiled pivoting mechanism. There were deep ledges at the base of both faces, and the whole thing was covered in the same taupe carpeting that also covered the walls of the exhibition galleries and the auction theater itself. Uniformed porters maneuvered the easel, setting the next item in place while the present lot was being auctioned.

Jeff had a moment of shock, seeing the famous Dupre gavel in Morgan's hands. The gavel was one of the legends of Dupre's. No one knew who made it, or exactly how old it might be, nor how it had come into the hands of the first Felix Dupre. The gavel was massive, with a handle of beautifully turned walnut inlaid with five brass rings. The hammer end was solid ivory, carved on its sides with an intricate pattern of scrolled leaves framed in delicately wrought ropes. The ivory had the yellow patina of great age. It was considered a good-luck charm, and it had been used in every Dupre auction since the 1920s. Jeff remembered the weird shiver of delight that had run through his twelve-year-old body when Felix had first let him handle it. *If we sell,* Jeff thought, *I must remember to keep that gavel.*

"Number twenty-three," said Morgan in a tone so understated it almost seemed conversational, until you realized it penetrated to the last row with vivid clarity. "A fine early portrait by Benjamin West, subject unknown, undated, but probably from 1784 to 1786. I will start the bidding at twelve thousand dollars."

Jeff fought the smile. He remembered this picture well. It was a portrait only a mother could love: a fat, red-faced, red-coated British Army officer from the period of the American Revolution. His little piggy eyes burned dully from a face that resembled a fallen tomato soufflé more than anything human. It was easy to see, from the skillfully painted likeness, why the British had lost. Jeff didn't know much about West other than the fact that he had been American working in London. He wondered if this were a flattering portrait.

Hands shot up in several parts of the room.

Jeff studied the crowd, trying to imagine who would want the West portrait, and why. West was a highly regarded artist, but this was a subject to make you reconsider lunch. Still, Polly had said that anything American and old was likely to be hot in the art market now.

The bidding went fast. In seconds the price reached twenty thousand dollars, then climbed more slowly to thirty. At thirty it seemed to stall. With genteel persistence Morgan St. James began milking the crowd.

"I have thirty-one thousand," he said, "for this superb example of West's early London period, a work that might well grace any museum . . . I have thirty-two . . . thirty-two-five . . . thirty-three."

The bidding was being done by signals more subtle than raised hands now.

Jeff remembered Felix's amusing tales about the elaborate codes some secretive bidders devised, winks and nudges and coughs and sneezes.

In the end the West portrait went to an invisible bidder at the front of the room for thirty-six thousand dollars. Of which Dupre's would keep $7,200: ten percent being paid by the seller and another ten percent by the buyer. That seemed, to Jeff, very good pay for a minute's work.

The Brueghel flower piece was number 139 in the sale, and Jeff decided to wait for it. Even it it went for the minimum estimate, Dupre's stood to gain seventy thousand dollars.

Suddenly Jeff found himself caught up in the gambler's excitement of it all. The glitter of huge sums changing hands in a few seconds was a surprise to him. An awareness that this happened was nothing at all like being there in the flesh.

He could feel the tension rippling through the crowd. It was electric, even to someone who wasn't bidding. Jeff knew now what Bunny meant when he had said he sometimes went to an auction just for the drama of it.

There was coolness, surely, and professionalism. Dealers were cool, usually, and art was an investment now. Institutions like the British Railway Workers' Pension Fund were now heavy investors in the art market. Study after study had proved that art and antique furniture increased in value far faster, and with less chance of deflation, than stocks or bonds. Jeff had heard stories of warehouses filled with objects held by syndicates of investors, waiting for the market to ripen, playing with fine paintings or signed French furniture the way some brokers play with sow bellies or soybeans or any other commodity.

But underneath it all there burned a passion that could never be spent on a soybean. There was a need to possess the unique, the rare, the prestigious, the beautiful. There was snobbery in it, too: the dream of social acceptance via the ownership of great art was known to many a recently rich striver.

There might, Jeff cheerfully admitted, even be a glimmering of interest in art for its value as art. Probably, he felt, it was many things, a web of motives, that brought people to the world's auction rooms.

The crowd at Dupre's today was an international mixture.

For people who had tens and maybe hundreds of thousands of dollars to dispose of on a painting, they were a motley assortment.

Few took the trouble to look rich.

There were perhaps a dozen glittering representatives of the international glamour set, sleek women of indeterminate age with perpetual suntans, lean bronzed men with awe-inspiring tailors, dowagers in operatic ropes of pearls and sensible walking shoes.

But for the most part the bidders at Dupre's this afternoon could have been anyone. The little white-haired man who had dropped out of the bidding on the West at thirty thousand dollars would have made a seamless fit into the faculty lounge of any university.

The plump, rather severe-looking middle-aged woman in front of Jeff might have been a librarian in a small town. Yet she bid sixty-three thousand dollars for a small landscape by Thomas Gainsborough, and Jeff heard someone murmur the name "Du Pont."

Many of the audience must be dealers, bidding for themselves or on commission. Dupre's would bid for customers who couldn't attend the sale, and it was possible to leave bids at a fixed figure.

There was the usual gaggle of Japanese businessmen, although Polly had told Jeff that the high point of the Japanese invasion of the art market had been a few years past.

"Now," she had said, "it's the Arabs who throw their money around, but their taste isn't ours, so in a funny way they're not competitive. They love bright colors, almost like children. If it isn't oversized and crusted with gold, they won't go near it. The Arabic market has completely revitalized the demand for all that hideous Louis Philippe stuff. They go mad for all those late-nineteenth-century Sèvres palace urns, you know, eight feet tall and wildly overpainted, gilded and what-have-you. Subtlety is definitely not their bag."

If there were Arabs in the room, Jeff couldn't see them.

Morgan kept the pace moving briskly.

At last the little Brueghel was carried to the easel. The easel revolved. There was a murmur in the room, a low vibrating sound like wind rippling through pine trees.

Even from the back of the sales room, Jeff could feel the power of the little painting. It glowed. Jeff had a feeling it could light up the night, vibrating with life, each brush stroke a drama.

Morgan paused for a beat.

The room was now absolutely silent.

Someone coughed.

As if the cough were a signal, Morgan began the bidding. "Number one-thirty-nine," he said quietly, as though this were just another old painting, as though everyone in the room hadn't felt the electricity in the air, or edged a little closer on their seats. "A floral still life by Pieter Brueghel the Elder, undated but likely to be from his late period, after 1560, unframed, oil on walnut panel. I will start the bidding at two hundred and fifty thousand dollars."

Jeff wondered how many private individuals there might be

in all the world who could spend that much money on a painting.

The bidding went very fast, almost too fast for drama.

Although the speed of it had a drama all its own. It was at four hundred thousand dollars now. Morgan had been right. And Jeff could tell the bidding would go higher.

Morgan changed the pace now. The bidding had gone up in increments of twenty-five thousand dollars. Now Morgan brought it up by tens.

At four-sixty, the bidding slowed and threatened to stop.

Four-seventy was bid. Now Morgan shifted down again, and reduced the increments to five thousand dollars.

Four-seventy-five was bid, and then four-eighty.

There was a pause. The pause extended into a brief silence.

Silence filled the room with an almost physical weight.

Jeff could feel it pressing down on him. Morgan raised his left eyebrow just slightly.

Jeff smiled. It was a subtle challenge, but a challenge all the same. Morgan had the timing of an accomplished stage actor.

"I have," Morgan said quietly, "four hundred and eighty thousand dollars bid. Do I hear four-eighty-five?"

There was another pause; then Morgan continued, "Four hundred and eighty thousand dollars . . . going . . ."

His head rotated slowly as he spoke, surveying the room expectantly. The expression on his face was that of a kindly schoolteacher waiting for the brightest student to answer an especially difficult question. Morgan conveyed a sense of great trust in his audience. He radiated confidence that he would not be let down.

And his confidence was soon rewarded by still another flurry of bidding.

The painting was sold for five hundred and five thousand dollars. More than a hundred and fifty thousand above the estimate.

Jeff sat very still for a moment.

He felt wrung-out. He tried to imagine how Morgan must feel. The artistry of Morgan's performance had impressed Jeff profoundly. A less sensitive performer—for it was a performance—might have knocked the painting down for much, much less. How much less was impossible to estimate.

Slowly Jeff found himself smiling at his own involvement. *Jeff Dupre, who had always scorned the materialism of the auction business!* Well, materialistic it surely was, but it was thrilling too. Very thrilling, in fact. He'd tell Polly that, and she'd laugh.

Thinking about Polly reminded Jeff she was coming back today.

He stood up and left the room, grateful that several others were leaving too. They must have stayed, as he had, to see the Brueghel sold.

As Jeff walked slowly down the hall to the elevator, he noticed his leg again. The excitement of the auction had erased the pain. The leg was hurting now. He went up to Felix's office and dialed the number of Polly's cubicle.

No answer.

He dialed her at home.

The phone rang six times before he hung up. He'd call her later on, from Minnie's house.

It was nearly four o'clock now. He decided to call it a day. Tomorrow he'd compliment Morgan, and find out who had paid all that money for the Brueghel. He said good afternoon to the ever-efficient Miss Winn at her reception desk and rode alone to the street level.

He considered taking a cab—the leg was hurting that much. Then Jeff decided that was silly, five blocks after all, and turned down Madison Avenue, moving slower than ever now, favoring the injured leg.

He turned the corner of Sixty-fourth Street and hesitated, looking left and right before crossing.

The fear came back to him now, strong and irrational, from wherever it had spent the afternoon.

The street was empty. Jeff grinned, but it was a false grin. Only the fear was real.

Hastings was at the door when Jeff opened it. "A message, Mr. Jeff, on the telephone. The Countess di Cavolfiore asks that you call her."

Jeff froze. Something must be very wrong for Carla to phone. She was so conscious of the cost of the telephone that she hesitated to call him even at Veii.

"She wants me to call her at Cavolfiore?"

"No, sir. The countess is at the St. Regis."

Jeff looked at the butler as though he had just arrived from Mars. Carla in New York? It seemed like some kind of a joke.

Realizing that he was gaping at Hastings, Jeff managed a smile and took himself quickly upstairs to phone in privacy.

26

Jeff could hardly have regarded his telephone with greater apprehension had it turned into a coiled viper.

He sat at his worn schoolboy desk and tried to make his head stop spinning.

His life was coming apart all around him, breaking up and reforming in new and unwelcome patterns. It had all worked so smoothly before, everything in its neat little niche: Harvard, the dig, women, Felix and Minnie.

Now his life had scrambled, and Jeff didn't know where to begin putting it back together again.

He tried to sort out his feelings about Carla.

Carla was wonderful. In Cavolfiore.

Jeff remembered that last beautiful night, how he'd asked her if she could ever leave, meaning to go with him to America. Her answer had been vague, hesitant.

And here she was. Jeff had always believed her stories of poverty. Now, here she was at the St. Regis. Jeff wondered who had subsidized her trip, and why. If there was scheming afoot, Beppo di Cavolfiore would be at the bottom of it. Jeff knew how intensely loyal Carla felt toward her feckless brother. And Carla, in her beauty and her unwavering truthfulness, would be an ideal front for . . . what?

Well, she was here, and Jeff would make her welcome. Maybe it was for the best. It would be good to see Carla in a different setting. Jeff had always thought of her as a natural part of Cavolfiore. What would she be like in Manhattan? How would she look to someone like Minnie? How would she look to Jeff Dupre? He thought of summer romances, of charming wines that didn't travel. He thought of making love in the afternoon in Carla's bedroom at the *castello*.

Jeff was smiling when he reached for the phone.

She answered at the second ring. Waiting. Suppose he'd been out of town? Suppose Polly had been in when he called?

" 'Ello?"

"Carla," said Jeff unnecessarily, for there could be only one voice like hers in all the world. "Darling, what a surprise." *And other banalaties,* he thought, wanting desperately to reassure her, the more so, maybe, because he felt guilty about Polly.

"I do not," she began softly, "want to intrude upon your sadness, Jiff. But Beppo has made for me an errand."

It was Beppo, then. He'd guessed right. Jeff felt little satisfaction in the correctness of his theory. It had been too easy.

"When can I see you, darling? Are you free tonight?"

"Oh, but yes. If . . . it is not complicated for you."

Jeff smiled. She should only know how complicated it was. "I'll pick you up at the hotel at seven."

"Seven, then. I have missed you, Jiff."

"And I."

He could feel the tension on the line. And he wasn't sure of the cause, or the remedy for it. Jeff set the receiver down softly and lay on his bed for half an hour. That made his leg feel much better. It did very little to relieve the confusion in his mind.

Jeff got up at five with the determination that he must, at the very least, treat Carla royally while she was in town. He called Bunny and asked the banker if he'd pull a string and get them into the famous restaurant on top of the World Trade Center in lower Manhattan. The string was pulled.

He showered, changed into his dark suit, and went down to have a drink with Minnie.

"Cavolfiore?" she asked, sipping Lillet. "Never heard of them."

Jeff laughed. "Thus might a Roman empress dismiss some unwashed provincial. Carla's provincial, but far from unwashed. Decayed minor nobility. She runs the old *castello* as a farm, damn near makes it pay, too. She's been very kind to me in Italy."

Minnie looked at him shrewdly. "Well, darling, I'd love to meet her. Why don't you invite her for dinner tomorrow, and I'll ask Bunny, or someone, and we'll have a little party."

"If it's not too much for you."

She smiled. "I've got all my life to fill up now, Jeffy. It isn't too much, in fact it's exactly what I ought to be doing. What he'd want me to be doing."

Jeff got up and kissed her cheek.

"I love you," he said. "You are an aunt in the great tradition."

Minnie laughed. "God help auntdom if I'm the tradition. Have fun, darling."

His leg hurt almost not at all now. Jeff walked the nine blocks to the St. Regis and stopped just before he got there to

pick up a dozen tea roses in a shade of copper-red that reminded him of Tuscany.

Jeff got off the elevator on the fourteenth floor and hesitated. He had never been in the hotel before.

But the real reason for his hesitation was that it bought
him just a few seconds' more time. Time to try to sort out
how he felt. What he owed to Carla. To Polly.

How was it possible to be this strongly attracted to two
women at once? Especially two such different women.

And why was life a question of who owed what to whom?
Who was counting?

Jeff couldn't stop himself from thinking about the problem,
even though he knew he had no answer. Maybe there wasn't
an answer.

He took a deep breath and walked down the deeply carpeted hallway.

Her room was number 1403. He knocked and heard the
familiar voice. The door opened and she was in his arms.
Fragrant with some old-fashioned scent, tanned from the
Tuscan sunlight, beautifully dressed in something that seemed
to be made from old lace. *Carla*. Jeff's confusion was melting
fast. It was a long, long kiss, and he held her for a moment
afterward, saying nothing. The closeness said it all.

Then he realized that he was still holding the flowers, and
that they had a hard-won dinner reservation.

Jeff stepped back a little, bowed, and handed her the
flowers.

"You look more beautiful than I remembered, Carla, and
it was a beautiful memory."

"You are not angry that I come so suddenly?"

"I'm delighted. Why would I be angry?"

"With no warning . . . it is not a good time for you, I
know this, Jiff. With your uncle, all that."

"If I am with you, it is a good time."

Her smile was the smile of a little girl who has worked
very hard at her lesson, and gotten it right, and been praised
by the teacher. It was a lovely smile. Jeff wondered if he detected something disconcerting in it, something just slightly
out of focus. *No, dammit, you're imagining things, you're
reading your own damn self-made problems into the poor
girl's smile. The poor girl. Why "poor"? Because suddenly
you see something waiflike in Carla, something you never saw
in Cavolfiore. Because she's been dropped on your doorstep
like a waif, asking for . . . what?*

Jeff looked out the window while she put the flowers in a

bathroom glass. He didn't want to start off their first night with a barrage of questions. She set the flowers on her night table. Then he took her hand and they left the room and walked down the richly carpeted corridor to the elevator.

Twenty-five minutes later they were seated at a window table looking down on the most spectacular view in America. The day had been clear. Now there was just a faint haze blurring the horizon. It was breathtaking: they were high enough to see the earth curve. All Manhattan stretched below them. Jeff performed as best he could, playing the tour guide. He pointed out the airports, the park, the two rivers and their bridges, and the rolling hills of Connecticut in the far distance.

She was impressed. "You dine here often?"

"Never before. It's a special place. This is a special night."

"Yes," she said softly, "special."

They sipped white wine. Menus were brought. They ordered. Jeff ordered a bottle of a California white wine made from the Pinot Chardonnay grape of Burgundy. It was crisp as moonlight, flowery, deep.

The sky was slowly darkening. Lights flickered on, making a bright frame for the dusky park, decking the bridges, defining the city streets.

Jeff decided that Carla's beauty had only improved in transit. She was fascinated by Manhattan's gridlike street plan.

"A city," she said, "drawn with a ruler."

He laughed. "Most of it was. It's the easiest city of any size to find your way in."

He looked at her. It was a big, cold room, and Carla warmed it. Carla could warm up the dark side of the moon. She was different here from Cavolfiore. Off her turf. Jeff felt different too, uneasy and excited at the same time.

As though he were seeing Manhattan for the first time.

He'd wondered, more than once, what she'd be like away from Cavolfiore. He should have known she'd be beautiful. Maybe even more beautiful, because Carla's warmth was the deep soft warmth of a peach that has ripened in the sun. The contrast with some of the other women in the room was quick and startling. Most of them seemed to be clothes hangers.

Carla di Cavolfiore was a woman.

Even out of her element. Even when she was probably here against her will, and obviously nervous about something.

Carla paused before she answered. Her eyes seemed darker

139

in the lowering light. "It seems," she said, smiling gently, "that I have found my way."

The food was good. It was only over coffee that she told him about Beppo.

"You know Beppo," she said, smiling. "Poor Beppo has always a scheme to make money. Now it is to be a dealer."

"In what?"

Jeff wouldn't have been surprised if she said heroin, or small boys, or hijacked aircraft. Beppo di Cavolfiore inspired that kind of confidence. If there was a way to be sleazy, you could be sure Beppo would take it. It was a source of continuing amazement to Jeff that the same family tree could sprout a pair so radically dissimilar as Carla and her brother.

"Beppo," she went on, "has many friends who are like us: old family, old houses, no money. Often in these old houses there is art. Or chairs and tables, decorations, statues. Beppo has noticed that such things are fetching high prices, very high sometimes."

"And he wants to become an art dealer?"

"A sort of middleman. He knows, as you say, where the bodies are buried. He has entrée into places that might not be accessible to . . . well, to a stranger." She stirred two spoonfuls of sugar into her tiny espresso cup. "This is true," she said, as though he might not believe her.

"I'm sure it is, and it might work."

"He has sent me to bring the goose to market."

"Why didn't he come himself?"

She averted her eyes, and Jeff wished he hadn't asked the question so bluntly. It was, after all, the crucial question. The question to which there might not be an answer, at least not a simple one. Carla smiled shyly, suspecting, Jeff thought, his low opinion of Beppo. She had made no pretense, in the past, that he was anything but a ne'er-do-well. The pause stretched out like an accusation.

Finally she spoke.

"He knows, of course, about us. He knows the House of Dupre. So—being Beppo—he uses me. I am the messenger. I bring the goose to market. I bring samples, a few things from Cavolfiore. And pictures of more. Of other things that might be available, were the price good."

"Well, darling, I'll help in any way I can, you know that. But I'm really not an active part of Dupre's. Quite to the contrary. I'm helping my aunt sell it."

"I know that, Jiff. I give in too easily, perhaps, to Beppo.

But this time, well, it was a chance to see New York, to see you. So I come."

He reached out and took her hand. The awkwardness was over now.

"I'm very glad you came. What did you bring?"

"You will see. Things of ours—of Beppo's, truly, for he is the heir of Cavolfiore. Two small paintings, very old, early Renaissance. One head . . ."—she laughed, and went on— "very heavy head, could be Greek. Marble. A tapestry, not too big, pretty. One of four. And the photographs. We know very little about these things, Jiff, about what they are worth."

"Well, Dupre's is full of experts who know precisely, and they'll be glad to help. This could be a good thing for the House of Dupre, too, Carla. Who knows what treasures might be hidden in some dark corner of Cavolfiore?"

"Yes," she said, smiling gently, "who knows?"

"The center of the art market is here now. The highest prices."

"So Beppo says. It is sad, Jiff. The money is all here now. People are leaving Italy, the rich ones, and their money with them. They are, you see, afraid. Since Moro was killed. Since all the terror, the kidnappings, that Getty boy. Sophia Loren and Ponti have fled. Others, less famous but none the less rich, flee too. To this"—she gestured at the dazzling sight below—"to where it is safe. For the moment."

Jeff asked for the check and paid it.

As Carla walked ahead of him up the stairs and out of the restaurant, she trailed a wake of staring eyes. Many men and not a few women watched Carla's progress.

She was quiet in the taxi. Jeff asked the driver to run through Times Square so that Carla could see the lights. But Broadway was a squalid anticlimax to the spectacle they had seen from the top of the World Trade Center. There is no dirt in the gutter from 110 stories up.

He went with her to her room.

It seemed natural as breathing. She locked the door and kissed him with a sudden urgency.

"Can you stay?"

His answer was a kiss and more kisses. In a very few minutes they were in bed and truly together, in a realm where no questions need be asked, nor answers given.

The night welcomed them.

Jeff forgot Dupre's, forgot his suspicions. He almost forgot Polly. He forgot the bandage on his left leg, and played down the accident when Carla asked about it. All he wanted now, and all he got, was loving. It filled his heart and blurred the pain of remembered doubts and fears. It comforted the small lost boy who always lived somewhere inside him. And it was beautiful.

Jeff woke to rain.

The light was gray, the windows streaked with rivulets. It was very quiet on the fourteenth floor of the St. Regis. Carla lay beside him, deep in sleep.

Jeff closed his eyes for a moment.

He had dreamed about the yellow sailboat again. It was always the same dream, waking or sleeping. It had come to him often since he'd been in New York.

The dream had no beginning and no end, and that was the most frightening thing about it. There was just the image of the yellow sailboat, empty, bobbing in the ocean, its white sail flapping.

He eased out of the big bed and went into the bathroom. Jeff showered and dressed. Thank God, he thought, looking in the mirror, for the blond hair and the suntan. I can go a day without shaving and not look entirely like a bum. In spite of the good dinner they'd had the night before, Jeff was ravenous. He came back into the bedroom and called room service for a big American-style breakfast for two. This woke her.

Carla sat up, yawning, stretching, utterly charming in the dishevelment of waking. Jeff came to her and bent to kiss her.

She smiled, slow, lazy, and closed her eyes and reached her brown arms around his neck and pulled him down to her breast.

"You must go, so soon, Jiff?"

He laughed, standing. "Was the whole night so soon? Yes, but I'm starving and I ordered breakfast. Why don't you show me what you've brought, and I can take them to Dupre's later on."

Carla slipped out of bed and walked to the bathroom. If Jeff had ever wondered why the Italians are such consummate painters of beautiful women, the sight of Carla that morning was answer enough. They'd had a lot of practice, and the subjects were never very far away. Water splashed and Jeff could hear the sounds of her singing. He'd never heard her sing before, but it didn't surprise him.

There seemed to be music in everything Carla did.

Breakfast arrived promptly, steaming hot. Jeff had ordered

English muffins, bacon and eggs, coffee, melon, and orange juice.

Carla laughed at the sight of the English muffins. She'd never seen one before.

She was wearing an old robe. her hair swathed in a big white towel. "I look," she said grimly to her reflection in the big bedroom mirror, "as though the elephants of Hannibal had walked over me."

"Lucky elephants. You look wonderful."

"Men! They teach you to say that in the cradle. And, what is more the trouble, they teach us to believe it."

Jeff stood up. He walked across the room and stood very close behind her, and encircled her with his arms. His voice was muffled; he had buried his face in the nape of her neck. "Would I lie?"

"No," she said, and her eyes when he caught a glimpse of them in the mirror were serious. "I think you would not lie, it is not in you. Which is why I am frightened to show you what Beppo has sent."

"They may be fakes?"

"Poor Beppo. With Beppo one never knows. These things, they are all from Cavolfiore, of that you may be sure. I have known them all my life. So this is a fact, that they were not made by—we say *sofisticazione*—they were not made fraudulently. But what they are, who knows?"

"I'm not an expert on Renaissance things, but we have experts, as I said last night."

She walked to the closet and dragged out a big heavy suitcase. He lifted it onto the bed. It must have weighed at least fifty pounds.

Carla opened the suitcase with a little brass key.

The first things she brought out were two small paintings, twins, perhaps six inches wide by twelve inches tall. They made a pair: one was a portrait of a saint facing left, the other had a similar figure facing right. To Jeff's eye they certainly looked old, very old, and they looked as though they had been designed to be the left- and right-hand panels of a triptych. The colors were bright, the drawing severe, the perspective very flat. The background was rich with old gilding. The saints were enthroned against a golden sky. They had golden haloes too, worked in a kind of shallow relief, and the slender frames, too, were encrusted with gilding. The saints' faces were elongated, olive in hue, with eyes that slanted so severely they appeared almost Oriental. Jeff thought the little pictures might be Sienese, and from the fourteenth century, perhaps earlier. The golden dawn of the Renaissance.

He held one close to the lamp. "They're lovely, Carla, and they surely look real to me."

"God willing."

She rummaged in the suitcase and produced a bulky package wrapped in white tissue paper. Then she unfolded a small tapestry. It was a hunting scene: three men in capes and feathered hats aimed curious-looking rifles at a stag. The stag rolled his eyes operatically, anticipating the blast to come. The colors must once have been bright. Now they had faded to an attractive near-monochrome, with here and there a hint of the vivid reds and blues and greens that had illuminated the tableau. Jeff found the tapestry stiff in its design and not really appealing. But it was almost certainly old, and he knew that old tapestries often fetched excellent prices.

"I know nothing about tapestries, darling," he said, "but I'll take it and have someone look at it who does know."

"Good."

Carla dug into the suitcase once again. Jeff was beginning to wonder if it were all a magician's trick, if the case were bottomless. He half-expected her to come up with the Albert Memorial.

What actually appeared was a marble head. It was a very idealized study of a young man in the Greek manner.

The statue's cold white eyes seemed to stare past Jeff into some eternal emptiness. Its lips were curled slightly as though the head were about to speak. Or sneer.

There was something wrong about the head, a coldness, a lack of real vitality. Jeff felt uneasy about the head, but he couldn't be sure. It, too, would have to go to Dupre's.

She showed him six photographs, badly lit but clearly focused. One revealed a dark, heavily carved table. Another showed a pouting, rather evil-looking cherub in a stone niche. There was a pair of elaborate bronze andirons, one topped with a goddess, the other with a god. And the last three photographs were of paintings.

Jeff finished the last of his English muffin and emptied his coffee cup. "Let me get going, darling. I don't know how long it'll take to have these things looked at, but I'll start today. My aunt invites you for dinner tonight at seven. I'll pick you up here."

She smiled, yawned, kissed him. "Today," she said, "I am a tourist."

Jeff stood in the doorway for a moment, just looking at

her, wondering how he could have doubted that she'd be as fascinating here as in Italy. Seven o'clock couldn't come soon enough to suit Jeff Dupre.

"Until seven, then," she said. "Stay well, Jiff."

"Seven," he said, leaving, "is a magic number."

Her heavy suitcase seemed light to Jeff as he walked briskly down the hallway.

27

Jeff took a taxi up Madison Avenue to Dupre's.

The fear hit him around Fifty-ninth Street, a sudden deep-gut fear, the bottom dropping out of the world.

Fear mixed with anger.

Suddenly he was sure the accident hadn't been accidental.

He sat back in the lumbering cab. The cab was air-conditioned. He sweated anyway.

Who in hell could it be? And why? Why him, why now?

It was all mixed up with the other confusion. The confusion about Carla, about Polly.

The confusion about himself.

For the first time in his life Jeff began wondering who he was, who he wanted to be.

There had been enough dodging, playing of social games, trying to avoid what Felix and Minnie wanted him to be, what the mothers of coveys of East Coast debutantes would have liked him to be.

It had all been so easy back in Veii.

Carla had been easy there, too, and natural. And, lovely as she was, had been last night, the transition from Tuscany to home made him wonder. He wondered how Carla would take to being a faculty wife in Cambridge, Massachusetts.

The cab got stuck in traffic. Horns blew. Other drivers swore. His own driver leaned on the horn until Jeff yelled at him to stop.

And then there was Polly. Well. And what about Polly? Polly was a very attractive lady. But Veii was waiting. And there was Carla. In that moment Jeff was glad he had Veii, his work, his trenches, his book. Veii was real. Veii had its own mysteries, but they threatened no one. The whole question of Jeff and Polly would have to be put on the shelf for the moment, maybe forever. She was a beautiful, busy girl. Her life must be full of admirers, maybe lovers. Certainly she wouldn't lack for chances.

The cab hit a pothole and Carla's suitcase bumped against Jeff's left leg, reactivating the pain.

It was good to have the artworks to study. That would be something specific to do today. Jeff felt a need to fill every moment, to keep busy, to keep moving.

If he kept busy, kept moving, maybe the demons of fear wouldn't catch up with him.

Maybe.

The rain was letting up as the cab pulled neatly to a stop at the front door of Dupre's.

Jeff hauled the suitcase through the lobby. He wondered if Polly's work ever took her to Italy. There must be a lot of silver in Italy. He thought of big church candlesticks, opulent trays, goldwork. The Winchcombe Chalice was Italian, when it came to that.

Polly in Veii. That was something to think about.

In the meantime, there were Carla's paintings, and the tapestry and the marble to be considered. Jeff brought the suitcase to Felix's office, asked Miss Winn to order coffee, and began consulting the Dupre phone book.

The old-master expert was Robin Caswell.

Yes, of course, Jeff could come right down.

Jeff did that. This was the important thing: to keep moving.

Robin Caswell stepped back from the two little paintings and squinted, made a faint growling noise somewhere deep down in his throat, like a lion about to pounce. Jeff watched the Renaissance-painting expert of Dupre's with the reverence he accorded all true scholars. He had never met Caswell, but the man's superb reputation was well known to him from Felix. Caswell was the first of three experts on Jeff's list this morning. He awaited the man's pronouncement with a strange mixture of eagerness and fear.

Fear, because he wouldn't trust Beppo any farther than he could throw the castello di Cavolfiore. Expectation, because if the paintings were valuable, it would have to help Carla.

There was silence for half a minute. It seemed to Jeff like days.

Caswell was silver-haired and gnomelike, and his voice belied the rather frail appearance he made. The voice, when it came, was deep, stentorian, and had the implacable ring of well-earned confidence.

"School of Lorenzetti," said Caswell, "painted during recess."

The expert laughed. It sounded like rocks rolling down a mountain. Jeff realized that the man might be poking fun at him, pulling the leg of the heir of Dupre's. It must seem to Caswell that Jeff was somehow testing his expertise. As indeed he was, but not from any ulterior motive.

"I have to tell you," said Jeff easily, "that I have no idea who Lorenzetti was."

"Sienese, around the middle of the fourteenth century, admirer, maybe even a pupil of Duccio's. But nothing like the same quality. He has all the mannerisms, but not the inner conviction. These"—Caswell gestured toward Carla's paintings with a casualness that failed to hide his disdain for their quality—"could almost be Lorenzetti himself on a bad day. Of which he had plenty. But we'd have to say 'school of' without an absolutely ironclad provenance, you understand, a note from Lorenzetti's mother, that sort of thing."

Jeff laughed, as he was sure Caswell expected him to do. "How much might they bring? I'm thinking of selling them for a friend. They come from the castello di Cavolfiore, near Veii, but the family doesn't know much about them."

Caswell picked up one of the panels and looked at it very closely, turning it around, peering intently at the back, where the walnut panel that made the painting's surface was joined to the intricate frame.

"Well, they're real, that's virtually a sure thing. These are not the sort of stuff anyone would bother to fake. It's too easy to fake Rembrandt, Matisse, Picasso, those boys . . ."

"Is it?"

Caswell looked at Jeff with an expression that conveyed both astonishment and pity. Astonishment for the young man's ignorance and pity that Dupre's should sink so low as to come into the hands of a half-wit.

"It is a major industry, Mr. Dupre. Every year, in every part of the world, millions—uncounted millions—of dollars are spent on forged or misattributed art of all kinds. The art world is a minefield for the amateur, a positive minefield. Even for so-called experts, it gets riskier every day, as the fakers get more and more clever. That's why provenance is so terribly important. And, of course, even provenances are faked now."

"But you're pretty sure about these, their being real, I mean?"

"Oh, yes, quite. I'd guess they'll bring between thirty-five and fifty the pair. Pity the middle's missing. They so often are."

"Thirty-five to fifty thousand? But isn't that a lot?"

Caswell blinked, then remembered that he was speaking to one of the great uninitiated, and replied gently, "Dear boy, if they were by Duccio, they'd fetch a million. Possibly more."

"I see. Well, let's leave them in the vault and I'll speak to the owner. She didn't leave me firm instructions on the price."

"Yes, do that. They're really quite attractive, mind you, considering."

"I thought so. Well, thank you, Mr. Caswell. I'll put them in the painting vault."

Jeff walked out of Caswell's little office sure in his heart that he would never, never understand the auction business.

His next stop was Mrs. Duckworth, Dupre's expert on Oriental rugs and tapestries. He found her after losing his way twice. Mrs. Duckworth was plump and pushing sixty. She was dressed entirely in black, warm weather or not, and Jeff found her perched on a bale of carpets sipping tea. Tea seemed to be the universal beverage at Dupre's, which suited Jeff fine. He preferred it to coffee.

"Fran," she said instantly when he introduced himself, "do call me Fran."

"If you'll call me Jeff."

"Jeff." She giggled. "Oops! Didn't mean to be irreverent, it just seems strange . . . after all these years."

"To be dealing with another Dupre?"

"All the changes." Fran Duckworth fixed Jeff with an appraising eye. He felt like a somewhat threadbare carpet must feel coming under her quick laser scrutiny. "Well, what can I do for you, Jeff?"

He produced Carla's tapestry. Fran asked him to drape it over another, larger bale of carpets that was on the other side of the hall. "Light's better, don't you know?" She stood, looked, sipped her tea, put down the teacup, walked slowly up to the tapestry, lifted a corner, sniffed, let it drop.

"Well, young man, you've latched on to a goody. Oh, yes. Yes, indeed. Probably stayed in Italy, too, didn't it? Faded as it is."

"It came from a castle in Tuscany."

"It was woven in a castle in Tuscany. Mid-sixteenth-century, almost sure to be Florentine, not signed that I can see, which is a shame, 'cause that would up the price—way up."

Jeff hardly dared speak. "I guess," he began, "I'd always thought tapestries came from northern Europe."

"Most of 'em do. Did. The great ones mostly all did. But it caught on. In fifteen-something Cosimo de' Medici set up a workshop in the Palazzo Vecchio. He had a finger in every pie, that one. This could be from Florence. Mid- to late-sixteenth. Fair condition—faded, don't you know? Bring about forty, maybe a bit more, it's hard to say. Forty would be fair."

Once more Jeff took a deep breath. Carla could be nearly a hundred thousand dollars richer, just from the two paintings and this worn tapestry.

"It is," he said with some effort at control, "part of a set. Four in all, all the same size."

"And in the same condition? You should have said so. Sets bring a lot more. Rare as hen's teeth, sets. If they measure up to this piece, then I'd say two-hundred-plus. Up to a quarter of a million. Of course, I'd have to examine them very closely indeed. Fly over, if that were necessary."

"The owner's a friend of mine," said Jeff, "and she just asked me to find out what they might bring. I think it'll have to be a family decision whether they really sell. But at prices like you mentioned . . ."

"Which go higher every week. Think of the Arabs."

Jeff thought of the Arabs. And of Beppo. And other things. At last he smiled and shook Fran's plump hand, folded the tapestry, and left.

The marble head was sitting on Felix's desk, gazing arrogantly up from the Out box. Jeff passed Morgan's door on the way down the hall. It was open. Morgan sat at his desk, gazing intently at a piece of ivory-colored notepaper. Jeff knocked. Morgan looked up with a start, his hands instinctively covering the letter, if letter it was. He must, thought Jeff, receive a tremendous amount of confidential correspondence. Jeff smiled. "You were very good with the Brueghel yesterday, Morgan."

Morgan smiled shyly and made a small, shrugging-it-off gesture of dismissal. "All in the day's work, as they say. The Brueghel made the sale. Other than that, it was fairly ordinary stuff. Even if we did total over two million."

"Who bought the flower piece?"

"The Chicago Institute, in reasonably hot contention with one of Mr. Simon's agents, the National Gallery in Washington, and one bidder I didn't recognize, which is very unusual, at that level. Still, they do sometimes creep out of the woodwork, buy something amazing, and creep away, never to be heard from again."

"Can I show you something? A marble head a friend is thinking of selling."

Morgan stood up at once, folded the note he'd been reading. "Of course," he said, smiling easily. "Where is it?"

Jeff took him down to the next office. Morgan looked at the head, picked it up, turned it slowly in his hands, then set it down again in the Out box. He walked across the room and looked at it again from that distance. Then, without saying anything at all, he walked to the telephone and dialed a three-digit number. "Hello, Dawkins? Yes. Yes. Could you join Jeff Dupre and me for a bit, in Felix's office? Thanks, Sam."

Dawkins was with them in a few seconds, a lean young man with intensely green eyes. Jeff smiled through the introduction, thinking that the sculpture expert must be even younger than Polly. Dawkins went through much the same routine as Morgan, holding the head, backing off, squinting, saying nothing. Finally he spoke.

"The Roman copies—it isn't Greek, of course—had a certain hard quality. The Renaissance copies weren't really copies, even though the people who made them might have thought they were, because the gentlemen in the Renaissance put their own stamp on the form, turned it into something else entirely. This is fine work, but it has no inner conviction. Doesn't know what it wants to be. I make it a fairly limp late-nineteenth-century bit of Victorian wistfulness. In the great marbles, from whatever period, even lately, even Rodin, you see the spirit of the thing, deep inside, burning to get out. It has thrust and strength and authority. This is merely decorative, 'in the manner of,' as we'd be forced to say in the catalog." He paused then, and blinked, blushed slightly when he realized to whom he'd been speaking, smiled too quickly, and said, "I'm sorry."

Jeff smiled back. "I didn't carve the damned thing, Dawkins. And I appreciate your scholarship. The head belongs to a friend, and she doesn't know a thing about it." As he spoke, Jeff wondered whether Beppo did, whether Beppo was trying to palm off the fakes with the good stuff. It was something to think about.

"You're an archaeologist?"

"Right this minute I'm late for a date in a trench in Veii."

"Then you know what I mean, about the conviction. An

out-and-out forgery might be tougher to detect, more skillfully made."

"There seems to be a lot of that going around."

Dawkins threw up his hands in mock despair. "Understatement. They'd fake Barbie dolls if they could make a buck at it. Art faking is an idea whose time has definitely come. It combines public ignorance and private greed in an irresistible manner."

Morgan laughed. "You talk," he said, "about the same way my aged mum speaks of New York, as though the streets run with blood, and no one's safe out of the house at any hour. Fakes exist, naturally, but possibly you overstate the volume. It's a glamorous subject, the hot crime of the minute. Faked art has replaced kidnapping and air hijacking in the headlines. Tomorrow, who knows what it may be, the crime of the hour?"

"Would we," asked Jeff, "sell a thing like this head? I don't really know where we draw the line."

Again, Morgan St. James laughed, a supple laugh, the laugh of a clubman. "In black ink, Jeff, in black ink, God willing! Yes, I think we might sell it, as a bit of nice Victoriana, which is getting more fashionable every day. Don't throw out your granny's Burne-Joneses, if she has any, because the trend is up, decidedly up!"

"I'm glad to hear it," said Jeff, smiling. "And what might it bring?"

"Not a lot." Dawkins frowned. "With luck, if the sun's out, maybe a thousand. If it were signed, maybe more. It's decorative, is all."

"I'll speak to the owner, who lugged it all the way from Italy. I doubt she'll want to carry it back. And thanks for helping."

"Not at all."

Dawkins left them, and Morgan, too, drifted out.

Jeff felt pleased with his morning's work. Carla, he knew, would be delighted at the news.

He sat down at his uncle's desk, feeling, as always, like an intruder. Then Jeff picked up the phone and dialed the St. Regis. Carla didn't answer. She had told him she'd be out doing tourist things today. Jeff wondered what they were. He should have arranged to meet her for lunch. It was getting close to noon.

He considered dropping down to see if Polly was in Dupre's. Then he reconsidered. Jeff wasn't sure what he'd say to Polly, or what he'd do. He wouldn't avoid her, but he wouldn't seek her out, either.

And she'd think he was the kind of guy who went in for one-night stands.

And maybe she'd be right.

Jeff looked at the marble head in Felix's In box. Arrogant son of a bitch. The head was mocking him: all cool and marble and narcissistic. The head didn't have to make any choices between Carla and Polly. The head didn't have to look left and right very carefully before crossing the street. Of course, Jeff thought, and smiled, thinking it, the head didn't enjoy many nights like last night, either.

Jeff got through the afternoon without leaving Felix Dupre's office. He sent out for a sandwich and spent the time going through all of his uncle's files.

He suspected it would be a goose chase, and it was.

Jeff didn't even know what he was looking for. Some indication of trouble at Dupre's, maybe. Something that might have upset Felix so deeply he'd smash up his car on purpose.

Felix had been orderly in all things. His files were in good shape and absolutely unrevealing. These were not the general, full-scale records of the House of Dupre, but rather Felix's private files. They contained records of special sales, of certain individual objects that must have interested him. There were personal notes; a file for Felix's doctor contained records of annual checkups only. He had been a remarkably healthy man. There was a file on Jeff, too, touchingly fat. It held school records, statements from Jeff's trust fund, and every letter Jeff had ever written the Dupres.

Jeff was sad that the letters, lately, had been so few.

There was a file labeled "Fleet." It recorded the sale of many items, dating from the early 1950s. Here were the treasures of Berwick, sold off one by one. Paintings, some by noted artists. A great deal of silver. A few fine rugs and tapestries. Some furniture, bits of jewelry. Nothing of the caliber of the Winchcombe Chalice. The Fleet file told Jeff nothing he didn't know. It was an old story and a sad one. Sadder, perhaps, because the duke was rather a friend of the Dupres. Of Felix anyway.

By the time he'd read his way through two big filing cabinets, it was nearly five o'clock. Jeff closed the last cabinet, feeling more than a little foolish. What had he hoped to find, anyway? Looking through his uncle's files was surely his right, and yet he felt sneaky. Like reading someone's mail.

He walked to the elevator, carrying Carla's suitcase.

The elevator door opened. There stood Polly, cool and beautiful. She smiled. Jeff did something with his face that he hoped would look like a smile.

"Hi," she said. "How are you?"

"I'm okay, Polly. I tried to call you yesterday and—"

"I was delayed in Dallas."

Jeff's mind became a whirl of options, a tangle of conflicts.

"Could we have lunch tomorrow?"

The elevator had stopped at her floor.

Polly looked at him intensely. Her face was unreadable. Then she smiled. "Sure, why not? Call me in the morning, okay?"

"Okay."

Mercifully, she stepped out of the elevator then, and the door closed behind her.

Minnie was out when Jeff got back to the house.

He left Carla's suitcase in the foyer and went upstairs to shower and shave and change his clothes.

At seven, Jeff took a cab to the hotel and delivered the empty suitcase and the good news. Carla was thrilled. She bubbled with plans: now there could be a modern electrical generator at Cavolfiore, new tractors, the roof repaired once and for all. "And there is more, Jiff, much more."

"Paintings and tapestries?"

"Some. And old chairs and tables, some religious things, carvings, old reliquaries, vestments even, from the time when Cavolfiore had its own chapel. An altarcloth from very long ago." She stopped her recital and laughed. "Of course, Beppo would sell Cavolfiore itself, stone by stone, and I must attend to it that he does not."

Carla looked lovely. She wore a simple dress of silk in a mysterious shade that was somewhere between gray and green, the color of the ocean on a day with both sunshine and clouds. The dress's neck was cut in a scoop. It had short sleeves and a rather full skirt. It looked, to Jeff's eyes, neither old nor new, but simply beautiful.

They met Bunny on the doorstep. Minnie was her sparkling best, telling Carla stories Jeff had never heard, tales of Felix and Minnie in Italy, of the Berensons, film people at Portofino, clergy in Rome, tycoons at Lago di Como.

Bunny acted the host, filling glasses, laughing, charming Carla and, Jeff thought, being charmed in turn. It was a very nice little party. Emmalee had outdone herself.

"I thought, Carla, that we'd have simple American things, things, perhaps, that you don't get in Tuscany."

There was cornbread and New England clam chowder. There was lobster taken out of its shell and sauced with drawn butter and fresh tarragon. There was corn on the cob and, for dessert, peach shortcake with whipped cream. The wine was a California Riesling throughout, spicy and cool, perfect with the lobster.

"It's a sign," Minnie said to Carla, "of good character in a girl to have a healthy appetite. It does an old lady good to see you, Carla."

Carla regarded her hostess, and smiled an urchin's smile. "I am a farmer, Mrs. Dupre, so I have a farmer's appetite."

"Yes, Jeffy told me you do wonders with your farm."

"I try. Now, thanks to Dupre's, we will be able to do more."

"That's lovely, dear. I hope to see Cavolfiore one day."

"We would be honored."

Coffee was served in the library upstairs. Bunny and Jeff each had a brandy, but the ladies declined. Jeff sat in his uncle's favorite wing chair and looked at the happy little group. It was the kind of evening the Dupres were famous for. There was a special grace in the room, a sense of ease and comfort and caring. It was the kind of evening that made those who shared it think: Yes, the world can be a splendid place, it is worth the struggle.

Felix and Minnie had always made it look easy.

Minnie was doing that now, with plenty of help from Bunny. It pleased Jeff to think of them together. Would Minnie ever consider remarrying? If she did, she could do much, much worse than Bunny Bartlett.

Soon it was nearly midnight and Bunny got up to leave. Jeff and Carla lingered for ten minutes, and then he stood up.

"I hate it to end," he said, "but I'd better get Carla back to the hotel. It was great, Minnie, just fabulous."

"Thank you, Mrs. Dupre," said Carla. "You are very kind."

"We'll be seeing more of you, I'm sure, my dear, so I won't even say good-bye, but *arrivederci*." And she kissed Carla on the cheek.

Jeff glowed. The kiss was surely a mark of Minnie's approval, and Minnie did not approve of people lightly.

They turned toward Fifth Avenue.

"Let's walk," said Jeff. "It's such a nice night."

"It was very special for me, Jiff. Your aunt made it so.

And the house is very beautiful. But you must tell me," she said with a child's giggle, "how does so distinguished man as Bunny get to be called after a *coniglio?*"

Jeff laughed. "Probably at school. Among a certain class of Americans, that kind of silly name is fairly common. Felix had a friend called Piggy Warburg. How did Beppo get to be called Beppo?"

"Beppo is hardly distinguished. But his name is unpronounceable even by Italians. It is a nursery name, Beppo."

They were about halfway up the block. No one was out on Sixty-fourth Street. An occasional taxicab drove down the avenue. Across Fifth Avenue was the entrance to the Children's Zoo, a wide opening in the stone wall, two fat low pillars brightly illuminated, behind them steps and darkness, and looming darker, the fake-medieval crenelations of the armory. The breeze stirred the trees and the clumps of dark laurels and rhododendrons that flanked the entrance. It was very quiet. The heat of the day was fading. It felt good to be walking on the handsome street, alone with Carla, holding her hand.

Jeff felt lucky.

One of the new calcium streetlamps blazed white light on the corner. Just before they reached the corner, Jeff's eye caught the bright copper gleam of a new penny on the sidewalk. It's stupid, he thought, my damned archaeologist's eyes are always on the ground. The Hindenberg could fly overhead and I'd never see it.

He squeezed her hand and quickly bent to pick up the penny.

"Good luck, darling, to find a penny."

She stepped in front of him.

"Penny?"

That was the last word Carla di Cavolfiore ever spoke.

Jeff heard a strange gurgling sound followed by the crack of a rifle shot. Her hand clenched his violently, then loosened.

She was collapsing to the sidewalk. There was blood on her face.

Jeff held her, stunned, unable to speak.

Slowly he eased her down to the sidewalk. He knelt beside her. Carla was dead. Jeff stayed there, holding her hand, not believing what had happened.

Then he believed.

And then he began screaming.

28

They had to pry him off her.

Jeff crouched beside Carla's body, trembling, holding her as though by holding her he could stop bullets, or turn back time. He heard voices, shouts, and soon there were sirens and red flashing lights. A police car. Hands on his shoulder, urging.

"All right, mister, you've done all you can. You can get up now."

And they helped him to his feet, very firmly. The hand was still on his shoulder. Maybe to keep him upright. Maybe to keep him from running away.

Jeff looked at the hand as though it were a part of him he hadn't noticed before. It was a big hand, strong, suntanned. It came out of a sleeve. The sleeve belonged to a big man with a lot of dark red hair and kind eyes.

"I'm Detective Kavanaugh, Nineteenth Precinct," said the voice behind the eyes. "Can you tell me your name, and what happened?"

Jeff blinked. There was another siren now. An ambulance. They were taking her away. He turned toward Carla. They had covered her with a plastic tarpaulin.

"No," said Jeff, gasping it, "no!"

The hand tightened its grip.

Jeff looked at the big detective. "She's dead," Jeff said. "Carla's dead."

Kavanaugh's eyes didn't waver. "I'm afraid so, mister. Can you tell us anything?"

Jeff felt something hot on his cheek. He touched it. Tears.

"My name," he said in a low dull tone, "is Jeff Dupre."

They were in the backseat of the patrol car. They had to go, Kavanaugh said, to the precinct house to fill out papers. It was just a few blocks away, on Sixty-seventh Street, a big, moldering old Victorian building floored in worn linoleum, its walls painted an evil shade of pistachio-ice-cream green. Kavanaugh's desk was in a big room with several other desks. There seemed to have been an explosion of papers, file folders, overflowing In boxes. Phones rang almost constantly. Policemen came and went. There was a low buzz of voices, an occasional laugh.

"Want coffee?" Kavanaugh asked, beckoning Jeff to sit down in a small iron chair by the desk.

"No, thanks."

Kavanaugh pulled some printed forms out of a drawer, found a pen, and began the interview. "Jeffrey Dupre," he said. "Your address?"

"One-forty-one Brattle Street, Cambridge, Massachusetts."

"Profession?"

"Assistant professor of archaeology, Harvard University."

It went on for nearly an hour. Jeff told the facts as he knew them. He told Kavanaugh about the incident with the speeding car. It was on the books. Jeff was interested that Kavanaugh thought it necessary to check.

"He was after me, Mr. Kavanaugh, I guess that's pretty obvious. I ducked, for that penny, Carla sort of stepped in front . . ."

"He must have been in the laurels to the left of the steps going down to the Children's Zoo. We found some of them broken, as though someone had been waiting. But no spent cartridge. It was probably a lightweight hunting rifle of some kind. I wonder why he didn't shoot twice."

"I think there was just one shot. She seemed to fall almost before I heard it. Then . . . well, I'm not sure what I heard, until you came."

"That's easy to understand."

There was a pause. Kavanaugh made some notes. Across the room, a foreign-looking old woman was weeping softly, steadily. She had been weeping when Jeff came in. She sat alone in a chair against the wall. No one seemed to pay any attention to her.

"What's the matter with her?" Jeff thought it was cruel for the police to ignore her that way.

Kavanaugh kept on writing. "That," he said quietly, "is Wanda the Weeper. She's one of the mild ones. She comes in about once a week, always at night, sits down, and starts crying. She'll do that for an hour or so, get it out of her system, then quietly go home. We've tried to get psychiatric help for her, but she won't have anything to do with any doctor. So she weeps."

"You get a lot of that?"

"Every police station is a magnet for them. For all kinds of crazies. And firehouses, too."

Jeff sat quietly. The blood on his shirt had long since dried.

He'd washed his face and hands in the precinct's bathroom. Kavanaugh filled in his forms. The old lady wept. Jeff felt as though he'd been kicked in the gut by a mule: sore and numb and aching all over.

"I have to say something, Mr. Kavanaugh."

Kavanaugh looked up, watchful.

"I'm scared. I am very frightened. I've never been scared before in my life, not really. Not like this. I don't have any enemies."

"Yes you do."

The detective's voice was soft with the softness of strength. "You may not know it . . . and there's always the outside chance we're dealing with two coincidences and the sniper is just your everyday madman. But I wouldn't bet on it. I wouldn't bet on it at all. Now, what we're going to do is this. I've ordered a round-the-clock guard on your aunt's house. Naturally, we can't keep that up forever, but we can do it for some time. There will be a patrol car on call, if you want to go someplace during the daytime. I'd stay close to the house at night. And we'll get going just as fast as we can to try to clear this thing up."

"I wish I could help you."

"You will. Let me take you back to the house now. We can talk more tomorrow morning. Or whenever it's convenient."

"Tomorrow morning's fine."

Jeff said it listlessly. Tomorrow morning wasn't going to be fine. Tomorrow morning was going to be just terrible. Tomorrow he was going to have to face Minnie. He was going to have to tell Beppo di Cavolfiore. And he was going to have to face the fact that someone was trying, and trying very hard, to kill Jeff Dupre.

Tomorrow was definitely not going to be fine.

"Tell me," Jeff asked, because the idea had just come to him, "how carefully do you look at smashed cars, when someone's been killed?"

Kavanaugh looked at him. "Your uncle? You think there was something funny about that?"

"I didn't, until right this minute. Something funny is happening to one Dupre, maybe it was also happening to Felix."

"Where did he crash, and when?"

"Not two weeks ago, outside of White Plains."

"They'll have the car. They always hold them, no matter how badly they've wrecked, because they're property. Your aunt owns it. So it'll be in some junkyard, probably, waiting for her to dispose of it. If they didn't suspect anything criminal, it's hard to say how carefully they'd look it over. I'll check into that myself tomorrow. We can make our own inspection."

"You don't think I'm going paranoid?"

Kavanaugh smiled. It was a big, slow smile, the first Jeff had seen on his broad Irish face.

"A little paranoia is a very good thing when someone's taking potshots at you, Mr. Dupre. A very good thing. If I were you, I'd try to cultivate it."

He got up then and led Jeff to a waiting patrol car and drove him to Minnie's house. A uniformed patrolman stood at the foot of the front steps. The sight of him was reassuring, and troubling at the same time.

Reassuring because the cop was there.

Troubling because he had to be there.

Jeff thanked Kavanaugh and went in. No one was up. Jeff had prayed they wouldn't be, that the noise and the confusion would have gone unnoticed. It had all happened half a block away. There was nothing to be done, no point in telling Minnie now.

Tomorrow would be soon enough.

Tomorrow he'd have to plan, analyze, think. Tonight all Jeff could do was feel. And the only way he could feel was rotten. The impact of Carla's death was too huge for Jeff to take it in all at once.

It seeped into his mind and his heart slowly, horribly, burning whatever it touched, acid on a wound.

Part of the pain was guilt.

The fact that she had died because someone wanted him dead made it worse.

Numb with sorrow, Jeff climbed up to his room. He took a long hot shower, but all the water in the world couldn't begin to wash away his grief, his guilt, his pain. He remembered the old western-movie cliché about the bullet with someone's name on it. There was a name on the bullet that killed Carla, and the name was Jeff Dupre.

And he had to live with that.

There would be times this night, and later, when Jeff would come close to wishing the bullet had found its target.

He sank onto the bed and turned off the light.

Sleep was a long time coming.

Jeff closed his eyes and saw Carla, smiling, eager. Carla in the warm sunset light at Cavolfiore. Carla, just last night in

159

the hotel. There was no way not to think of her. After a while he stopped trying.

Jeff opened his eyes.

Trees outside his window cast mottled shadows on his ceiling. He had always liked those shadows before tonight. Tonight they seemed menacing. Tonight everything that wasn't sad was threatening.

Jeff knew a lot about sadness, but in all his twenty-eight years he had never felt threatened. He had never been seriously frightened.

It wasn't a discovery he needed to make.

Jeff lay there watching the slow-moving shadows on his ceiling. He closed his eyes.

The image of Carla had gone.

It turned into another image, equally sad but insulated by layers and layers of time.

Now Jeff saw the yellow sailboat, empty on the sunlit sea.

Finally, mercifully, he fell into a restless, dozing sleep.

29

Berwick Castle, England, April 1969

Neville Fleet stood in the rose garden and forced himself to look up at the tower from which his only son had jumped three years before.

More than the heir of Berwick had died that night.

Young Neville's death had marked the end of his father's pretending. All the artifices he'd used, big ones and small ones, had been designed to create an illusion of normalcy for his son.

He'd never know, now, whether the illusions had worked.

The walls of Berwick loomed overhead, and the towers rose above the walls. Berwick was what it always had been: citadel, fortress, prison. Only, now there was no one to make the struggle worthwhile. Miranda lived so much in her own fantasy world that all one really needed to keep her happy was an endless supply of Thorazine, Valium, and rest. And the occasional very costly visits from the psychiatrist.

Neville sighed, a long slow sigh. He had invested more of himself than anyone would ever know in the hopeless effort of giving his son some semblance of the kind of life his own father and grandfather had given him. At what unreckoned loss to his pride, to his sense of the fitness of things, had he begun selling off the treasures of Berwick? And for what? For the intolerable smugness of the revenue man Smythe-Davies?

Smythe-Davies had grown, like some terrible cancer, to fill a great portion of Neville's life. He was always there, waiting, faintly gloating at the triumph of the working class over the likes of Neville Fleet. Not that Smythe-Davies would ever be so indelicate as to express the thing so plainly.

But there it was, the slow bleeding of Berwick to pay her majesty's death duties. Now there was talk of a new wealth tax, a sort of super income tax on accumulated capital. Not that there was any danger of Neville's accumulating any capital.

The government was only one of Neville's creditors.

Taken all in all, the debts of Berwick loomed larger and more intimidating than the castle itself. The motor people had quietly—but firmly—repossessed the fire-red Aston Martin that the duke had given young Neville the summer the boy destroyed himself. Other creditors were discreetly turning the screws tighter. Only the ancient title, and the deep reserves of snobbery that still animated the duke's tailors, shirtmakers, and bootmaker, allowed him to dress with some degree of decency. His name, his title, his custom, were all of some value to these people. They wouldn't press too hard, but even their patience must know an end.

He had come to dread the mail. The telephone, which rang only rarely now, never brought good news.

Felix Dupre had been his only salvation. Felix came to Berwick at least twice a year. And he never left empty-handed. One by one the great paintings had gone. And while they fetched good prices, sometimes amazing prices, it was never enough. What Smythe-Davies didn't consume, Berwick itself did. The huge sum that had been owing on Grandfather's death duties had been extended and extended and at rates of interest that seemed to make it impossible for Neville to ever pay off the principal. The old duke had been dead nineteen years now, and his grandson—it was mockery to call himself heir—hadn't paid the government ten percent of what was owed.

Neville knew he'd probably grow old with the wretched Smythe-Davies haunting his every step. Into the grave.

The Dupre connection was sustaining, but only sustaining. A holding action. There were many things that simply could not be sold. Neville had sold more than a dozen paintings, but the greatest paintings in Berwick were of his ancestors, and he could not bring himself to sell those. He could never sell the chalice, although some other, lesser objects had gone on the block. It seemed infinitely tacky to be forced into selling off furnishings, chairs, and carpets, even though Felix assured his old friend that these things were worth very substantial sums.

The time would come, Neville knew, when he'd have to sell everything. This was certain, unless some miracle intervened.

Neville stood in the rose garden and looked up at the tower and thought of miracles. As he stood there, Father Devlin walked out through the small pointed archway in the barrier wall, saw the duke, nodded, and continued on his regular afternoon walk. Miracles, indeed! Neville wondered what might happen if he went into the chapel and, for the first time in years, prayed.

Slowly he walked back up the gentle hill to the wall. Five minutes later, feeling faintly guilty and sure that Devlin would be gone for at least an hour, Neville Fleet opened the oaken door of the Berwick chapel, walked up to the altar, knelt, and tried to find the words of a prayer. He rummaged in his memory as though it were some deep and crowded closet.

No prayer came leaping full-blown into the duke's mind.

Instead, he knelt and silently prayed for help, for guidance, for some kind of intervention.

Everything had seemed so utterly hopeless these last few years, since Miranda's madness had become an established fact, since the boy's death. He knelt there for perhaps ten minutes. The worn stone floor was hard on his unaccustomed knees. He looked up at last. The Winchcombe Chalice stood where it had always stood, in the center of the simple altar, gleaming.

The old duke's dying words came back to Neville. The promise that all the old Fleets were here, somewhere just out of his sight, watching. The old duke would be with them now. *Make me a sign, Grandfather, get me out of this intolerable mess!* The chalice seemed to give off its own special radiance, beyond the light that it reflected.

Neville smiled at his folly. Communicating with the dead, indeed. Next he'd be reading tea leaves or seeking out Gypsies. But he felt better as he stood, creaking a little in the knees. He regarded the chalice for a long moment, then turned and walked out. At least Berwick had one superb treasure left. For whatever good it might do him.

He walked down the hall and out of the main door into the courtyard. It was a fine April day, clear, with a promise of the warmth to come. Some of the earliest daffodils were blooming, and armies more had shot up with astonishing speed, legions of them on the grassy borders of the courtyard and thousands more on the lawns that swept down to the river.

Neville decided to walk down to the village.

He'd pick up a novel or two for Miranda. In her deepening madness, Miranda had conceived a fondness for a certain kind of light-headed romantic fiction of the kind churned out by blue-haired old ladies for the edification of shopgirls. These books were all set in times past. They all featured innocent but resourceful virgin heroines, wicked noblemen with dark desires, gallant horses, castles, and happy endings. For Miranda, Duchess of Berwick, heiress to Loweswater House, to indulge in such nonsense would have been amusing under normal circumstances. As things were, her taste in reading was only pathetic. It did no harm. There was a good lending library in the village bookstore, and Neville patronized it regularly. Doing so was one of his few luxuries, although no one in the tiny hamlet of Berwick Village would have guessed that. They were most indulgent to the eccentricities of the rich. Neville was, after all, their own liege lord, and, more often than not, their landlord too, since much of the village property belonged to the castle. Not that the rents amounted to anything.

There was another reason to come into the village.

He might see Bess Williams.

Bess ran the bookstore in partnership with a dour older woman named Mrs. Garvey. But Bess was not old, and she was anything but dour. Bess was a widow in her late twenties, with a young daughter to raise and a small pension. The husband, a local boy, had been in some minor Foreign Office position in Africa when one of the emerging bandit chieftains there had decided to emerge a bit faster, with much blood spilled, including that of young Williams.

Bess was a cheerful sort, not a great beauty, but much given to laughter. She was rather a tall girl, freckled, a tennis player, and entirely alive. She wouldn't remain a widow long; Neville was sure of that. In the meantime, she could make him laugh. And making the Duke of Berwick laugh these days was a far more challenging proposition than Bess Williams had any reason to know.

Neville liked to walk in the village.

Here, everything seemed as it had always been. Here he was a Fleet of Berwick, unchallenged, unchanged. The villagers were polite, respectful without toadying. They thought he walked for pleasure, or perhaps from a sense of *noblesse oblige*. In fact he walked because he begrudged the high cost of gasoline for the old Daimler that was the last working motorcar in the Berwick stables. Grandfather's Bentley was too costly to keep up. It was there, carefully shrouded in canvas, on blocks. Felix Dupre had told him it would be worth money one day. That day might come very soon, if things didn't get better.

Neville walked down the village's one main street, nodding, smiling. He was the Duke of Berwick to his toes now, gracious, lordly, admired by all. If only they knew. His step picked up as he neared the bookstore.

Maybe Bess would be there. Maybe.

30

Jeff lay in bed with his eyes determinedly shut.

There was no way to keep the day from beginning: it had begun in sorrow long before he'd dragged himself to bed. But maybe he could put off the reckoning a little.

He wondered how much would make the papers. He wondered how to tell Beppo di Cavolfiore about Carla's murder.

And most of all Jeff wondered what the rest of his life was going to be like, now that there was no possibility of Carla sharing it with him.

As much of his life as was left to him.

He had awoken thinking of Carla. Now he thought about his own situation too. His situation was about as bad as it could be. Bad and dangerous.

Kavanaugh had said it. Kavanaugh had offered only the most slender hope. Jeff wondered if the people who wanted him dead would follow him to Veii.

What made you want to kill someone? Especially someone

to whom Jeff was so little a threat, he had no idea what it was all about.

Well, someone had attacked him first. Twice.

Jeff opened his eyes then. A fine bright day. The small corner of the sky that he could see from his bed was clear blue and cloudless. A day to run outdoors and do something. But there would be no running outdoors for Jeff today.

He forced himself to get up, washed, shaved, dressed. It must feel a little like this if you're condemned, in prison, he thought, facing the grimness for what it was: solid as a rock.

Minnie was at breakfast.

"Did you hear us last night, Minnie? The sirens?"

"I thought I heard something, but there always are sirens. Why?"

Jeff sat down. "I was walking Carla toward Fifth Avenue. Someone took a shot at me from the park. Only, they hit Carla."

Minnie put down her coffee cup. For a moment she said nothing. "Someone shot at you? Oh, Jeffy. Jeffy. Is . . . ?"

"She's dead, Minnie. They killed her."

It was the first time he'd said it outright. Jeff's tongue felt heavier than a brick, and as dry.

"I didn't wake you, there wasn't any point in that. I spent some time with the police. Afterward."

"From the park?"

"From the park. A sniper. He probably would have got me, but I'd seen a penny on the sidewalk. Bent to pick it up. It's good luck, you know, to find a penny."

Then he was crying. She got up and came to him, put her arm around him. Tried to think of some magical thing to say that would help him. "Darling, you couldn't help it."

"She died because of me. Because some maniac is after me—us."

Minnie held him close and said nothing.

Only when Jeff managed to look up at her did he know that she was crying too.

He had never seen his aunt in tears before, not for Felix, not for him.

Jeff felt the sobs shaking him, building, heaving, uncontrollable. And still she held him. He couldn't tell for how long.

Finally it stopped.

Finally she spoke. "Darling, you're home now. You just cry all you want. I may join you, Jeffy. She was a lovely, lovely girl."

"Yes," he said softly, "she was."

He managed to drink some orange juice, to eat an English muffin, to drink a cup of coffee. The food tasted like cardboard.

"There's this detective, named Kavanaugh," Jeff told his aunt, "who said he'll come around sometime this morning. I guess he'll want to talk to you, too."

"Naturally, I'll help any way I can. But, darling, shouldn't you be getting back to Veii? It seems safer."

Jeff broke off a small piece of muffin.

"I'm not going to run away, Minnie. There are things I have to find out here first. No one knows what, or why, or anything. I asked the detective about Felix. I asked him to look into the car crash."

She looked at him, frowning. "Felix?"

"I know, Minnie, it's not easy to think about. Who'd want to kill Felix? But, who'd want to kill me? It is a possibility. And when they begin taking potshots at you in the dark, you've got to explore every possibility. Even the scariest ones."

"Of course. It's just that, well, everyone loved him so."

Jeff laughed. He hadn't planned on laughing. It came out, quick, brittle, heavy with the weight of an irony he couldn't control.

"I'm sorry, Minnie. I'm hardly in a laughing mood. It's just that my life isn't exactly crawling with enemies, either. I mean, how many enemies can you make in a ditch in Veii?"

"I don't think this has much to do with Veii."

"I suppose not. What does it have to do with?"

Hastings came in then. "The phone, Mr. Jeff."

It was Kavanaugh.

Jeff had forgotten the voice. It was a gentle voice for such a big man. He remembered Kavanaugh's hand on his shoulder. A gentle hand, backed by a vast amount of muscular leverage.

"How are you feeling, Mr. Dupre?"

"I've felt a lot better. How are you?"

"Anxious to get this thing in gear. Could I drop by in half an hour?"

"Absolutely. We'll be here."

Of course we'll be here. There's a goddamn cop on the doorstep to make very sure of that. And to make sure they don't actually invade the place.

"Ten-thirty, then."

He hung up. Other than a few traffic tickets, Jeff had never said three words to a policeman. Kavanaugh had been fine last night, considering the horror of it, and the confusion. He had been in control, even if there was really nothing to be in control of. Yet.

Jeff went back to the dining room and told Minnie about their appointment.

"I don't know how he'll want to handle it, both of us together, one at a time, whatever."

"Well," she said very quietly, "we'll see soon enough." Then Minnie looked up. There was an expression in her eyes that Jeff had never seen before: utter puzzlement. "What do they want from us, Jeffy? What in the world do they want?"

Ted Kavanaugh smiled at the patrolman and bounded up the steps to the Dupre house. It was a day for action, and he was ready. Ready for what? For whatever would happen. And it better happen fast. The bell was brass and old-looking and immaculately polished. He rang it and was not surprised when a butler in full rig opened the door.

Ted stood in the spacious foyer while the butler went to fetch Jeff Dupre.

It never failed to amaze him that people still managed to live like this in New York, in the final quarter of the twentieth century. The Nineteenth Precinct was one of the richest in New York, and Ted had been in many of its private mansions and luxury cooperative apartments. He'd been in one co-op last week that had thirty-nine rooms. Astonishing.

Jeff walked into the foyer, smiled, extended his hand.

Ted Kavanaugh knew Dupre was only two years younger than he. But Jeff looked hardly out of his teens. They never worry, he thought. It's all handed to them, wrapped up with a bow.

"I want to thank you," Jeff said quietly, "for being so good to me last night. I was a wreck. Still am."

"You were fine."

"Let's go into the library, it's more comfortable than the drawing room."

Kavanaugh followed Jeff down the hall and into a beautifully paneled library. *Just like that he says "drawing room" and never thought twice about it, and we aren't in some Noel Coward play. Or are we?*

"Sit down, lieutenant. Would you like some coffee?"

"Thanks, yes."

Jeff was sitting in his uncle's favorite wing chair. There was a small buzzer on the table at his elbow, a cube of black onyx with a small brass button to press. He pressed it.

Hastings appeared in less than a minute. Jeff ordered coffee for two. Kavanaugh watched all this in fascination.

"Where do we begin, lieutenant?"

"Maybe I'd better begin by telling you how weird this really is," Kavanaugh said quietly. "Smart people, people in comfortable circumstances, hardly ever kill each other. There are so many alternatives. As you go down the scale economically, educationally, violent crime increases in pretty much mathematical proportion until, at the very bottom, life gets very cheap indeed."

"Where does that leave us?"

"It leaves you in the middle of a real mystery. Most crimes aren't mysterious. They're almost all done by blood relatives, or lovers, or as part of a rape or a burglary. You seem to have only one close relative, and I guess we can be pretty sure it wasn't her."

"We can."

"And you don't even live here, usually, do you?"

"I only come on holidays, and maybe drop in on my way to or from a dig. I might be here three or four times a year."

"And—understand I've got to ask it—there aren't any jealous lovers hanging around?"

"No. I mean, not that I know of, and I guess I'd know."

"I guess you would. How about on the lady's part? Could someone have been gunning for her?"

"Almost certainly not. No one knew she was here: her visit was a surprise even to Carla. Her brother knew, of course, but it was Beppo who sent her. If he'd wanted to kill her, why not do it at home? And he wouldn't want to kill her. They were very close. This is going to be a sad blow to him."

Hastings appeared with a tray containing a big silver coffeepot, cups, spoons, cream, and sugar. Jeff thanked him and asked Kavanaugh how he liked his coffee.

"Black, please. Thanks. This gets us down to the next ugly question, Mr. Dupre. And that is, who benefits from your death?"

Jeff stirred a spoonful of sugar into his coffee, thinking, as he did it, that he'd learned to like sweetened coffee from Carla.

"No one. I mean, I have no dependents. I've had a will for years, just because Bunny Bartlett—he's a friend of my uncle's, and he advises us about money—wanted me to. And what it says is everything goes to Harvard and a couple of charities. And there really isn't a whole lot, anyway."

"Your aunt, for instance, doesn't benefit?"

Jeff looked at him, wondering how he could even think what he was obviously thinking. Cops probably had to look under all the rocks, however stupid it might seem.

"No. There are no individual bequests. We talked about it at the time, and Felix said it would only complicate things. Plus, of course, it seemed pretty unlikely that I'd die first. So unless the trustees of Harvard are after me, I don't see how it could be anything like that."

Kavanaugh sipped the coffee. It was very strong, the way he liked it. The cup was so thin you could see light through it, thin and pale and painted with flowers. Old-looking. Probably worth a fortune, like everything else in the house.

"What about the firm, Dupre's? Is there anyone there who might feel threatened, if you were to come into the business, for instance?"

"Maybe if I were coming into it. I do inherit, after Minnie, and she's asked my advice about selling, even though it is her decision. But I've made it very clear, at Dupre's, that I'm not interested."

"Dead ends and dead ends. Of course, there is such a thing as coincidence. We could be dealing with two random events. The car could have been a real accident. And the sniper could have been your typical crazy shoot-everything-that-moves kind of guy. But I don't think so."

"Neither do I."

Jeff poured himself some more coffee. Kavanaugh declined.

"How much," Jeff asked, "would it upset your plans if I went back to Italy?"

"It would probably upset Mr. X. Mr. X might not be able to simply hop on a jet and continue his little tricks overseas. But what it would also mean is that we might not find out who he is, or what he thinks he's doing. And there's another element, Mr. Dupre. I don't want to alarm you more than you may be alarmed already, but there is a possibility that our Mr. X might also be interested in your aunt."

Jeff had thought of that, and dismissed the thought. Now, hearing it from the big, confident-looking Kavanaugh, it didn't seem like such a wild idea.

"The way he might have been interested in Felix?"

"We have to think of it. Things that normally might seem just too weird, too beyond the pale, have got to be considered. Because we're dealing with someone weird. Someone who's already gone—or been driven—beyond reason."

Jeff smiled. "Here we go: the mummy's curse. Someone

wiping out all the Dupres, one by one, the result of some old grudge. Do things like that happen?"

"They do, but not to people like the Dupres. In some cultures, absolutely. Serbians. Greeks. Some Latins, especially Mexicans. You get real vendettas, whole families going after whole other families, generation after generation. The Capulets and the Montagues are enemies, and no one remembers quite why. The grudge feeds itself. On blood. But if there were anything like that going on in your family, you'd be very aware of it."

Suddenly, in the bright comfortable room, Jeff felt a chill. He saw the empty yellow sailboat. It seemed crazy to connect his father's death with anything that was happening now. But crazy things were exactly what Kavanaugh said they had to be thinking about.

Jeff thought for a minute before he spoke. "I guess you ought to know, Detective Kavanaugh, that in 1960 my father died mysteriously. He took his sailboat out one day and disappeared from it. They found the boat, but not him."

"Could it have been suicide?"

"Of course. It could have been anything, including an accident—the boom swung about on him suddenly, something like that. But he was a fine sailor, very at home on the water. They ruled it death by misadventure. No one in the family thought he was suicidal. Things seemed to be going well for him. To me he looked happy, and to my mother. I was only ten at that time. I guess you never know. There wasn't any note or anything like that."

"You never do know. But eighteen years is a long time for someone to nurse a murderous grudge and not act on it. If your dad's death was murder, why did the killer wait so long to strike out at Felix?"

"It makes my flesh creep to think about it."

"If there were no more Dupres, who benefits?"

"You mean, no Minnie, no Jeff?"

"Exactly."

"I'm Minnie's principal heir, other than some charities and some rather small bequests to servants and old friends, things like that. The firm—Dupre's—is privately held, and now Minnie owns all of the shares. It would, naturally, be sold in the event of her death and mine, but it's going to be sold anyway, more likely than not. That's a well-known fact. So killing us wouldn't really affect the sale of Dupre's very much."

"And you're not the repository of anyone's fatal secret?"

"Not likely."

"No rivals in love, at your job, that kind of thing?"

Jeff laughed. "You flatter me. This is getting to sound like an insurance physical exam: did you ever have measles?"

Kavanaugh smiled. "It is just that. And it seems equally stupid. But we've got to start someplace. For example, if you were going at it hot and heavy with the wife of a Sicilian mobster, that would mean something. I have to know. Everything."

"I realize that. And I want to help. But there just isn't anything like that. I was . . . very fond of Carla."

Kavanaugh looked away, out the window. It was a moment before he spoke. "Look," he said gently, "I know how tough this must be for you. It's like pulling teeth. Maybe I ought to talk to your aunt for a while."

"I'll be okay, really." Jeff said it quickly, too quickly. He didn't feel anything like okay. Not even semiokay. "It's just that I can't seem to think of anything that's useful to you."

"Everything's useful. Even negatives are negatively useful. We've eliminated the Sicilian mobster, for instance. Tomorrow I'm going up to take a look at your uncle's car. Would you like to come?"

Jeff smiled, relieved. It would be something to do, something physical, whatever the results. To get out of the house. To move.

"You bet I would, and thanks."

"I'll pick you up around ten. Now, could I meet your aunt?"

Jeff went to get her.

Kavanaugh stood up and looked at the books on the library shelves, and at some of the paintings that hung on the paneled walls.

A small pen-and-wash drawing attracted his eye. It was several studies of a young girl's head, quickly done and with a vivid freshness. In one corner of the paper she gazed coyly over her shoulder. In the center of the sheet her head was thrown back in a peal of laughter. Ted could almost hear it now. It would be light, silvery laughter. Just off-center on the paper the girl was drawn full-face, her eyes cast down as if deep in thought, or even in prayer. The little drawing was more than beguiling. Ted didn't know who the artist might be, but whoever it was had loved the girl, all girls, life itself.

Minnie Dupre's voice was soft when she spoke to Kavanaugh. "It was his wedding gift to me, lieutenant, but

I think that even if it weren't, it would be my favorite drawing."

Ted turned, smiling. "Who drew it?"

"Fragonard."

"I was just thinking," Ted said, "that he loved her."

"That's what Felix and I think. Thought."

She sat down where Jeff had sat.

"I'm sorry to trouble you, Mrs. Dupre. There are a few questions I have to ask you, and it won't take much of your time."

"You're no trouble, lieutenant. The trouble came, and maybe you can help us get rid of it. Jeffy—my nephew—said you were very kind last night."

"He's holding up pretty well, considering."

"Jeffy is, always has been, a very interior sort of boy. A bottler-up of emotions. That isn't always healthy, but that's the way he is."

"He's in double shock, first from losing the girl, then from thinking someone's after him."

"And what do you think?"

Ted looked down at his empty coffee cup, then back at Minnie. He wouldn't have expected the wife of Felix Dupre to be anything less than very bright. "I don't know what to think. The shooting, plus the incident with the car, that adds up. Maybe. But we can't take the chance that these things weren't planned. I've posted a watch on this house, around the clock. In the meantime, anything you can tell me about your nephew, about the family, anything that might indicate a motive . . ."

"I've been thinking, and thinking hard, lieutenant. I can't pretend to know much about the details of Jeff's life, but I do know his character, which is just fine. We raised him. Did you know that? Both of his parents were dead by the time Jeffy was eleven. He lived here, we treated him as the son we never had."

"You seem to have done a fine job."

"Well, of course, I'm prejudiced. To me he's perfect, or damn near it. But, that aside, there really isn't anything in Jeffy's character that would create enemies. He's not the kind of boy who has a million pals, never has been. There's nothing of the playboy about Jeffy, thank God."

"Love affairs?"

She smiled. "Ah. He's a cool one. They come after him, as you might imagine, looking as he does, and being a Dupre. And even when he was very young, Jeffy just went his own way. He always had a girl, but she usually wasn't the girl you'd expect. They came and went. Of course, since college, he's been away nearly all the time, on his digs, then teaching. If he'd ever been truly serious, to the point of marrying one of them, I am sure we'd have known. I met Carla only once. Last night. . . ."

"It must be painful for you, Mrs. Dupre. If you like, we can continue another time."

Minnie smiled. "You are very kind, lieutenant, but thank you, I'd rather get it over with. I think that Jeffy was fonder of Carla than usual. He never said anything specific, but seeing them together, well . . ."

"Her visit was a surprise? He didn't invite her to America?"

"A complete surprise, even to Carla. Her brother wanted her to get some things—art objects—evaluated at Dupre's."

"Did it ever occur to you that there might be something out of the ordinary about your husband's death?"

Her eyes changed. She looked down at the rug for a moment as though some secret message was to be read, wreathed among its Aubusson scrolls. Then she looked at Kavanaugh. "Death is always unusual, lieutenant, when it comes so suddenly. I thought of suicide, because, well, I guess one does when a driver as skilled as my husband cracks up. But he was in excellent health and good spirits. We were very close. Very. If anything had been troubling Felix, I would have known. I would have known, lieutenant, even if he hadn't confided in me. Which he would have done. He always did."

Ted asked her more routine questions, details of the household, schedules, dates, trivia. He was charmed by Mrs. Dupre and troubled by the absolute lack of anything to build a case on.

"I think that about does it, for the moment at least, Mrs. Dupre," he said at last. "If you can think of anything about Jeff that might make someone want to kill him, you will call me?"

"You can count on it, lieutenant, but as I've said, while Jeffy may not be perfect, there isn't anything in his character to even make anyone mad at him, let alone . . . this."

"I see."

Thus, thought Kavanaugh, did Mrs. Ripper speak of her little boy Jack. He stood up, smiled, extended his hand.

"Thank you for being so patient, Mrs. Dupre. We'll keep our men out front until further notice. You'll oblige me if you don't go out for a few days. If it's something urgent, I'll send you a car."

Minnie stood, frowning. "It's that bad, then?"

"It could be. We can't take any chances."

"No," said Minnie softly, "I guess we can't."

She saw him to the door, and stood there as he walked down the steps onto the street. The patrolman was posted where he'd been all night and all morning. Minnie felt like a prisoner, and not just because of the policeman outside. She felt trapped and threatened, and for the first time since she could remember, Minnie Dupre felt afraid. Afraid because she had no idea in the world who was after Jeff, or her, or who had killed Felix. If Felix had been killed. If, and if, and if. She shuddered, although it was a bright and sunny day.

Then she turned and closed the door and locked it.

31

Berwick Castle, July 1970

Neville sat at his desk, trying for the third time to compose a letter to Inland Revenue Service. To Smythe-Davies. It should have been easy. Neville had written similar letters many times over the last fifteen years. The content was always the same: asking for time. Begging for indulgence. He choked on the words, writing them, as he would have choked if he had been forced to speak them. As he sometimes was.

He would grow old writing these letters. He was barely able to keep up the payments on the interest he owed in death duties. To reduce the principal was a dream that had once seemed possible. Now, Neville wasn't so sure.

Smythe-Davies had grown fat and prosperous in the Revenue Service. He oozed confidence now, feeding, Neville felt, on his aristocratic victims. Smythe-Davies was a bureaucratic vampire, sucking, sucking, draining the lifeblood of families like the Fleets. From the young and enterprising, Smythe-Davies and his kind took away the hope of accumulating any substantial fortune. For those lucky enough to have inherited something, he took away the prospect of enjoying it. A very depressing man, in a very depressing job. Neville would have enjoyed killing Smythe-Davies in some particularly horrible way. But there were armies of Smythe-Davieses. The country specialized in breeding them now, the creeping, half-fawning, half-threatening bureaucrats. Only nuclear fission or the ultimate collapse of England would get them all, and by that time it would surely be too late.

Neville was plagued with a feeling that it might be too late already.

He had run through the Berwick paintings now. They were beginning on the family silver, and on some of Grandmother's Chinese porcelains.

There was a discreet knock on the library door.

"Come in."

Neville looked up, ashamed to be grateful for the interruption.

His wife's maid, a wispy-gray-haired countrywoman, kindly but myopic, poked her head in, blinking.

"Oh, sir," she said, "she's gone. The duchess is gone."

"Gone where, Dorothy?"

Neville frowned. Miranda hadn't left the castle for years. From time to time she'd take a walk in the rose garden, if the weather were especially fine, or ask for luncheon on one of the terraces. But gone? Miranda couldn't be gone.

"That's just it, your Grace, I don't know. She was there only an hour ago, about to take a little nap after lunch. And I came to wake her up, and she's gone."

Neville got up. It would be too disconcerting if Miranda took to wandering physically, as she had wandered in her mind these many years.

He remembered the London psychiatrist suggesting a psychiatric nurse. A very expensive psychiatric nurse. It had been out of the question then—when?—some years ago. It would be equally out of the question now.

They went up to Miranda's rooms. The rooms he had shared with her in those first happy years. Neville had moved out of Miranda's bedroom thirteen years ago. Thirteen very lonely years ago. If Miranda noticed his absence, she never mentioned it. Her world was well-populated with people and animals and events from the past. It made Neville shudder to think that he must be part of that past, too. Miranda treated him with unfailing kindness and even with affection. Just as she treated her dead brother, Johnny, or the dog she had loved as a ten-year-old.

They looked through the suite; it was, of course, empty.

"Can you tell," he asked the maid, "what she might have been wearing? If she wandered off, it might be necessary to call in the police."

The maid looked at him, boggling.

Miranda's condition was never mentioned to the duke. A fine pretense was kept up that she was perfectly well, just a bit vague. There had never been an incident. Until now.

It was understood, naturally, that the servants would keep an eye on the duchess and make sure that her medications were forever at hand. This they did, quietly and kindly, and until today Neville had had no cause to regret not having employed someone more scientific. What Miranda's idea of her condition might be, Neville had no way of knowing.

He couldn't bear to confront her with it.

When he walked in, as he often did in the old days, on a conversation between Miranda and one of her imaginary companions, she smiled sweetly and went right on with it, including Neville.

The maid went through Miranda's closets, muttering softly.

"The pale green garden-party dress," she said at last, "and the white pumps. Was there to be a party, your Grace?"

"Not that I knew of," he said dryly, wondering what in creation Miranda was up to. "I think we'd better speak to Father Devlin, and cook, and old Hilda, and try to make our own little search through the forest and the gardens, before we go alarming anybody else."

Dorothy nodded.

They went downstairs. It was a strange little group that fanned out through the rose garden, moving toward Berwick Forest. Neville had felt awkward approaching Father Devlin. Devlin had been the Berwick priest ever since Neville was a lad. But he wasn't quite a servant. Berwick kept him, and there had always been a small allowance, sometimes, lately, in arrears. But Neville had long since drifted away from the faith. Father Devlin was a kind old man and far from stupid. But Neville found little to say to the priest, and saw him seldom. Devlin preferred to dine with the servants, although he surely could have taken his meals alone in his rooms, and he was invited to dine with the family on holidays like Christmas and Easter.

But it had been years now since there was a family at Berwick worthy of the name.

The two men walked, separated by some fifty yards of grass and an infinity of spiritual differences.

They walked through the forest, and from time to time Neville called her name. She had been lost to him for so long that the physical fact of her disappearance was unreal.

They had walked for more than an hour when Neville signaled them to turn back. The shadows were lengthening. It would be nearly dark by the time they got back to Berwick.

Then it would be time to call in the police.

Searching for Miranda forced Neville to think of her in an unaccustomed way. Her illness had been so much a part of him for years now that he had almost stopped thinking of her as a person. She had become just another of his burdens, something to be dealt with as best he could.

Miranda!

He felt his eyes misting. His heart was suddenly full, filled with images of what she had been.

What they had been to each other.

Miranda had drifted away from him slowly, slipping into the gentle madness that now ruled her poor mind completely.

He stumbled on a small rock, blinked, came quickly out of his reverie.

Neville tried to recall who was in charge of the little local constabulary now. It used to be old Higgins. Maybe it still was. The worst crimes Berwick village ever saw were occasional fistfights at the pub. Now and then a car smash, or some very petty burglary. The police force consisted of three men, as closely as Neville could remember.

The little search party came straggling out of the forest.

Neville looked at his castle as it caught the last yellow rays of the slanting sunlight. The yellow light on the yellow stone of Berwickshire made the castle seem to be built of gold. It looked like happily-ever-after. Neville found himself smiling faintly at the irony of it. He, who had married the fair lady with the golden hair and brought her to live in this enchanted place. And all the enchantments had turned into the blackest sort of black magic. There was no room in a fairy tale for the likes of Mr. Smythe-Davies.

Neville paused on the lawn, looking up at the castle.

He didn't see the gardener's boy until young Slucutt was almost on him.

"Oh," said the lad, "begging your pardon, your Grace, but I found these. By the river, there."

Neville turned, startled.

The boy was about eight or nine, small for his age, brown from the sun. His eyes were brown too, and big in his head with awe at the discovery.

He held Miranda's white pumps gingerly by the heel straps, as though they might burn his hand.

Neville stared. He reached for the shoes, and tried for a smile.

"Thank you, Tommy," he said. "You're clever to have found them so quickly."

Then he went inside and called the police.

He did it calmly, mechanically. All Neville felt was a great numbness, a chill.

It was as though his heart had been transmuted from some brighter metal into lead. There were none of the immense racking waves of sorrow, of outrage that he had felt when the boy leaped from the tower.

Miranda was gone in fact now, but she had really been gone for a very long time. This final madness only put the seal on it. What Neville felt now was pure despair. It was as though all hope had gone out of his life. Everything he had lived for and cared deeply for was gone now.

Poor Miranda. At last she was at peace.

Neville wondered if he would ever find peace on this earth.

32

Jeff dragged himself through the day.

The feeling of being trapped got worse the longer he stayed in, and Kavanaugh had asked him not to go out.

Minnie was as thoughtful as ever, but nothing she could do made much difference. They found, quite quickly, that talking about Carla's death didn't help. Nor did speculating about who might be after Jeff.

The possibilities were so limited, they seemed not to exist at all.

Jeff took down three different books from his uncle's library, and found he couldn't get more than ten pages into any of them.

He resorted to magazines and picture books.

In midafternoon he realized he'd promised to call Polly for lunch. He couldn't face describing what had happened. Instead, dreading it, he put in a long-distance call to Cavolfiore. Beppo must be told, and Jeff knew he'd never forgive himself if he didn't do it personally.

The call was person-to-person.

Beppo was not at the *castello*. They didn't know when he might return. Reprieve. Jeff put down the receiver with a guilty rush of gratitude. At least the ugly moment was delayed. It would be so much better, if anything could make Carla's senseless death better, for Jeff to be able to tell her brother they'd caught the killer. Jeff wondered what the chances were of that ever happening.

In the late afternoon he went up to his room, changed into shorts and an old sweatshirt that said "PROPERTY OF THE HAA," and did exercises. One hundred each: sit-ups, push-ups, knee-bends, elevated scissor kicks. Then he took a very long, very hot shower and changed. Jeff dressed carefully now, as if for an occasion. Old gray flannel trousers, white button-down shirt, a paisley tie from Liberty's that Minnie had given him years ago, dark blue blazer. His one other decent pair of shoes. If he was going to hang around New York much longer, he told himself sternly, he'd better invest in some new clothes. He could probably use some new clothes anyway. Somehow Jeff never thought about buying clothing, until the old stuff wore out.

He felt better after the workout. He'd do that, and more, every day of his confinement. Jeff had read someplace about a prisoner of war who'd done the same thing. He felt like a prisoner of war. At least if you were a prisoner of war, you knew what side you were on. And who the enemy was. And where you were.

Jeff went downstairs, all the way to the kitchen.

Emmalee was bustling about, stirring something in a big mixing bowl with an enormous wire whisk.

"I have come," Jeff announced, "to raid the icebox."

He hadn't been able to eat much lunch. The exercise had made him ravenous. Emmalee's eyes lit right up. So did her smile. "You just raid away, then. You are all skin and bones. There's chocolate brownies in the cookie jar, there's leftover peach cobbler, there's three kinds of that fancy ice cream your uncle likes . . ."

She stopped then, quickly. They all did it, Minnie especially, but Jeff too. Referring to Felix as though he might walk in the door at any minute. He wondered how long it might be before he—or any of them—could absorb the fact that Felix was dead.

He smiled at her. "I'll start off conservatively," he said, "with some brownies and a big glass of milk."

Emmalee's brownies and her infallible good spirits made Jeff feel a little more human. How bad could a world be that contained Emmalee Jefferson and her brownies?

Bad enough to kill you.

179

He made plans. Maybe tomorrow he'd call Veii. For the first time in days Jeff thought about the dig, what he hoped they'd find, and what he'd do about it if they did. He thought about the *tombaroli*, about Corky and Fred and the diggers. How good it would be, to be in the trenches again, in the sun, sweating, putting the past together bit by bit, making it make sense.

He had to keep reminding himself that there were things in the world that made sense.

Jeff thought about Minnie and wished there might be some specific thing he could do to help her. To protect her, if protection was necessary. As Kavanaugh seemed to think it might be.

It would be so easy to simply step on a jet and disappear.

Minnie could go on some long, luxurious cruise and forget all this. For a while. But what would be waiting for her when she came home, as she surely must come home? And what would be waiting for Jeff? He was right, he felt it, in staying here. In trying to face out the danger. Because the danger wasn't going to get better if he ran away from it.

By long-established custom, Jeff and Minnie had cocktails in the library at seven.

They talked of many things, dancing around the issue. Jeff mentioned the sort of cruise he'd imagined for Minnie. Minnie showed more interest in Jeff's digs than she ever had before. It was hard going, try as they did: rolling the rock uphill. Their unstated dread filled the room with its own ominous weight. The air itself seemed hard to breathe. Jeff felt they should be doing something, something physical, barricading the windows, sharpening swords, anything.

He knew that if this kept up long enough, it would drive him frantic.

He also knew that maybe someone was counting on just that.

They got through supper, had coffee together, making small talk like very polite strangers who have just met on a rainy day in a resort hotel, prisoners of the weather. Jeff had never been good at small talk, but all the questions he wanted to ask of Minnie had been asked, and all of the answers led him nowhere.

He thought of tomorrow.

Kavanaugh would be here tomorrow, they'd see Felix's car, maybe some sense could be made of that. Maybe.

Minnie, as always, had made an effort in the way she

dressed. But the tension showed in her face, caught in her voice, crept into her fine dark eyes. There was a special wariness about her now. The Minnie Jeff knew from boyhood had no need to be wary. That Minnie was relaxed, easy, quick, and funny. This Minnie was haunted. Jeff would give a lot to exorcise the ghosts that made her look this way. To let Felix Dupre rest easy.

It was too late now to call Cavolfiore again. That could wait until tomorrow. And it was too late to call Polly Kunimara.

Carla's killing hadn't made *the New York Times*: maybe they didn't bother with such incidents. Maybe it happened too late at night. Tomorrow he'd call Morgan. Maybe he'd call Polly. He owed her an explanation. It would be a tough explanation to make. That seemed to be the standard, now, for Jeff Dupre in New York. Never let it be easy when it could be tough, maybe impossible. He looked at his watch. Ten-fifteen. He'd made it through one day, however gracelessly, however without profit. Jeff picked out the biggest picture book he could find, a study of medieval portraiture, kissed his aunt, and went to his room. There he paged through the book, trying to make some sense of it.

All the people in the book looked very stern to Jeff.

They did not look happy. They seemed to know that bad times were coming. It was not the book he should have chosen on this night.

He put the book on his bureau and looked, for the first time since he'd been in town, at the bookshelf in his bedroom. Schoolbooks, mostly, assigned reading from high school and college. Many a battered paperback stalked Jeff out of the past.

He pulled out a collection of Edna St. Vincent Millay.

It fell open at a page he'd marked one romantic seventeen-year-old afternoon. A poem about a death in winter, the death of a buck deer.

Now he lies there, his wild blood scalding the snow.

How strange a thing is death, bringing to his knees, bringing to his antlers

The buck in the snow.

And more, about the doe, waiting, vainly.

There had been much wild blood in old Edna. Edna had meant a lot to Jeff when he was sixteen, seventeen. He loved the extravagance of her, the generously spilled emotions, the candle burning at both ends. Her wild world seemed so very far from his own carefully constructed one: it was more exotic than China could ever possibly be.

How strange a thing is death.

Even when both his parents died, Jeff had never thought about death as death. As tragedy, as abandonment, sure, but not as the unfathomable emptiness and permanent mystery it seemed to be.

He put away the verse and turned off the light.

Tomorrow couldn't come fast enough for Jeff Dupre.

Jeff opened the door himself. There stood Ted Kavanaugh, grinning a Saturday grin. Jeff had forgotten it was Saturday. The lieutenant was wearing old blue jeans and a red alligator shirt and pilot-type sunglasses. Parked at the curb was an immaculate racing-green MG TC with lacquer-red gleaming from the underside of its bicycle-slim fenders.

"All set?" asked Kavanaugh.

"Sure. Would you like some coffee or anything?"

"No, thanks, I just had some."

Five minutes later they were snaking onto the FDR Drive with the midmorning get-out-of-town mob scene. Once they gained the drive, the traffic began moving briskly. Kavanaugh drove with effortless mastery. The MG was tuned to a fare-thee-well. It made a contented rumbling sound, such as might occur in the chest of a large and well-fed tiger.

"This," said Jeff, "is some beautiful machine."

"Thanks. It is my mistress, my religion, my obsession. And, they tell me, a good investment."

"We auction cars, sometimes. I could check it out for you, if you like."

"Hell, thanks, but I do that every week in the Sunday *Times*. The going rate for a good TC is between twelve and fifteen, sometimes a little more. Which isn't so bad when you consider I paid less than three, about five years ago."

"You do the restoration yourself?"

"All but the chrome and the leather."

"Lieutenant, you continue to amaze me. Us. You amazed my aunt a little too, yesterday."

"She's not a lady who amazes easily."

"No. She is not. I guess we all grow up with very distorted images of cops. Police."

"Cops is cops. There are good ones and bad ones. Mostly, we're sort of average."

Jeff looked at him. Kavanaugh was anything but average.

They drove in silence for a few minutes, the lieutenant inscrutable behind his dark glasses.

"The next question," said Kavanaugh absently, "usually runs something like, what's a nice guy like me doing in a job like this?"

"Very well, it looks like."

"My banker wouldn't say so. My parents think I'm wacky to go through law school and end up a cop. I think they have this picture of me directing traffic in the rain."

"And my family—my uncle at least—thought I was crazy to spend my life digging ditches, living on a schoolteacher's salary."

Right on, thought Kavanaugh. It's not too tough digging ditches out of a marble mansion on Sixty-fourth Street, is it, pal? "Flying," he suggested aloud, "in the face of tradition?"

"They wanted me to take over the family store."

"Some family store. Why didn't you, if that isn't too personal?"

"It's too commercial, somehow. I mean, logically—intellectually—I know there's nothing really wrong, or dishonest, or immoral about the auction business. But it's all so naked. The greed."

"That," said Ted, turning to his passenger with a grin, "is about what I felt when it came to joining a law firm."

"You don't find a whole lot of bureaucracy?"

Kavanaugh laughed. It was not a bitter laugh. "Well, you had a good look at my desk. Sure, there's enough paperwork to sink the Pentagon. And personalities, and problems, a rat race in blue. My boss has all the warm, human sympathy of Vlad the Impaler. But still, there is the possibility for improvement. There is just a chance, if I can hang in there, if I get a little lucky and don't lose my nerve, there's just a chance I can help. Change things. Do good. Plus, I enjoy it."

"I can see that."

"Probably not. I mean, your case is exceptional. It definitely isn't all riding around in MGs to look at smashed Jaguars. As a rule, rich people don't get themselves murdered. Like that old saying that rich people don't hang, which is also true. I spend most of my days on petty burglaries, assaults, family quarrels. This is a rich precinct, and we get very few murders."

"When you say you can change things, what do you mean?"

"I mean Hamlet Bendito. Sixteen. No father. His sister's a hooker with a three-hundred-dollar-a-day heroin habit. Hamlet works as a delivery boy at a liquor store. The sister's pimp thought he was doing the kid a favor by letting him run a little coke. For which the market in this neighborhood is bigger than you might imagine. This came to my attention. I had a little chat with Hamlet. Hamlet Bendito is a good kid all set to go the other way. Hamlet is now back in school, from whence he'd dropped out a year ago. He's playing on the varsity in basketball. Still working at the store. Not seeing his sister, who may be beyond repair. But Hamlet has a chance now. Maybe he won't make it. I think he will. Well, if I can bring off one of those, just one, in a year, that's better for me than all the wainscoting on Wall Street."

"That's amazing. You make me seem frivolous in my ditch."

Again the policeman laughed. "To each his ditch. You're not doing anyone any harm."

"Sure, but how much good am I doing?"

Kavanaugh casually flipped some coins into the maw of the exact-change machine on the Triborough Bridge. He shifted the sports car and they sped off.

"Who's counting? We do what we do. I am very, very far from being a saint myself."

The little green car darted through the thinning traffic with the quick, effortless precision of a gamefish. Soon they were winding along the Saw Mill River Parkway. They said little now, enjoying the sun and the wind they created by their own motion. There was a long straight stretch in the parkway, followed by a 180-degree curve that swung to the right. At the apex of the curve, the road cut under a big bridge built of handsomely rusticated stone.

"This," said Kavanaugh, "is where he lost it."

Jeff looked at the bridge, at the abutment on the far left where the Jaguar must have hit. There was no sign of a disturbance, no stain, no scratch or nick. Well, it was two weeks ago, and they must have cleaned it. Still, it looked unreal in the friendly sunshine of this Saturday morning. It was as though no accident had ever happened.

The Jaguar was not a pretty thing to see.

It was in a sturdily fenced lot in North White Plains, at the back of a large Sunoco station. The police, it seemed, leased the space for storing wrecks until their investigations had been completed.

"But," said Kavanaugh, "as far as we were concerned, the

investigation was completed. We had no reason to suspect it was anything but an accident."

"So it would have stayed here how long?"

"Until your aunt decided to sell it, which she still can, for parts. After two weeks' notice, she'd be billed for rent."

The car was in a corner, facing out. The elegant lines of its hood were crumpled like used Kleenex. The windshield was cracked and broken, and Jeff caught a glimpse of a smear that could only be dried blood. He quickly looked away, and prayed he wouldn't be sick. A plump man in bib overalls was prying open the hood of the Jaguar with a small crowbar. Kavanaugh introduced Jeff to Mr. Rankin, a retired master mechanic who free-lanced on such investigations.

Rankin poked and prodded the engine, which looked to Jeff like chromium spaghetti. Jeff couldn't tell whether this was because of the crash, or if it might be the natural state of Jaguars. Rankin made small noises of sympathy, as an old lady might, visiting some terminal sickbed.

"Pity, pity, it's a lovely thing, that Jag V-12," said the mechanic.

Jeff and Kavanaugh took a melancholy walk around the lot. It was numbing, the graveyard of bright metal and brave paint, dozens of cars, most of them new, crushed and broken and sometimes defiled beyond recognition.

"The fifty-five-mile limit," said Kavanaugh, "only helps a little."

"Catch Felix Dupré going fifty-five," said Jeff. "He was a good driver, but a fast one."

"And if anyone knew that, maybe they fixed up a little surprise for him?"

"I guess, if you knew enough about cars."

"I asked Rankin. He instantly came up with four sure ways to throw a Jaguar out of control. Of course, none of them would really guarantee a fatality."

"He hated seat belts. Thought it was part of a creeping fascist conspiracy on the part of the government. Infringement on civil liberties."

"If he'd worn a seat belt, he could be alive today."

They circled the lot, and came back to find the mechanic flat on his back under the jacked-up front end of the Jaguar. He was reposing on a little wheeled platform. His plump-sausage legs maneuvered the thing. More grunts and murmurs emerged, but they were undecipherable.

Finally he rolled himself back into daylight. In one hand he held a flashlight. In the other, he held a clear plastic bag containing four large wing nuts. He was grinning. "Very clever," he said with a professional's admiration for a job well done. "Very, very clever."

"What," asked Kavanaugh, "is so damned clever?"

Rankin stood up, puffing with the effort of it, brushing off his hands.

"There are probably three, maybe four easy ways to fix a Jaguar so it'll crash. Whoever did this used the one that's least likely to be proved. He loosened the wing nuts that control the front suspension, which would have the effect, at speed, on a sharp corner, of making the whole thing collapse. You'd lose control absolutely. And who can say how a nut got itself loose? Or, in this case, four of 'em. All the other ways, like changing the pads on the disk brakes, or fiddling with the pinions in the rack-and-pinion steering, or maybe setting up the front wheels to fly off, well, they're all possible, but fairly easy to detect. This? You'd have a very hard time proving they didn't work loose in the crash, or some kid was fiddling with the wreck since it's been here. Like that."

"But you're morally certain the suspension was fixed?" Kavanaugh's voice had an edge to it now.

"Beyond doubt, and I'll testify to that if you like. And you can dust these for prints, but if I'm right, naturally you won't find any."

"Naturally." Kavanaugh took the four nuts, in their clear plastic bag. Then he looked at Jeff Dupre. "And now," he said, "the fun really begins."

Jeff just looked at him. A big redheaded cop, broad as a barn, flat-muscled, quick, confident. Behind Kavanaugh Jeff could see the wreck of Felix's Jaguar. There could be no doubt now, no equivocating. There could be no playing around with possibilities. Someone had killed Felix. Maybe not in a way that could be proven in court, but murder all the same.

And someone had tried to kill Jeff.

And someone might just be after Minnie, too.

The feeling was visceral. Jeff had heard all the byplay between Kavanaugh and the mechanic. He had seen the wrecked Jaguar, cringed, didn't look too closely. He heard the words, and they seemed unreal, as though it was all part of a movie he had watched long ago, a film whose name he couldn't quite remember. Nor its ending.

There was this sinking sensation, as though the ground had turned into quicksand.

Nothing was what it seemed to be.

Yesterday Jeff had been afraid. He was still afraid. But now he was angry, and the anger felt good to him. It burned. He could sense it rising, hot, high-pressured, seeking an outlet. He knew that Kavanaugh wasn't a target for his anger. But Kavanaugh was there, waiting.

Jeff turned to him, trying to cool it, not trying hard enough. "You really promise that? That it's going to be fun?"

33

Berwick Castle, October 1971

It had been a very small wedding. Now it was over, and the guests had gone home. Neville looked at his bride. Bess smiled. Her smile warmed him. Neville had despaired of ever knowing happiness again.

And now there was Bess, and Bess was his, and there was light in his heart again.

The wedding night would hold no surprises for them. Even this seemed fitting. They had been lovers for more than six months now, during the year-long period of mourning that Neville felt obliged to observe in memory of Miranda. How fine Bess was, how strong and warmhearted and kind. Neville knew perfectly well that tongues were wagging, that people might say his second marriage was beneath him. And let them be damned. Bess was good stock, an officer's daughter, nothing fancy but nothing disreputable, either.

Miranda had been fancy.

Bess pleased him enormously. She had laughter in her, she was a realist, she had no girlish illusions. But she was young enough still, at thirty, to give him an heir. Her own child, Holly, was proof enough of that. A delightful child: he'd adopt her soon. Holly had been the flower girl today, five years old and carrying it off beautifully.

Bess knew how bad things had been at Berwick castle. The fact that Neville was nearly twice her age bothered her not at all. Bess wanted what Neville wanted: a happy home, a little comfort, some security. And poor as Neville might be, he could provide her that.

Neville's mourning for Miranda was a formal thing. In his heart he felt that she had left him long ago to wander in the netherworld of madness. When Miranda stepped into the river, Neville felt regret for the girl she had been, for the love they had known together, long ago.

The wet, muddy thing they had dragged from the river three miles downstream had nothing to do with the Miranda he remembered, with the girl he had loved. She had drowned in madness long before she drowned in fact.

Sometimes, to this day, Neville could see the image of the gardener's boy, eager and apologetic all at once, standing beside him, holding Miranda's white party shoes.

Bess had helped. She had helped a great deal.

It had started innocently one day soon after Miranda's funeral—she was buried beside her brother now, whose death she could never admit—when Neville had gone into Bess's bookshop-cum-lending library in the village to return one of Miranda's damned novels. Bess was just making tea, and asked if he'd like a cup. He'd like nothing better. He invited her to lunch at the castle not long after that. With, of course, the child. Little Holly Williams had been enchanted. For her, Berwick Castle was a fairy-tale thing, and her joy in it helped ease some small part of Neville's pain.

He got out the old Daimler and took them for long drives and pub lunches he could ill afford.

Eventually, Bess Williams came to Berwick not for lunch, but for dinner, and not with the little girl, but alone. It had flowed simply, easily, one small pleasure into other, greater pleasures.

One night they had found themselves in bed.

Neville had been afraid of sex, wondering if he could meet her expectations, young as she was, and vibrant with health. Bess reassured him, warmed him, loved him. No one would have called her brilliant or a beauty, and the Duke of Berwick might easily have captured almost any woman. But Bess suited him, fit into his life, matched his diminished expectations.

With Bess, he began to hope again.

It was even because of Bess he'd found the silversmith. And the silversmith was going to change Neville Fleet's life.

He'd wanted to give her a splendid wedding present, a jewel, a fur coat, whatever. He showed Bess what remained of his grandmother's jewels. Some of them were quite impressive. Bess looked intently at the contents of box after box. Most of it was Edwardian, some older, all quaint.

She leaned over and kissed his cheek. "You're a dear, Neville, and I suppose I'll wear some of it if we ever do anything fancy. But what I'd like is a simple gold ring, and if you must give me a wedding present, a small silver tea tray will do just beautifully. You must have those by the dozens."

That he did. They went to look in the silver closet. It was a small room, really, not a proper closet at all. The trays had a wall all to themselves, dozens and dozens of trays in felt-lined sleeves, musty and many of them black with tarnish. It had been so very long since any large-scale entertaining had been done at Berwick.

Bess had chosen one simple piecrust circle perhaps fourteen inches in diameter. Neville decided to have it engraved with her initials and the ducal crest.

Bess, as it happened, had heard of an excellent silversmith. "And not too dear, either," she had said with a laugh, ever mindful of the budget.

Neville had gone alone. The man lived in the next town, and it was the devil to find him. Almost as though he didn't want to be found. Tauranac, for this was his name, lived in a small thatched cottage at the end of a winding graveled lane. There was no sign, no indication of the occupant's profession. Rather diffidently Neville knocked on the weathered door. Silence. He knocked again.

A strange feeling came over Neville then. He looked left and right. He had a feeling of being watched, and not by friendly eyes. It was very lonely at the end of the silversmith's lane. There was a slight movement at the nearest window. Neville looked there.

Two dark eyes bored into his own eyes from behind the curtain, from under an unruly mass of dark brown hair, from under a high white forehead.

Neville knocked again.

The door opened.

A man stood there, the owner of the dark eyes, the unruly hair, the high white forehead.

Tauranac did not look as though he belonged in the countryside, and he did not look as though he welcomed visitors.

"Yes?"

Neville smiled. The man needed taming.

"Mrs. Williams, in Berwick, sent me to you. You are Tauranac?"

"I might be. What do you want of me?"

"To engrave a tray, if you would."

"Silver?"

"Silver."

Neville decided it was going to be tough sledding. He'd half made up his mind to forget the budget and take the tray to Asprey's, as he'd intended at first. Before Bess put him onto this odd creature.

"If it's too much trouble . . ."

"Come in, then."

The cottage had two main rooms and a small kitchen behind. One room was fitted out as a workroom. There was a sturdy workbench, with a metal lathe and what looked like a surgeon's battery of tools, and a chemist's burner, retorts for melting metal, hammers, punches, gravers, buffers, and many odd-looking instruments whose function the duke could only guess at.

A magnificent pear-shaped silver teapot stood on the bench. It was the only silver object in sight.

Neville unwrapped the tray. Bess had polished it herself.

Tauranac took it without a word, squinted, held it up to the light from the window, turned it slowly.

"It's fine work, sir. I make it Henry Cowper, London, about 1790, give or take a bit."

Neville knew nothing of silver. He was pleased if the thing were old and of some worth, because he wanted his Bess to have the finest he could provide. He handed the silversmith a sheet of stationery with the Fleet crest on it.

"What we want," he said, "is this crest and my wife's monogram, EWF, done whatever way you think would look best."

Tauranac looked at the crest, at the tray, at Neville. "You realize, do you, that this is a fine old piece, and you'd have me desecrate it. Sir, for fifty or so pounds I can duplicate this tray, crest and all, and Henry Cowper himself wouldn't know the difference. And you'd be saving the value of the original. I've often done that, recreated missing parts of sets, you know, or matched a piece for someone wanting a pair."

Neville looked at the man.

An idea was coming to him.

"Do you include the hallmarks and things like that?"

Tauranac looked at him. "It wouldn't be a true reproduction without 'em, now, would it?"

"Fifty pounds, you say?"

"More or less. Not much more. Less if you provide the silver, like an old damaged thing I could melt down."

Neville thought of the silver closet at Berwick and smiled. Provide the silver, indeed. He could plate Berwick Castle in silver and not feel the lack.

"Do it," he said. "I'll be back in an hour with the silver. I think," he said softly, not wanting to press his dream too hard, "that you and I may do quite a bit of business, Mr. Tauranac."

The dark eyes regarded Neville implacably. "If you say so, sir."

Then Tauranac smiled. He smelled money, and for the scent of money the silversmith had an infallibly accurate nose.

"In an hour, then," said the duke happily, shaking Tauranac's big, competent-looking hand.

"In an hour."

Tauranac stood in the doorway as the duke drove off. His smile was a thin, mocking smile, and it flickered on his lips like a flame.

34

Kavanaugh drove fast coming back from the automobile graveyard in North White Plains. The little MG flew down the Saw Mill River Parkway. Jeff found himself wondering what happened when a cop stopped a cop for speeding. Kavanaugh was a good driver. Jeff never for a moment felt insecure, small as the car was, open as it was.

Jeff had yet to get used to being a target. He didn't think like a target, darting and bobbing and doing whatever else targets are meant to do if they want to stay alive.

Jeff thought about that, too, as they drove.

There wasn't any point in talking. The wind took their words before they became audible. Kavanaugh tried once or twice, and shrugged, grinned, and drove faster.

The MG belonged to the road. It had an easy grace, moving, that was unlike most other cars Jeff knew. It greeted every bump and turning as a challenge to be met, quickly, defiantly, with the jaunty awareness of those nimble forest creatures who compensate for their small size with the deftness of their maneuverings. Driving with Ted Kavanaugh was an adventure of the best kind. Jeff was grateful in spite of the grim result of their investigation.

The air rushing by seemed fresher. The open car gave Jeff a sense of having escaped from a prison, which he cherished all the more for knowing that it would soon be over.

Kavanaugh slowed for a toll booth. Jeff fished in his trousers and handed the detective a quarter.

Kavanaugh grinned. "Thanks," he said. "Another sleazy payoff."

Kavanaugh's big hand moved lightly on the stick shift. The MG was doing fifty before they reached the end of the toll lane, and seventy by the time they'd gained the unrestricted highway. Like many big men, Kavanaugh moved with a deceptive smoothness. His hand on the stick shift might have been stroking a guitar, or a woman. Jeff could imagine the velocity of those hands, unleashed.

They drove in silence until Kavanaugh slowed again for the Triborough Bridge toll. Again Jeff handed him money. Again, the grin.

"I want," said Kavanaugh in the slow-moving traffic on the bridge, "to talk. Do you mind stopping by my place?"

"Of course not."

Kavanaugh said nothing, only nodded.

Jeff felt embarrassed because of the simple inescapable fact that going to wherever Kavanaugh lived suddenly put Jeff's relationship with the detective in a new dimension. Jeff had never bothered to think about what a policeman's life must be, where he lived, what he ate, who loved him. Jeff had considered the detective as a kind of public service, an appliance to be turned on and off like a light switch, handy when you wanted it, out of mind when you didn't. Even though your life could depend on it.

Suddenly, on the bridge, Jeff felt vulnerable. The MG offered no more protection than a roller skate. The traffic seemed to crawl. After the freedom of the open road, it was oppressive. They eased onto the exit ramp and Kavanaugh picked up some speed.

From the ramp they could see traffic inching down the FDR Drive. Jeff could feel the city closing in on him. The early returners were coming back from wherever they'd been.

Impulsively Kavanaugh pulled the MG onto 125th Street.

Heat danced in the thick air. Windows in Harlem were opened to the nonexistent breeze, and it seemed that half the radios in the world were blaring. Disco fought reggae. Sultry Latin beats and the mindless repetitive chanting that someone had mislabeled soul joined a sad, obsessive Dixieland saxophone as part of a mad, tragic symphony whose theme was not-enough. Not enough money, not enough hope, nothing to do but fry your brains. They stopped, trapped by a red light.

Jeff thought the tires might melt, or his brain, if they didn't get moving soon.

They moved.

Kavanaugh cut down Second Avenue. The character of the neighborhood changed block by block, improving. The change wasn't dramatic, just a small abatement of the noise, fewer burnt-out buildings, more trees. Jeff felt that he could almost breathe again.

They stopped for another red light at the corner of Ninety-eighth Street. Three stick-skinny little black girls, maybe eight years old, were jumping rope. They wore immaculate pastel-colored party dresses and vast grins. One girl wore blue, another pink, another lemon-sherbet yellow. The two girls who swung the rope were chanting, singing a song whose words Jeff couldn't quite make out, keeping up the rhythm. The girl jumping seemed to soar, her eyes half-closed in an almost religious ecstasy, entirely lost in the game, not missing a beat, holding on to the moment.

The MG pulled away. Jeff thought that the happy little black girl might go right on jumping, blissfully, forever.

He wished he could join her.

Kavanaugh lived in the middle of the block between Second and Third Avenues on East Eighty-fourth Street. It was a mixed sort of street, with some fashionable town houses, some shops, the occasional plastic high-rise. Ted pulled up to a shabby structure that seemed to be a carriage house from Victorian times, yellow paint peeling, a big "PRIVATE DRIVE: KEEP OUT" sign painted in large white letters on a flaking black carriage-entrance door. The policeman deftly turned his MG into the drive, at the same time pressing a button under the dashboard. With startling speed and almost unearthly silence the carriage door rose. In the darkness beyond, a light clicked on. Ted drove in, far in, all the way to the back of the deep space, then pushed the button again. The door rolled shut with a decisive thud.

The light from one narrow fluorescent fixture only partly illuminated the huge echoing space. Jeff could make out the contours of a big old-fashioned touring car that stood draped in a tarp in the far corner. It might have been a Rolls-Royce. He followed Ted to an old iron staircase that paralleled the wall, climbing to the next floor, a climb of some thirty feet. The old staircase echoed beneath their feet with the thunder and clang of some Wagnerian elf banging his heart out in a dark cave.

The door was double-locked and heavy, thick wood, Jeff

guessed, plated in steel. Ted found his keys, unlocked it quickly, and swung it open.

Jeff stood amazed. He'd never seen a space quite like it.

They stood in a small foyer floored with softly polished teak. Beyond them stretched one enormous room, its walls and soaring ceiling all painted white, with straw mats on the floor. The back wall was one sweep of window maybe thirty feet wide, perhaps fifteen feet high. Beyond it was a narrow terrace massed with green plantings and flowers. There was no free-standing furniture in the great room, but only a simple wooden bench which ran around all three of its walls and seemed to serve as couch and coffee table.

Ted smiled, seeing his guest's reaction. "I'll have to ask you to take off your shoes, Mr. Dupre, but there are plenty of slippers."

To prove it, he reached into a closet and produced a pair of flat, heelless scuffs woven of the same straw as the matting.

"Incredible," was all Jeff could say, and he sensed it wasn't enough.

"A guy I know," said Kavanaugh, "keeps it as a workshop. Lets me live here for—are you ready?—a hundred bucks a month. It gives him some sort of a tax break. And he likes the idea of fuzz on the premises."

"Wow. And wow again."

They took off their shoes, put on the slippers, and walked into the big room. The light was almost dazzling. Jeff saw, against the back wall, one old Japanese scroll hanging in dramatic contrast to the white sweep of the wall behind it. The scroll was mounted on old silk brocade, hung from a lacquered wooden rod. It depicted three stalks of bamboo bending in a wind, painted in shades of gray and black, with just a few brush strokes. Yet the thing was absolutely alive. Beneath the scroll, on the bench, was a black lacquer tray filled with polished black pebbles. From the pebbles sprouted three perfect blue irises. They were the only touch of color in the room.

"Am I," Jeff asked, "dealing with New York's first Zen Buddhist police officer?"

Kavanaugh laughed. "Not quite. But I like what they do with space, and—the sparseness, the balance—that is part of it. Part of their religion. Now. How about a drink, a beer, coffee, tea . . ."

"Beer sounds great, thanks."

Jeff walked around the room. The benches were beautifully crafted from some warm-toned wood, not teak, whose name he did not know. The bench tops were thick, and the legs had been perfectly dovetailed into the thickness of the top. Corners were precisely mitered. The benches were deep, perhaps three feet. Underneath them, neatly spaced, but plainly in view, were tucked rows of wicker trunks, their strawlike color and uneven texture playing nicely against the warmth and smoothness of the surrounding wood. Everything had been thought of, calculated, sculptured, balanced, weighed. Now Jeff began to see that the big, simple room wasn't quite as simple as it first appeared. Set with precision into the wall nearest the window on the left were three flush doors, white, invisible at first glance. One must be a bathroom. He wondered what the others were: closets, maybe, or a bedroom. The kitchen, too, was sunk into the same wall, all white, flush-doored white cabinets, butcher-block counters, a big flush-doored white refrigerator-freezer. The terrace outside had no furniture either, but only plantings: bamboo, bonsai trees in decorative tubs, dwarf pines of an Oriental aspect, and planters filled with bright impatiens: pink and white and lacquer-red.

Ted handed him a beer in a tall, heavy Danish pilsner glass.

"Cheers," said the policeman.

"Cheers, yourself. I really am amazed."

"My folks saw it and all but accused me of taking big fat bribes. But the owner gutted the space for me and put in the window and the kitchen, and I built the benches and the other stuff myself, piece by piece, in my dad's workshop. The scroll, I just plain went into hock for."

"Well worth it."

Jeff sat on one of the benches. He sipped the beer. It was some kind of ale. Jeff smiled. He liked ale better than beer anyhow. Kavanaugh sat cross-legged on the floor. He sipped the ale, then set the glass down.

"The precinct house is no place to talk," Ted began. "It can be a zoo. And please don't think I'm paranoid or anything, about your aunt's place, but we really can't take chances. What I want, Mr. Dupre, is for you to tell me a story. In your own words, what you think might be happening here."

"Is it permitted for you to call me Jeff?"

Kavanaugh grinned. "It sure is, Jeff, and thanks—if you call me Ted. One thing I need more on—one thing of many—is the Countess di Cavolfiore."

Jeff blinked, picked up his glass, drank. More than a sip

this time. He hated to admit to himself that, ever since he'd climbed into Kavanaugh's car that morning, he hadn't once thought about her. He put the glass down slowly and rubbed his eyes. It didn't erase the sudden chilling image of her lying on the sidewalk.

"We've got to find her brother. Beppo di Cavolfiore."

"I'm glad you reminded me."

Ted stood up, lifting his lean frame in one fluid motion, and walked to the far side of the room. There, on the bench, was an inconspicuous walnut box. He opened the box to reveal a phone system, one receiver and three call buttons. Ted quickly dialed a number.

"Martha? Kavanaugh here. Can you get Interpol in Rome? Yes. Italy, Martha, where the pope is. Right. A find-and-detain on an Italian citizen, Count Beppo—that's B, as in bummer, E as in Ex-Lax, P as in pistol, P again, as in St. Peter's, O as in Omigod. Last name, same as the lady in the morgue, di Cavolfiore. You have that somewhere, I don't have to spell it? Right, Martha. I love you too. Thanks. No, not criminal. We just want to talk to him. He should call me."

He put down the phone.

"She's lovely, is our Martha. Mother of us all."

"I'm going to have to tell him. And then you may have two people after me."

"He's given to violence, Count Beppo?"

"Not that I know of, and I'd guess not. But he's surely not above using his sister. He might have thought of her as a possible meal ticket. The family finances at Cavolfiore were not very good at all. As you know, she came here with a few of the family treasures to sell. Such as they were."

"Fakes?"

"No, they're real enough. One very good tapestry. Two minor paintings, two-thirds of an old altarpiece. And a marble head that's probably a hundred-year-old copy. Minor, all of them, but far from worthless. Worth possibly a hundred thousand, all told, and more if they sold the complete set of four tapestries."

"Jeff, you have to realize people have killed in this town for less than ten bucks. I mean, what might seem minor to a Dupre . . ."

Jeff laughed. "I get it. But Beppo sent her here, there's no point in his killing her. Or me. Hell, I was all set to sell them, if she wanted me to."

"Could they be stolen? There's a lot of that going around. Out of some cathedral in France yesterday, on to Rio tomorrow. The jet age has done wonders for fences. And half the stuff isn't properly recorded at all."

"I know," said Jeff, "it happens in my line of work too, the grave robbers and all. But Carla was very specific about that, and I believed her."

"You were very close?"

"We were very close. Unless it was for some enormous reason—not just because her dumb brother asked her to—Carla wouldn't, probably couldn't, say a thing that wasn't true. She said the stuff, the good stuff, such as they had left of it, was all stored in her mother's bedroom at Cavolfiore, and I surely have no reason to doubt that."

"But you never actually saw the things there?"

"No. No, I didn't."

Jeff stood up and walked across the big room to the scroll. He grew calmer just looking at it. Those bamboo stalks had been swaying gracefully in some unfelt wind for hundreds of years now. They'd probably go right on swaying for hundreds of years more, long after Jeff and Ted and the House of Dupre had turned to dust. Somehow it was reassuring. He noticed a small photograph in an antique bronze frame, an oval delicately wreathed in tiny laurel leaves, with a magnificently carved ribbon bow on the top. Jeff looked at the photograph in the frame. It was a young girl, no older than mid-twenties, with startling almond-shaped eyes. She was laughing. And she was absolutely lovely, the kind of face that might burn holes in your memory for years. Jeff stared at it dumbly, not wanting to believe his eyes.

"The lady," said Ted's voice softly from behind, "who wouldn't marry a cop."

It was Polly Kunimara.

Jeff turned slowly and looked at Ted Kavanaugh. "I know Polly. She works at Dupre's."

Ted's recovery was quick, maybe too quick. He smiled. "Yes. Well, it was five or so years ago, Jeff. She's a very special lady."

"You're right."

Jeff looked around the room once more. Polly! Well, why not? They might have met in a dozen ways, both living in the neighborhood. Hell, the precinct house was just around the corner from Dupre's. Then why was it so disturbing? For Kavanaugh to want Polly. To have wanted her, rather, and not gotten her.

He blinked, turned away, walked back to the bench where his drink waited. He took a gulp of it. "I have a friend," said

Jeff quietly, "who insists that there are only two hundred people in the entire world."

"Less," said Ted. "Our numbers get fewer every day."

Shadows were crawling across the terrace. Jeff found himself thinking, unavoidably, of a five-years-ago Polly, of Polly with Ted, of this room, and how much of her must be in it, of what they might have done here. He thought these things, and hated himself for thinking them. The ale tasted more bitter than ale should.

Ted's eyes never left his face. "Maybe you think my heavy Japanese number up here is Polly's doing. Well, would you believe it started with my karate teacher? Who definitely does not resemble Miss Kunimara. I keep the picture because I keep very fond memories of the lady. But I have no claim on her, Jeff."

Jeff looked at him. Sure. Some karate instructor. He'd never thought that Polly had been waiting all her life for Jeff Dupre to come along. But it was weird, all the same, her and Kavanaugh. There had been a rapport between Jeff and the big detective, a special kind of tension. Now there was more tension. If the case involved Dupre's, it might involve Polly. Kavanaugh would be seeing her, questioning her. Hell, it was his job. But Jeff wondered where that would leave him.

"It just took me by surprise. Hell, I barely know the girl. But then, everything today has been a surprise. What's the next step, Ted?"

"I call a patrol car and you go home in it. And you give these to whoever's in the car"—he handed Jeff the plastic bag with the Jaguar's wing nuts in it—"and we get them to the lab, which will probably find nothing, because if someone really did fix the Jag, he'd be smart enough to wear gloves. More likely, he'd use a wrench, or pliers."

"But the mechanic would testify, if it came to that?"

"He would give a professional opinion. And his opinion is very widely regarded."

"So we're morally certain someone killed Felix."

"We've got to assume that."

"I'd better be going."

Ted went to his hidden phone again, and in five minutes a patrol car was at the door. Ted walked down with him, opened a small door in the big panel of the carriage entrance, smiled, and shook hands.

"It may not look like it, Jeff, but we made some progress today."

"Thanks. And thanks for the drink. We'll talk on Monday?"

"Right. So long, then."

Kavanaugh watched him to the patrol car. Jeff climbed into the backseat and the car moved off. He felt as though he'd fought all the wars in history. Images raced through his mind, bounced off other images, crashed, exploded, turned into other, more frightening images. Felix and Minnie and Jeff all adrift in a yellow sailboat, headed for the rocks, the crashing surf, and there was no sail, no rudder. Polly, laughing up from the photograph frame. Kavanaugh's MG, and the unexpected elegance of his apartment. Ted and Polly together.

Jeff and Polly.

Jeff and Carla.

The patrol car pulled up to the Dupre house, not a minute too soon. Jeff got out. He felt like a target now. Kavanaugh had said that was a healthy way to feel. Unintentional irony. The healthy target.

Jeff walked quickly up the steps, nodding at the patrolman.

The healthy target.

Any other day, Jeff might have smiled.

35

Minnie Dupre looked up expectantly.

All the way back from Ted Kavanaugh's apartment Jeff had thought about this moment, about what he'd tell her, and how much. It wasn't a hard fact. Yet. Still, he loved her too much to play games.

He sat down. There hadn't been time to rehearse any slick speeches. Jeff wasn't much good at slick speeches anyway.

"The answer," he said gently, "seems to be maybe. The car might have been fixed. So it's a possibility we've got to face, even though it isn't one-hundred-percent sure."

She looked at him and past him. Without turning, Jeff knew her eyes were focused on the little Fragonard drawing Felix had given her as a wedding present so long ago.

"There is," she said at last, "some sort of relief in knowing you have hit the absolute rock bottom, isn't there?"

He got up and went to the little settee, knelt, and took her hand in his. Her hand was cold. It was trembling.

"Oh, Minnie," he said, "what can I do?"

She stroked his head as though he were some faithful old dog.

For a long moment they said nothing.

She sighed. "I feel so empty, Jeffy," she said. "Empty as a dry well. I'm not even sure there's any hate in me now, for whoever did this thing."

"I'm learning," he said. "Slowly but surely, I am learning how to hate."

It wasn't a lesson he'd ever wanted.

"Tell me," she said at last, "all about it. About what you did today."

He told her quickly, not dwelling on the ugliest parts. Except that the whole thing was pretty ugly.

They sat alone in the library, trapped.

Jeff had a sense of being locked in, and in fact they were locked in the big house. The sentinels changed, working eight-hour shifts. The house was guarded, in front at least, all around the clock. Jeff wondered—he hadn't thought to ask—how long the New York police could afford to keep that up. And if it would do any good.

You had to hope it would do some good.

You had to hope the thing would wind up, that Kavanaugh would find the missing evidence.

If there was any evidence to find.

It was all too neat: they had gone over the critical areas just inside Central Park, where the sniper must have stood, and found nothing.

There was no evidence at all about the speeding car that had struck Jeff.

And today's adventure had developed nothing that would bear up in court. Unless, by some miracle, there were fingerprints.

"Well," he said at last, "we don't know for sure. We may never know. But Kavanaugh had a good man out there, a mechanic, and he thought it had been tampered with."

"I see," she said. "Or maybe I don't. Isn't this a rather serious question to leave hanging?"

"We aren't leaving it, not for a minute. The crucial parts are being looked at right now, in the police laboratory. But Kavanaugh warned me—it might not be provable."

"What a thing to live with. I'm not sure I can."

Jeff looked at his aunt, sharing the feeling of helplessness.

The worst thing was, you did live with it. With anything. You just went right on breathing, and Carla was just as dead as ever. And the grief and the rage were too big to handle. They handled themselves, somehow, but you couldn't measure them or classify them or roll them up and stash them away in some nice little pigeonhole for future reference. They were there, burning in your heart, tearing at your nerves, churning and seething inside you. And you lived with it, and there was very little in all the world anyone else could do to help.

"If the car was fixed," Jeff said, "then it has to be the same people who are after me. Small consolation."

Minnie looked away. "I am beginning," she said flatly, "to understand vengeance. The desire to get some of one's own back. And I hate . . . whoever this is even more for making me feel that way. It's such a cheap feeling."

"We'll get him—them. I was impressed by Kavanaugh today. He is not, whatever your image of a typical cop may be, typical."

"No," said Minnie, "I rather think not."

Hastings came in then. "Telephone for you, Mr. Jeff."

It was Beppo, calling from a friend's house on Sardinia. He had already heard the news from Kavanaugh. Jeff had rehearsed what he might say when this moment came, and hated himself for rehearsing, and now he forgot the words he'd planned to say. His sadness was too big to be covered by set speeches. Beppo held up surprisingly well in his grief. Jeff had been prepared for almost any kind of outrageous behavior; what he got was quiet dignity. Maybe some fragment of Carla's strong character was lurking in her brother's chromosomes after all. Their talk was brief. Carla would be buried at Cavolfiore. Jeff offered to accompany the casket. Beppo declined, too politely, his voice tense and frosty with the unstated accusation. It would be unnecessary. As for the art objects, if Jeff would submit a written estimate, Beppo would, indeed, consider selling. Thank you and good-bye.

Jeff was touched by Beppo's attitude. The poor bastard had lost everything now that Carla had gone. He'd lost the center of his gypsy existence. Who would keep up Cavolfiore now? The old castle was half in ruins as it was. Poor Beppo. He hadn't even asked about the objects Carla had brought to Dupre's. Jeff made a mental note to write him the details tomorrow.

Jeff's relief was a quick and palpable thing. He would never have to see or speak to Beppo di Cavolfiore again. Another door had closed on his sorrow now. If he could contain it, Jeff hoped, it might be easier to deal with. And there would have been no chance of containing it had Beppo decided to become a continuing presence in Jeff's life.

Minnie was reading again when Jeff got back to the library.

"Carla's brother," he said, "from Sardinia."

"How was he?"

"Way better than I expected. He was fine. As fine as you could be, hearing something like that."

Minnie smiled a small sad smile. "When people come up to you and say they know just how you feel, I could stick pins in them. No one knows how you feel. In the first few days or so after Felix's death, I didn't know myself how I felt. The idea that grief can be diffused by sharing, as though it were some kind of yard goods, is simply not true."

Jeff laughed then. It wasn't his happiest laugh, but it came quick and uninvited and he let it out. "If you keep on like that, Minnie, I'm going to tell you I know just how you feel. Because, in a way, I think I do."

"Maybe you do, darling. I won't deny it."

Then they went down to dinner and talked of happier things.

It wasn't easy to feel threatened in Felix Dupre's house.

This didn't make Felix one bit less dead, nor Jeff less in danger. It was what might happen out of the house that mattered. And Jeff wanted to be out in the air, breathing free, without the frightening necessity of keeping his back to the wall.

It seemed a simple thing, to be able to walk outside without thinking twice about being in danger.

A simple thing, surely. But suddenly it was the most important thing in Jeff's world.

36

Berwick Castle, December 1972

For the first time in many years Neville Fleet felt that he was in control of his fate. It was a good feeling, warming his heart, adding new vigor to his walk.

In the village they attributed the duke's newfound happiness to his marriage. And Neville was happy with Bess, with the little girl, and with the news Bess had brought two months ago, that she was pregnant. A new heir for Berwick! Another chance, just when Neville had given up hoping.

It gave new urgency to his plans for the silversmith Tauranac.

For it was through the skills of the enigmatic silversmith that Neville planned to restore the tattered glory of Berwick.

The plan was a simple one, like all the best plans. And for a year now it had worked. Tauranac made reproductions of antique silver from the Berwick collection, and the reproductions were sold as real by the House of Dupre in New York. The profits were huge.

A teapot that might cost a hundred pounds to make could sell for ten times that. The risk seemed negligible. How, after all, could Neville be blamed? He was merely selling off the castle's cupboards. If an object turned out to be a copy, then one of his ancestors had been cheated. Of course, he interspersed certain real pieces with the copies. And Neville continued to sell the occasional authentic painting, tapestry, or chair.

It was a shame to pull such a sly trick on his old friend Felix. But hadn't the government played tricks on Neville? The additional income generated by the Tauranac copies was keeping Smythe-Davies at bay. Neville could even imagine expanding the operation, copying paintings, maybe, or furniture.

But that would be in the future. He had Tauranac, and Tauranac's skill, now.

There was something deliberately secretive about the silversmith. Neville never asked why he chose such a solitary, almost hermitlike existence. And Tauranac, typically, volunteered nothing.

There was some dark shadow over the man's past. He should, by right of accomplishment, be working for one of the top London or Paris jewelers. Instead, he lived alone, in the very heart of England's farm country, barely getting by on repair work and the occasional commission like Neville's tray.

All that would change now.

The entailed estates of Berwick Castle included slightly more than ten thousand acres, most of it forest. In the forest were several cottages very similar to the one Tauranac had chosen on his own. Neville offered him one of these, rent-free, and a salary that must be far more than he could be earning now. A pittance, by comparison with the profits to be gotten from selling his copies as real.

The rent-free cottage was most appealing to Tauranac, especially after Neville fixed it up a bit. It was even more secluded than where he'd lived before.

Part of Tauranac's cottage was outfitted as a silversmith's shop, with all of the man's old tools and several new ones, power drills and buffers. In the silent fastness of Berwick Forest, no one was likely to come upon the cottage. And if they did, thought Neville, what of it? Surely it was permitted for the Duke of Berwick to engage his own court silversmith, as it were.

If Tauranac guessed what was happening to the copies he made, he never hinted at it. No more did Neville volunteer. Three of the Tauranac replicas had already been sold at Dupre's. The profit was well over one hundred thousand dollars. Neville was pleased. He looked forward to Morgan St. James's visit this afternoon.

St James came to Berwick now, instead of Felix Dupre.

St. James was being groomed, Neville knew, to take Felix's place in the House of Dupre. A very smooth article was St. James. They got on well, although there was nothing of the rapport that Neville had shared for so many years with Felix. There was always something a trace too eager-to-please about St. James, a hint that he might not quite belong on the first team.

When Morgan St. James arrived, Neville served him tea, then brought him into the red drawing room, where several objects were laid out on a table, ready to be considered for sale at Dupre's.

Morgan looked at an old folio of etchings, botanical prints from the sixteenth century that might have been, but were not, by Besseler. "Very fine," he said, "very fine. This sort of thing is getting to be quite fashionable nowadays. I make them at no less than a thousand per plate, and there are . . . how many?"

"Twenty-six plates, and in good condition."

Neville had long since stopped feeling timid about the sales. Now he became something of a salesman, polishing the goods, promoting their quality wherever he could.

Morgan moved down the table. There was a handsome silver tankard that must hold nearly a quart, lidded, absolutely simple but for thick turned moldings at the rim and at the base. An irregular row of four roughly square hallmarks appeared on the side, near the top, adjacent to the handle.

He picked the tankard up, squinted a bit, turned it in his hands. And he looked at Neville with an expression Neville had never before seen on the bland face of Felix Dupre's general manager.

St. James was mocking him.

Gently perhaps, but unmistakably, the fellow was letting it be known that he knew about the tankard. Which had come up from Tauranac's workshop only last week, patinated, buffed to simulate wear, tarnished, and only fairly well-polished.

"Very convincing, your Grace," said St. James smoothly, "but I really can't allow you to go on cheating us like this. You are asking us to take a serious risk, you see, and for very little reward."

It had been a shrewd guess. Neville was thunderstruck.

"I don't know what you mean, St. James!"

Morgan smiled. "Come, come. Of course you do. The Cowper platter. The Bateman salt cellars. The Fountain tureen. In all, you've passed no less than a dozen replicas through Dupre's in the last few years. I feel it is time we came to some happier arrangement."

Neville felt flushed. Suddenly he had some trouble breathing.

"You can prove nothing!"

It had been the wrong thing to say. He knew this as soon as the words were out. The look on St. James's face was one of undisguised triumph. Damn!

"Try me."

"But . . ."

"Of course, it will be a festival for the press."

Neville simply looked at him, not willing to believe what his ears plainly heard.

"They do so love a scandal, especially when it involves a peer of the realm."

"You wouldn't dare!"

"Would I not? This piece aside—and it is a handsome one, isn't it?—there are two other copies in New York, awaiting sale. I have only to unmask them. And you. It can be done with a phone call, and at no risk to me. I'd emerge as some sort of hero. You, on the other hand . . ."

His words trailed off like smoke. The silence that followed seemed to ring with the echoes of shattered expectations.

Finally Neville spoke. It was the voice of a haunted man. "What," he asked, dreading the answer, "do you want me to do?"

A smile formed on St. James's face. It was not a pretty thing to see. When he spoke, it was softly. He might have been recommending a new vintage of Burgundy. "You'll see," said St. James persuasively, "that I can be a considerable help in this venture."

When St. James left, soon after, he took the replica tankard, the folio of etchings, and two small paintings.

Neville went with him to the door.

Neville stood in the open door for a long time after St. James had driven his little rented car out through the perimeter wall of the castle. All the good feeling of control, of triumph even, had gone. To be found out so easily! St. James never said precisely how he knew. It didn't matter: he knew. And was ruthless enough to act on the knowledge.

The little bounder!

Neville made himself a promise as he stood in the open doorway of Berwick Castle. He promised himself that one day he would regain control of his destiny, for once and forever.

In the meantime, he would wait, and make such compromises as seemed necessary. But he would not wait forever.

It would be impossible for him ever to really trust St. James. Yet, before very long, Neville knew that the arrangement was working better than it ever had done. The sales continued, shrewdly planned and smoothly executed. On Morgan's advice he began making occasional trips to New York, opened a bank account there in which St. James could deposit the proceeds discreetly. Smythe-Davies and that lot need never know!

And in the spring Bess gave birth to a boy.

An heir for Berwick! Maybe the luck of the Fleets had turned, after all. Neville kissed Bess and the small pink object on whose tiny shoulders reposed the entire future of Berwick. There were tears in Neville's eyes, but he managed not to shed them. Not then.

"You have made me happier than I can say," said Neville to Bess, who lay beaming in their bedroom at the castle, "happier, dear Bess, than I dared to hope I might be, ever again."

The baby screamed. Bess drew him closer and offered her breast. Little Neville fell silent, reaching with small red hands, making eager gurgling noises as he drew nourishment from his mother.

The House of Dupre seemed very far away then.

37

The news of the Berwick Castle auction vibrated through the art world with the insistence of an imminent earthquake.

There were so few great objects left outside of museums, that a kind of desperation infected everyone who lusted after the chalice.

In New York, the curator of Roman antiquities of the Metropolitan Museum, Frederik von Kronholtz, got to work earlier than usual. He didn't even stop at his small, crowded office, but continued down the musty hallway and through an inconspicuous door that led into the main exhibition galleries.

Now was the best time, before the mobs came. The guards were just beginning to take their places. Alone, dwarfed by the immense space of the great staircase, von Kronholtz slowly climbed it. How Roman it was, with its vast columns, its soaring vaults and arches, with a resonance of marble and bronze.

It was a place to dream Roman dreams.

Frederik von Kronholtz had many dreams, but today one was predominant, sweeping all the other, lesser schemes aside.

Today he must convince his boss to find perhaps four million dollars to buy the Winchcombe Chalice. And convincing the elusive Billy Berkeley of anything was never easy.

Von Kronholtz had spent most of his life building the great Roman collection of the Met. The Winchcombe Chalice would be the keystone of this collection, beyond question the finest example of late-Roman goldwork extant. He had seen the cup, of course, but only once, and many years ago. Still, the memory of it sang in his soul. Berkeley was new at his job, flashy, charming, young. A man who prided himself upon the diversity of his interests. Dilettantism was more like it, in von Kronholtz's disciplined mind. Still, he must have the chalice. The Met must have it. Trustees must be persuaded to write large checks. Very large checks. Even then, it wouldn't be a sure thing.

The competition would be fierce.

Oswald Webster, damn him to hell, would probably be after it. Not to mention the vastly well-endowed Getty Museum in Malibu. And who-knew-what Arabian oil magnate or Japanese tycoon or Swiss gnome.

Von Kronholtz reached the top of the huge staircase and moved directly into the European-painting galleries. He did not need to look at his own wing for inspiration: he knew every object in it by heart.

But the great Velazquez portrait always cheered him.

Not only because it was possibly the best portrait he had ever been privileged to see, but because the story of its pursuit and eventual capture by the Met was precisely the sort of coup he hoped to pull off with the Winchcombe Chalice.

Velázquez had painted the thing in Rome, in 1649 or 1650. It had come into the possession of the Earl of Radnor at Longford Castle. And when the earl decided to sell the painting, a hue and cry went up that reverberated through all England. Painted by a Spaniard in Italy, a portrait of a mulatto servant, still it was considered to be an English national treasure. But—like the Winchcombe Chalice—it was also the owner's personal property. Only if a matching fund could be raised might the painting stay in England. And when asked to put their pounds and shillings where their outrage had been, the English failed sadly. The portrait was auctioned off in London, and the Met took it for a most uncool five million dollars, by far the highest price ever paid for a painting until that time.

Von Kronholtz walked into the gallery and smiled. There was the honey-skinned servant, Juan de Pareja, glowing, his dark eyes alive with secrets. Not for the first time the curator wondered just what ethnic mixture was displayed here. The man was almost Polynesian. A touch of African, perhaps some Moorish, what else? The portrait seemed about to speak. In that moment von Kronholtz knew he would do anything in his power to gain the Winchcombe Chalice for the Met. Such masterpieces must live in each other's company!

Now it remained to convince Berkeley.

He bowed a slight Teutonic bow to the painting, turned, and walked briskly out of the gallery. The guard nodded a greeting, but von Kronholtz did not see him or acknowledge him.

The guard looked after the curator and grinned. They were crazy, these scholars, crazy as loons. It was a miracle a guy like von Kronholtz remembered to put his pants on in the morning.

High on a bluff overlooking Santa Barbara, Oswald

Webster stood in his vast art gallery of a living room scowling at a small first-century Roman bronze statue of a dancing satyr. It was a charming little statue, full of merriment, not deserving of Webster's wrath.

But it was not the Winchcombe Chalice.

And the Webster collection must have the Winchcombe Chalice. It was as simple as that.

Webster stood in the big white-walled, glass-fronted room. It was so very high above the sea, and farther still above the humble beginnings of its owner. The accountants told him he was in a cash bind. How could the owner of forty-two percent of Webco be in a cash bind? They'd damn well better unbind him before the sale. The chalice would go for no less than three million, more likely four. And he must have it. Webster could feel the familiar tingling in his fingertips. When would he meet the woman who would excite him as much as the thought of possessing some rare new artwork? He smiled. It seemed ironic that all his wealth had started with the coarse, ugly tomato plants of the San Fernando Valley.

At any minute in any day of the year, thousands of ounces of Webco catsup were oozing their way onto millions of hamburgers, hot dogs, and french fries in seventy-three countries around the world. Often the hamburger in question was also accompanied by Webco pickles, Webco mustard (hot, mild, and Old Heidelberg), and Webco chili sauce.

An ocean of condiments had made Oswald Webster very rich, one of the ten richest individuals in America and possibly in all the world.

And from his immense wealth, Webster had amassed one of the world's greatest private art collections. The collection was all the more remarkable for having been assembled within the last twenty-five years.

The Webster collection was every bit as ambitious as its owner.

It ranged through history, touching every form of art from primitive in New Guinea to the highest of High Renaissance; impressionists; temple art from India, Cambodia, and Bali; Kamakura carvings and screens from Japan's finest period; priceless Chinese ceramics; old masters; English court painters; and palace carpets from Persia.

One day all this would furnish a spectacular museum. His lawyers were hard at work even now, setting the thing up, much to the distress of the United States Internal Revenue Service.

The museum would have Oswald Webster's name on it.

But what Webster wanted was not fame or social recognition or any kind of immortality.

He wanted the objects themselves. He wanted to possess their fineness, to bask in the pulsing glow of their rare beauty, to cherish them and love them, to absorb whatever he could of their distinction. He wanted to become part of them, like a lover, and to have them become part of him.

From the first, as an uneducated clerk in the pickle factory in Salinas, Webster had had an uncanny instinct for aesthetic quality. When he first visited the Los Angeles museum, poor as its collection was, it became a revelation to him. And from that moment on Webster lived only for art. Not to see art, but to consume it. For this he worked eighteen-hour days, seven days a week. For this he schemed, drove himself harder than anyone he knew. And one day he owned the pickle factory. Then the tomato cannery. Then Webster Industries, whose most profitable enterprise was Webco. The condiment business flourished, and eventually the empire expanded to include vast stretches of farmland in the California valleys, housing tracts and industrial parks, oil, natural gas, and three truck lines.

It was all in the hands of managers now. Oswald Webster still watched his companies, shaped policies, created new opportunities. But the details were left to others now. The driving force in Webster's life was the collection.

And the driving force of the Webster collection, right now, was an insatiable desire to own the famous Winchcombe Chalice.

At the whims of Oswald Webster, empires trembled.

He *would* have the chalice.

In five minutes, five of his most trusted art-buying agents would walk into this room and report on their plans for the acquisition. Each one of them, Oswald knew, would have a different approach. It would be interesting to pit them one against the other, competing for his favor and the chalice itself. For the man who came up with the winning strategy was sure to rise in the complicated world of Webster Industries.

Oswald Webster put down the statue. He placed it gently on a table of polished ebony banded with bronze. He turned the little satyr so that the satyr seemed to be looking out over the seething blue Pacific.

Then Webster smiled, a rare, thin smile. He had long since learned to trust his intuition. And his intuition told him that, one day soon, the Winchcombe Chalice would also be in this

room, overlooking this rare view. He turned and looked at a
Frans Hals cavalier on the opposite wall. The cavalier gazed
insolently out over a Ming-dynasty fruitwood armoire on
which reposed three Tang horses of the utmost rarity. The
chalice would be in good company here. Webster could almost
see it now.

38

It rained all Sunday.

Jeff felt the house closing in, getting smaller. The pressure
was almost a physical thing, as though someone had wrapped
a rope around his head and was twisting it tighter, tighter.
And he still didn't know why.

Why wasn't Kavanaugh doing anything?

There was the Sunday *Times*. Jeff had forgotten the sheer
weight of the paper. He plowed through it: something to do.
The only way to read the damned thing was sitting on the
floor. He did that, on the old Persian carpet in the library,
coffee cup at his side, flipping pages, not really seeing the ads,
the articles, the pictures. He was finishing the sports pages
when the phone rang.

Kavanaugh. Jeff was having mixed feelings about the detective. Ted Kavanaugh was disturbing. He refused to stay
put in one category. That apartment. Polly. His whole attitude, irreverent and dead earnest at the same time.

"Negative," said Kavanaugh, not bothering with pleas-
antries. "The lab found zero on those bolts. No fingerprints,
nothing."

"Couldn't that mean someone wiped them clean?"

"Sure. In fact it's likely. But it is called negative evidence,
Jeff. Proves nothing in a courtroom. And that has to be at
the bottom of all our thinking, everything we do."

"What next?"

"For today, just sit tight. Think. Who could it be, and
why? Tomorrow, let's both begin finding out whatever we can
about Dupre's. Top to bottom. The finances. Disgruntled employees. Is there the possibility of some sort of scam over
there, like smuggling, maybe?"

Jeff paused, trying to sort out everything Kavanaugh had

said. It was embarrassing to know so little about Dupre's. "Well," he said at last, "Bunny Bartlett knows all about the money flow. So that's easy."

"It's easy if nobody has been, shall we say, diverting the old flow a bit."

Jeff thought of Bunny. He felt himself flushing. Kavanaugh had no damned right to cast suspicions around quite so freely.

"You don't mean you think Bunny—"

Laughter.

"Jeff, look. The first rule of the game is, we don't rule out anyone, okay? Not your long-dead grandmother. It's a narrowing-down game, Jeff, eliminating possibilities. Bartlett is a possibility, simply because he could be up to some kind of hanky-panky and how would you know? Or your aunt, either? Unless he got very careless."

"You're right, of course. I guess I just hate thinking that anyone that close . . ."

"A girl is dead, Jeff. I don't need to tell you that. And maybe—quite likely, I think—your uncle was murdered too. Nearly all the killing in the world is done by someone the victim knows well. Loves. Lives with. You can't afford the luxury of eliminating anyone. Not anyone."

"What a way to live."

Again Jeff heard the mocking laugh. "Beats hell out of the alternative."

"Yeah. So we're under house arrest?"

"If you have to go someplace, just ask the patrolman to call you a car. I wouldn't even walk to Dupre's."

"Swell."

"And don't linger at open windows, all right? Draw the shades at night."

"It's that bad?" Jeff was standing in the hallway. He looked around the empty space, half-expecting to find ticking bombs, lurking thugs.

"It could be, Jeff. Consider it preventive medicine. Not fun, but way better than the disease, okay?"

"Okay."

"There's one other thing. What you said about your dad. Is there anyone, some distant relative, someone who just might have some long-running hate against the House of Dupre?"

"If there is, Ted, we've never heard of them."

"No ancient curses, revenge, stuff like that?"

"You're getting a little heavy, Ted. Absolutely not."

"Death," said Kavanaugh a shade too patiently, "is heavy."

"And I am jumping out of my skin—what's left of it."

The laugh was warmer now. "I know. That's the hard part. The action kind of takes care of itself. But this job is one percent action and fifty percent waiting. You never get used to it."

"What's the other forty-nine percent?"

"Paperwork."

"I'd give anything to have something happen, Ted, to get it all over."

"You're doing fine. We'll talk tomorrow, all right?"

He hung up.

The next day, Monday, something did happen. Something entirely unexpected.

It might have been the architecture, or the cool professionalism of the guards and receptionists at Dupre's, but to Jeff the venerable auction house seemed unchanged. It was astonishing. Felix might never have died. There might never have been a gunshot from the park. People came and went. There was a schedule of this week's sales. Today was "Important Jewelry and Objets de Virtu." Jeff knew how carefully adjectives were used in the artworld. "Important" jewelry was good, but "Very Important" would have been better, and "Magnificent" was best of all. Tomorrow was rugs, Wednesday Chinese snuff bottles, Thursday autographs, Friday Shaker furniture and related items, Saturday a mixed estate sale.

Dupre's went on.

Jeff wondered where he'd be on Saturday. And he wondered if he'd be alive.

The elevator rode smoothly to the fourth floor. Just as it had always done. Jeff smiled as he caught himself thinking that it might suit his mood better if the elevator clanged and rattled like a ghost, if people were wailing and shrieking in the hallways of Dupre's.

The elevator glided smoothly to a stop and the attendant smiled as Jeff walked out onto the executive floor.

He was sitting at Felix's handsome desk, having his first sip of coffee, when Morgan walked in, beaming. He hadn't knocked. On the other hand, the door had not been closed.

"Good morning," said Morgan brightly.

"How are you, Morgan?"

"Pleased, very pleased, if I must say so. The Duke of Berwick asks us to come over and just make one last check, in case there's anything not included in the sale that we might

213

want to stick in. It's a bit redundant, naturally, but he does want to be very sure that this is the sale to end all sales. And, the truth is, we've put it together so hastily, there might well be something we've overlooked."

"Does that 'us' include me?"

"Precisely!" Morgan smiled. "Precisely. Had Felix been here, naturally, he would have gone over. More for form's sake than anything else. But the duke specially asked for you, his sense of correctness, as it were, to have a member of the family on the scene."

"It really isn't the most convenient time for me, Morgan. When would we go? And for how long?"

"Oh, soon, presumably this week. But not for long. Just for a few days. Just to check. I thought," he said with a little smile that might or might not have a hint of mischief in it, "that it would be just you, and Polly, and me. The change might do you good, Jeff. I know what a strain all this has been."

Jeff looked at Morgan, hating the suspicion that came creeping into his mind. Morgan, good old Morgan. He hadn't specified what he meant by "all this." Felix's death? The attempt on Jeff, and Carla's death? Jeff hadn't talked about these things, not within Dupre's. The papers had kept Carla's death quiet. That might have been Bunny's doing. But there were no glaring headlines, no flocks of reporters. None of the B-movie stuff. Just lonely death, and not knowing why.

But Morgan was right. Getting out of New York might not be such a bad idea. Maybe Minnie could come, too; they were old friends, after all, she and the Duke of Berwick.

But maybe Kavanaugh wouldn't want that. He hadn't wanted Jeff to go back to Veii, not just yet. Finally Jeff answered. "I'll have to check, Morgan. I can't promise you one way or another. You know, of course, that I'm trapped in this damned police investigation?"

"I'd imagined you might be. Is there . . . do they have any idea who did such a terrible thing?"

"Not a clue."

"Well," said Morgan after a pause, "I'm sure they'll get onto something soon. And in the meantime, I would consider it a favor if you could come. I realize that you feel, how shall I put it, less than deeply involved with the future of Dupre's, but it would help. The duke's business is a valuable thing for us."

"Never think I don't care about Dupre's, Morgan. I do

care. It's just that I've never wanted to run the business myself."

"Of course. Forgive me. We're all on edge, I guess, however much we'd like not to be."

"I'll try to come with you. Let me make a few phone calls. I'll get back to you before the end of the day, all right?"

"Fine. And thank you."

He left then. Jeff sipped the coffee. Kavanaugh had asked him to call. Jeff picked up the phone and dialed the precinct house. Ted Kavanaugh was out. Jeff left a message. There was a knock on the office door as he put down the receiver.

Polly walked in. Not smiling. Jeff looked up at her and realized he shouldn't be as startled as he was. And that he should have called her sometime over this last weekend, no matter how rotten he felt about Carla. About his own peril.

"Hi," he said.

"Hi," said Polly, smiling a little at the sheer inadequacy of the greeting. "Jeff, I just wanted to tell you how sorry I am about your friend, and . . . well, if I can do anything at all, I'll be happy to."

For a moment Jeff just looked at her, remembering their one night together. It had been a wonderful night.

The night someone had tried to kill him with a car.

"Thanks," he said at last. "Would you like some coffee or anything?"

"Sure. Tea, if you have any."

Jeff ordered tea, and more coffee for himself. Then he got up and closed the door. "Sit down. I met someone who knows you. Believe it or not, he's in charge of my case."

"Ted? Ted Kavanaugh?"

"Detective Lieutenant Ted Kavanaugh. Nice guy."

"I knew him well about five years ago. He is a nice guy. Does he still have that quasi-Japanese apartment?"

"Some place."

"He would take you there. He's very proud of that pad."

"So would I be, if it was mine."

Jeff liked the way she was handling it. Very gently, with a good measure of cool. He wondered if Ted had been trying to prove something by inviting him up to his apartment, and what that might be.

Miss Winn knocked then, and came in with a tray. She set it between them on the little tea table in front of the fireplace. Jeff sat on one of the twin settees, Polly on the other. She squeezed some lemon into the teacup and stirred it

215

slowly with a silver spoon. The silence just hung there, building.

It was Jeff who broke it. "Kavanaugh asked me to do a little probing around Dupre's, Polly. He asked me to find out what I can about Morgan. Tell me what you think."

Polly said nothing for a moment. Instead, she picked up the teacup and its saucer, lifted the cup to her lips, and sipped. "The cup," she said quietly, "is old Spode. The tea is Lapsang Souchong. The silver is American Federal. Felix Dupre had very good taste."

"And it was Felix who promoted Morgan?"

"Exactly."

"Was that a lapse of taste?"

"I don't think so. You've seen Morgan on the platform. He knows his job very well, and he performs well. In public and in private. Felix wasn't a kid—he was looking forward, or, more likely, *not* looking forward, to a time when he'd have to phase out of Dupre's. So he was phasing Morgan in, and in a handsome way. I won't insult your intelligence, Jeff, by pretending he's my idea of the world's most perfect person. But I've never seen him do any harm, and he's good at his job, smart as a whip, and he can be charming on a certain level."

Jeff laughed. "You're going to break your neck before you say anything bad about the man." He liked that. She was trying, with the diligence of a whole hive of bees, to be fair. Not every girl her age would have gone to that trouble.

"Don't you do that when you sort of instinctively aren't too enthusiastic about someone? I mean, he is not on my list of people to take to that hypothetical desert island."

"I've known him forever," Jeff said, "since I was sixteen, anyway. He's always been very kind, showed me the ropes a bit that one summer I worked here. But I don't really know Morgan. I mean, what his life is like, his friends, lovers, any of that. If I see him once a year, that's a big deal."

Jeff wondered who was on Polly's list to take to her desert island, and hoped it included him. A desert island with only Polly on it would suit him very nicely right now. In fact it wouldn't even have to be deserted. Just with some nice secluded coves and beaches and broad-minded natives.

"What's Ted up to?" Polly took another, long sip of the tea. "Asking about Morgan, I mean."

"Well, the chances are someone's trying to kill me."

There was a crash. Polly had picked up her teacup again. Hearing Jeff's words, she had dropped it onto the floor, where it broke into dozens of pieces, at the same time showering tea in several directions.

"Shit," said Polly quietly as she rose. "Jeff, you shouldn't drop news like that on anyone without preparing them a little."

"I'm sorry," he said, feeling stupid. "I thought you'd realize that."

She stood there for a moment looking at the floor. "And it was such a pretty cup. Damn. I'm sorry. I'll get some towels."

She turned then and almost ran from the room.

Jeff stood up, walked the length of the room and back again. The phone rang just as Polly came rushing back, her hand filled with paper toweling.

It was Kavanaugh. "You called?"

"Morgan wants me to go over to England for a few days, to Berwick Castle. How do you feel about that?"

Jeff was watching Polly. She looked up, then went back to cleaning up the mess.

"Interesting," said Kavanaugh, then paused. "I say go, if it isn't for very long."

"Just a few days. I'm sure I can make my own schedule, if it comes to that. It's a piece of diplomacy."

"Go. It couldn't hurt, and it'll keep you from going stir crazy."

"I worry about my aunt."

"She'll be fine, Jeff, I promise."

"I don't mind going, but let me talk to her, okay?"

"Do what you think is best. Are you finding out anything about . . . what we discussed yesterday?"

Jeff hesitated, thinking about Kavanaugh's careful phrasing. Was someone tapping the line, or just plain old-fashioned listening in? Obviously the policeman thought so, or that it was likely.

"I'm right in the middle of it. Can I get back to you?"

"Absolutely. If I don't hear from you by five, I'll call you at the house later, okay?"

"You're on. So long, Ted."

He put down the phone and went back to where Polly was now sitting, presiding over a newly cleaned-up tea tray. The shattered cup was neatly piled on its unbroken saucer.

"These things can be fixed, but they're never the same. I'll look into it."

"Don't bother, Polly. It was my fault anyway. I'm learning

to live with this . . . threat, and I may pretend to take it more for granted than I really do."

"Yes," she said softly, "I can see how you might."

"He wants me to go. To Berwick."

It was only then that she smiled. "Good. I was hating having to go with only Morgan."

"Have you met the duke?"

"A few times. The last few years, he's come here rather often. He was, you know, something of a pal of your uncle's."

"They had dinner together the night before Felix died."

Polly looked at him for a moment, and said nothing.

Jeff thought about Felix, and the duke, and their having dinner together. There was nothing unusual about that, they were old friends. The duke looked up Felix whenever he was in town. They did business. Quite a lot of business, judging by Felix's records. Still and all, it might be worthwhile asking Minnie about that night. If Minnie could bring herself to talk about it.

Finally Polly spoke. "Did Morgan give you a timetable?"

"He said it would be this week."

"It's odd, but I guess the client's always right."

Jeff poured more coffee and tasted it. Cold. "Why," he asked, "is it odd?"

"Well, the catalog's in the works already. We've sent a photographer over to take the pictures on the spot. The sale begins in two weeks. I'm not sure we can add anything to the catalog this late. I haven't checked, but it should be at the printer's. And even with that, it's a rush.".

"I wonder," said Jeff, as much to himself as to Polly, "why all the hurry? When you're the Duke of Berwick, you don't exactly plan on skipping town."

"The word is, pressing debts, so he's trying to accumulate a lot of capital in one fell swoop."

Jeff paused, thinking.

"It doesn't ring true, does it?"

She smiled.

"Why would he make it up? Morgan, I mean? It could be that we're all getting a shade too suspicious."

"I hope," said Jeff, "that you're right. I hope it's possible to be too suspicious."

Polly looked at him long and hard, and this time she didn't smile.

Jeff stood there stewing. *Now she'll think I'm suspicious of her. Very good, Dupre, foot in mouth as usual.*

Suspicious of Polly?

Would Ted be?

Jeff tried on a smile and hoped that it fitted.

Polly.

Not a chance. He thought of Polly's body, her warmth mixed with some subtle coolness, the natural-born elegance of her, head to toe. Polly!

Somebody had squeezed that trigger, driven that car.

Jeff was having to face the black realization that it was almost certainly someone he knew.

Maybe someone he loved.

Finally Polly did smile, said something inconsequential about work, and walked out.

Jeff stood there for a long time, looking at the empty space she left behind.

39

On Tuesday Ted Kavanaugh came to see Jeff at Dupre's. Jeff had found out a few basic facts about Morgan, but nothing suspicious, nothing startling. The man was paid a substantial salary: sixty-two thousand dollars per year. There was a Dupre profit-sharing plan, too, which would have added to that amount, although, as Jeff had known, the profits had been slim during the past few years.

Still, it was enough to explain a private town house. Especially since Morgan lived in only half of the place and rented two floors, the lower duplex, for eighteen hundred dollars a month.

"Probably," said Kavanaugh, who had found out about the rental income, "he lives just about free."

"It doesn't sound like motive for a life of crime, then, does it?"

"You never know. He might have an expensive habit."

"Like drugs?"

"Possibly. A lot of habits are expensive. Collecting art, for instance. Girls. Boys. Gambling. You never know. And some people don't need a conventional motive. Although nine times out of ten it's either love or money."

Kavanaugh had never been to Dupre's before. He paced Felix's office, looking at the pictures, touching the furniture, frowning, smiling, and all the while keeping up a running dialog with Jeff. Jeff sat on one of the settees by the fireplace, drinking coffee.

"You are," said Jeff, smiling, "the image of a sleuth, Ted. I keep expecting you to be on all fours, on the carpet, sniffing."

Kavanaugh turned, grinning. "Don't think I haven't done that. Carpets can have secrets." He turned to the window and gazed out across Madison Avenue. "It has to be centered in Dupre's. I'd bet anything on it." He paused.

Jeff said nothing.

"Have you thought about smuggling?"

Jeff looked at Ted's back.

Then Kavanaugh turned. He wasn't kidding.

"No. No, I hadn't thought about smuggling. Why should I?"

"Because Dupre's might be a pretty good cover for anyone who wanted to bring something small but valuable into the country. Something like heroin. Or maybe diamonds. Your name is like Tiffany's. You've been around for a long time. You've got a perfect record—never anything shady, and de facto, all the stuff that comes to Dupre's is duty-free because it's either old—no duty on antiques—or works of art, and there's no duty on art, either. So if a customs inspector sees a consignment going toward Dupre's, what do you want to bet he doesn't give it his closest scrutiny? And even if they do look carefully, think of the hiding places! Huge old chests of drawers, some with secret compartments, I'll bet. Chinese vases with false bottoms. Those big, deeply carved old-fashioned picture frames. You have to realize that as much pure cocaine as would fill this vase here," he said, pointing, "would be worth . . . well, I don't know exactly, but hundreds of thousands on the street."

Ted paused and sat down again. He looked at Jeff quizzically. Jeff felt confused, tentative, out of his depth. He he tried. "It could be. I mean, anything could be, right? But wouldn't that imply a steady pattern of shipments? Once a month from so and so? And that, it seems to me, is what we don't have."

"I'm not so sure." Ted put down his empty teacup. Jeff filled it. "I'm not sure about that," Ted continued. "Say I'm your permanent roving dope smuggler on the Continent. All I have to do is pick up the stuff regularly from wherever I get it. Then I hop over to . . . Paris, let's say, and consign something to my pal at Dupre's. Comes from Paris this month, Amsterdam next month, someplace else the rest of the time.

Different names, different objects, practically untraceable. Until, of course, someone tumbles onto the contact here."

"Who's doing so well, he'll kill to protect the racket. You may have something, Ted. It sounds very plausible. What do we do about it?" Jeff tried to control the anger that rose in him because the policeman was forcing him to think about the unthinkable. Jeff knew it was Ted's job to do this. But knowing that did nothing to dull his revulsion. It was like finding a snake in your boot.

"The first step is to check up on your processing. When an object comes to you from overseas, exactly where does it come? Who handles it? What's the system of confirming arrival? We could be dealing with someone as unexpected as a porter, one of the mail-room people, someone like that."

Jeff thought of calling Polly, then decided not to. "I know roughly what happens," he said. "Small items often come to us by registered mail. Even jewelry. All mail goes to the mail room on the first level of the basement. If it's registered, the head mail room guy signs for it and gets it to the appropriate department head. Unopened. Then, we have a regular freight entrance on the side street, big steel double doors, and there's a huge storeroom down there, and vaults for especially rare items, and a big freight elevator that has to be twenty-something feet wide, to take the stuff up to the exhibition and sale galleries. Who, exactly, uncrates things, who's the first to get their hands on a shipment, I'm not quite sure. There are lots of what we call porters, all union men—"

"And we all know how honest the unions are."

"Well, most of them have been here for a while. It's easy to check into. There'd have to be a code of some kind. Or the smuggled items would have to be all addressed to one person, one department head, for instance."

"Unless," said Ted, "it is someone in shipping."

"That's easy to check. But I kind of doubt it would always be just one guy in the shipping room, or the mail room either."

"Then maybe it's someone deeper in the mechanism."

"Maybe." Jeff found himself wondering how much cocaine could fit into a Hester Bateman wine cup. He looked at his watch. "You getting hungry? Let me invite you to lunch. In or out?"

"If we go out," said Kavanaugh, grinning, "you'll have a police escort for sure. And the food'll be better."

"Out it is."

On an impulse, Jeff took Kavanaugh all the way down to

the shipping room. One level below the main lobby, it was a huge battleship-gray area brightly illuminated by banks of double-bulb fluorescent fixtures. Six black men of various sizes, shapes, and ages were relentlessly uncrating a large shipment of dark Jacobean-looking furniture that seemed to have just lately arrived. They all wore faded khaki uniforms that reminded Jeff of the United States Army summer issue. One tall, grave-looking black man in a dark suit was issuing orders, softly, but with an unmistakable air of command. Jeff tried to remember the man's name. Finally, luckily, it came back to him from that summer twelve years ago. Marcus Aurelius Jones, Head of Dupre's Security, ex-FBI, fit and very efficient at age sixty.

"Mr. Jones," said Jeff as the man walked over to where he and Kavanaugh were standing, "let me introduce Detective Kavanaugh, of the Nineteenth Precinct, who's checking our security measures."

Jones grinned quickly and unexpectedly. "How're you, Mr. Jeff?"

"Fine, sir, and you?"

"Gettin' on, gettin' on. Well, Detective Kavanaugh, anything I can do, or any of us can do, we'll be glad to. Haven't lost one yet. Worst happens down here is, we drop a big old bastard on our toe, maybe, or—you didn't hear this, Mr. Jeff—maybe we adds a little bitty scratch to the patina, if you take my meaning. But, security-wise, no one's ever complained yet. Anyone tries to take anything off us, well, we are ready and able."

"I'm sure you are," said Kavanaugh. "What I'm really interested in is the way you check things in, as they get here."

Jones paused for a moment, as though the question puzzled him. "Well, we do that on a piece of paper. I do it personally, have done for nearly fifteen years." He walked to a small and notably battered gray steel desk and picked up an equally battered clipboard. Clipped to the board was a sheaf of ruled paper with lines and boxes for shipping numbers, a brief description of the item, and the time and date of its arrival. Jones's handwriting was astonishing: so precise and elegant, it looked almost like steel engraving. He handed Ted the clipboard.

Ted looked at it briefly, flipped through the other pages, smiled, and handed it back. "I admire your penmanship, sir," said Ted.

"These papers," said Jones as though Kavanaugh hadn't interrupted him, "make their own little carbon copies, as you see. Now, one of those—the carbon, which is yellow—stays here in that old file cabinet. The original and one other go upstairs, where only the good Lord knows what happens to them. But, like I said, we never lost one yet."

"About how many objects go through your department every day?" Ted looked around the big room as he asked the question, but it was impossible to get even a vague idea.

The black foreman wrinkled his high forehead in puzzlement. "Darned if I ever counted. I'm sure someone has that kind of number, though, but if we stopped to count everything, we'd get no work done, and that's for sure. So I guess I can't help you too much on that one."

"You've been very helpful, thanks, Mr. Jones," said Jeff. "We just wanted a rough idea how you handle all this, and you gave us just what we want. Thanks again."

In a few minutes they were out in the dazzle and heat of a New York Indian summer noon.

"Now," said Jeff as they eased into a small table at the little French bistro Polly had shown him, "don't tell me you're casting old Marcus Jones as the archcriminal. Hell, he's ex-FBI. He's been with us for . . . I don't know how long. Used to call my uncle 'young Mr. Dupre.'"

Ted laughed. "Somewhere, and don't ask me how, most of you straight folks acquire the idea that all criminals spend their time sneaking around dark corners, scowling and drooling, and looking suspicious. If anything, the opposite is true. I mean, think about it. The most plausible-looking people are the ones most likely to get away with a crime. The records are filled with sweet-looking little old ladies who've fleeced people out of fortunes. Charming kids who just happen to be psychopathic mass-murderers. Beautiful girls who'd cut you into coleslaw for cabfare. And so forth."

Jeff smiled. "You keep nice company."

"Doctors hang around with a lot of germs, too."

"That's how you think of yourself, Ted? Preventive medicine?"

"That's how it should be. The way it is, we often get called in too late—only after the infection, if you will, is out of control."

"Like it was with Felix."

Ted frowned. "Like it isn't—yet—with you."

"I've always wondered how they feel, people who kill, the first time."

"Plenty of 'em are simply incapable of feeling at all. The shrinks have a name for that: sociopath. Might as well be

223

stepping on an ant as pulling the trigger that kills—let's say, your friend the countess."

Jeff closed his eyes for a moment, hoping the image would go away. It didn't.

"I guess," Jeff said finally, "it has always been that way."

"Until very lately," Kavanaugh said softly, almost as if he were speaking to himself, "life was so brief, and so cheap, that death was the great subject. There was so much of it going around."

"The fascination is always there. Ask any poet."

"And," said Kavanaugh, raising his wineglass, "Hemingway ended up sucking on a shotgun."

"What's next?"

Ted's grin came and went. It was a ripple of a grin. "For you, for me, or for Hemingway?"

"For us. For this damned case. If it is a case."

The grin was gone now.

"It's a case, Jeff. It is definitely a case. The lady's dead."

Jeff reacted quickly. He took Kavanaugh's comment personally, and knew that he shouldn't take it personally, that he should be calm and rational. But he wasn't calm, and he wasn't rational. Jeff started to say something, something sharp, something bitter. That was how he felt, sharp and bitter, deeply sour. Instead, he changed the subject. "We're going to England tomorrow."

"Good."

There was a pause. Jeff took another bite of the hot quiche.

"Just you and St. James?"

"And Polly."

Ted's eyes were on his plate. He spoke very carefully. "How is she?"

"Seems to be fine. A great lady."

"Yes. It should be interesting. And while you're gone, I may be able to get more of a line on Mr. St. James."

"Searching the premises?"

"Why not?" Ted put down his fork. He looked at Jeff, then at his own half-eaten quiche. It was a delicious quiche. Ted just didn't feel hungry. He picked up his wineglass and took a drink. The glass was nearly empty. Then he put the glass down and looked at Jeff.

The silence seemed to thicken. The restaurant was filled with a happy lunchtime crowd, but the sound of their voices was blurred somehow. Finally Ted spoke. "This may not make a whole lot of difference to the case, Jeff, but did the Countess di Cavolfiore come here to tell you she was pregnant?"

For a moment Jeff simply sat there, stunned.

"No," he said, and it was more like a moan than human speech. "Oh, no." He had thought, grieving, that nothing could be more terrible than Carla's death, the manner of it, the sudden irrational senseless destruction of it. And now this. Jeff was in some cold place beyond shock, too hurt for anger, too sad for words. His child. His and Carla's. He'd never thought of himself as a father. He'd assumed, easily, comfortably, that one day, one vague day, he would marry and have a family. But it wasn't real to him.

This was real, too real.

"I'm sorry, Jeff," said Kavanaugh. "I thought you knew."

Jeff managed to look at him. For a moment he just stared, trying to master the rage that was building in him. It wasn't Kavanaugh's fault. It wasn't anyone's fault, except for the monster who pulled the trigger.

So now there were three murders.

Jeff reached up with both hands and covered his face, pressing hard, holding his eyes shut. It didn't make the horror go away. Finally, slowly, he lowered his hands. But still he said nothing.

There was nothing in the world to say.

40

Berwick Castle, late February 1974

Father Devlin walked down the hallway with a step whose spring belied his seventy-eight years. The priest felt any age but old. His eyes sparkled with interest in all that went on around him. He delighted in teaching the workers' children who came to him for religious instruction each Wednesday after school, and every Sunday after Mass. Few enough they were, but what could one expect from times like these?

There were pleasures in Father Devlin's life sufficient to allay any pain or doubt that might come sneaking past his formidable barriers of faith and good cheer and good humor.

He knew, in his keen mind and in his intuitive bones, that he would be the last family priest at Berwick.

And he wondered sometimes just how long he had left.

God had seen fit to give Frederick Devlin rare good health. Even now, there was only the occasional touch of arthritis that plagued him. But all in all, he'd been well blessed in the health department. And in other departments, too. For wasn't it an honor and a privilege to serve the dukes of Berwick? He never knew, and never asked why, of all the young men in his class at seminary, he had been chosen to go to Berwick straight off after ordination.

And hadn't some of his classmates ragged him for that? "Doing good works among the rich, are ye, Freddy?" The priest smiled. As though the rich hadn't souls worth the saving. Not that there weren't others, and sometimes a handful, to be served. For Berwick chapel was the official church for the village and all the farms around, off the great estate or on. In all he could count two dozen families who were more or less consistent in their faith. How many of them came just to be more familiar with the castle? How many more came because of the ancient fascination of the Winchcombe Chalice? It was better not to ask such questions too often, for the answers might be troubling.

And Father Devlin considered it a part of his holy office to keep troubling matters forever at bay.

God himself surely must know that the ducal family had suffered more than its share of troubles lately, without any additional burdens.

Father Devlin had served three dukes of Berwick in his time, and served them with all the pride that might be consistent with his bone-deep humility.

The story of the spiritual life at Berwick Castle was far from a happy one for Father Devlin.

He felt in his most secret heart that he'd gone very wrong somewhere.

For hundreds of years, it had been a matter of family pride for the Fleets of Berwick that they had sustained their Catholicism through all the ravages of the Tudor dynasty and through all the encroachment of the blasphemous Protestantism that followed. Never had the Berwick chapel been deconsecrated, as so many others had been defiled. No king would dare incur the wrath of Berwick.

How beautifully the old duke had sustained the forms! Not a Sunday went by when he was in residence but that the old duke would appear at young Father Devlin's service and the family with him. The son—they were all called Neville Fleet, every last one of them, first sons of first sons—well, the son had been a good man, but vague. Forgetful of appearances he was, but meaning no harm. As for the incumbent duke?

Father Devlin frowned a frown that was more avuncular

than spiritual. He had known the present Neville Fleet since birth.

And something, somewhere, had gone very wrong. The priest often asked himself what he might have done that would have made things come out differently for the poor man.

This, too, was a question with no answer.

And then there was the unspeakable and not-to-be-thought-about subject of the dead heir.

Buried in consecrated ground, and at what cost to the conscience of Father Frederick Devlin? Squiffed and fallen from the tower was the official view. How easy it must be to mold officials' views if you were the Duke of Berwick and they virtually your chattels. And hadn't the duke also molded the official views of Father Devlin, too, so who was he to condemn?

And in fact the priest condemned no one but himself. In truth, no one knew what happened on that tower.

It was done, the boy was dead and best forgotten. As for the death of the duchess, she was mad, poor creature. There were different rules for the insane.

The things that had happened since were best forgotten, too, but easy forgetfulness did not come readily to Father Devlin's mind.

The present duke had never been deeply religious. But in these last several years Father Devlin had a sense of losing contact with the duke. It was almost as though the man were slipping away into some dark inner life of the soul where it was impossible to follow. For a time, Father Devlin attributed the duke's withdrawl to the illness of his wife. It was partly that, he was sure, but it was also something bigger, deeper, and infinitely more sad. Father Devlin knew, as who in the household could not but know, of the duke's financial problems. He knew when the pictures and silver began to make their way to the auction house. It was a common predicament for the nobility these days, and none the less sad for its frequency.

The unaccustomed poverty of the duke was one thing, in the priest's view.

The duke's response to his predicament was quite something else.

To sell, if sell he must, was a hard thing.

To sell the chalice was sacrilege. Father Devlin was a quiet man, and there was little anger in him. The selling of the chalice stirred unwelcome feelings in the old man.

And then there was the unsettling matter of the silversmith. Father Devlin saw much on his afternoon walks. And one of the things he had seen was the hasty restoration of Tauranac's cottage, deep in Berwick Forest. As for the man himself, the duke had never bothered to introduce him. A dark, secretive-looking man. Father Devlin had heard clanging, hammering sounds from the cottage one day while strolling through the forest nearby.

He had knocked on the cottage door.

There was a silence, then a pause, then the sound of chains being removed and a bolt being drawn. The door opened halfway. That had been Father Devlin's first view of the silversmith.

Tauranac was surprisingly young to be so surly.

The priest could glimpse into the workroom behind the man. One glimpse was enough: the man was obviously a master silversmith. The priest was very familiar with such silver as was displayed in the castle. And he knew, from servants' gossip, that some of it had been sold off. Why, then, the regal expense of the duke's maintaining a private silversmith on the estate? Father Devlin wondered. The man was curt to the point of rudeness. He did not invite his visitor inside. The priest walked away saddened and confused. He thought of the chalice being sold, and that made him sadder yet.

Not, of course, that the chalice wasn't the duke's to sell. Surely no modern judge would dare to prosecute Henry VIII of England, dead these 427 years, for stealing the thing. Perhaps, the priest had dared to dream, just perhaps there might be some Catholic rich enough and religious enough to buy the chalice and install it upon the altar of St. Peter's in Rome, which would be a fitting and glorious end for the much-traveled goblet.

From Rome to Rome! The idea sang to the old priest, but he had no idea how to begin implementing it. Surely the Vatican must be aware of the upcoming auction, suddenly and secretly as it had come together.

The duke had not seen fit to tell his own priest that the most precious of all the Berwick treasures, the sacred altar chalice, would be put on the block with no more regard for its spiritual import than if it had been some wordly pot or painting.

And that had hurt Father Devlin more deeply than anything else about the decline of the house of Fleet. It would have been so easy for the duke to have a private word with him. But the duke had not done that. The duke was more likely off tooling about the countryside in his gleaming new motorcar, or scheming what new treasures might be added to the trove marked for auction.

Father Devlin was saddened to see a Fleet of Berwick sink so completely into materialism. It denied his own early training, and it cheapened a great and ancient heritage. For the Fleets of Berwick had ever been patrons of the arts, collectors, endowers of universities.

With a curiosity so far removed from any consideration of his own personal comfort that it was purely abstract, Father Devlin wondered what would happen afterward. After the auction, after the walls and the silver and china cabinets were stripped bare. Then what? Would there still be Fleets at Berwick? He thought not. Would the castle be transformed into some echoing museum, as had happened to so many of the other great houses up and down England? He thought of the castle at Leeds, lovingly restored by an American heiress's money, deeded to the state, and empty now but for the odd caretaker, used for the occasional conference where extreme privacy was desired. Many sad fates might await a house as vast as Berwick.

Father Devlin often included among his prayers a special wish that he would not be around to see the day when all this tarnished glory crumbled once and for all. He came straight from Tauranac's cottage to the chapel.

He knew as he stood silently before the small altar, that his prayer would very likely be answered by the attrition of time if not by God himself.

Father Devlin stood there for several long moments.

The chill of a Berwickshire winter seemed to flow up out of the paving stones of the chapel's floor and into his bones. Or perhaps the chill he felt was no more than sorrow. Surely he was at least partly to blame for the sad times that had befallen the Fleets of Berwick. Surely there was something he might have done along the way, some word said to young Neville, some bit of advice.

But whatever was unsaid now must be unsaid forever, for the time was long past when any words of his could have even the smallest influence upon the duke. A quick, wan smile came and went on his pale face. He imagined the interview.

"Please, your Grace, you cannot sell the chalice. It means so much to me."

Would the response be scorn, laughter, puzzlement, or a

quick phone call to the nearest hospital for the mentally deranged? Possibly all of the above responses might come into play. Father Devlin was so far removed from the duke's confidence that he could hardly guess.

As a young priest newly installed at Berwick, the attendant grandeur of his situation had caused many a rich fantasy to create itself in the lively imagination of Father Frederick Devlin.

In such dreams, he saw himself as the Richelieu of Berwick, adviser to the great, and not only on spiritual matters, either.

And as the seventy-eight-year-old man who had once dreamed those dreams stood in the chill silence of the ancient chapel, he smiled again. For folly breeds folly, and who, in such matters, was entirely without guilt?

Then he knelt before the altar, before the Winchcombe Chalice, and prayed. He would say his daily Mass later on, perhaps in the evening. It was a fine thing, of a winter evening, to celebrate a Mass, to light the holy candles and see their dancing flames refracted from the glowing surfaces of the chalice.

The chalice. Father Devlin had never presumed to consider it his, even though he'd said his Mass with it every day for going on to sixty years. His long, thin fingers knew every bump and twist of that grapevine, the curve of the lip, the subtle irregularities of the banded rubies. He knew the contours of the chalice better than he knew his own face. It was impossible to imagine life without it, even though the moment when that empty life must begin was rushing at him with the unstoppable force of an express train.

Father Devlin finished his prayer, stood up, crossed himself, and looked once more at the Winchcombe Chalice.

Even in the cool winter light, the golden cup radiated an almost alarming power. The priest turned and walked out of the chapel as slowly as he had walked in. He wondered if the Vatican would think him balmy if he wrote, discreetly suggesting that a suitable Catholic buyer might be found to bid for the Winchcombe Chalice.

41

Minnie Dupre sat in the old wing chair in Jeff's room and watched him pack. "I'm glad you're going," she said. "For all his troubles, Neville Fleet is a charming man, and although I haven't met the new wife, the reports are that she's a fine person."

"I guess," said Jeff, "it's sad, him having to sell all that stuff. I've never seen Berwick."

"Berwick is something to see, Jeffy. Felix and I were at his coming-of-age party there, just before the war. Footmen. Footmen in powdered wigs and livery. The women wore important jewels in those days, huge diamond dog collars, things like that. Oceans of champagne were poured that night, and the castle was illuminated so that it seemed to be made of gold. The roses were in bloom. Berwick's rose garden is famous—I do hope they haven't let it go. It was a magical night, in a magical place. And it seemed impossible it could ever change, let alone fall to ruin."

"They seem to have lost the will to live."

"I'm not sure what they've lost, Jeffy, but it's something. Or maybe what we thought was there was an illusion: the force, the gallantry. We all grew up stuffed with their legends, and so did they. Maybe all they were, were legends."

"The duke has a new heir, Morgan said."

"And at his age! More power to him."

Jeff's answer was to laugh.

"Poor England," said Minnie then, softly, sadly. "The ruling class has nothing left to rule, yet they will not change. One knows only certain carefully selected people, and one definitely does not try too hard, at anything. It won't do, don't you know, to do anything so vulgar as to compete. The entire nation assumed that its superiority of the nineteenth century was the gift of God, that it would go on forever on its own momentum. Poor England. Every industry is on its knees, and in the meanwhile the whole establishment is being wrecked from within, by a monster of its own devising. England resisted every invasion for hundreds of years, and now they've created their own Visigoths. The working class is in permanent rebellion. The North Sea oil will maintain them for a while, but it's artificial, like tubes into a terminal case. It makes me sad, Jeffy, because I love England. They had so much, and they threw it all away."

"I notice Morgan asked me to bring a dinner jacket. I have this vision of the duke in full fig, eating off orange crates."

She laughed. "I doubt it's come to that."

He paused, rummaged in his sock drawer, and wondered, not for the first time, if it was a good idea to leave her alone. "I'm glad I'm going. I wish you were coming along."

"Don't worry about me, darling. I'm pretty tough, and I'm also pretty mad. It was only a freak of luck, you know, that I wasn't beside Felix when the car crashed. It's not an easy thing to live with, the idea that someone might be trying to kill you."

"No," said Jeff quietly, "it sure isn't." Neatly, professionally, he stacked several shirts in his shirt case. "I forget sometimes. But not for long."

"And I," said Minnie, "keep trying to tell myself we don't know for sure, that maybe his death was an accident."

"Let's assume the worst. That it was murder. Did he know anything, some secret, something the killer couldn't have known?"

"He'd have told me, Jeffy. I'm sure of that."

"Even if it was threatening to you?"

She frowned. "I hadn't thought of that. Possibly not, then. But what might it be?"

"God knows." Jeff paused. "I'm afraid for you, Minnie. Come with us to Berwick."

"No, my darling. Neville would have me, I guess, but I just don't feel up to it. Berwick takes a lot of living up to. And, Jeffy, you are not to worry. There's nothing to be afraid of. For me, I mean. I have moments when it would be a blessing if—"

"You don't mean that."

She smiled. It was not a happy smile. "Some things are beyond helping, darling. You only fear death when you have something to lose. I have lost what I cared most for in this life. Not that I don't care very dearly for you, Jeffy, but I can't—won't—do what I've seen some parents do, who turn into vampires, eating their children, living their lives. You have a fine life, darling, but it is yours to live, not mine."

"It's that bad?"

"It was very good while it lasted, Jeffy, and it lasted a

long, long time. We had better luck than anyone has a right to. So I'm not, you understand, complaining. Just stating a fact."

He had a crazy thought then. "Minnie, if Felix had left a message, a secret one, where would it be? I've looked in the office and there's nothing unexpected."

She smiled at the concept. "Felix was anything but secretive. I looked through his desk, hating every minute of it, but there was nothing unusual. There is the safe-deposit box down at Bunny's bank, and we'll have to go through that officially one day, for the will."

"But you haven't done that yet?"

"I didn't think it was important, Jeffy. I know what's there."

"Are you sure?" Maybe while I'm in Berwick, you could take a look, okay?"

"I could easily have done it before. But I do know what's in it, just papers and a few of my mother's jewels I never wear."

"There's probably nothing to it. But why not be sure?"

Jeff tried to imagine his uncle in possession of someone's guilty secret. What kind of secret would it be? He thought of Kavanaugh's idea of Dupre's being the fulcrum for a smuggling operation. If Felix had stumbled on something like that, it might very well be dangerous enough to make someone kill him.

Killing Felix was one thing. The attempts to kill Jeff were quite something else. Felix might have known something dangerous. Jeff knew that he himself didn't.

Which left only one possibility, and that was that the killer imagined Jeff knew . . . whatever it was. Crazy. Pure and simple madness. But then, a killer would be mad. Mad like a fox. Jeff closed the suitcase. He couldn't get to England fast enough.

42

New York, August 1978

Neville had misgivings now about having accepted an invitation from Felix Dupre.

It was one thing to filter the Tauranac fakes from Berwick

to Morgan, and through the House of Dupre. It didn't seem personal, viewed from the lofty towers of Berwick.

But here in New York, in Felix Dupre's own house, Neville felt uneasy. And Neville had promised himself he would never feel uneasy again.

He smiled at the elegance of his scruples as he stepped out of the taxicab at Felix's house on Sixty-fourth Street. One must learn to cultivate a touch of ruthlessness.

Felix opened the door himself. He smiled, a quick mechanical smile.

Something's wrong, thought Neville. Something is troubling the fellow. And he wished, once again, that he'd made an excuse.

But it wasn't possible, just now, for the Duke of Berwick to elude Felix Dupre. Felix was essential. The House of Dupre was essential. Even the damnable blackmailer Morgan St. James was essential.

It was all working so very smoothly.

If Neville had been a contemplative sort of person, he might have questioned whether things weren't working out just a bit too smoothly. But contemplation was not in Neville's character. Fleets acted. Let others think, let others dream. A dream was of no use to a Fleet of Berwick unless it could very quickly be made to come true.

Neville's dreams had done much better lately than merely come true.

His whole life, these days, seemed more like a radiant miracle. There was Bess. There was the baby—more than a baby now, a fine healthy little lad of five. And there was the very profitable enterprise of selling Tauranac's replicas.

Neville would always despise Morgan St. James. But St. James had been enormously helpful.

It was St. James who regulated the flow of objects, and the flow was a gentle one. They might do two major pieces a year, and three or four minor ones. And it was Morgan who suggested what might bring the best prices, what might be hard to detect.

Only the deLamerie teapot had thrown them, and that was a fluke.

Even Felix himself had passed on it as genuine.

There were some things, naturally, that could not be controlled.

And even in the frightening case of the deLamerie replica, they had made money. A lot of money. The delivery and collection were Morgan's part of the business. How he handled it, Neville was never quite sure. But handle it he did, and well. Never using the same courier twice. Lucky it was that the auction house never bothered to check up on people's credentials when they brought in objects for sale.

Through it all, Neville had been very lucky.

There was more than five million dollars in the account at the Knickerbocker Trust Company, securely invested in short-term U.S. Treasury notes, yielding at least ten percent. The fund was building itself now. Selling the last of Berwick's treasures would make Neville secure forever. That was why he wanted to do it quickly, dramatically. To get the whole business over with, once and for all. To end the traffic with Tauranac, to end his arrangement with Morgan. They had been useful, both of them, but their usefulness was ending. It would end very soon, with the great Berwick Castle auction. Neville could feel his life taking a permanent turn for the better. His smile was a warm one as he greeted Minnie.

He'd always been fond of Minnie Cartwright, even before she married Felix. How very lovely she'd been, a quick dark thing, all flashing wit and laughter. Not his type, precisely, but undeniably a charmer. And she was a charmer still.

Minnie charmed them that night.

The night needed charming. Felix was tense, obviously under some strain. If Minnie noticed that, she gave no sign. And Neville played the gallant Duke of Berwick to the hilt. It was a role he had been rehearsing from childhood, and he did it, on occasion, very well.

Tonight was such an occasion.

Neville was beginning to feel the delicious release of not worrying. Of not fearing the paper revenge of the revenue man Smythe-Davies.

How glorious it would be to see the last of Smythe-Davies! In his darkest dreams, Neville had contemplated many a horrible end for the smarmy little man. A rogue he was, a fiscal vampire, thoroughly and unquestionably a blight on England's honor. Whatever honor poor besieged England had left.

They were just three at dinner, the sort of party Neville liked, not a party really, but more family than formal. That's how it usually was at the Dupres'. That was not the way it was tonight.

After coffee Felix asked Neville to come into the garden, to see some Exbury azaelas Neville had brought from his own gardens last season. The Dupre garden was lovely, as city gardens go. Felix and Minnie had not made the typical mistake of keeping everything tiny; there were several big rhododendrons flanking a tall, theatrical cypress, beautifully planted underneath with flowering perennials and annuals too. White and pink impatiens illuminated in the soft moonlight. The big houses on the next street seemed very far away.

For a moment they spoke of simple things, of planting and flowering. Then, slowly, painfully, Felix came out with the thing that had so conspicuously been troubling him that evening.

"There isn't," said Felix carefully, "any easy way to say this, Neville. It hurts. It hurts me deeply. So let me be blunt. I know. I know what you've been doing at Dupre's. The question is, what do we do about it?"

Neville Fleet stopped in his tracks and simply stared at his host. A flush went through him from his toes to his ears, tingling.

He shuddered, gasped, said nothing.

Felix went on. "I see how it must be with you, Neville. How you could be driven to such a thing. It makes me sad that you found it necessary to play such tricks on me. On us."

His compassion cut Neville more deeply than rage might have done.

There was a weathered teakwood bench. Neville sat down on it heavily. He leaned forward and covered his face with his hands. His sobs were dry sobs, but they came straight from the depths of his soul. Neville felt the touch of his old friend's hand on his shoulder and looked up suddenly, eyes blazing. It was too much, much too much. That Felix should know, and be sympathetic. This was a time for outrage, for duels and accusations, for revenge!

"We won't prosecute, you know, Neville. But it will have to cease. And we'll have to see about some . . . shall we say reparations? That deLamerie teapot cost us more than eighty thousand dollars. Out of pocket."

The rage left Neville's eyes now. "You won't tell?"

He felt like a small child caught raiding the pantry. The disgrace was a physical thing, swelling, choking him. He thought of Bess, of the child, of Berwick.

Felix stood in the darkness, thankful for having chosen the garden to confront his old friend. To do it in the light might not be bearable. "I won't prosecute, Neville. There are some key people who must know—to be completely sure this won't happen again. Morgan, for instance. My nephew, Jeff, because he may one day own Dupre's. I haven't told Minnie, and I won't, if you like."

"Your nephew," said Neville softly.

"My brother's boy. He's in Italy now."

Neville said nothing, but merely stared into the darkness.

"You must promise me," Felix went on, "that this will stop, at once and forever. We'll go on with the sale, selling the chalice. It's been announced, we can't back out. But that must be an end to it, Neville. Do you promise?"

Slowly, painfully, the Duke of Berwick got to his feet. He was taller than Felix. He felt about one inch high. And the rage that had left him was coming back now, hotter, riper, more dangerous. By what right did this shopkeeper pretend to extract promises from Neville Fleet? Far as he was from the castle, Neville could feel the eyes of all his ancestors staring at him down the ages, accusing. He well knew how the Fleets of old would handle this threat or any other.

"I promise, Felix, and I thank you."

The words came out softly, and that softness in itself was an effort.

The two old friends stood close together in the midnight garden.

Neville could feel the gap between them opening wider, deeper, cold, impassable. How very naive the Americans were! To extract such an insulting promise and actually expect him to hold to it.

It was beyond effrontery.

It was also mortally dangerous.

Neville felt himself cornered, trapped. Desperation seeped into his brain slowly, burning hot on the heels of the relief he had felt when Felix Dupre promised not to prosecute.

Something must be done, quickly and decisively.

From some dark corner of his mind Neville could hear the trumpets of old ringing out. Calling the Fleets of Berwick to battle.

To defend what was rightly theirs.

Little echoes of glory, tatters of pride, came fluttering and dancing in his head. Glory to be regained. Pride to be avenged.

Felix Dupre was just a dark looming shape now. Menacing. A thing to be eliminated. The honor of the Fleets was in the balance!

Neville felt the sweat on his forehead, although the night was not warm. He smiled. "You have been more than kind, Felix."

Then, in silence, the two men walked back into the house.

43

Jeff could feel the power of Berwick pulling at them long before the old castle came into view. The anticipation affected all of them.

The flight over had been predictably swift and luxurious, reflecting all the economically doomed opulence of the Concorde.

A rental car was waiting for them. Morgan took the wheel.

Polly had been rather quiet during the flight, pensive, sitting across the narrow aisle from Jeff. Maybe she didn't like flying. Maybe she was reconsidering Jeff Dupre.

Maybe she was reconsidering Ted Kavanaugh.

It felt very good to set foot on British soil.

Jeff hadn't been in England for some years. It was as green as he remembered, as disorganized, as polite.

But the best thing about Britain right now was that it wasn't East Sixty-fourth Street, New York, New York.

Jeff had slept part of the way across the ocean. He had tried, for the thousandth time, to sort out the last few weeks in his head. The result was more confusion, loose ends leading nowhere, half-formed hopes, and deeply regretted sorrows. Every time he thought of Carla, and that was often, a horrible sinking feeling happened in the bottom of his gut. A feeling like stepping into an open manhole on a dark street. That sudden. The sensation that you were falling and falling and there was nothing like a parachute to save you.

Morgan drove quickly and well. The villages were clean and perfect: they seemed like antiquated toy villages or illustrations for some forgotten fairy tale written in a happier time. The little scrubbed and smiling villages looked as though nothing bad could ever happen there. It was only fitting that this fairy-tale-looking kingdom should be crowned by a fairy-tale castle.

Morgan, who had been rather quiet throughout most of the drive, was the first to see Berwick. "Behold," he said softly over the rushing of the wind, "Camelot."

And there on the crest of a distant rise were the honey-gold stone towers of Berwick.

Some trick of perspective made the great castle seem close, but in fact they had a full half-hour's drive before they got there. Jeff's sense of history was sharply tuned, and he had a special interest in Berwick and its treasures. He could feel the weight of Berwick's power and the force of its legends. For a thousand years and more Berwick had dominated this part of England, vast and impregnable. Berwick had sent its sons to the courts of kings and emperors, to war, to make love and sometimes to die. The history books were filled with men named Neville Fleet, different individuals, surely, but in many ways the same. Jeff wondered what kind of man this present Neville Fleet was, he who had chosen to preside over the final and irrevocable dissolution of Berwick Castle.

Minnie had spoken of him as a rather sad case, a man to be pitied.

How could you pity a man who owned all this, not to mention an art collection that included the Winchcombe Chalice?

The car wound through the village of Berwick. The village was tucked against the looming battlements of the castle, clusters of neat little stone and stucco houses, some with their old thatched roofs, others roofed in slate or red tile. They seemed to be huddling against the eternal walls of Berwick Castle as though to draw warmth from it. The road was a lane now, with barely room for two cars to pass. Morgan turned right, and suddenly they were on the graveled drive that led straight to the castle's main entrance. This appeared to Jeff's eyes as a mere slit in the rock, and it struck him as unlikely that their car could squeeze through. The entrance was cut into the base of a fat five-story tower crowned with merlons and embrasures, arrow slits being carved into the solid segments of the crenellated wall in the form of rude Maltese crosses. The great oaken door that had once been the first barrier to uninvited entrance had long since vanished. But the sharp-spiked iron grille of the portcullis hung in deadly readiness above the arched entrance to the tunnel.

As the car squeezed into the tunnel, Jeff half-expected the sinister-looking machine to come crashing down, slicing them like salami.

The tunnel was nearly forty feet long, the thickness of the tower, and another grim portcullis was suspended at the far end.

"It's a pity," said Morgan as he eased the car down the narrow chute, "that we can't see the murder holes. I'll show them to you later on."

"And what," asked Polly, "is a murder hole?"

"They're arrow slits cut into the roof of the tunnel, accessible from the tower armory, so that if anyone should breach the front end of the tunnel, they could be shot at from above, and trapped by the final portcullis you see ahead."

"Charming," murmured Polly in a voice that did not sound charmed.

Jeff looked at her and grinned. "And you can guess," he said, "what they do if they aren't pleased with the way you dress for dinner."

"Boiling oil?"

"Iron maidens?"

Morgan was not amused. "You really ought," he said rather sternly, "to ask the duke if he'll take you round the dungeons. They're most impressive."

Polly giggled. "I'll sleep on it," she said. "Restlessly."

Morgan pulled the car up close by the impressively carved door to the state apartments of Berwick Castle. Jeff looked eagerly around the great walled courtyard. The perimeter wall was punctuated by towers of varying sizes, and the wall enclosed a large rolling lawn planted with mature trees, a huge paved central court, and, of course, the principal wing of the castle, which held the state apartments and the residence of the Duke and Duchess of Berwick. *What a prison they made for themselves,* he thought, *when they went to all this trouble to keep the world at bay.*

The courtyard looked well-kept, but there was something forlorn about it too. There was no sign of life but for the three occupants of the rented car as they extracted their luggage from the car's trunk.

The front door of the castle swung open, and a tall, slightly stooped man came walking toward them, dressed in old but beautifully cut tweeds, wearing a large smile of welcome. Jeff knew at once this must be the duke.

"Dear Morgan," said this personage, pumping St. James by the hand with enough vigor to move water. "How very kind of you to come so soon. And," he said, beaming at Polly, "my old acquaintance from Dupre's, Miss Kunimara. Welcome, my dear, and to you, too, Mr. Dupre. We are desolated about your dear uncle, a great, great loss, my boy." With these words he shook Polly's hand and Jeff's and shepherded them into the castle.

Jeff was no stranger to castles, but he had never seen anything quite the equal of Berwick. Fundamentally a medieval fortress more than a residence, the castle had been expanded and redecorated by generations of Fleets. There were rooms and entire wings of the place in a diversity of styles that made up a living museum of architectural fashion from the time of the Tudors through Victoria Regina. It was all there, and it had all stayed there virtually untouched through the ages. Here were wainscots from the thirteenth century, carved to resemble folded linen, and elsewhere could be seen the lavish, richly sculptured wooden festoons of the famous Grinling Gibbons, great swags framing overmantels, capping windows, turning low-relief pilasters into somber festivals of fruit and flowers and trailing leaves. The prince regent's taste for things Oriental was evident in great lacquered cabinets whose surfaces were painted with Chinese figures in gold and muted colors. Victorian ponderosities flirted with Edwardian attic.

It seemed, to Jeff's eyes, that the Fleets had never thrown away anything: it was all still in place, a living museum.

Here and there, sadly, he could discern squares and ovals on the walls, clearly places where pictures and mirrors had hung before being sold off. The distinction was subtle: a brighter square of painted wall where the sunlight had been unable to fade it. There was a sense of abandonment in these chambers, and even a musty, empty odor, faint but insistent. The general effect was dark, and somehow threatening.

The duke led them through room after room, until they were drunk on decor. There seemed to be no servants. Finally he paused at the foot of a vast stone staircase where a tiny and withered little maidservant was waiting.

"Perkins will show you to your rooms," said the duke. "Mr. St. James, I believe, already knows the way. You'll probably want to freshen up a bit before dinner, which is at seven-thirty. We'll meet in the blue drawing room for cocktails."

"How," asked Jeff, "will we find the blue drawing room? A stranger could get lost here, for weeks."

The duke laughed. "Of course. In fact, it has happened. Just ring, dear boy, just ring. Someone will fetch you. It isn't really all that difficult, but there is a knack to it."

"Thank you."

"Until seven-thirty, then."

The duke smiled and bowed slightly, and Jeff and Polly followed the tiny maid up the stairs. At the first landing, the maid led them down a long vaulted hall. It seemed to lead into infinity. There was something cold about the hallway, a feeling of being in an institution. They passed over carpet after worn Persian carpet. In groups, against both sides of the hall, were arrangements of chairs and settees that seemed to be awaiting guests who had long since vanished and would never come again. The furniture was splendid to look at. But it gave Jeff the uneasy feeling that no one had ever been comfortable sitting in it. They passed door after door, each elaborately carved and paneled, leading, Jeff guessed, to guest rooms. Between the doors and above the furniture hung paintings of an almost impenetrable darkness. The hallway was only intermittently lighted, and although Jeff could make out a window at the far end of it, the window's light made only the most feeble inroads on the prevailing gloom.

Suddenly it all began to seem funny to him. He turned to Polly. "It's not much," he said softly, hoping the maid might not hear, "but it's home."

She giggled. "It's not the price, it's the upkeep. You could burn out a vacuum cleaner a day on this hallway alone."

Their rooms were on the same side of the long hallway, about halfway down its length.

The maid opened Polly's door first. Jeff caught a glimpse of a great canopied bed, tall windows, fresh flowers. It looked like a pleasant change after the grim hallway. He turned to Polly. "When you've finished polishing your tiara," he said, grinning, "give me a knock. Say about seven. We can search for the blue drawing room together."

"You're on."

Jeff's room was huge and very beautiful. It was paneled in some dark wood—walnut, he thought, without being sure. The windows were many and deep-set into the paneling so that each one had its own window seat. There was a fireplace with logs and kindling and twists of old newspaper waiting to be lit. Summer it might be, but this was England. Jeff wondered if Berwick had central heating. There was a low sort of buffet table set against one wall, and on it was a large silver urn filled with flowers. On the small table next to the bed was a reading lamp and three current magazines. Someone had taken a bit of trouble.

After a little searching Jeff located the bathroom, which had obviously been converted in the expansive past. The tub could have held three men Jeff's size. It stood arrogantly on claw-and-ball feet, its brass fittings gleaming. The sink was porcelain and enormous, decorated with stylized Greek key motifs in apple green and gold. There was no shower. Jeff decided he'd fill the tub and go swimming.

An hour later, bathed and unpacked and dressed in his well-worn J. Press dinner jacket, Jeff stood gazing out the window across the river and over the rooftops of Berwick village to the endless forests beyond.

He suddenly felt quite ducal, and grinned at the image.

There came a knocking at his door.

Polly stood there, glowing. "Is this the blue drawing room?" she asked, smiling a slow smile.

"I think it may be a bad movie, the castle, the monkey suit, all that."

"Not so bad as you may think. Are you going to invite a lady in?"

"I'm sorry." He stood aside and she walked into the room. "Nice."

"You look nice, Polly. No boiling oil for you." He wanted her then, urgently.

She walked to the window. "It's my basic little castle-hopping number. Or is it castle-crawling these days?"

"Is it presumptuous if we ring for a drink?"

"I'll tell you a secret, Jeff. I couldn't find what to ring with."

They both looked. Finally, on a side table that held several small objets d'art, Polly located a thick disk of malachite set with an ivory button. Winding out of its base was an old-fashioned electric cord covered in braided silk. She pressed the button. "That'll either bring a servant or we've launched missiles against Ireland."

"He told us to ring. His . . . what do we call him?"

"His grace, can you believe?"

"His grace asked us to ring. I'll never get used to it. We don't have his graces in Veii."

But you have countesses, thought Polly, and hated herself for thinking it.

"I was so dizzy from all that splendor," said Polly, "when the duke was showing us around, that I couldn't focus on any one object. It would take months to really catalog this place."

"I think that's what Morgan intends will happen. Several sales, over a period of time. Starting with the spectacular one."

"It'll be spectacular, all right."

The maid knocked. Jeff let her in. It was a different maid from the tiny old one who had shown them up. This maid was plump and blushing and couldn't have been much over twenty. She looked like a Boucher milkmaid.

"You rang, sir?"

"Yes. Could you show us the way to the blue drawing room?"

"If you please, sir, and follow me."

They retraced their steps down the hallway, which was even gloomier now in the fading light. Down the great staircase and down another long hall, past chamber after splendid chamber, past the chapel, the library, and another, smaller library, and the maid reciting the names of the chambers softly as they walked.

Finally they reached their goal.

"The blue drawing room, sir."

"Thank you."

They walked in.

Polly gasped. It was a room meant for crowds, for spectacles. The walls soared. The ceilings retreated into space. The room was a disconcerting shade of peacock blue, details of the molding picked out in old gold. Against the still-brilliant blue were hung dozens of paintings, landscapes for the most part, with here and there the occasional still life. Wherever the ancestors were kept, thought Jeff, it wasn't here. There was a vast fireplace crowned, literally, by a carved and crested white marble mantelpiece. Over the mantelpiece was hung a mirror of imperial proportions, webbed and festooned with a half-acre of elaborately carved eighteenth-century giltwood chinoiserie. There was an enormous Aubusson carpet, obviously specially woven for the room, for it defined the fireplace and echoed the family crest. The carpet was peacock blue and gold and ivory and rose. There was one predominating suite of furniture, carved and gilded within an inch of its life in the opulent, ostentatious manner of Louis XIV, and upholstered in the same demanding blue, this time a self-patterned silk satin brocade.

"Well," whispered Polly, "it certainly is blue."

Jeff laughed out loud, and the laughter echoed in the vast room. They were entirely alone, and the scale of the place made them seem even more alone than they might have been in a more normally proportioned space.

"It just shows," said Jeff, "what you can do with a little imagination."

"And a thousand years."

"And God knows what demented decorator."

"Did someone say something about a drink?"

Jeff was still studying the room. He located a small table on which reposed a silver tray, glasses, an ice bucket, and several decanters. "Let us assume," he said, "that it's self-help. What can I get you?"

"Something very stiff, because I'm afraid my upper lip isn't. How about some Scotch on the rocks?"

"Consider it done. I feel just the same way."

He sniffed at three decanters before locating the whiskey. "Cheers," he said, handing her a glass.

"Cheers yourself, Jeff. We seem to be in this together."

Jeff was about to reply when the duke's voice interrupted them. "Ah, children, I see you've found the hooch. Were the rooms in good order?"

They both assured their host that everything was just as it should be. He poured himself a large Scotch on the rocks and lifted his glass.

"Tchin-tchin," said the duke merrily.

"To your good health," said Jeff, "and to the auction."

"Yes," said the duke, "to the auction."

Morgan joined them then, sleek in his dinner clothes, smiling. "Am I the last?"

"Not at all," said Neville. "Bess will be with us shortly, from the nursery. She's dotty about the boy, but then, so am I."

Minnie had mentioned the duke's second marriage, and the sad death of his first wife. Jeff wondered what it must be like to marry into Berwick. Especially to marry into a Berwick so thoroughly on the skids.

He didn't have to wonder for very long. Bess Fleet came in just then, smiling, dressed simply in a white silk shirt and a subdued tartan skirt to the floor. Polly's instinct had been right, and her dress was similar, understated, a rich-looking shirt over a long velvet skirt, the shirt deeply pink, the skirt of the darkest burgundy. Neither woman wore jewelry.

"Welcome," she said, shaking hands all round. "The monster is finally in his cage for the night, at least we hope so."

The duke laughed. Too quickly, Jeff thought.

"Young Neville," said his father, "is in an exploratory stage at the moment, much to the detriment of anything small and breakable."

"Such as his mother's nervous system," said Bess, smiling.

The duke looked at her, thinking, perhaps, of Miranda.

They went in to dinner, the duchess having declined a cocktail. The room they entered after much walking down corridors and turning of corners was misnamed the small dining room. It was anything but small. At a glance, Jeff guessed, it would hold the entire ground floor of his aunt's house on Manhattan. The chamber might have been fifty feet long by thirty feet wide. The ceilings were enormously tall.

Jeff wondered how a lifetime spent in rooms like these might affect your perception of ordinary spaces. They were seated at a table whose size would have made an adequate dance floor. It gleamed with centuries of devoted polishing. And the silver candlesticks gleamed, and the centerpiece, also silver, added to the flash and glow. Their place mats of antique lace made white islands on the glass-smooth mahogany sea that was the tabletop. Four tall-stemmed wineglasses flanked every plate, and the plates themselves were of an age and intricacy that made Jeff wish he knew more about antique porcelain. The flatware was hardly flat, encrusted as it was with deeply carved scrolls and flowers and cherubs.

The smallest of the four wineglasses was already filled with an amber-colored liquid.

The duke raised his glass. "Welcome to Berwick," he said, "and may luck be with us." He lifted the intricately etched wineglass a bit higher, so that it was nearly level with his eyes. Then he looked from face to face to face before drinking, in the old German style, his eyes meeting and holding those of each guest in turn. There seemed to be more meaning hovering somewhere just behind the duke's glance than mere welcome, but Jeff had no conception of what that might be and decided not to try guessing. Maybe the old turkey had the hots for Polly. It would be easy to understand, with her looking the way she did tonight.

"We are enchanted," said Morgan, easily assuming the leadership of the small group of visitors, "to be here. Cheers!"

"Cheers!" said Polly, smiling gently.

"Cheers!" said Jeff, not feeling especially cheerful.

The wine proved to be an ancient *fino* sherry of an almost crystalline dryness and delicacy. It made a remarkable partnership with the clear turtle soup that quickly appeared, served by a maid who hadn't been seen before. The meal was long and sumptuous but not, Jeff felt, especially well-cooked. There was an unidentifiable white fish, elaborately sauced, roast duck a shade too fat, excellent beef, also roasted, but a touch too well-done. Then came a small salad and a fine, old-fashioned custardy trifle laced with rum. The wines, throughout, were poetic and generously served. Jeff was nothing like an expert on wine, but even an amateur accustomed to living on a budget could tell that these were extraordinary. With the fish came a Montrachet of great depth and clarity, followed by a red Bordeaux soft as flower petals and almost equally well-perfumed. With the beef, and compensating to a

246

great degree for the beef's dryness, was a triumphant old Burgundy.

Jeff complimented the duke on his wines and got another dose of unexpected frankness in reply.

"If I drank like a fish from morning till night and lived to be a hundred, dear boy, I couldn't work my way through the wine cellars of Berwick. So my attitude is, as with the chalice and all the rest of it, well, I can't take it with me, as they say, can I now?" And he laughed, and rang for more wine.

Jeff had an inkling of what it might have been like at Berwick in the great days of the castle's power. The lord of the castle, extravagant and extravagantly powerful, decreeing this and denying that, master of all and completely invulnerable. Jeff could see the duke glorying in the role, and he could see, too, that his host was aware that it was a role. And that the show was definitely going to close, possibly one day soon.

Jeff sipped the wine. The ladies said little; Morgan and the duke did most of the talking.

Coffee was served in the library. This room, surprisingly, was not large. It was warmly paneled in a honey-colored wood that made Jeff think of the color of Berwick stone. The books were richly bound, mostly in gilded leather. An old Persian hunting carpet adorned the floor. Mythical animals chased each other around the carpet, blue deer being attacked by white leopards, a bright red lion scampering among improbably yellow foliage. The colors had faded and blended with time: there was nothing shrill about the carpet now. Its violence had been subdued by the softness of passing years. The coffee could have been stronger. They sipped and chatted of nothing in particular. The duke offered cordials, but only Morgan accepted, and the duke himself. The two older men swirled cognac in huge balloon glasses. A silence fell on the library.

Polly broke it with a yawn that was only half-stifled. "Oh!" she said, smiling lazily. "Please excuse me, your Grace. It's been a long day, and there's so much to do tomorrow. I think what I need is some sleep."

"Of course, my dear," said the duke kindly. Bess and I are very early to bed ourselves, more often than not. This is quite a festive occasion for us. I'll see you up, then."

"Don't bother, I can find it now." She stood up.

Jeff stood also. "I'll see you up, Polly," he said. "I was just thinking the same thing, about being tired."

"Whatever," asked Morgan in a voice laced with mockery, "is happening to the younger generation? Why, it's hardly eleven o'clock."

"Airplanes," said Jeff, "always make me sleepy. I think it's the altitude."

"Or," said Polly, laughing, "the terror."

"Something, anyway. Good night, then, and thank you for a great meal."

"It was," said the duke, half-rising out of his chair, "nothing, dear boy, nothing at all."

Jeff and Polly walked side by side down the long hallway to the stairs. They could hear soft voices in the library behind them, but the cavernous spaces of Berwick seemed to devour the sound: no words were distinct to them, even when they were just a few feet away.

The lighting in the hallway cast eerie shadows.

"If," said Polly quietly, "a person were given to seeing ghosts, this would be just the place."

"I'd love to see a ghost. I often wonder if my Etruscans had ghosts. They sure believed in all kinds of crazy gods and spirits and magic. So much so that it's hard to figure out just who was worshiping what at any given time."

"So they don't scare you?"

"Not really," said Jeff, thinking how many more recent mysteries did scare him.

They were climbing the dark stairs now. The castle seemed to be completely silent. There were no echoes. Even their footsteps on the ancient stone stairs seemed to vanish as they fell. It seemed quieter to Jeff than any place he had ever been.

They reached the landing.

"Our host," said Jeff, "ought to give us flashlights and a map."

"We go left," said Polly. "I think."

"Stopping only for ghosts?"

"Don't say that!"

She reached for his hand and squeezed it. He squeezed back. It felt good, her hand in his, as they made their uncertain way down the long hallway.

"Like everything else," he said in a voice so low it was almost a whisper, "there are good ones and bad ones."

"The ones I imagine are all bad. I must have a creepy character."

"Right, very creepy. I couldn't tell which door's mine if my life depended on it."

They walked in silence for a moment. Now they were nearly halfway down the length of the hall.

"It's either this one or the next," said Jeff, knocking on a door. There was no answer. He tried the knob. It was open.

248

He pushed the door back. It moved on silent hinges. There was no light in the room but for a faint grayness that seeped in through the windows. Jeff could just make out the bulk of a big canopied bed. He couldn't tell whether it was his. Still holding Polly's hand, he felt along the wall, hoping to find a switch. He stumbled against a small table. Objects on the table jiggled, tinkling. Luckily, nothing broke. He felt for the tabletop. There was a lamp. He switched on the lamp. It was his room after all. His bed had been turned down, and there was a small silver dish on the night table with chocolate candies in it.

"Home free." He had imagined bursting in on the duchess, or some other such embarrassment. Jeff turned to Polly, suddenly very aware that her hand was still in his. She was trembling. She looked to be on the verge of tears.

"What's wrong, Polly?"

She pressed against him, still trembling. Her other hand wound its way around his back. He held her tight.

"Hey," he said gently, as if to a child, "it's all right. Everything's just fine."

Finally she spoke. "I'm sorry, Jeff. Something about this place gives me the creeps."

She looked up at him in the dim amber lamplight and smiled.

Polly was not a short girl, but Jeff had to bend down a little when he kissed her. It was a long kiss. It got longer. Finally she pulled away. Her arms were still around him, his around her. Jeff was very aware of her body, and of his own. The silence was complete.

"Feel better?" he asked, his hand moving against the silk of her blouse where it covered her slender back. Then she kissed him again, and that was all the answer he required.

Time dissolved for Jeff then. Soon they were together on the great old bed, lost in a magical world of giving and taking, of urgency and joy, of pleasures that were infinitely the more sweet for being shared. Part of the magic in her was that she made him forget where he was, forget the past weeks. She almost made him forget the specter of death itself, and Carla, and the unborn child.

Much later, Polly lay silent in his arms, wondering what might be going on in Jeff's mind and not daring to ask. She tried to sort out her own feelings, to separate the good thoughts from the fears. Polly knew she was given to unfounded doubts and trepidations. But the knowing didn't make them go away. She had liked Jeff from the first, and she had liked him in bed more than any of the other few men she'd known. And what did any of it mean? What would he think tomorrow? For that matter, what would she think tomorrow? Whatever happened, nothing between them could ever be the same. Jeff, she felt, was far from casual, definitely not your love-'em-and-leave-'em type. But only time could prove her right about that. Right or wrong.

He moved beside her. "Polly?"

"I'm here."

"I didn't think it could be the duke."

She laughed. He kissed her. They made love again. And again.

Jeff woke in an empty bed.

He looked around, startled. His dinner jacket and trousers were neatly folded over a chair—not by him. His shirt, tie, socks, and underwear were in a heap on the floor. He hadn't imagined it, then. The light was pale. He looked at his watch. Five-thirty. He wondered when she'd left him.

Jeff stretched, yawned extravagantly, and rolled over in the huge old bed. *Polly!*

He closed his eyes and saw her. He smiled. *Polly, Polly, Polly*. How strange and unexpected, the way they'd finally gotten together again. And how delightful. Then he slept again, and for a few blessed hours Jeff forgot everything that had happened. He forgot the deaths of Felix and Carla. He forgot the troubles at Dupre's. He forgot his dig at Veii.

He even forgot to be afraid.

44

Jeff found his way to the breakfast room. It was predictably huge, but sunny and informal by contrast to the vast chamber where they had dined last night. Sun streamed through enormous small-paned windows. He could catch a glimpse of greenery outside. One of the windows had been opened. A fine curtain of some white material flapped slowly in the breeze. The air smelled of hay.

The Duke of Berwick sat alone at the dining table, reading the London *Times*. He wore an open shirt with a silk scarf firmly knotted at the throat, a dark blue blazer, and old flannels. He looked absolutely at ease. On a sideboard a huge breakfast buffet had been set up, silver chafing dishes of scrambled eggs and sausage, a large partially sliced ham, several kinds of fruit, coffee and tea, and thick, thick cream.

"Ah," said the duke, "there you are, dear boy. I'm afraid you and I are the lazy ones. Miss Kunimara and Morgan are hard at it already."

It was nine-thirty. Jeff was still warm with the memory of last night. Of Polly. Berwick seemed warm, too, and utterly secure. Out beyond these thick walls, empires might be falling, and you'd never know.

Jeff helped himself to toast, eggs and sausage, to fruit juice and coffee, and sat down near his host. "Lovely morning," said Jeff, wondering why he had been asked to come.

"Yes," said Neville absently. "Later on, I want to give you and the young lady a proper tour."

"I'm eager to see the chalice."

The duke laughed as though Jeff had told the funniest joke in the world. "I'll wager you are, being a Dupre! Oh, you'll see it, dear boy, have no doubts about that!"

Jeff ate sparingly.

Last night had taken him by surprise. And it had taken him places he wasn't sure he wanted to go. Even thinking of another woman seemed treacherous to the memory of Carla. But it had happened, and happened naturally, and in the rush of his feeling for Polly, he had forgotten Carla. Or had he made love to Polly in order to forget? Or was he kidding himself on several counts, about the depth of the feeling he'd had for Carla, about this new feeling for Polly? Thinking about it was painful. He tried not to think. Impossible. He looked at the duke, to find the duke looking at him, slightly puzzled. *Well he might be puzzled. He probably thinks I've gone bonkers, and he may be right at that.*

"The Concorde took away your appetite?"

"Oh, not at all, it's just that I'm not used to your big English breakfasts. In Veii, it's coffee and a roll, and that's it."

"Veii. What a lovely name. I've never been to Italy. There was the war, and then, afterward, one didn't travel."

"Perhaps now . . ."

"Ah, yes, indeed. Now. Now many things will become possible. Would you . . ."—the duke paused, suddenly shy—"show us your dig?"

"I'd be delighted, although there isn't much to see just yet. The glamour, the big finds with lots of gold, Schliemann at Troy, Carter at King Tut's tomb, that's all Sunday-supplement stuff. It does happen, but so rarely you could wait your whole lifetime and it might never happen to you."

"What's the fascination, then, if you'll excuse a rude and ignorant question?"

Jeff paused, and spread a bit of marmalade on a piece of toast. The toast was too soft for his taste, but the marmalade was perfection. "The jigsaw part of it. Putting the pieces together. Adding, with luck, some small grain to the mountain of human knowledge."

"Then you are a historian."

Jeff laughed. "Professional historians sometimes get mad at us. We tend to upset some of their most cherished theories. It seems that historians like to generate theories, to promulgate whole philosophies of who did what, and when, and why, all following some grand design that's clear only to the historian. In real life, it almost never happens that way. This king is crazy, that one has wanderlust, an unstoppable drought or plague breaks out: these are the things that change history. And they're so much at random, it drives historians up the wall. The concept of random is unscientific, you see."

"Come with me through Berwick, dear boy, and I'll make an historian of you yet."

The duke rose. Jeff finished the last of his coffee and got up too.

"No one," said the duke as they walked down a wide corridor, "has ever counted all the rooms, but, taking in dungeons and armories and various chambers tucked into the perimeter walls, there must be well over three hundred. It was a city, really, more than a house: fortress, spiritual headquarters, center of temporal authority for the county."

They came to an ancient oaken door set into a pointed archway. The duke swung it open. "The chapel of Berwick. Catholic forever, my grandfather used to say. We don't know what the National Trust will make of that—if the Trust ends up with Berwick there may have to be some sort of heavenly intervention, as it were. To keep it consecrated and all that."

"It was never changed?"

"Henry wouldn't dare. Nor Mary either."

Jeff was amused to note that the duke spoke of King Henry VIII and his benighted daughter as though they were a pair of not very reputable tradespeople. The duke stood aside and beckoned Jeff into the chapel.

The room had a certain austere dignity, all gray stone and wood so dark it might be called black.

But what drew Jeff's eye was the chalice. It seemed to

reach out to him, beckoning. A few shafts of morning sunshine struggled down from the narrow windows high overhead. They were enough. The chalice had the power, or so it appeared, to capture what light there was and amplify it, making it bounce and sparkle.

Without being aware of it, Jeff had walked the length of the room. Only when he bumped into the altar rail, and only then did he realize how far he had come. Often in his lifetime Jeff had come upon some famous sight for the first time and found that it fell short of his expectations.

This was not true of the Winchcombe Chalice.

For all of its undeniable beauty, age, and history, for all of its immense value on the market, the chalice had an extra dimension of appeal. It was more than the sum of its legends. Jeff Dupre, accustomed to old and beautiful things from childhood, was deeply moved by the thing.

The duke's hand touched Jeff's shoulder. "But you must touch it, dear boy. After all, the chalice is yours now, so to speak."

The duke opened a gate in the altar rail and stepped casually up to the altar and picked up the cup.

Jeff was a little shocked. The cup must be sacred, even if it was the duke's own private property!

The duke handed the chalice to Jeff as though it were a teacup.

Jeff reached out to take it, and quickly withdrew his hand, as though the cup might burn him.

Neville Fleet laughed. "It's perfectly all right, Mr. Dupre. God will not strike you dead."

Jeff took it. How many people, after all, in the whole history of the chalice, had actually handled it? The texture of the gold was astonishing. The raised surfaces were bright from the touch of a priest's hands, or from attentive polishing. The leaves had a different finish, delicately veined, naturalistic, and the stem of the cup itself was textured too, for contrast. Each grape in each grape cluster seemed to have its own personality. The rubies looked wet, as if some rare old claret had been transformed into burnished gemstone.

He stroked the cup. It felt alive. Jeff had never touched a decorative object that had such tactile beauty combined with its legendary past. A blind man would covet it too, he thought, as his fingers caressed the chalice from top to bottom.

Then Jeff turned and proffered it to the duke. "You're very brave," said Jeff, "to part with it."

"Oddly, and I guess luckily," replied his host, "it's never meant that much to me. A pretty thing, to be sure, and crammed with all sorts of history. But we Fleets haven't been all that keen on art lately, not these last hundred or so years. Run more to horseflesh and the ladies, I blush to confess."

Jeff looked at the duke and tried to imagine him at either pursuit.

"Suddenly," said Jeff, "I'm beginning to understand why people pay the amazing amounts they do for certain things at auction."

"Bless them," said the duke with a chuckle. "God bless them, every one."

They walked out of the chapel and down the corridor. They passed through rooms that Jeff remembered, if vaguely, from the walk they had taken on arriving yesterday. Room led to room, hall to hall, vault to arch to mullion. Suddenly they were in the great dining hall of the castle. Jeff understood now why the room they had eaten in last night was called "small."

An army could have dined here, thought Jeff, and armies probably have dined here. The ceiling was supported by black oak beams that met at the roof peak perhaps sixty feet overhead. The walls were paneled in the same dark oak. Two immense trestle tables stretched, side by side, nearly the complete length of the room. At widely spaced intervals on the tops of these tables, islands of old silverware glittered. There were many-branched candlesticks that seemed to want to be trees. There were punch bowls, ladles, mugs, wine coolers, service plates, and vast aggregations of spoons, knives, and forks. Sitting in isolated splendor next to the biggest assortment of silver was Polly Kunimara, businesslike in trim blue slacks and a white turtleneck of some thin material. She was writing furiously with one hand and reaching for little self-sticking tags with the other. Each little tag was precoded with the Dupre sale number. All Polly had to do was attach the tag and write a short identifying notation in her sale book. Further research, if necessary, could be done in New York.

She looked up at the sound of their footsteps, smiled rather perfunctorily, and went right back to her cataloging.

"Good morning," said Jeff, his brain churning.

"Hi," she said.

Hi. Hi! She says "Hi" with about as much feeling as the stones in the floor. Jeff knew he was being foolish. Maybe he wanted to be foolish. Maybe it was time for a little foolishness, a touch of the old careless rapture. He tried to think of something clever to say. Something that would tell her how he felt without tipping off the old duke.

So he said, "How's it going?"

If there was a message for Jeff in her glance, he didn't find it.

Her answer was really more for the duke. "We have enough material here for a dozen big sales, your Grace, and that's just the silver alone. It's extraordinary. Of course, there is a lot of Victorian stuff, but even that's bringing good prices these days. Some people seem to prefer it."

Polly said that in a manner that left no doubt as to what she preferred.

"Wonderful, wonderful," said the duke happily. He actually rubbed his hands together in a cheerful pantomime of greed. "Every bit helps, then, doesn't it?"

"We're having a grand tour." Jeff had felt useless when he first saw Polly so diligently at work. Now, announcing his recreation, he felt even more useless.

"How nice," she said, looking at Jeff directly for the first time.

"I was hoping," said the duke, "that we could lure you away for a few minutes. To see . . ."—he paused for effect—"the dungeons!"

"I'd love to," said Polly quickly, maybe too quickly, "but . . ."

"Duty calls? Well," said the duke, "one can hardly quarrel with that, can one?"

"How long," asked Jeff, "would it take?"

"To do the dungeons? Dear boy, people have spent decades down there, ha-ha. Perhaps half an hour, if we are brisk. Do come, Miss Kunimara, I insist. You make me uneasy, working so hard—you are sure to ruin your health."

Polly sighed. "If you promise—"

"Not an instant more than half an hour, on the honor of the Fleets of Berwick."

Polly put her pen into the sale book and closed it. She stood up, stretching. "After the first hundred or so items," she said, "I begin to get cross-eyed anyway."

And without saying another word to either man, Polly joined them as they passed through the great dining hall and down the corridor to the dungeon stair.

The door, when they came to it, was surprisingly small. They had come into a very old part of the castle.

"Not older, truly, for the entire thing is ancient," said the duke, "but the state apartments and such have been rather recently fixed up, don't you know, seventeenth-century and later, whereas the basic hulk of the place is really twelfth and thirteenth."

The door was arched and framed with oak so old it seemed on the verge of petrifying. Thick bands of black wrought iron formed the door's hinges. The door swung out, and the duke led the way, first pressing a light switch that was just inside the door on the left.

"I'll lead," he said. "Parts of the dungeons are a bit tricky, and you want to know what you're doing."

The stairs were cut into the living rock of Berwick. They spiraled down in tight little corkscrew turns, round and round. Down and down. But for their footsteps, the silence was complete. Jeff could hear himself breathe. Or maybe it was Polly. The duke led the way, Polly followed the duke, and Jeff brought up the rear. The lights had been strung rather crudely at intervals along the top of the stairwell. Jeff had to bend to avoid bumping his head.

At last, after many turns of the corkscrew stairs, they came to a landing. Tunnels branched out in two directions, and both of them were pitch black.

"This," said the duke, "is the first level, and not all that interesting. Storage mostly, and Grandfather's wine cellars, for which I shall be eternally thankful. The fun begins on the next level. That's where we'll see Mortimer."

"Who," asked Jeff, "is he?"

"Ha-ha, Berwick has its secrets, and Mortimer is one of them, dear boy. If I told you, it wouldn't be a surprise, then, would it?"

Jeff looked at his host, wondering for the first time if perhaps the Fleets had developed a little strain of madness. He couldn't see Polly's face, and there was no room, descending single file as they were, for him to take her hand. They continued down the spiral stairs.

The second level of the Berwick dungeons was even farther below the first level than the first level had been below the living quarters. Jeff tried to calculate precisely how far they had gone down. But the turnings of the stairs confused even his trained archaeologist's mind. More than a hundred feet, surely, and probably more. Much more. The air, oddly, was nothing like as stale as Jeff expected to find it at this depth. He mentioned this to the duke.

"Vents, dear boy, vents. The thirteenth century's own air-conditioning system. All through the cliff face are cut small slits of air vents that lead right to these passages, and the wind whipping down the river does the rest."

"Ingenious. Are there other entrances?"

There was a pause before the dúke answered. Jeff wondered if he was perhaps debating whether to reveal another of Berwick's secrets.

"Two that I know of for certain," said the duke. "And there are rumored to be still others, family legends, escapes during sieges and so forth, but no one has yet discovered them."

The light remained dubious at best.

Finally they reached the second level. Here, from a larger landing than the one above, three tunnels penetrated the honey-colored rock. There was a rude table pushed against the rock wall, and on it a large and efficient-looking flashlight.

The duke picked up the light and motioned them on. "Stay close, my dears," he said. "This is where we all must watch our steps."

"Why?" asked Polly.

"Mortimer will tell you that," said the duke with a chuckle.

Jeff felt Polly's hand reach for his. He smiled. If it was going to be a creepy walk, there was no one he'd rather have next to him. As he had before, the duke led the way. The tunnel was illuminated only at very long intervals, and at that with small bare bulbs whose rays made only the most feeble inroads on the prevailing darkness.

The tunnel meandered through the rock, curving slightly this way and then that. Here and there little rooms, rough-walled and doorless, had been hollowed out of the rock. There was an unidentifiable dusty smell to the place.

They moved cautiously forward in the dancing, changing shadows thrown by the duke's powerful electric torch. There came a sudden bend in the tunnel. The duke threw out his arm to halt their progress. Jeff and Polly came up close beside him, wondering why they'd stopped so abruptly. The flashlight's beam wandered along the walls. The rock walls were rough-hewn. Jeff could see the marks left by ancient tools. He could imagine sweating, grumbling serfs hacking away at the eternal rock, spending their whole lives in anguished toil for the glory of the Fleets of Berwick. Here and there a rusted iron hook or ring had been fitted into the rock. Prisoners, the duke had said, once hung there in chains and iron cages. The beam of light darted lower.

There was a square black hole cut into the tunnel floor,

directly in their path. Jeff could tell the hole was deep. The flashlight beam danced about the rim of the hole, teasing.

Then the duke moved half a step aside and focused the beam at the bottom of the pit.

Polly gasped and grabbed Jeff's arm.

The pit was perhaps ten feet deep. Its walls were straight and smoother than the tunnel walls. Up from the floor of the pit grew regiments of sharp iron spikes set into the rock at six-inch intervals, rusted now but obviously meant to kill.

Impaled on the spikes was the skeleton, white and grinning, his bony right hand still clutching the short sword. There was a helmet near his skull, and fragments of ancient armor were strewn near the bones where the leather fastenings had rotted away, letting the iron plates slide free.

The duke laughed. "Mortimer," he cackled, "welcomes you to Berwick!"

Then the light went out and they were trapped in utter darkness.

Polly screamed.

Jeff grabbed her, pulled her close, held her tight. Then he backed slowly, quietly away from the pit. The rock was solid behind him. He remembered that.

For a moment, after Polly's scream and its echoes died away, there was no sound at all in the dungeon but for the three people breathing hard. Jeff wondered why he'd allowed Fleet to lure him down here so easily.

Lure.

The duke himself had used the word.

Suddenly it had a terrible significance.

Jeff pressed hard against the wall behind him.

They wouldn't dare.

Whoever they were.

Or would they?

He tensed, waiting for the unknown, and completely unprepared for it. Whatever it was they had in mind.

45

On the night table next to Oswald Webster's enormous bed was a telephone programmed to dial any one of sixty-two numbers around the world, automatically, at the touch of a button. One of these numbers was Hong Kong; others were in all the capitals of Europe; there was one in Moscow, several in the United States, and three on private oceangoing yachts. Still another button was connected to Webster's aircraft, the only 747 in the world owned by a private individual.

It was 2:20 A.M. in Santa Barbara. Oswald Webster lay in bed, alone, idly flipping through a Parke Bernet catalog from the year 1931. His mind seethed with opportunities missed. What treasures had slipped away from him simply due to the stupidity of fate, that he hadn't been rich and in New York in 1931. Or almost any other year. Or in Florence, the time of Cosimo the Magnificent.

He put down the catalog and picked up the telephone receiver. He pressed a button.

In a studio loft in SoHo in Manhattan, a red light flashed. The loft was huge, one vast room with forty-foot ceilings, forested with fluted iron columns. Seventeen deciduous trees grew in tubs near the vast windows. Against one wall was a small but well-fitted-out gymnasium. A slender brunette woman with very long hair pedaled a chromium exercise bicycle. As the light flashed, she reached out and picked up a telephone receiver, never missing a turn of the pedals.

"How many miles so far?"

"Nineteen and a half, more or less."

Webster knew she got up every morning at five and did an hour's worth of exercises. The woman was one of his consultants. Oswald Webster employed twelve such experts. They were on the Webco payroll at substantial salaries, but the real money they earned came from commissions on anything Webster purchased on their recommendation. To last as a Webster consultant, his employees quickly learned, meant being at Oswald's beck and call virtually around the clock and around the calendar. But the rewards were significant, both financially and artistically. Most of the consultants were either practicing artists, chosen for the sensitivity of their perceptions, or working scholars, chosen for the precision and depth of their knowledge. Webco made it possible for these people to live comfortably without fear of compromising their artistic or scholarly integrity.

All Oswald wanted was assurance that whatever he bought would be the best of the best.

"What," he asked the pedaling lady, "is new on the chalice?"

"Big hoo-ha in Britain. Basil Palfrey's up to his old tricks. Wants to raise a matching fund so Customs and Excise can refuse the export license. Which, theoretically, they could do. But there's no chance, not the way the economy is today. They couldn't do it for the Velázquez, and they won't for this. So, never fear, the sale will go on. You may have to go over four. Von Kronholtz is definitely interested, and he can swing a few biggies. But they'll probably put a limit on his bidding, whoever bids for him this time. Berkeley's not entirely keen. Or, rather, he's keen in theory but maybe not where he lives, if you get me."

"I get you, my dear. What do you think of a direct offer to the duke?"

There was a pause while she considered this. Webster could hear the rhythmic sounds of her bicycle clicking across three thousand miles of copper wire. Finally she answered, slowly, still weighing her answer. "If I knew the man, you'd get a yes or no. But I don't. It's hard to tell with the titled nobbies. Some are daffy as ducks. Some are crafty old devils. Or young devils. Basically, I think—gut feeling—that direct offers stink. There's no doubt but that the thing'll go for a lot. I think you'd have to make an offer well over the estimate. And the estimate—"

"I know. Three to four million. However they arrived at that figure."

"Unprecedented figure. Unprecedented item. Could go higher. You're not reconsidering?"

Now it was his turn to pause, to ponder. His funds, though immense by any standard, were not unlimited. If he had to spend, say, six million for this one item, it would cool down his buying activities for some time. Not because of any strict budgetary considerations, but rather because of the emotional factor. Oswald Webster had to feel the need for an object in his bones, feel it deeply and intensely. Only then would he call in his experts to authenticate the thing. In the case of the chalice, the need was intense.

"No," he said. "Nix. I am definitely not reconsidering. I'll have to find someone who knows the duke. Thank you, my dear. Have a nice ride."

Frederik von Kronholtz had not slept really well since acquiring the chalice had first become a possibility.

Now he turned in his bed. Shadows chased each other across his bedroom ceiling, formless, dark, and vaguely threatening. Many things seemed threatening to von Kronholtz these days. One was the director of his own museum. Berkeley was an odd one, for sure. Showman, figurehead, anything but a classical scholar. Sometimes von Kronholtz thought the man had gone quite off his rocker. Turning the place into a circus, that's what he was up to. If it made headlines, then it was good for attendance, and attendance was good for fund-raising, and fund-raising was good for match grants. It was a vicious cycle, all based on body counts. Rather like the horror in Southeast Asia. Body counts. Never mind if they came to gape, with never a glimmer of the artistic significance of what they were gaping at.

Well, the chalice would make headlines, no doubt of that. Thank God it was gold! Even Berkeley had heard of the Winchcombe Chalice. Even Berkeley knew the sensation it would cause, a distinctly Velázquez-like sensation. Of which he, Berkeley, would inevitably be cast as the hero. Well and good—let him cast himself as Jesus Christ if it snaffled the cup for the Met. He'd never get an argument from von Kronholtz on that subject. Again the curator turned in the empty bed. His wife was in Europe, visiting relatives. Just as well. He hadn't been fit to live with these last few weeks. Maybe Delia sensed that when she decided, rather suddenly, to make the trip. Whatever.

He stretched, relaxed, forced his eyes shut.

He needed a good night's sleep. But he would not resort to drugs to get it.

The misty specter of Berkeley shoved aside for the moment, the curator considered his other-rivals. They were not many, but they'd be both crafty and determined.

There would be Oswald Webster, the great white shark of the art world, his greedy jaws dripping with catsup from the infamous Webco corporation that was the source of all his damnable money. Webster could sniff out a masterpiece with an almost supernaturally accurate sensitivity. And he could—damn him!—move in and strike while his betters were still struggling with their respective bureaucracies. Oswald Webster could buy an object as fast as the ink would dry on his unbounceable checks. This made him more formidable than any dealer or museum.

Frederik von Kronholtz was very well aware of Webster, too well aware. By nature a gentle man, von Kronholtz frequently caught himself wishing the most dire misfortunes to befall Oswald Webster. The government, in one of von Kronholtz's best fantasies, determined that tomatoes caused cancer, and Webco went bankrupt overnight. And there were other, more violent pitfalls waiting for the unsuspecting Webster in the dreams of Frederik von Kronholtz.

He wondered, too, what other individuals might surface in pursuit of the cup. What oil magnate, what South American quasi-dictator, what treacherous Japanese? The possibilities were hardly infinite, but von Kronholtz's mind seethed with them nevertheless.

Again he turned, onto his stomach this time. He reached for the pillow and pulled it over his head. The ostrich with his head in the sand, he thought wryly. As though the pillow would make all the other bidders go away.

If there were any justice at all left in the world, then the Winchcombe Chalice would go to its most suitable resting place, the Roman wing of the Metropolitan Museum.

But Frederik von Kronholtz had lived too long, and in too many places, to have that much faith in simple justice.

Poor Justice. She was, indeed, blind. Justice might not be able to see what von Kronholtz saw in the chalice.

Justice might need a little help.

And as he lay unsleeping in the first anemic light of dawn, his mind churned with a hundred impossible schemes that might win him the Winchcombe Chalice, for the museum, and for all the time to come.

46

Jeff's first reaction was physical, purely instinctive. He grabbed Polly and drew her very close. Then he inched backward, remembering that the tunnel wall was just a foot or so behind. Touching the wall with his back offered some small feeling of security.

The feeling of security quickly vanished.

Fear came welling up in him like a sickness.

If something happened to them down here, who'd know? Who'd be able to stop it? Why had the duke brought them here? The image of the skeleton in the death pit was clear and alarming. *A warning? Or a prophecy?* Jeff could see him now, for, dark as it was, the yellowed bones and the cruel spikes that impaled them glowed in his memory.

Jeff tensed. What he expected was to be attacked out of the darkness. Just where was the duke? Jeff didn't have to wait long for an answer.

"Damn!" The duke's voice was very near. The outrage in his voice seemed real. "These contraptions," he continued, "are terribly unreliable. Are you all right, then, Miss Kunimara? Mr. Dupre?"

Jeff waited a beat before answering. If the duke were trying to locate him by the sound of his voice, maybe it would be better to keep quiet. Then he decided he was imagining things, and spoke. He spoke quietly. "We're all right. Mortimer took us by surprise. But I guess you intended he would."

"Yes, yes, ha-ha, he is our little joke. Mortimer's been scaring people forever. At least since before I was a boy."

"Do you," Jeff asked, calmly, "think you can lead us back safely?"

"Oh, yes, never fear. There are other pits, but they lie beyond this one. The way back is rough, but quite safe, really."

Jeff's eyes were slowly becoming accustomed to the blackness. Neville Fleet's voice was coming from the black void somewhere to Jeff's left. The duke had been ahead of them, and to the right. Jeff froze, waiting. He could hear the duke's tentative shuffling footsteps, coming closer. A knife thrust in the dark, a shove into the pit: it would be so easy, so hard to disprove as anything but a tragic accident. Jeff made himself ready, crouching.

The footsteps came closer still.

"It might be a good idea," said the Duke, "if we joined hands until we get to the end of the tunnel."

The duke's hand came out, probing, caught Jeff in the chest.

Jeff managed not to exclaim. Instead, he reached for the hand. *If he tries anything, he's coming with me.*

Polly was tight in the crook of Jeff's arm, silent. Jeff held them both, firmly.

"That you, Dupre?"

"That's me."

"Oh. Good. Shall we go, then, hand-in-hand?"

"Let's."

Jeff kept his voice even. It could have been an accident. The duke's flashlight might really be broken. In a few minutes that stretched out like hours, they regained the tunnel stairs. They climbed in silence. At the top of the stairs the duke apologized again and asked them if they'd like a drink. Polly declined, saying she must get back to the silver. Jeff accepted. They went to the library where coffee had been served the night before. There was the inevitable silver tray with decanters and glasses. The duke poured Jeff a sherry and, for himself, Scotch whiskey on ice.

"Cheer-ho," said the duke, smiling.

Jeff felt the presence of death in Berwick. He had felt it in the dungeon and he felt it now. Not just in the form of the theatrically splayed-out skeleton in the death pit, but all through the castle. Even the brilliant sunlight outside couldn't dispel the feeling.

"To your health," said Jeff, "and Mortimer's."

"Dear old Mortimer, ever reliable. I'll miss him, should we ever leave Berwick."

"You'd consider leaving?"

The duke laughed. "Bess—my wife—would leave in a second. And the child, like all children, could be happy anywhere. For me, it would be wrenching. But, yes, we have considered it. The place just eats money, and God knows we've little enough of that."

Jeff said nothing, but sipped the rare old wine. It had been bottled before he was born, and its flavor managed to be both dry and flowery at the same time, haunting, exquisite. "The sherry," he said at last, striving to fill the silence, "is beautiful."

"Compliments of my grandfather, bless his decadent old heart. He damned near bankrupted us, but he had a superb palate always."

"We sometimes auction fine wines, you know. It's illegal in New York, but we do them here, and in Los Angeles."

"Well, it hasn't quite come to that yet. But thank you. I hope, in fact you might say I pray, that the sale of the chalice will hold us for a long time."

"I hope so too," said Jeff, feeling restless, wanting action and not knowing how to go about finding it.

Jeff put down his empty glass and refused a refill. The duke escorted him through Berwick, down the rambling hallways, through dozens and dozens of rooms, out across the courtyard and into the perimeter walls, to the armory, up onto the towers and parapets. If there were other dungeons, Jeff didn't see them.

Once he asked his host about the other death pits in the dungeons.

"Oh, my, yes," said the duke softly. "Six in all, that we know of. There may be others. It isn't sure, you see, whether anyone's truly explored the place. Scientifically, I mean. That sort of thing would be more in your line, I suppose."

They walked back across the courtyard and into the state apartments. The duke then excused himself, saying he must visit his wife.

Jeff felt more than a little useless. Polly and Morgan were busily correcting the catalog and seeking new objects for the big auction, and here stood Dupre himself, idle. He wondered once again why Morgan had felt it so important that he come. Surely the duke hadn't indicated any lack of confidence and need to speak directly with the owner. If Jeff could rightly be described as the owner.

He wandered down the great hallway. It was cool and silent, a shadowy contrast to the bright day outside. The hall was getting more familiar now. Jeff noticed that the chapel door was ajar. He went in, thinking to catch another glimpse at the chalice.

Jeff paused halfway through the door.

An old man in a simple black soutane was kneeling at the altar rail, deep in prayer. Two shafts of sunlight cut into the deeply shadowed space. The golden chalice commanded the simple altar, sparkling on the plain white cloth that covered the ledge. The priest's prayers were silent. The old man was so perfectly still, he might have been a statue. Jeff hesitated, not wanting to intrude. The priest obviously thought he was alone.

Suddenly, with surprising agility, the old man got to his feet. He made the sign of the cross, bowed to the altar, turned, and saw Jeff. He smiled. It was a kindly face, very white, crowned with a sparse fringe of silver hair. The old priest's eyes sparkled with pleasure at the sight of his unexpected visitor.

"Welcome, welcome, come in, sir." The priest extended his hand. Jeff shook it. The man was old, very old, but his grip was firm. "I," he said, as though his priest's robes were not explanation enough, "am Father Devlin, the Berwick-chapel priest."

"I'm Jeff Dupre, Father. You have a lovely chapel."

"Yes, yes, I suppose so. One takes it for granted, a terrible mistake. You are American, of course. One of the . . . appraisers?"

There was sadness in his voice as he asked. Jeff wondered what would become of the old man if Berwick became Trust property. Where did old priests go? There must be some place.

"I'm with the firm that's doing the auction. We're making the catalog."

"Ah, of course. The catalog." The priest turned and gestured toward the chalice. "You will be wanting this, then?"

"Not for the moment. Eventually it will come to New York, and we'll photograph it. But the chalice is so well known that cataloging it isn't much of a problem."

"Poor old cup. I had thought its wanderings were over. I suppose that was presumptuous of me. Perhaps our wanderings are never over: a question to think on, and so I shall."

Jeff smiled, imagining the old gentleman debating with himself.

"I was just about to take a turn through the gardens, young man. Will you join me?"

"With pleasure."

The priest led Jeff back down the hallway to the main door. They crossed the courtyard again and passed through a small oaken door in the perimeter wall.

Jeff had heard Minnie speak of the rose gardens at Berwick, but the vista that appeared with dramatic swiftness as they passed through the small opening in the wall was startling in its scope and beauty.

At his feet, a wide rolling lawn billowed down to the riverbank, landscaped with the artful simplicity of the famous eighteenth-century garden-maker Capability Brown. There were enormous clumps of rhododendrons, huge beech trees, and several large rose borders in roaring bloom. The air was ripe with the scent of them. Jeff looked at the priest, who was watching his reaction.

"It's lovely, isn't it?"

"Breathtaking. How many gardeners are there?"

"Just one, not counting the village lads who help. But old Perkins has a motorized gadget, you know, for the mowing."

They walked down to the river, a slow and pleasant excursion. The castle was situated on an easily defensible cliff that rose directly out of the river to their left. The gardens had been carved out of the hill at the castle's side. The perimeter walls made a rough rectangle, but if Berwick could be said to have a front yard, it must be the river. So there had been no temptation to create a formal terraced sort of garden.

The priest said very little. Jeff was happy with the man's restraint. There was an old teakwood bench facing the river. The priest sat on it and patted the space next to him. Jeff sat too. The river ran merrily. There were fat white ducks, and every now and again the splash of a frog. The day was warm enough to make Jeff wish he'd brought a swimsuit. Idly he picked up a pebble from the path that ran parallel to the river. Just as idly, he tossed it into the stream. A large duck swam disdainfully by. "I envy the duck his swimming," said Jeff.

"You wouldn't, though," said Father Devlin, "if you got a mouthful, for the stream is sadly polluted, I fear."

"That's a shame."

"Yes," said the priest, "a shame." He looked at Jeff. "These are sad times for England, young man, and for Berwick, too."

For a long moment they watched the ducks.

The ducks were fat and seemed smug. They glided, to all appearances effortlessly, propelled by the velocity of their own self-esteem. Jeff knew that was an illusion. He knew that, pompous as they looked, just below the surface of the river webbed feet were churning, churning. And below that, below the glib complacent expressions of the birds, their might lurk predators and perils. Still, they made him smile, and it was good to smile at something simple. At something that could hold no threat to him. Jeff held on to the moment with the tenacity of a frightened child building sand castles, knowing in his heart that when he left, the golden plaything would disappear with the tide.

Finally he turned to the priest and found the old man looking at him. "Tell me, Father Devlin," said Jeff, risking it, feeling he had nothing to lose, "tell me what's happening at Berwick that the duke doesn't want me to find out."

There it was, the shot-in-the-dark question that might have no answer. Something had been going on in that dungeon, and Jeff had no idea what. Was it a threat, a hint, a warning to back off? The old priest might know, or guess. Or he might go straight to the duke and blow the whistle.

Father Devlin was beyond astonishment. The keen blue eyes had seen much and forgiven most of it in their time. He stroked his chin. Jeff reflected that, in an auction, such a gesture might be a signal to upgrade the bidding.

Then the priest began speaking softly. "The story," he said, "is a long one and a sad one. . . ."

47

Ted Kavanaugh stood on the north side of Seventieth Street and looked across at the neatly kept brownstone owned by Morgan St. James. It was a typical 1870s row house, one of four identical houses, still in good shape, next to an elegant twelve-story brick cooperative apartment house. Morgan's house was narrow, probably no more than twenty feet wide. There were four stories: one below the stoop and three above. Morgan, Ted knew, lived at the top of the house in a duplex, and rented the bottom duplex to a Greek ship broker who was seldom in town.

The condition of the house and its fashionable location made it valuable. Morgan, Ted had learned, had bought the place five years ago for ninety-something thousand dollars. Today it would be worth no less than three hundred thousand, and maybe more. With the income from the bottom duplex, Morgan must be living very nearly free.

Ted felt the two keys in his pocket.

He had already gotten a warrant to search the place, and he'd sent a police locksmith to make keys. He didn't want to be found fiddling with the locks if the tenant should accidentally show up. It was seven o'clock. The sun was just lowering enough to bring on the lights. There were no lights in

Morgan's duplex, nor in the two floors below. Ted crossed the street and let himself in.

The key worked perfectly. It worked so perfectly that Ted wished he had one little idea about what he might be looking for. There was a small outside foyer and another pair of tall arched double doors, twins of the outer door. Inside these doors was another foyer, perhaps ten feet square, with the tenant's front door on the left and the door to the sealed-off staircase straight ahead. All locked. Ted opened the staircase door, flicked on the light, and walked up. The paint matched the downstairs foyer: a subtle beige, with white trim. The carpet was thick, an unobtrusive coffee brown. At the top of the stairs was a simple Victorian archway with deep moldings to frame it, and inside the archway was Morgan's apartment door.

On the entrance level, Morgan's apartment consisted of twin parlors, each with a white marble fireplace. The front room was a living room; the back parlor was a library with a dining table in one corner. Behind it was a small but well-equipped kitchen. An antique wrought-iron spiral staircase led upward. Ted climbed it, to discover two bedrooms and one large bathroom. Handsome spaces, handsomely laid out.

He started his search at the top.

It was a science, searching, and it was also an art. Books had been written about where and how to look: the hidden drug, the smuggled gem, the stolen bank notes all had their typical hiding places. And in Morgan's apartment, Ted might have been looking for any of these things, or just about anything else. In the bedroom that was obviously Morgan's, there was a neatly filled-in address book on the night table next to the phone. In the table's one shallow drawer was a current copy of the *Social Register*. Of course: Morgan's best clients were probably within its covers. Ted scanned the private address book. The addresses were almost all very good ones except for two that were in Harlem and probably belonged to servants. Some of the names were familiar to Ted and would have been familiar to nearly anyone: legendary names. If these were pals, then Morgan moved in fancy circles. Ted decided to take the little book, copy it, return it, and check out every name. It wasn't easy to imagine people at these addresses being Morgan's partners in crime. But you never knew. Certainly Ted Kavanaugh didn't know. He pocketed the address book and explored the closets. They held no surprises. Morgan's wardrobe wasn't extravagant, but what there was was very good. Most of it from London. Swiftly, smoothly, Ted felt every pocket. Nothing. He looked in every drawer. Nothing. There was a kind of desk, a writing table really. Ted checked it out: nothing. A small stack of unanswered mail: bills, invitations, two personal letters in what looked like women's handwriting. One of which came from a country house in Pennsylvania called "The Cliffs." A bill from Cartier's. Something from the Racquet Club. Fancy. Very fancy.

Impersonal. Very impersonal.

The whole apartment, handsome as it was, had an unlived-in quality. It was hard to imagine anyone laughing loud here, or making love. Ted found himself wondering what a stranger, searching, would make of his own apartment. Lots of luck.

He searched the smaller bedroom, the bathroom, the guest closet. Nothing. He went down the spiral staircase. Both parlors had tall bookshelves sunk into the wall on either side of the central fireplace. There were hundreds of books, some with old gilt-leather bindings. Perfect hiding places.

Ted didn't know much about European furniture, but Morgan's two parlors appealed to him. The furniture was strong-looking and quite simple, with a lot of wood showing, good old walnut and mahogany, faded and softened from use. Touches of brass, and faded Persian rugs. Here and there was a piece of old silver. Which made Ted think of Polly. She'd tried to teach him about silver, but there hadn't seemed much point in learning.

He thought of Morgan in Berwick Castle, and of Jeff and Polly.

He thought of the deLamerie teapot. It had to be a deliberate forgery, not someone mistaking Aunt Hepzibah's reproduction teapot for the real thing. Because when they had tried to look up the woman who brought the thing in, there was no such address. The woman had collected her check in person, and cashed it immediately. That was unusual: ordinarily, these things went out through the mails. But the lady had called in, saying there had been some problem with her mailbox being broken into—and God knew that was common enough—and she didn't want the check mailed. And that was that. The fake wasn't detected until a few months later. And Dupre's had paid up, even though they weren't legally obliged to do so. It said clearly on every catalog that Dupre's could not accept responsibility for the authenticity of an item. They could, however, and did accept responsibility for maintaining their own good name. And that was what the forger had been counting on. Very cute.

Ted had been trained to look for patterns. He wondered if the deLamerie fake were part of a pattern. If there had been other fakes, of silver or anything else. He knew that art theft and forgery were fast becoming one of the most lucrative of international rackets. He knew that Dupre's—like all the major auction houses—just could not take the time to check out every item that came to them. How the seller acquired the object was a question almost never asked. And even if it were asked, who could deny that you found the thing—whatever it was—in Granny's attic? The possibilities were infinite, and as market prices soared, the temptation soared right along with the prices. There were even rumors that the Mafia was interested. And why not, when a few square inches of old canvas could be worth millions?

Ted stared at the books, scanning. It would be a few days' work to take them all down and examine every one. *If you were hiding something in a book, which book would you choose?* Probably everyone in the world would have a different answer, choose a different book, and for a million different, very good reasons.

You would not hide anything in a book that was likely to be used. Not, for example, the dictionary. Or any current best-seller. Or Shakespeare. You would hide it in the dullest, most intimidating, least-tempting sort of volume. Maybe. Or you'd hide it in a book of special significance, that meant something only to you.

He read a row of titles.

Most of them were well along the road to dull and intimidating. Maybe some of them were worth money. Hadn't somebody just spent more than a million for old Guten-something's Bible lately?

Maybe some of these old chests and tables had secret drawers. He could ask Jeff to lend him the Dupre secret drawer expert.

He went into the other parlor, the back one.

More books.

He scanned the titles. His eyes came to rest on an old favorite, Kipling's *Kim*, a book Ted had read . . . when?—as a teenager. He wondered if this were the same edition, remembering the pictures, remembering how the book had thrilled him then with its blending of mysticism and adventure.

He reached up for it. The book was on the topmost shelf.

As he touched the book's spine, the phone rang.

Ted froze. Let it ring. I'm not home. Nobody's home. He pulled out the book, brought it to eye level, and opened it.

Three cards fell out. They were perfectly ordinary three-by-five white, lined filing cards, with writing on them. With names. With addresses. The book was an old edition, not the edition Ted remembered. It had someone else's name written on the inside cover. The kind of book you bought for fifty cents at a country sale. The file cards, on the other hand, looked quite fresh. Ted felt a familiar throbbing in his fore head. There was one antic vein up there that throbbed when he was very excited, when he was making love.

He looked at the list. The names did not seem to be names from the *Social Register*. He looked quickly over his shoulder, half-expecting someone to be lurking there.

Maybe the list was meaningless, a forgotten bookmark.

It couldn't hurt to find out.

He'd take the list back to the precinct with Morgan's address book, copy them all, and get right to work tomorrow. St. James had at least three more days in England. The famous sale was in three weeks.

Maybe by the time Jeff and Morgan and Polly got back, Ted would have a little surprise for at least one of them.

Carefully, stretching, Ted put the book back in the slot where he'd found it. If the names didn't pan out, he could always go over the books one by one. Not a happy prospect.

He walked out onto the street. A stranger smiled at him.

Ted returned the man's smile with a smile and a half. He suddenly felt lucky, very lucky. He felt like something was going to happen in this damned case at last.

48

The sky over the San Fernando Valley was a startling blue, more blue than sapphires, perfect.

A custom-designed helicopter whirred like a demented steel insect. It was white, and on its egg-shaped fuselage was painted the legend "WEBCO" in huge, tomato-red sans-serif letters that had been designed at great expense by a haughty Swiss architect-turned-image-polisher in New York.

Oswald Webster sat directly behind the pilot in the luxurious craft. They flew low over chocolate-brown farmland. Even from the air it seemed to throb with fertility. Webster clenched his teeth. He didn't have to see the damned acreage to believe it. He believed everything—well, nearly everything —that Jim Desmond told him. That's why Desmond was worth better than a hundred thousand dollars a year as Webco's treasurer.

Oswald Webster remembered a day when the treasury decisions and all the other decisions in his business were made by him, instantly and with a shark's quick, sure, and entirely visceral accuracy.

Webco was too big for that now.

Now you had to hire the sharks, and Desmond was one of the best.

The only trouble with hiring sharks was that sometimes they showed signs of turning on you.

Today, Webster thought he could detect such signs in his head financial adviser. In his office, in the chauffeur-driven company limousine, even here in the chopper, Desmond had given his boss a stern lecture on corporate expenditures on art.

What it amounted to was that Webster had a so-called "cash-flow problem." Money people loved cloudy images. They loved, too, "scenarios" and "parameters" and "game plans." Any one of them could have gotten a job with the Watergate set in an instant, and felt right at home. "Cash-flow problem" meant that Oswald Webster was, in effect, broke. Not broke, of course, in the sense of did he know where his next meal was coming from. But broke in a way that buying the Winchcombe Chalice made out of the question.

Always, in the past, Oswald Webster had used his own private funds to buy art, and also the corporate funds of Webco. For Webco to buy an object made it tax-deductible. Decorations for the corporate headquarters. And if the chairman of the board wanted to borrow an object from headquarters, who would deny him?

It worked out very well. At least, it had worked out well in the past. Now, it seemed, the corporation had its own cash-flow problems. Oswald Webster owned forty-two percent of the outstanding Webco shares, by far the largest single voting block of stock, and his largest personal financial holding of any sort.

These shares could be used as collateral, and they had been so used, extensively. Now the prime rate of bank interest was

273

soaring to unprecedented new highs. It was already past thirteen percent and climbing.

And hurting.

The helicopter cruised over the immense patchwork that was Webco's San Fernando Valley avocado ranch. Twelve thousand prime acres, waiting to be a subdivision. Webster had bought it cheap during World War II, when gas was scarce and avocados were an exotic curiosity. Today the Webco avocado ranch supplied sixteen percent of the national demand. There were innumerable offers for the property every year. Webster had always turned them down. The land was growing money. Considering the low purchase price, considering that the taxes would remain relatively low as long as it was farmland, the avocado ranch was, almost literally, a gold mine. The treasurer droned on, filled with scenarios.

Oswald felt his attention span shortening, felt his temper heating up. He looked down at the rich fields. What he saw, startlingly clear, hovering over the farmland like a desert rat's mirage of heaven, was the Winchcombe Chalice. The golden cup beckoned him.

"Jim," he said, "cut the crap. What are you getting to?"

The treasurer looked at him, startled. Webster was usually a monument to cool logic. Desmond had never crossed swords with his boss on a question of the Oswald Webster art collection. He was sensitive enough to sense the dangerous glint of naked steel in his employer's eyes. The ring of it in Webster's voice. But it was too late to back down, and Desmond wouldn't have backed down in any event.

"We're getting to the point where Webco can't afford to buy you that cup."

He spoke, Webster noted, with barely concealed scorn for the chalice, for any work of art.

It was as though Webster had suggested spending the money to subsidize the finger-painting exercises of apes.

When Webster replied, it was slowly, with the precision of a time bomb ticking away toward the inevitable blast. "Webco," he said, echoing the treasurer's words, "cannot afford to buy the chalice?"

"Not without getting you—the corporation—into a very vulnerable situation. The interest rates are murder. And the cost overruns on the San Diego plant are out of sight. We really don't have an extra penny, Oswald, and to borrow at these rates for a venture like the Winchcombe Chalice would make us the laughingstock of Wall Street."

Webster turned to him. "Fuck Wall Street."

Desmond flushed. "It's possible they might not be willing to lend us that much money for such a purpose. Do you want it known that someone refused a loan to Webco? Can you imagine what effect that would have on the stock?"

Webster held back his reply.

The helicopter had flown for nearly ten minutes now, and they were still over Webco land. Far away, where the farmland ended and before the hills began, Webster could see patches of suburbia creeping like mildew over the horizon. He thought of the chalice. He could see, in his mind's eye, the sinuous curves of the golden grapevine that adorned the stem, that embraced the cup itself. He could see the rubies, glowing. He could almost feel the weight of the thing. His mind danced with legends. It was impossible that he couldn't get the cup.

Webster turned from his reverie to find his treasurer staring at him.

"Sell," he said.

"Sell?"

There are a thousand things that Webster might sell if he wanted to, including the entire corporation.

"Sell what, Oswald?"

Oswald Webster looked out the Lexan window of the helicopter. He raised his hand like a benediction. "This," he said. "Sell the ranch, Jim."

Desmond only stared at his boss, utterly convinced now that he was dealing with a certifiable madman.

"If you say so."

"I say so. And never, never tell me I can't buy something I want, okay?"

"Sure. Sure thing."

Desmond forced a smile. In his head he was reviewing his résumé. Something told him he'd need it soon.

The helicopter droned through the immaculate blue sky.

Frederik von Kronholtz worked fast.

From Morgan St. James he had obtained a printer's proof of the Dupre catalog of the Berwick sale. Its centerpiece was a four-color photograph of the chalice with a brief description.

#103 The Winchcombe Chalice. Roman, circa A.D. 50. A very important example of Roman goldworking with some Greek influences. Fourteen inches tall, six inches in diameter. The chalice came into possession of Winchcombe Abbey in the eleventh century, after which it was appropriated by the crown in the dissolution of the monasteries in 1531. It was presented to Phillip II of Spain by his wife Queen Mary Tudor, and is thought to have sailed with the Spanish Armada. It disappeared at that time and was lost until acquired by an ancestor of the present Duke of Berwick, in Venice in the eighteenth century. It has been in the collection of Berwick Castle since that time.

The pictures said it all.

The chalice had been photographed, at the castle, against a backdrop of antique burgundy-colored velvet. This enhanced the color of the rubies, made them glow with life. The gold, too, seemed alive. Von Kronholtz carried the catalog wherever he went.

He showed it to Billy Berkeley, and Berkeley was impressed.

"If," he said, "we can get the trustees to free the money for it, new money, I mean, not current funds, then, hell, let's go for it."

Go for it. Von Kronholtz smiled. It was so typical of the trendy young museum director to sprinkle his speech with expressions the teenagers had dropped six months ago. But, inside, the curator was pleased. This was the first step, the essential preliminary. Without Berkeley's blessing, nothing would happen. Now they must persuade the trustees. That was never an easy thing to do. In today's inflationary money market it would be even harder.

Von Kronholtz would not admit to himself that it might be impossible.

It couldn't be impossible.

He gave a list to his secretary, and began setting up private meetings with the ten most influential trustees.

Berkeley had already called a special meeting next Monday.

But the real battle for the Winchcombe Chalice would be won or lost in the drawing rooms of upper Fifth Avenue, in the luncheon clubs of Wall Street, in intimate dinner parties in chic restaurants. And the persuader would be von Kronholtz. His job—every high-ranking museum official's job—was part scholarship and part diplomacy. Charming the funds out of the very rich was not a thing von Kronholtz enjoyed doing.

Public money should be available for such a worthy cause. But public funds were barely adequate to heat the vast museum and to pay its guards. Great collections sprang from the checkbooks of wealthy patrons, and he stalked these exotic individuals with all the skill and cunning of a big-game hunter pursuing the elusive snow leopard. It required the delicacy of a high-wire walker performing without a net. It required a measure of flattery, a soupçon of psychology, plenty of charm, and an immense amount of plain hard work.

Von Kronholtz was prepared to go to almost any lengths to get his chalice.

Already he thought of it as his. As he thought of the entire Roman collection of the museum as his. The public who trooped through the halls every day, the museum itself—these were only secondary, unfortunate appendages to his work. The work was creating the best Roman collection in America. And now that it was available, no Roman collection in any of the world's museums could fairly call itself best if the chalice went elsewhere.

Of the ten top trustees, the most influential was unquestionably Dorothy Dutton. Dorothy's influence transcended her wealth, although her wealth, like that of all the trustees, was stupendous. Dorothy was a mover-and-doer, a dynamic force in the city's cultural life. She supported dance and the opera, underwrote scholarships at a dozen universities, and, not incidentally, sat on the board of the Metropolitan Museum.

To say that Dorothy Dutton sat on any board understates what really happened. She drove the board, as much as the board would let her. And it often was very amenable to her enthusiasms, to her vendettas, and to her generosity.

Conventional wisdom had it that no one was invited to be on the Met's board unless capable of writing seven-figure checks on short notice to aid the museum's acquisition fund.

Dorothy Dutton had done this on several occasions.

But if Dorothy dug her heels in, if Dorothy opposed a project, that opposition could be more formidable than the enthusiasm of all the rest of the board put together. Dorothy could be infuriating. But Dorothy got her way.

Most of the other members were businessmen deeply involved in their banks, insurance firms, or oil companies. Dorothy, who had inherited one of America's famous tobacco fortunes, had all the time in the world. Five times married, she now divided her time among her palaces in England and France, in Mexico and on Bali, and her double town house on

Sutton Square in Manhattan, while all of the financial details of her existence were expertly managed by others.

Dorothy was in her sixties now, between husbands, restless.

Frederik von Kronholtz knew all this as he rang the doorbell of her Sutton Square town house. She had invited him to tea.

Von Kronholtz knew that somewhere behind this dark green door lay the key to securing the chalice. What it would be, what magical lever must be pressed to activate Dorothy Dutton's support, he had no idea. Tense, he shifted the florist's package under his arm.

A butler answered the door, dark but not African, perhaps Indian. Madame would see him in her boudoir.

How long had it been since von Kronholtz had heard the word "boudoir"? It conjured up a special rosy brand of wickedness, indulgence, romance.

Maybe Dorothy was setting the scene for a bit of romantic diversion. As the butler led him up the impressive freefloating curved staircase, von Kronholtz found himself wondering precisely how far he would be willing to go in order to obtain the Winchcombe Chalice.

The house was not old, but it had been made to look old. Paneling had been imported from several châteaus and installed, flawlessly, throughout the big rooms. Antique hardware gleamed from the doors and window fittings. The floors were parquet, in mahogany, in a pattern that Thomas Jefferson had designed for Monticello. The quality of the furnishings was breathtaking. It was all light, never showy, always authentic. She favored Louis XVI, but the effect was of a mixture. Some fine English pieces were well-integrated with the French. Here and there a touch of the Oriental. Two magnificent blue dragons danced on an old Chinese carpet with a background of honey gold.

The door to Dorothy's boudoir was at the end of the second-floor hallway. The butler knocked softly, then opened it and stood aside.

Von Kronholtz was startled.

There knelt Dorothy Dutton, her head bowed, all in black, praying at an old French prie-dieu. She crossed herself and rose, beaming with a transcendental glow. Von Kronholtz smiled, blinking away his astonishment. This was a new Dorothy. He had often wished for the amounts of money this lady had spent, in her sixty-something years, on massage, cosmetic surgery, and all the attendant huge investments required for a lady of her age and stylishness to preserve an appearance of youth.

Every other time, and these had been many, that von Kronholtz had met Dorothy Dutton, she had been superbly coiffed and made up, dressed by the master couturiers of Paris, Rome, and New York, glittering, a spectacle.

Now she was very simply dressed and wore almost no makeup at all. Her hair was drawn back into the plainest of chignons. She looked older, but she also looked better. There was an inner radiance.

"Freddie!"

It was a gentle explosion: she always called him Freddie and he grinned and put up with it, hating diminutives as he did.

She presented her cheek to be kissed.

"You're looking marvelous, Dorothy."

"Flatterer. What's this?"

He handed her the wrapped flowers. "I make no bones about it, my dear," he said with what he hoped was a twinkle. "I'm here to bribe you and cajole you with freesias."

"Sweet Freddie. I'll put them on the altar."

She accepted the flowers, kissed him on the cheek, turned, and rang for a maid. Von Kronholtz watched this with increasing astonishment. There was, indeed, a little altar on the wall opposite the fireplace. A tall, shallow Italian Renaissance-looking cupboard had been covered with a richly embroidered wine velvet cloth fringed in dull gold. Centered on this cabinet was a magnificent free-standing crucifix in old ivory, Gothic in appearance, splendidly carved. Flanking it were two simple silver-gilt candlesticks, also old and valuable. When Dorothy got religion, she went first class, as in all other things. He smiled as he imagined a first-class ticket into heaven.

He smiled, too, because here, on this altar, he had found the magical lever with which he could move—if not the world—at least the board of directors of the museum. And that would be sufficient.

The maid appeared, took the flowers, arranged them in two low bowls, and put the bowls on the altar. The yellow-and-white freesias made a delightful contrast to the rather somber arrangement that stood there.

"Lovely," said Dorothy, "just lovely. Now. Shall we have some tea?"

Tea was served. They talked of mutual friends, of the museum, of politics. At last, as she slowly stirred an artificial sweetener into her Limoges teacup, Dorothy came to the point. "All right, Freddie, what do you want?"

He laughed. "I want all our directors to be so direct, for one thing. You know I am your devoted servant, Dorothy, you know I love seeing you under any circumstances. But I cannot deny it, today I have a special mission."

Now it was her turn to laugh. "I have a feeling those freesias may cost me dearly."

He smiled.

"Well?"

"I need your help."

"Moral support—which you already have—or in my long-running star role as Mamma Bigbucks?"

"Maybe both. Surely I need your support in persuading the board. At next Monday's meeting. No one can move them like you can, Dorothy, you know that. They are putty in your hands."

"Are we doing something simple, like taking over a small South American country, or what?"

Von Kronholtz was interested to learn that Dorothy's new spirituality hadn't dulled the razor edge of her tongue. An astonishing and sometimes very earthy frankness had always been one of her most disarming qualities.

"One of the great treasures of Western art is coming up for sale. Billy's given me permission to go after it if I can persuade the board to endow the project, above and beyond our operating budget."

"What are you after, Freddie?"

"The chalice. The Winchcombe Chalice."

She looked at him expectantly. "Whatever is that?"

For a moment von Kronholtz was taken aback. It seemed almost incredible that a woman so cultivated could be unaware of the cup. He turned his head for another look at her altar, forming the words that might make or break his project. Then he leaned forward, looked into her eyes, and spoke softly, confidentially, as though he were afraid someone might overhear. "It was found," he began, "under miraculous circumstances. An early Roman chalice of pure gold, all twined with grape vines, buried in the earth of medieval England with . . . an iron cross. The speculation was, the chalice had been used in illicit Christian Masses in Roman England. It was found by the abbot of Winchcombe Abbey, on the site they had chosen for their new monastery. So it became the great treasure of Winchcombe, and they endowed it with miraculous powers. Cures, pilgrimages, you know. Then, when the monasteries were broken up, it went to Henry Tudor, Henry the Eighth, and from him to Anne Boleyn, back to Henry again, from him to Mary, from Mary to Phillip of Spain, sailed—we think—with the Armada. Then it vanished completely for over two hundred years, only to surface in Venice in the eighteenth century, when one of the Fleets bought it. It's been at Berwick ever since. But aside from the spiritual aspect of the thing, it's a very great work of art. Unique, really. So much has been melted down or simply lost over the centuries. There is nothing, that I know of, of this quality, in any collection."

She sipped her tea. "Very impressive, Freddie. What does it look like?"

He produced the catalog.

"This is a fair representation, but nothing can convey what it's like to see the cup, to touch it."

"We'll be able to see it, naturally?"

"Naturally. In about ten days. The duke is breaking up the entire collection—what hasn't been sold off bit by bit over the last few years. The chalice will be the star, of course."

"And the estimate?"

He took a deep, silent breath, looked at her altar once more, and prayed. "No less than three million, and no one knows how much more. My guess is four-million-plus."

"Wow," she said, half under her breath. "It better have miraculous powers."

Dorothy got up and walked across the room to her altar. She looked at the crucifix, reached out and touched it, then turned to her visitor. "Suppose I buy it and give it to St. Peter's?"

He looked at her, aghast, as the room trembled and spun. Of course, it was possible. And it would be difficult to deny the logic of such a gift. He must tread very softly, for fear of offending her newfound religious sensibilities.

"What we need to ensure," said von Kronholtz carefully, "is that the best care is taken to display the cup properly, that the most people can derive the greatest possible pleasure from it. I hardly need to tell you about the crime rate in the churches in Italy. Why, only—when was it?—that madman got into St. Peter's itself and nearly ruined the *Pietà*. In broad daylight. With a hammer. The security is minimal, Dorothy, and while I understand the spiritual rightness of such a gift, wouldn't it be a tragedy if the cup fell victim to thieves or terrorists after someone invested so much money in it?"

"I hadn't thought of that, Freddie. You're right, of course. They do not care for things properly. And, well, you've seen the Vatican treasury. They hardly need more gold, or rubies either."

Von Kronholtz felt a small but definite rush of relief coming over him. Maybe there was still hope. Now came the critical moment. Now he must ask for a commitment. "Money aside," he said smoothly, "what I truly need from you, Dorothy, is your support, your enthusiasm at the board meeting. You have the strength of ten men."

She laughed then, her old roaring uninhibited laugh. He was pleased to see she hadn't donated that to the church: it was one of her better qualities. "Freddie, you are priceless. Your restraint. Your diplomacy. Your freesias. I love you, I swear it. You'll get your support, and if I have anything to say about it, you'll get your damned chalice too. Ahem. Not damned." Quickly, like some small French schoolgirl, she crossed herself. "Forgive me. Your *blessed* chalice. I don't know that I can promise . . . well, I don't know how much I can promise. That's for the accountants. But I'll back you in the meeting, and I promise . . . something. Something tangible."

He felt the sweat on his upper lip. Something tangible from Dorothy Dutton meant something large. Maybe something very large. He stood up then, bowed, and kissed her once again. There was no point in prolonging the visit. He had gotten what he came for.

She walked him down the elegant staircase to the marble foyer to the door.

"I won't even try to thank you, my dear," he said. "I think you can imagine what this means to me, to the museum, to the whole country."

"You're sweet, Freddie," she said. "I do thank you for the freesias."

He kissed her hand and walked down the five front steps to the street.

It was only by a major effort of will that the distinguished curator of Roman antiquities of the Metropolitan Museum restrained himself from dancing across Sutton Square.

49

This time Jeff went to her.

Polly's room was the next one down the hall. Jeff knocked on her door in the quiet, dusky time just before sunset. They were supposed to be dressing for dinner.

She opened the door a crack, smiled, opened it wider. "Hi," she said softly. "I thought it might be Mortimer."

She was wearing a plum-colored robe of some silky material. If there was a curve it didn't cling to, Jeff couldn't imagine where. He took her hand, and suddenly felt light-headed. "Thank you," he said, "for last night."

She turned away, still with her hand in his. "You say that as though I did all the giving." Her face was somber when she turned back to him. "And that isn't true."

"For a while there, this morning," he said, "I thought I'd imagined you. It was that beautiful."

"Maybe you did."

She was smiling now, a sad smile. She wanted to tell him she understood about Carla, but Polly didn't know what—if anything—there was to understand. She only knew Jeff had been hurt, and would break his own back before he inflicted any portion of that hurt on someone else. And she liked him all the more for that, irrational as it was.

"No," he said, "I definitely did not imagine you. I don't have that good an imagination."

She smiled, and the smile faded as quickly as it appeared. Polly put both of her arms around him then, and held him. Quivering.

Jeff's voice was soft as a wish. "What's wrong?"

She sighed. "Whenever I like a guy, it scares me."

"Can I tell you you're about the only thing in my life right now that doesn't scare me?"

She held him tighter. The trembling stopped.

The bed in Polly's room was smaller than Jeff's. It was big enough. Part of his pleasure was the blessed relief of not thinking. In her arms, in her bed, Jeff didn't have to think about anything at all. The moment was sufficient, more than sufficient. He needed her as urgently as he needed air to breathe or water to drink. Their union was complete, intense, distilled.

She looked at him in the half-shadowed twilight room, her face glowing. It was the face of a small child who has been given an especially nice surprise.

He touched her cheek, her lips, gently sealing them with his strong brown fingers. "Still afraid?" he asked.

"There are worse kinds of fear."

They were lying side by side on the antique bed. Jeff's arm encircled her.

She reached up and touched his throat wih one finger. "You have," she said speculatively, "a very low pulse rate for such a good lover."

He laughed, and kissed her. They shifted, settled in closer. The urgency of his need came throbbing back. He stroked her breast. "They'll be looking for us," he whispered, "in the blue drawing room."

"Fuck the blue drawing room."

"If you say so."

Thirty beautiful minutes passed before they decided it would be too rude and too conspicuous to delay dinner any longer. Jeff was cautious enough to get fully dressed before slipping back to his room. He tried to remember just how he felt that first night—it seemed years ago—when they'd had dinner and ended in her bed. Before Carla had come to town. Before he knew for sure about Felix.

The attraction had been strong then.

It was stronger now.

Even knowing about Polly and Ted. Polly was the sum of many mysteries. Jeff was never quite sure what she was thinking. He knew, in the first moments of shock after Carla's death, that he might have needed a woman, any woman, just to prove he was alive.

His feeling for Polly was much more than that. Mixed as it was with guilt about Carla, about the baby he hadn't known existed, Jeff knew it would take a lot of sorting out.

He was too well used to keeping the various parts of his emotional life tucked into neat little pigeonholes. Which might have been fine except that emotions like the one that gripped him now could not be easily classified, much less filed away. This was a big, fine, messy feeling that threatened to dominate his whole life.

Jeff wasn't at all sure that would be a bad thing.

He liked the fact that he knew so very little about her. Except for her brief mention of Ted, Jeff had no idea what her life had been like during the last few years. She had mentioned her parents, the Irish mother, the Japanese-American father, the two basketball-freak kid brothers. Polly seemed fond of them all. Hers had been, she insisted, a most conventional childhood in suburban New Jersey. That was the best argument Jeff had yet heard for conventional suburban childhoods.

Hand in hand, they walked down the long hallway to the stairs. It felt very good, just doing something as simple as walking and holding her hand. They said nothing.

Jeff was the first to break the friendly silence. "You have to be either a big-game hunter or an archaeologist to find your way around this place."

"What, exactly, was the duke up to in the dungeon?"

"I'm not sure."

Jeff was still thinking about his conversation with Father Devlin. He hadn't mentioned it to Polly. It was too disturbing for that. Polly was involved deeply enough as it was, just because of Jeff's feeling for her. If they were together—and he wanted that—and he was a target, then she might become a target too, de facto. Even as Carla had been a target. Jeff shuddered.

They reached the blue drawing room, where the duke and duchess and Morgan were laughing merrily.

"There you are, my dears!" The duke was bubbling with good cheer. "We feared you'd gotten lost."

"We did take a wrong turning, but mostly it was because Polly's been telling me about the silver."

She shot him a look, questioning. They hadn't mentioned silver at all.

"The chalice sale," she said quickly, as Jeff handed her a drink, "is just the tip of the iceberg. You have enough for at least two major sales besides that. I found two Paul Storrs, a Digby Scott, six matched Bateman salt cellars—but I'm not sure which Bateman—and a possible deLamerie. I say possible because I am not committing myself on Mr. deLamerie these days without the opinions of rafts of experts."

The duke smiled benevolently. "Well, Miss Kunimara, that is good news indeed. Bess and I have come to a conclusion. We will be leaving Berwick soon. It is simply too much, even with the sales. There is no realistic hope of keeping the old place in proper condition, and as you may imagine, it breaks my heart to see it any other way. So it will go to the National Trust, who will give it decent care. We'll keep a family apartment here, but we shall actually live, quite simply, elsewhere. Somewhere where the tax people will leave us in peace."

There were small, polite murmurs in response to this startling announcement. Jeff wondered with the legalities of the duke's situation might be. He knew Dupre's had advanced the duke one million dollars against the sale of the chalice. Maybe that million was being used to obtain some tax haven—where? Jeff didn't know much of such things. He vaguely supposed them to be in Central America. Where had that fellow Vesco taken off to?

"Well," said Morgan with more indignation in his voice than Jeff had ever heard there, "I call it shocking. It's no better than highway robbery, that's what it is."

"We're beyond all that, dear Morgan," said the duke quietly. "Bess doesn't care for the grand life, and I daresay I've had more than my share. The proceeds of the auctions should let us live in some comfort, in a simple way, and Berwick will still be here should the little fellow want to use it. The trust are quite decent about that sort of thing, actually."

"Of course," said Bess. "It's done all the time. Just fancy, not having to heat this old pile!"

She was quite merry about it.

Smiling, they went in to dinner.

And, Jeff thought, looking at the two of them, just what was going on in that dungeon this morning? He thought of the old priest, too, and decided to say nothing.

Not just now, anyway.

50

All through the long meal, Jeff debated with himself. To tell Polly what he had discovered this afternoon was to gain a sure ally. It was also, maybe, asking her to share his danger.

But Polly was sharing his danger already. Every time he touched her, she was in danger. The best thing, the logical thing, would be to put a lot of distance between himself and Polly. Or any woman. Jeff knew what the chances of that happening must be.

Jeff carefully watched the duke, who sparkled. He laughed.

He leaned affectionately toward Polly, who sat in the place of honor at his right.

It all made sense now, deadly sense.

Assuming the old priest wasn't altogether off his rocker, which was a possibility.

At Berwick Castle, almost anything was possible.

A tame silversmith smithing away deep in a thatched cottage in the forest. Elves in the enchanted wood. Magic. Black magic. Tricks at midnight, deeds done in darkness. Faked deLamerie teapots and God only knew what else.

Maybe murder.

And no way of proving any of it.

Yet.

How many fakes had been knocked down by the famous ivory gavel of the House of Dupre? How many of them had begun their treacherous existence right here at Berwick? How long had it been going on?

The why of the thing was easy. You only had to look at the dark squares on Berwick's walls, where famous paintings had hung. It was no trick to understand someone's being hard up. Fraud and violent death, though, brought the thing onto a new plane. A dangerous new plane. The thought ran through Jeff, tingling like electricity.

For dessert they had wild strawberries, clotted cream, and a 1926 Sauternes.

It was hard to associate all this splendor with the kind of desperate poverty that would drive a man like the duke to forge silver.

Or to kill.

Jeff found this hard to imagine.

Hard, but not impossible.

He spooned up some of the tiny dark red berries, wondering if they might be poisoned.

Killers were thugs. The duke was anything but a thug. And here was Jeff Dupre, trapped at the ducal dinner table as surely as though he were chained there. Trying to outrun the fear.

But the fear was gnawing at him now, scratching and fraying every nerve, persistent and elusive as a rat at midnight, teeth sharp, scampering nimbly away when confronted, dangerous, very dangerous if cornered. Unavoidable.

There was no escaping the fear now.

It had come with him from New York. It lived, thrived here at Berwick. The incident in the dungeon this morning ignited it.

Jeff felt the fear aging him. It was almost funny, how guilty he'd felt leaving Minnie by herself in New York. Not knowing that the real danger was a portable one. This traveling fear, this movable threat. This threat that seemed to live and thrive in Berwick Castle.

Coffee was served, as usual, in the library.

Flames danced in the pink marble fireplace. Jeff tried to be calm, to be analytical about the tension that clutched at his gut with the tenacity of a ravenous limpet. Each smile was an architectural accomplishment. Each laugh cost him dearly.

"This afternoon," he said to the duchess, "Father Devlin kindly showed me the gardens." He turned to Polly. "They're really spectacular, Polly. How about taking a look by moonlight? If there is a moon."

It was the kind of invitation that does not take readily to other company, and no one else volunteered to join them.

"That," she said, grinning, "is the second-best offer I've had all day."

She rose to join him, leaving their three companions to imagine what the first-best offer had been.

Jeff knew, and he treasured the memory of Polly this evening, just a few hours ago. Maybe a lifetime ago, as Jeff measured his life now. Each hour being an achievement.

"Enjoy yourselves, my dears," said the duke festively, "and we'll see you in the morning."

Morgan said nothing, but merely smiled, twirling the cognac in its crystal balloon.

Tomorrow would be their last full day at Berwick. They'd leave the following morning. If nothing terrible happened before then.

Polly loved the gardens. Spectacular as the rose gardens were by day, they were more beautiful at night. The moon was only half-full, but so bright that it bounced off the quiet river in an explosion of silver sequins, dancing, shimmering, magical. The paler roses caught the light and seemed to hold it, glowing. The balmy night was heavy with the scent of them.

Jeff held her hand and led her onto the path Father Devlin had shown him this afternoon. It was a well-packed dirt track that led straight into the forest.

For a while Jeff said nothing, trying to organize what he would say, trying to measure how far he should go.

The priest had been deliberately vague. At least, Jeff had felt the vagueness to be intentional. He didn't want to be quoted, did Father Devlin. He didn't want to take the role of accuser.

On the other hand, the old man had been sufficiently disturbed by his suspicions that he must tell someone. Even if the telling took the form of hints, innuendos.

For Jeff Dupre, a hint was quite enough.

The duke's financial troubles were news to no one. It would have been news if someone like the Duke of Berwick were not feeling a squeeze. Even the selling off of Berwick's treasures was a logical, if unfortunate thing to do.

The resident silversmith, secretive and surly, was something else altogether. Father Devlin knew it. Jeff knew it.

And now, through the highly educated eyes of Polly Kunimara, Jeff intended to do some quick in-depth investigating. Spying.

The path would be a sea of mud in bad weather. Now it was packed firm as concrete, smooth but for the occasional pebble. Even in the dense shade of the forest it was easy to follow. The pale sandy dirt reflected what moonlight there was.

Polly sensed his mood and fell in with it, silent.

Finally he spoke. "You have to tell me something."

"Sure," she said softly, as though someone might overhear them. "What?"

"Tell me if you want out of this."

There was a pause. He looked at her. She was looking at him. He could feel her glance, the intensity of it, more than he could actually see it.

"Out of what, Jeff?"

"Out of the mystery, the investigation, whatever you want to call Ted's case. It could be dangerous, is why."

"It's dangerous already, isn't it?"

"Very. But only to me, maybe to Minnie."

"I don't want out. I want to help you any way I can."

"Thank you."

"You learned something today." She bent, swiftly, gracefully, and picked up a dead stick. "What was it?"

He told her.

"God. Jesus H. God. Then it has to be Morgan too."

"It has to be someone in Dupre's."

That hung on the night air for a moment.

They had walked a good distance into the forest now. The path wound out before them, curving, glowing dully, inviting and threatening at the same time.

Jeff found himself imagining shots out of the darkness. The

farther they got from the castle, the farther they were from any help. Not that the castle itself was a sure refuge.

Finally Jeff spoke. "I'm too new at the game, suspecting people. I'm not good at it. It's hard enough to imagine the duke . . ."

"Let alone whoever else it might involve. I know."

Now in the distance they could see a faint gleaming that must be the silversmith's cottage with a lamp burning. The priest had mentioned that only the silversmith cared to live down this lonely lane.

They walked in silence for a minute or two.

Now they could see the dark bulk of the cottage, and the light in a front window. It had the soft yellow gleam of some nonelectric source. Kerosene, probably, Jeff thought, or even a candle. There was, he knew, a gas-powered electric generator to drive the lathe, to heat the crucibles for molding and casting, to power the welding and brazing tools. The priest had been specific about that, the expense of it, how unlikely it seemed when the duke's shaky finances were a basic subject of concern.

Jeff wondered what he'd say, what he'd do, if they should bump into the silversmith.

A guest at the castle, taking an evening's stroll. Perfectly natural.

Only, nothing was perfectly natural at Berwick Castle.

They came a little closer, then paused, just off the path, in the shadow of a big old rhododendron. Jeff tried to imagine what might be visible from inside. Unsure of himself, he played it as though they were in full sunlight. There were no sounds from inside the cottage, no smoke from its chimney. How did the man cook, what did he eat, how did he live, who were his friends, his women? Devlin, the priest, had no answers for any of these questions. The man was nearly a recluse; maybe that was its own answer, logic enough. Maybe he had sufficient reason for keeping himself hidden. It was strange, a skilled silversmith, a man capable of earning a substantial living, of making a name for himself.

In a world where everything seemed strange, any new eccentricity fitted in seamlessly.

They edged closer.

Jeff could see into the room now. The man was working. Good. That meant he wasn't roaming the woods, stalking intruders. All Jeff could see was Tauranac's back. He sat on an old spindleback chair, leaning over some unseen object, working a tool with his right hand. He made repetitive stroking motions, holding a gleaming tool that looked almost like a surgeon's scalpel. Engraving by hand, or so it appeared.

Jeff urged Polly closer. They were about ten feet from the window now, and that was as close as Jeff cared to come. To the left of the silversmith was a large silver ale mug. It must have been more than a foot tall, with capacity to hold a quart or more. The form was simple, straight-sided with a gracefully curving handle that described an elegant S, curling up at the bottom and under near the top.

Polly nudged Jeff and pointed. "If he made that," she whispered urgently, "he's our guy."

Almost as though he'd heard them, the man stood up then, quite without warning. Jeff froze, expecting him to whirl and grab a weapon.

The man put down his graver and stretched, a long, slow, luxurious stretch. It gave Jeff and Polly just enough time to duck back behind the rhododendron before he turned. He walked to the window, which was open, and looked out, but not suspiciously. Then he shrugged, turned, and went back to his bench. The ale mug gleamed like a beacon. They couldn't make out what he'd been engraving, probably something flat, like a small tray.

They pulled back. They pulled back all the way behind the bush, then turned and walked briskly down the lane in the direction of the castle.

It was several minutes before they dared to speak.

"I'd have to get a closer look, naturally," said Polly, "and, even if he is—and I'd bet anything he is—the source, you have to prove intent. Criminal intent. Otherwise, it's just a nice little hobby, a harmless pastime. Van Meegeren can paint and paint until the cows come home, but it's only when he begins selling his own stuff as Vermeer that the whistles start to blow."

Jeff put his arm around her, as much in a gesture of protection as affection. She moved closer, and the two of them moved as one.

"I think," Jeff said quietly, "that it's time to do some whistle-blowing."

51

Ted Kavanaugh sat in a shabby coffee shop on lower Fifth Avenue, staring intently into a half-empty cup of a dark brown fluid that might or might not be coffee. Ted was used to frustration. It came with the territory.

But seldom had he run into a situation as hopeless as the Dupre case. Ted had spent the better part of the week tracking down every name on the list he'd discovered in Morgan St. James's apartment.

The results were sub-zero. Nothing.

There had been twenty-eight names in all. Fifteen of these didn't exist at all—not at the addresses listed. Every New York cop knows how many hundreds of people disappear each year, often without any traces. But fifteen out of twenty-eight?

Ted had no way of knowing how old the list might be.

Maybe it was several years old, which would explain a lot. Still, he was frustrated. The few people he had reached—and four of those existed but were not at home—all denied any knowledge of St. James.

Ted looked at the liquid in his cup and frowned. Tiny globules of grease shimmered in miniature rainbows. Probably there was a painter someplace who might find that beautiful. For Ted the undrinkable coffee was the logical end of a maddening day. The kind of day that would make an Eagle Scout want to kick dogs. Then he grinned. Things could only get better. He thought of Jeff Dupre in England, and hoped that Jeff was having a better time of it at Berwick Castle.

Jeff Dupre felt sick, and tried to hide it.

He looked at his watch surreptitiously, even though he was alone in the depths of Berwick Forest with Polly. Or he hoped they were alone.

It had been nearly an hour now since they'd left the castle. An hour in which he'd discovered their host was almost certainly a forger, probably a murderer.

It was not an easy thing to absorb, or react to.

You killed my uncle. You tried to kill me. Several times. You killed Carla. And my baby.

These were the thoughts that dragged through Jeff's mind in slow, agonizing measure. Hurting. There was a great reservoir of anger in Jeff, anger built on grief, on a deep sense of betrayal.

The son of a bitch had killed Felix.

Maybe.

Faking silver didn't necessarily mean that Neville Fleet had to be a killer. It also didn't mean he wasn't.

Proof. There wasn't any, really. Not what Kavanaugh called proof. It would all have to be checked out. When was the duke in America? If the times coincided, that would only be part of the battle. So he'd been there when Felix was killed. If Felix was killed. Or Carla. He'd been there—maybe, along with a couple of hundred million other people. Jeff could see the lawyers laughing over that particular piece of speculation. Still and all, someone had pulled the trigger. Jeff's fists clenched in the darkness. His fingers wanted to be tight around the killer's throat—whoever the killer was. And he wanted to be away from this place. Quickly.

They walked, arm in arm, through the night, fragrant with roses. They sat, very close together, on the same old bench where Jeff had sat that afternoon.

There was no sign of the ducks.

Jeff remembered, once long ago, in Amsterdam, coming upon a small lagoon in a public park. The miniature bay was filled with complacent ducks, all sound asleep, their heads tucked into their wings, looking exactly like decoys. Zonked-out ducks in broad daylight. He wondered if the ducks of Berwick were sleeping now, and what dreams they dreamed.

"At least one thing feels good," he said, kissing her.

Polly said nothing. They sat in silence for a few minutes. Finally she spoke. "I guess we can't even make a phone call safely, not from the castle anyway."

"I wouldn't risk it. It's only a day. Who do you want to call?"

"Ted. I think it's time to stop playing amateur. We look in the window and see a man and a silver mug. Maybe he made it, maybe not. Maybe someone's going to sell it as authentic. Maybe not. We've got a lot, and we've got nothing at all."

"If Ted comes over, that really blows the whistle."

"What harm can it do?"

"We'll talk about it, naturally. See what he thinks."

He put his arm around her. She leaned her head on his shoulder.

"Probably," Jeff said softly, "you're right."

He kissed her then.

Morgan's laughter rang out of the darkness. Jeff tightened his grip on her shoulder so suddenly it hurt.

"Oh," said Morgan St. James lightly, "here you are, my dears!" He materialized out of the night, smiling. "I thought I'd never find you. Now, what sort of mischief have you been up to in the moonlight?"

Ted Kavanaugh put down the wineglass.

"Sure," he said, "unlike New York's finest, the British have a fairly sophisticated art-fraud department. Ours consists of one frantic guy: Volpe. But they take this kind of thing more seriously over there, as we ought to."

"Why don't we?" Jeff and Ted were having lunch in the little bistro near Dupre's. Jeff was feeling jet lag, Concorde or no Concorde. He had come home last night, late, to find Minnie in good spirits and the patrolman still vigilant in front of the Sixty-fourth Street house.

Ted laughed. "Unpopular subject. Too effete, until you're the one who got stung by some art scam, or your Rembrandt turns up missing. Someone's always going to say, why spend public bucks tracking down the Chippendale when old ladies are being mugged in broad daylight for their grocery dollars? And, of course, there's a point in that. Old ladies really are being mugged. America's priorities haven't grown up enough regarding art, not patronizing it, not protecting it."

"But you can go over there and look into it?"

"If Dupre's will spring for the expenses, I'm sure of it. And if money's a problem, we can do a lot by phone. I don't really know how it'll balance out, the international part. I'm not sure who has what authority, or where. If the stuff is made there and sold here, it's probably a crime on both sides of the ocean. Here, for sure."

"There won't be any problem about the money. Ted, do you think I'm crazy? With all this about . . . my recent host?" Secretiveness did not come naturally to Jeff Dupre. But he was getting plenty of practice. Now he spoke in a tone so soft it was almost a whisper. You never knew who might be at the next table.

Ted grinned. "It always seems crazy, for a good reason. We're dealing with craziness. Some of it's bound to rub off. It fits. There's a wacky kind of logic to it. Provable?—well, we'll see about that. If I didn't think we have a fair chance of getting something positive, I wouldn't spend my time or your money, believe me."

"I believe you. How tough is it to track the gentleman's coming and going in and out of the country?"

"It'll take some time, but it isn't hard. Assuming, of course, that he travels on his own passport. A few days, I guess. I'll have someone on it within an hour. What we don't know," Kavanaugh said, signaling the waiter for more coffee, "is how they set it up—who's the bag lady."

"He's coming over soon," Jeff said. "My host. For the hoo-ha before the auction. In a few days, he wasn't sure just when, but I can find out."

"When he comes," said Kavanaugh thoughtfully, "I go."

Minnie Dupre stood in the foyer of her house and looked out at the sparkling afternoon she was not allowed to enter. Outside, at the bottom of the stairs, stood the eternally vigilant policeman. Silently she prayed that his vigilance would be sufficient.

Jeff had been safe in England.

Here, every moment he was out of her sight was a threat, a new source of worry.

And the worry was made more bothersome by the constant necessity to hide it.

She tried to think of the patrolman's name and couldn't. Hastings would know, and Emmalee. They kept the policemen in coffee and pastries. She felt sorry for the young policeman. There must be many more exciting things for him to do than guard a frightened old woman.

Just forming this thought startled Minnie.

She was not used to thinking of herself as old, nor frightened, either. Felix's death had changed so many things, permanently, irrevocably. Minnie's fear was not for herself. It was for Jeff. Jeff, who hadn't wanted any part of Dupre's. Jeff, who had been so happy in his trenches, with his pretty countess.

Jeff, who would be coming home any minute now, driven like a condemned man in the police car. Not even free anymore to walk the few blocks from the House of Dupre.

Tomorrow they had an appointment to open Felix's safe-deposit box. Minnie doubted it would hold any surprises. She had been intending to go there every day Jeff was away, and hadn't. Somehow it seemed important that he be there. It was a ceremony, sad and inevitable, but a ceremony all the same.

Yet another good-bye to Felix. Bunny had set it up, there had to be someone official there to make sure they weren't plundering the estate. A charming thought. Minnie turned and walked down the hall to the library. She caught a glimpse of herself in an old Venetian mirror.

Frightening. She smiled at the ravaged face in the mirror. The mirror was clouded by time, and her face grimaced back through a blue haze. She hoped Jeffy wouldn't find her as depleted-looking as she found herself.

The phone rang then.

Minnie let it ring.

Tauranac was not given to smiling readily. He smiled now, looking at the thing he had wrought with such exquisite care these four long weeks. He preferred to work in silver, but the duke had insisted on the purest gold.

He stood now in his cottage looking at the replica of the Winchcombe Chalice.

The replica was on the right, the original on the left.

They were indistinguishable.

Only the shape of the rubies varied slightly, but such variations were intentional; they existed on the original chalice too.

He had made it in the old way, first forming the shell of the cup by molding it in the lost-wax technique. Then he had made each leaf and grape cluster and vine separately, brazing them on the stem, his strong fingers twining them round and round even as the old Roman master had done—whoever he was—and with no less pride. Then, at last, the aging and buffing. He had buried the chalice in the damp earth of Berwick Forest for five days, buffed it for three days more, the lamb's-wool buffer simulating a thousand years of wear in a few hours. The size, the scale, the weight—all were correct to the merest fractional measurement. And the duke was coming soon for the final inspection.

Tauranac had no doubts whatever of the result.

The duke would be pleased.

Tauranac knew why the duke wanted the replica. He knew, too, what had happened to his other replicas, to his silvery improvisations on themes of the Bateman family, or deLamerie, or the others.

For years now the duke had kept him thus, secreted, busy, well fed, and more than adequately paid. It had been very comfortable. It had kept him far from the roving eyes of Interpol. But in making the replica of the chalice, the silver-smith felt restless stirrings inside.

It was time for a change, time to move on. It was time to make another arrangement, with the duke or without him.

He reached out for the real chalice, lifted it, admired it.

Then he placed it very close to the replica.

Its own mother couldn't have told the difference.

What a simple thing it would be to switch the two.

The duke didn't bother to knock. The door swung open, and there he was, dressed as if for hunting, in an old tweed jacket and well-worn corduroy trousers.

He said nothing, but just walked up to the workbench. For a long moment Neville simply stared. He felt the old Fleets crowded in with him. It seemed as though they could see him, urging him on, encouraging him to preserve what little might be left of the honor of Berwick Castle.

"Amazing," he said finally, "truly amazing. Let me say right off, Tauranac, I can't tell the difference."

"I thought of that," said the silversmith, "and made a little mark, here." He lifted the replica and indicated a pair of small parallel scratches on the base. "This is the replica. To the eye, they will be undetectable."

"There will be a bonus for you this month, Tauranac," said the duke. "Your work gets better and better. But, come, let's take a bit of a walk. It's such a fine day."

Tauranac frowned. He did not admire nature the way the English did. Still, the duke was his employer, and maybe the walk would serve as a convenient time to negotiate for a bigger salary, or perhaps even a large cash settlement.

"Negotiate" was the polite word for it.

What Tauranac really had on his mind was blackmail. He knew what immense profits the duke must have been making from the replicas. He had no proof, but even to cast suspicion upon Neville Fleet would be ruinous. Especially if the suspicions proved true.

They walked into the forest.

Berwick Forest was old as time itself. The trees had ruled this land since before there was a Berwick Castle or a dukedom. Great thick oaks towered overhead, with here and there a splendid beech. Their branches intertwined, dense with leaves. It was always dark and cool in Berwick Forest, dark and cool and quiet. So little sunlight penetrated here that the undergrowth was sparse.

They walked on a soft carpet of last year's leaves. Now and again they surprised a deer. The Berwick deer were half-tame, unafraid. It had been years since any serious hunting had gone on there.

Tauranac said little, as was his custom. The moment would come, and he would seize it. His sensitive perceptions of moods in others detected that the duke wanted something of him, something special. Something beyond replicating the famous chalice. Whatever it was, Tauranac promised himself, the duke would pay, and pay well.

The walk seemed aimless. To Tauranac, one tree was much like another.

"Let's stop a bit," said the duke as they came upon one especially large oak tree. "A call of nature, don't you know?"

Laughing, Fleet stepped behind the tree.

Tauranac felt no such need. Faintly amused by the ducal modesty, he turned away, hands on hips, and gazed into the shadowed depths of the forest. A fawn walked delicately into view some fifty yards ahead. The fawn paused and regarded Tauranac as if making up its mind whether to invite him for tea.

When the explosion came, the silversmith had no time to act. Neville's first shot took half the man's head off.

Tauranac was dead before he hit the ground.

He crumpled gently and fell with hardly a sound.

The shotgun's roar echoed in the woods; then the silence closed in again. The young deer froze at the gunshot, then leaped into the distance with three great soaring bounds.

Neville sighed.

It had been necessary, of course. The preparations had been exact. A heavy plastic tarpaulin was hidden behind the great oak where the gun had been. The grave was already dug, and not a shallow one, either. Grimacing with disgust, Neville rolled the silversmith's corpse in the heavy plastic sheeting, tied it like a sausage at both ends and twice around the middle, and dragged it to the grave. Filling in the hole was quick work. He scattered leaves on top and rearranged twigs until a remarkably natural effect was built up.

You'd never know, glancing at the great oak, that it was the only marker for the silversmith's lonely grave.

Neville hid the spade and the shotgun in a crevice of a nearby rock. He would come back later, tomorrow maybe, and retrieve them.

Then he walked back to Tauranac's cottage, tidied it up to give what he hoped would be a disused appearance, wrapped the chalice and its replica in soft towels, and carried them back to the castle.

He went straight upstairs.

Five minutes later, having washed the imaginary stench of death from his hands and face, Neville Fleet walked into Berwick chapel and placed the replica upon the altar.

If he could fool old Devlin, he could fool the world.

And Devlin would be fooled—Neville was as sure of that as he had ever been of anything.

The golden cup gleamed from the altar.

It seemed to belong there. As he stood in the empty chapel, admiring it, Neville began to doubt himself. Had he really taken the replica?

He walked briskly to the altar, picked up the chalice, and scrutinized it closely. Yes. There were the two little scratches, just where Tauranac had shown him. Pity about Tauranac. Sad, but quite essential. The man couldn't live on, knowing what he knew.

The duke had plans, and the plans could not be upset.

Not by secretive silversmiths.

Not by Jeff Dupre.

When he left the chapel, the Duke of Berwick was smiling.

52

Father Devlin closed his eyes and lifted the chalice. His thin fingers cradled the cup, stroked the vines and leaves and clusters or ripening grapes. They passed over the rubies, counting silently as though the gemstones were beads on some celestial rosary.

Then he gripped the cup tighter.

Something was wrong. The priest knew that his old eyes weren't always as sharp as they had been. But his fingers did not lie. And his fingers told him that the cup in his hands was not the same cup the duke had removed from the altar some weeks before.

His lips formed the word of an old introit. Odd, after all the years, that the Latin came sooner to his lips than English.

"Dignus est Agnus, qui occisus est, accipere virtutem, et Divinitatem et sapientiam, fortitudinem, et honorem." *Power and Godhead, wisdom and strength and glory are his by right, the Lamb that was slain: and glory and power are his through endless ages.*

How lovely if it were that simple, that true.

Father Devlin had never doubted his belief, and he did not doubt now. No one had ever said it would be easy.

He opened his eyes, and the first thing they saw was the false chalice. For it must be false.

A great wave of sadness engulfed him. He thought of Neville as a baby, in the old days when he, Devlin, was new to Berwick. When it was all golden and peaceful and nothing bad could ever happen within these immense stone walls. And he thought of the silversmith, sullen in his little cottage.

It fit so very well.

Father Devlin set the chalice reverently upon the altar. Real or false, it was to be used in the Mass and therefore a sacred object. He turned, determined to walk into the forest and talk with the silversmith.

Father Devlin moved briskly now. He opened the black oak door of the chapel and stepped into the hallway just in time to see the duke disappearing down the hall in the distance. Walking toward the passage that led to the dungeons. Carrying something wrapped in a towel. Something very much the size of the Winchcombe Chalice.

Discreetly the priest followed his master.

He needn't have been discreet, for the duke seemed to move in a sort of trance.

Feeling guilt in his heart for doing a deceptive thing, the priest nevertheless kept on following. The duke turned from the main hallway and opened the little arched door that led to the dungeon stairs. Without hesitating, except to flick on the light, he went down the stairs.

Father Devlin paused at the open door, listening.

The sound of Neville's footsteps echoed in the narrow, twisting stairwell. Down and down. In all his years at Berwick, Father Devlin had been in the dungeons only twice, both times during the war, when they had been used as air-raid shelters. The shelter had been on the first level down. From the sound of it, the duke had passed that level. Then the footsteps stopped. There was, the old priest knew, a second level down, and perhaps other levels below that. The whole cliffside was honeycombed with dungeons and passages long forgotten and rarely used. But the duke was using them now, and to what dark end, Father Devlin promised himself he would soon discover. He closed his eyes again, for just an instant, and prayed for some sign to guide him. Then he walked down the hall again to the main door, and out the door into the forest. He must see the silversmith. He must find out the truth, and know, once and for all, if his feeling about the chalice now on his altar was the truth or merely some trick of old age.

Jeff felt suffocated. The air didn't move in the densely carpeted steel vault under Bunny Bartlett's bank, and the hush seemed eternal, the silence of tombs. Minnie said nothing. Bunny led the way, and the man from Internal Revenue followed.

There was something ceremonial—funereal, really—about the occasion, and Jeff was glad he was here to help Minnie. Or maybe it would be Jeff himself who needed helping.

Doors swung open as if by magic. Bunny had the power to make bank guards melt.

Finally they were in a little room walled with small individual vaults. Proof, Bunny had mentioned, against nuclear attack.

But not proof against murder.

There was a plain steel table in the middle of the room, and four severe chairs. The kind of furniture you might expect on a battleship.

Bunny opened the vault. The heavy outer door swung out on inch-thick steel hinges. Behind it were four drawers, also of steel, about twelve inches wide by six inches deep. This was, Jeff noticed, the medium-sized safe-deposit box. On another wall there were boxes double this size, and on the other walls, smaller sizes. Bunny removed the drawers one by one and set them on the table. The revenue man produced a pocket notebook and began making an inventory. The first drawer was all papers: the deed to the house, a copy of Felix's will, long-term bonds, papers relating to Dupre's. The second drawer had miscellaneous family jewelry: fat gold pocket watches from the nineteenth century, stylized art-deco pins and bracelets, an elaborate collar of garnets. Minnie wore very little jewelry, and what she did wear was simple: pearls, maybe, or her engagement ring, an occasional gold bracelet. Jeff could see that the things in the drawer were far too fussy for her.

"Collectively," Bunny said quietly as she sifted through them, "they're probably worth quite a lot. Maybe you should just give them to Dupre's next sale, Minnie, and invest the difference."

She looked up at him and smiled. "Oh," she said, "such a

bother. And Jeffy might want them one day, for his wife or daughters."

Jeff laughed. "My hypothetical wife."

He laughed because the alternative was to cry. The image of Carla di Cavolfiore came back to him then, all at once, alive and warm and glowing. And he saw her crumpled on the sidewalk of Sixty-fourth Street, dead from a bullet with his own name on it.

The next drawer held a small suede pouch with a drawstring closing. In the pouch was an exquisitely carved erotic ivory netsuke, lovers entwined, her legs gripping him tight, arms intensifying the closeness: you could sense the tension. You could almost feel the heat of the moment.

"My, my," said Minnie with a little laugh, "I never saw that before."

"It's lovely," said Jeff.

"Then it's yours, my darling," said Minnie. "Not the sort of thing I'd wear."

"Really?"

She laughed louder this time.

The revenue man frowned. "We'll have to get a valuation," he said formally, his eyes roaming anywhere but on the object itself.

"I'll do that," said Jeff, reaching for the carving, turning it over and over, then slipping it back into its pouch, and the pouch into his pocket. "I know just who can give us the estimate."

The last drawer held three letters. Two of them had been written to Felix. One was addressed to Jeff Dupre, in Felix's hand.

Jeff looked at Minnie's eager face, at Bunny's reassuring face, and at the professionally impassive countenance of the revenue man.

Then he sat down at the cold steel table and opened the thick ivory envelope.

The envelope was familiar: the house stationery of the Sixty-fourth Street house.

He read the letter in silence.

It was dated the night before Felix died.

Dear Jeff,

I know you will read this someday, but I hope it will not be soon. Even at my advanced age, there's a lot of

302

fight in me yet, and I hope to enjoy my life in the next several years as much as I have in the past.

I write not because I am sentimental, although you know that I am. I write because there is something you must know about the House of Dupre, a thing so surprising and possibly dangerous that I cannot bring myself to share it with Minnie, with whom I have always shared everything, happy and sad. You know, Jeff, that for some years we have been liquidating certain objects for Neville Fleet, the present Duke of Berwick. Poor Neville has had a bad time of it, I'm afraid, worse even than I suspected. He has had such a bad time that he has been driven into, well, putting a kind label on it, deception. In plain fact he has passed off some reproduction silver as the real thing. I have no hard evidence of this other than the best evidence of all, Neville's own confession, which I received tonight, in the garden of Sixty-fourth Street. I came to my conclusion about his involvement by watching—over some years—certain patterns. I am convinced that Neville has a confederate at Dupre's, but at this moment I have no hard evidence of that, either, and will not burden you with my suspicions. It could be any one of four or five people. Perhaps, by the time I die, this will all have been cleared up. I hope so, for it is only after my death that you will be asked to read this.

Tonight Neville promised to make full restitution for the eighty-some thousand dollars we lost in the case of the deLamerie-teapot forgery. My inclination, naturally, is to have nothing whatever more to do with the poor man, but the Berwick Castle sale has been announced, and to withdraw now would be to endanger the reputation of the House of Dupre, which I will not do under any circumstances. And selling the Winchcombe Chalice will be a fine and prestigious thing for Dupre's.

Well, Jeff, these may be the rantings of a confused old man, and I fervently hope that the messy business I describe on these pages will be long forgotten by the time you come to read them. Should the opposite be true, however, please remember this: that I have always loved you as much like a father as I was able, that Minnie and I cherish your affection and take deep pride in your success at Harvard and as an archaeologist, and that I know you will do whatever is best for the House of Dupre. Because when all is said and done, it takes a Dupre to do that.

I am always your loving uncle,
Felix

There were tears in Jeff's eyes as he handed the letter to Minnie. And even through his tears Jeff found himself wondering just how far Felix's letter would stand up as courtroom evidence of murder.

53

Jeff called Veii.

He picked up the phone, dialed the operator, asked for the familiar number. The guilt weighed on him, solid and heavy as any millstone. Whole days went by when he hardly thought of the dig, of Corky and Fred, the trenches, the *tombaroli*, the Etruscans.

The sacred grove was farther away than it ever had been.

Jeff remembered, too clearly, when the grove had been the biggest thing in his life. The Grove of Voltumna, and Carla.

He almost hung up. He was calling only to call. He didn't have anything to tell them, no orders to give, no urgent questions to ask.

All of a sudden it didn't seem to matter very much, what was or wasn't happening in a ditch in Tuscany.

Through the sputter and hiss of five thousand miles' worth of bad connections, the cheerful voice of Corky Cabot assured him that they hadn't been robbed again, hadn't found the Sacred Grove of Voltumna, but that they were enlarging the trenches at a good pace, and everything was just fine.

"Shit," said Jeff quietly, half to himself.

"What was that?"

"Nothing." Jeff smiled as he said it. He was about as useful in Veii as he was in New York. Zero and zero. He thought of the time he'd spent in New York, time stolen from his work, from his book. He might have done some work here. If he had his notes, his manuscript. If he hadn't been playing hide-and-seek with a killer. Killers?

"Hang in there, Corky," he said, "I'll be back soon."

"So long, Jeff."

"Take it easy."

Click.

He felt better after making the call. Even if they were doing just fine without him.

Ted was on a jet to England and the duke was arriving sometime this afternoon. There were two weeks until the sale.

Ted's feeling was that the letter was hard evidence, but nothing like grounds for arrest. It did, of course, provide Neville Fleet with a clear-cut motive for wanting to kill Jeff Dupre. If he knew of the letter, or even suspected its existence, Jeff was as good as dead.

Ted had arranged for a round-the-clock police tail on the duke from the moment he arrived in New York.

"And you," Ted had said, pointing his finger at Jeff, "just keep your ass indoors. If you have to go to Dupre's, get yourself driven. But you don't have to."

"There is such a thing as stir-crazy."

"And there's such a thing as dead."

They looked at each other.

"You got it, Lieutenant Kavanaugh," said Jeff softly. "You got it right where it lives."

"I'll be back in three days, maybe two."

"Consider me cloistered."

"It's closing in on him, Jeff. We can't nail him yet, but we know—ninety-nine percent—who to nail."

Jeff smiled, and thought of Polly.

It wasn't going to be easy with her. Seeing her. Overcoming his memories of Carla. Deep down, Jeff knew he'd never really overcome the way he felt about Carla. And why should he? The fact that Polly was here, and alive, and that he was deeply attracted to her did nothing to lessen the intensity of his pain.

Maybe the pain was worse because of Polly.

And none of it Polly's fault.

In a way, being forced to hibernate at Minnie's house might help. Might force Jeff to think. Felix's letter had been copied at the bank. The original was still in the safe-deposit vault. Ted Kavanaugh had two copies. Jeff had another. Minnie hadn't wanted one.

"Neville," was all she had said, "poor, poor Neville." She sighed, closed her eyes for an instant, and said, "We still don't know for sure, do we?"

"Not for sure, Minnie," Jeff replied, "but very close to sure."

So Neville was coming over, hand-carrying his precious chalice. Neville was coming for the parties and the viewings.

And maybe he was coming to kill Jeff Dupre.

Now Jeff sat at Felix's desk, thinking about the Duke of Berwick. Who had been a guest at Sixty-fourth Street the night before Felix died. The night Felix wrote that letter. It would have been easy for Neville to discover where Felix kept the Jaguar. Surely they'd driven in it together often enough. Minnie had said that, too: how they'd drive up to Connecticut on a Saturday, have dinner at some country inn, show Neville the sights, poke into the antique shops.

It had all been so charming.

Jeff wondered what kind of car the duke drove, if he'd have the knowledge, the skill, to fix a Jaguar so that its front suspension would cave in. Ted was sure there were just one, maybe two people in the conspiracy. Jeff wasn't quite so positive. Still, the fewer who were in on a thing like that, the fewer chances of someone making a mistake.

But the mistake had already been made.

Jeff remembered the duke's offhand reference to the fact that they were considering leaving Berwick.

One last killing in the auction market.

One last killing to seal the lips of Jeff Dupre.

The door opened and Polly walked in, closing it behind her. She walked to the desk, bent over, and kissed him. "Hi," she said. "How are you?"

He hadn't told her about the letter yet. He did that now, speaking quietly, hoping the room wasn't bugged.

"Well," she said when he finished, "it figures."

"It figures. But it isn't enough to arrest him. Not according to Ted."

"And Ted's going over there?"

"He's on his way right now."

"We know what he'll find. He'll find that cottage, some tools of the silversmith's trade, maybe a reproduction or two, that mug . . ."

"He's going after the man himself. Tauranac. If Tauranac can be persuaded to talk, that's evidence."

"If Ted finds him."

"Yeah. If. In the meanwhile, the duke will be tailed round the clock while he's here."

"And we'll have to see him and be polite, and pretend nothing's wrong." She frowned, not liking the idea.

"If we can. And—for a few days, anyway—it's going to be tough for me to see you. After work, I mean."

She grinned. "I understand, Jeff. He's got you under house arrest, kind of."

"Something like that. I feel I'm imposing on the police as it is. They've got a cop at the door, my aunt and I are asked to stay inside all the time. I can't even walk from here to there. Five blocks. It's like the old joke, I'm running away from home, only I'm not allowed to cross the street."

"I'm glad you mentioned it."

"I didn't want you to think—"

"It's okay," she said. "I'm a big girl, and I have a lot of homework. Trying to make some sense out of all the silver I saw at Berwick, for instance. Although, based on your uncle's letter, I doubt we should even consider it. And I'd feel better if we got some very expert outside opinions on the stuff in the chalice sale."

"The silver anyway."

"Anything and everything can be faked, Jeff. Silver's easier than, say, a Renaissance painting or some elaborate bit of furniture. But it's all been done, and the higher prices rise, the more we'll see it."

Jeff thought about that. "Could he fake the Winchcombe Chalice itself?"

The thought was startling enough to make her pause. The question hung heavily in the quiet air of Felix Dupre's office. She spoke at last, slowly. "It's conceivable, I guess, if he had a real master craftsman. But why?"

"Why fake anything? If he could fake the chalice, it might be possible to sell it twice. Aboveground and underground. If he's going to cut and run, and he may be, what's he got to lose?"

"It would be tough, and it would be risky."

"Riskier than faking silver?"

"Much. They can fake old silver using a base of old silver: melted-down monstrosities that wouldn't have much value today. So the silver itself is the same. And silver, in the old days, came from just about everywhere. From coins, from other ornaments melted down, from all over. Gold, very ancient gold—that's another story. They had one basic source, in North Africa, what we call King Solomon's Mines. They really existed, those mines, and they were the source of Egyptian gold, and most Greek and Roman gold too. That gold had a specific composition. I forget what, but the refining techniques were relatively unsophisticated. It wasn't anything like pure. That can be checked out. It is very unlikely that someone as conspicuous as the Duke of Berwick could accumulate—or afford to accumulate—enough authentic Roman gold to make the weight of that chalice. Modern gold is far purer. I suppose a very sophisticated chemist could find out the composition of Roman gold and make gold soup—adding a bit of this and a trace of that. But not in thatched cottages in Berwick Forest. At least, I doubt it very much."

"So when he brings the chalice in here this afternoon or tomorrow—he's hand-carrying it—we can have it checked."

"Indeed we can, and should."

"How big a deal will that be? I mean, physically, would the cup have to be taken out of Dupre's?"

"I'm not sure. That's how it's usually done. You just send an object to the lab. But they can take a little scraping—I've heard of that being done too."

"And you know the people to do it?"

"I know who to ask. Discreetly."

"Very discreetly. If the art world gets even a breath of a suspicion, the whole sale would be blown right out of the water."

"It's awfully unlikely, Jeff. That any modern goldsmith could bring a thing like that off successfully."

"They can do deLamerie teapots, why not Roman chalices?"

She looked at him, and something flashed in her dark eyes.

"I'm sorry," Jeff said at once, "I didn't mean . . ."

She laughed. "But you're absolutely right. I'm too sensitive about that. The child who got burned."

"We all got burned. Felix and Morgan, too."

"Yes," Polly said softly, "Morgan too."

She left then. They made plans for lunch the next day. Jeff sat at his uncle's desk thinking about Morgan St. James.

The obvious link. Morgan, who had become the pipeline from the House of Dupre to Berwick Castle. Charming Morgan, successful Morgan, rising star of the art world, owner of a fancy town house. Why would a man like Morgan stoop to conspiring in a forgery scam? *Because it was a way to make very big bucks very quickly. Because he was in the ideal situation to pull any string he wanted to in the House of Dupre.*

Restless, with the caged-in feeling that had troubled him since the day of his arrival in New York, Jeff suddenly stood up and began stalking the halls of Dupre's, looking for he knew not what.

Morgan, for starters, was not in his office.

Downstairs, they were setting up the exhibit for the Berwick Castle sale. The catalog was already selling out at fifteen dollars for the paper edition. All of the other objects were in the house now. There would be just one hundred and seven of them, ranging from medieval Limoges enamels to a small Holbein portrait of young Prince Edward to a set of brilliant Netherlands hunting tapestries, a diamond necklace that had been a wedding gift from Queen Anne to the incumbent Duchess of Berwick, to the chalice itself.

The House of Dupre was vibrating with excitement.

The international press had made much of the coming sale. England had tried, and failed, to raise funds to buy the chalice, to keep it in Britain. Even as they had failed on another, similar occasion to keep the famous Velázquez portrait of Juan de Pareja. The duke had become an instant celebrity in a town that consumed its celebrities like popcorn.

Extra guards had been brought in for the sale.

The public exhibition would begin tomorrow and run for an exceptional two weeks before the sale.

Jeff felt the anger building. He wanted action, confrontations, he wanted to break things, to wring the Duke of Berwick by the neck. He wanted to do everything he couldn't, shouldn't do. The helplessness made it all worse. His outrage must be contained, and with every passing hour Jeff wondered just how much longer he could keep it up.

He had lunch at his desk and at three o'clock called for the patrol car to pick him up.

The elevator doors closed on him.

For a moment Jeff thought he was hallucinating. Because what he saw before him was not the familiar walnut-paneled doors of the Dupre elevators.

He saw an ocean of the purest sapphire blue, and on it one lonely sailboat. A yellow sailboat, luffing in the breeze. Empty.

The downward motion of the elevator could hardly keep up with the sinking feeling Jeff had in his gut.

The car was waiting. Jeff got into it quickly, feeling, as he always did on these occasions, like a fugitive. *Well, you are a fugitive.*

He knew Felix's letter by heart now.

After he had read the letter, Minnie read it, then Bunny Bartlett. Later, of course, Kavanaugh read it. Bunny had made quite a fuss about arresting the fellow right here and now, the instant he landed.

But Kavanaugh prevailed. That would only mean a long and complicated trial, in which the duke would have an excellent chance of getting off. The letter was heresay. There was nothing real to back it up. You had to get a confession somehow, or catch the man so thoroughly red-handed there could be no reasonable doubt of his guilt.

Just as easy as that.

The thought that Neville might go forever unpunished was intolerable.

The car pulled up in front of Minnie's house.

Jeff opened the police car's door and got out. Then he stopped in his tracks, blinking, not believing what he saw.

There, big as life and smiling, there on the top step of Minnie's house, crisp in tan linen and carrying flowers, stood Neville Fleet.

54

Ted Kavanaugh had to keep reminding himself what his priorities were. Were supposed to be. This was not a good sign, and he knew it, and hated the knowledge.

The Dupres had offered to send him first class. He rode coach and wished he'd taken their offer. Jeff had said it so casually, not realizing that the difference in symbolism went far beyond the price spread. Ted grinned at the weird scruples that kept him in coach, and a little defiantly, ordered champagne. What he really wanted was a big stiff Scotch.

The problem wasn't Jeff Dupre, or even Polly. Or the Dupre money. Plenty of people had money, and some of them were good people. The Dupres were good people. Jeff was a good guy—better than average. And Ted had known the minute that Polly left him she wasn't going to be anyone's wallflower.

So the resentment was irrational.

That didn't make any of it hurt less.

It was Jeff, it always came back to Jeff Dupre. Everything zeroed in on Jeff. God knew it wasn't Jeff's fault. But Jeff had it all, and always had. Including Ted's girl. Good things seemed to come so easily to Jeff Dupre, to all the Jeff Dupres of the world. There was a certain look they had, an unstudied quality, an air of not trying too hard. Ted tried to like Jeff. Some days he even succeeded a little. The other days, he kept his mouth shut and did his job. Hell, he'd do the job just as well if his client were Attila the Hun.

The jet landed on time. Ted rented an MG, drove around London a little, checked into Brown's Hotel. That had been Minnie Dupre's suggestion, Brown's. Ted loved it: homey, if your home was a fancy one and the time was a hundred years past. He showered, changed, called Scotland Yard.

An hour later, Ted was being served tea in the small but astonishingly neat office of Detective Leonard (Nipper) Muir of the Yard's well-known Fine Art, Antique, and Philatelic Squad. Ted smiled at the sight of Muir's surgically clean desktop, thinking of the avalanche of paper that would be waiting on his own shabby desk when he got back.

Leonard Muir redefined the word "roly-poly."

Everything about the man was rounded. There were no hard edges at all, not in his voice or in any part of his body. When the man stood up, he reminded Ted of those weighted dolls with rounded bottoms that always come bouncing back when you knock them over. A round face framed a circular smile. Muir's eyes, blue globes, seemed to dance behind perfectly round gold-rimmed spectacles. His shoulders sloped into plump arms that seemed to be parentheses for his predictably rounded belly. His thighs had the form and substance of well-cured hams, and they terminated in the roundest knees Ted could recall seeing. If there were such things as round feet, this man would have them. Yet for all the roundness, Muir gave no impression of being soft, or even obese. He was quick on his feet and curiously graceful.

Rich shortbread cookies came with the tea. Ted realized he was ravenous.

"Yes," said his host cheerfully, "we've only been in business a bit over ten years. Sixty-eight it was, and me one of the first, the hard core as it were. That was when art crime became epidemic, the late sixties. Now only dope's bigger, and we seem to be giving them a run for their money. Sad as it is."

"How many are you—in the art squad?"

"Going on to two dozen. We feel," said Muir, sipping the tea, "for your Mr. Volpe."

Ted thought of the one-man, underfinanced NYPD art squad, Robert Volpe.

"I'm afraid," said Ted ruefully, "that we're still the colonies when it comes to that."

"If," said Muir, "we could only teach the people who own

art to photograph it, to register it in a central file, the vultures would have a much harder time of it."

"Is there such a file?"

"Several of us are working on it," said Muir, "including your man Volpe. But it's tough, maybe almost impossible. So many people don't know what they own, don't want to bother. And others, for various dark reasons, don't want it known that they own something very valuable. What we do have," he went on, rising nimbly to his feet and producing a loose-leaf folder from a nearby filing cabinet, "is good information—at last—on what's missing. In here is a computer printout of every reported art and antique theft of international significance in the month of August. Let's see—there are thousands of items, of course. Two fine fourteenth-century altarpieces missing from a church in Ravenna. A major Picasso gone from someone's beach house in Rio. Three postage stamps worth more than five million dollars gone from New Orleans. Of course, this is just what's reported. Half of those dark little churches in Italy have no concept of security, or of what they have or have not in the way of art. Have not, more often, these days."

Ted was impressed, and said so.

"Ah, Mr. Kavanaugh, we are only scratching the surface. And our recovery record is nothing to brag of. So much of it just disappears."

"Goes underground?"

"If we knew that, we'd know all. The myths of gangsters and oil potentates with huge secret collections, placing orders for thefts, *may* be exaggerated. Then again, they may not. Statutes of limitations vary, too: usually it's seven years. But you must know all that."

"Not as much as I'd like to. And you deal with forgeries, too?"

"Oh, yes," he said, "the lot. Faking's a slippery part of the business, and sometimes it's hard to prove. Experts vary like the bloody weather. This one swears on his mother's grave it's a Rembrandt, that one can prove six ways the butcher's boy painted it yesterday. And in the end they prove only that experts aren't always as expert as they'd like us to believe."

He laughed. The laugh was round, too. Kavanaugh smiled. Whatever he'd expected, it wasn't Leonard Muir, aka Nipper. Ted liked him almost immediately.

"About Berwick, Inspector Muir . . ."

"Nipper, lad, call me Nipper." His eyes changed as he

spoke, and Ted could see a hint of the inner Muir, all precision and incisiveness.

"If you'll call me Ted. Well, here's what we think we know . . ."

Ted told his story quickly and well. The forgeries at Dupre's. The letter from Felix. Felix's suspicious death. What Jeff had heard from the priest at Berwick, and what Jeff and Polly had seen in the little cottage in the woods.

When Ted finished, his British colleague was silent for a moment, stirring sugar into a fresh cup of tea. The tea was strong, amber-brown, and very good. Ted accepted another cup, too.

"I think," said Muir at last, "that it would serve us well to nip on down to Berwick. Poor Neville Fleet."

Ted remembered Mrs. Dupre saying almost the same thing. Odd that they seemed to feel sorry for the man. Who among them, Ted wondered, was saying, "Poor Felix"?

At nine the next morning Ted's rented MG was speeding south of London toward Berwick. From New York, Polly had arranged for a silver expert from Sotheby's to consult with them should they need another opinion. Nipper Muir felt that their first approach should be purely investigatory. The experts could come later, if at all. Muir was dressed casually, as if for a grouse-shoot, in an earth-colored linen jacket, open shirt with ascot, and billowing corduroy trousers. Ted wore blue jeans and an open shirt and carried a windbreaker. Nipper Muir had made a point of his intention not to alarm anyone at the castle. The only equipment the Scotland Yard man brought was a small, powerful electric torch, and a compact 35mm camera equipped with flash. Ted asked about search warrants.

Part of Nipper's laugh was lost on the wind. "Ha, ha," he said, "a man's home is his castle, right? Right. We take that sort of thing very seriously over here. Yes, I've obtained the warrant, but the chances are we won't need it. The badge does all, more often than not. Very law-abiding lot, we British."

"I wish," said Ted, "that I could say as much for our side of the ocean."

"Ah, but that's a rum situation, lad. You have guns."

"Yes," said Ted grimly, "and plenty of maniacs to use them."

"Well," said Muir, "never think we are morally superior, Ted. We have crazies by the score, famous for 'em, and plenty of crime, for all that. There's many an Englishman who'd sell his old mother into white slavery for another go at the football pools. And we've seen our rippers and poisoners and who knows what all. But guns do make the difference. It's a hard thing to go on a rampage with a toasting fork, then, isn't it?

Now it was Kavanaugh's turn to laugh.

They were at Berwick village by eleven. Jeff's descriptions had been useful: Ted found the castle's entrance on the first try. The open car moved into the chill of the tunnel that penetrated the perimeter wall of Berwick Castle. They moved slowly into the great courtyard, crunching the neatly raked gravel.

Ted pulled the car to a stop near the main door, climbed out, stretched, and stood gaping up at the nine towers of Berwick. "Not exactly my idea of a nest of crime, Nipper," he said gently, smiling.

"Nor mine. Of course, they were a pack of bandits, really, in the old days. Successful bandits, mind you, with well-placed friends. What they wanted, they took, and look out if you're in their way."

Nipper Muir, the spit and image of a well-fed country gentleman, then knocked at the door of Berwick Castle.

A maid answered his knock.

Muir asked for the priest.

"Oh, sir," said the maid with a hint of Ireland in her speech, "I'm afraid you're too late."

Muir turned from the maid and looked at Ted. There was death in his look, more concern than he had shown thus far.

"Too late?" Muir's voice was gentle.

"It's most peculiar, sir. Father Devlin is an old, old man. And he up and went to America, just like that. Said he must see his grace the duke, and off he went, only yesterday."

Kavanaugh thought of the indecipherable maze that was Heathrow Airport, and how he might well have crossed paths with Father Devlin. Damn and damn!

Nipper Muir got to work then.

He identified himself, not mentioning Kavanaugh. He produced an official-looking identification card. The maid's eyes grew wider. Muir explained quietly, reassuring her, that this was only routine, that it was not necessary to disturb the duchess, that they just wanted to look around, with particular reference to Mr. Tauranac.

"I'm afraid, sir, that you'll not find him, either."

Another look was quickly exchanged between the two policemen.

"He's gone too?"

"Well, sir," she said, looking down, "sometimes I take a bit of a stroll, like, into the forest, it's so pretty there, and pass the cottage where he lives. Only, he's gone away."

There was regret in her voice, enough regret to make Ted wonder if her strolls in the forest had been entirely casual.

They asked the way to Tauranac's cottage. The maid was happy to oblige them at last.

"I can't imagine," said Ted as they walked down the dirt path that led through the forest, "why Father Devlin took off like that."

"Perhaps he discovered something urgent. Surely," said Nipper Muir, "the man must have felt it was urgent."

"Whatever 'it' may be."

They walked through the ancient wood.

It took fifteen minutes to get to the silversmith's cottage.

The cottage was immaculately neat on the outside, but the air of abandonment was unmistakable.

The door was open, as the maid had assured them it would be. "We never lock things, sir," she had said, proud of the immense security of Berwick Castle. Her attitude reminded Ted of all the old tales about knights and serfs and dragons, and the common folk huddling into the castle for protection in the bad times.

Bad times had come again to Berwick Castle, seeping through the chinks in the old stones, curling around the mullioned windows. But these were subtle, modern evils. They could not be exorcised with prayers or driven off by force or fire. Poor Neville.

The cottage was clean as a broom could make it, neat, dead.

The silversmith's bench lay ready, but it was immediately apparent that no work had been done here in some time. Dust was everywhere in a uniform film. It had settled in lately. Ted wondered if there was a system for measuring the elapsed time indicated by a coat of dust. There must be.

The workbench was long and well-equipped. There were retorts for melting metals, gravers and burins and all kinds of steel hammers with worn, well-cared-for walnut handles, cloths and a large electric buffer, and a drill contraption that reminded Ted of things you might see in a dentist's office. There were cloths and chamois rags and solvents and pots of polish and jars of dark red jeweler's rouge. Clamped in a

315

special padded-grip vise was a lovely pear-shaped form of spun silver. It lacked both base and handle, and Ted couldn't tell whether the smith had intended it to be a teapot or a large mug or possibly even a vase.

"He intended to come back, then," said Nipper, almost to himself.

"Looks that way."

Muir began poking in boxes, pulling out drawers. The long, sturdy, obviously recently built workbench had shallow drawers the length of it: eight drawers in all.

Muir opened the sixth of these drawers and sucked in his breath. "Coo! Look here, Ted. The sorcerer's hoard, or me name ain't Nipper."

Ted grinned at the cockney put-on. Then he walked up to the drawer.

Four gleaming ingots of pure gold were stacked there, as casually as if they were worthless.

"Credit Suisse" was stamped rather crudely on each thick rectangular slab, and a purity rating, and some hallmark-looking numbers that Ted couldn't figure out.

"My, my," said Nipper. "Someone has been quite careless, don't you think, lad, leaving the likes of this in an unlocked drawer in an unlocked cottage in the forest?"

"Someone left in a hurry."

"Someone . . ." said Nipper softly, "someone may not have left at all, if you take my meaning."

Ted looked at the man, at the gold, at the empty room. "It figures," he said softly. "It scares me, Nipper, but it definitely figures."

55

Hastings was just opening the door when Neville Fleet, hearing Jeff's footsteps on the stairs, turned. He smiled and extended his hand. "How very good to see you, dear boy," said Neville smoothly. "I was just paying a call on your dear aunt."

Jeff managed the smile and wondered how well he managed it.

There was something in the man's eyes—Jeff wasn't quite

sure what. A touch of sadness, a hint of mockery. His smile was the smile of a road-company actor, practiced, broad, not entirely convincing.

They went into the cool, shadowed hallway.

Minnie had been expecting her caller.

She sat on her favorite settee, near the fireplace in the library. The fire itself had been replaced by several potted orchids casting sprays of tiny white and pale golden blossoms that looked like flights of butterflies. Minnie rose, smiling. It wouldn't have surprised her nephew if she had whipped out a rapier and plunged it into the heart of Neville Fleet.

Instead she smiled and beckoned him to sit beside her.

"Dear Neville," she said, taking the flowers, which proved to be small yellow tea roses, "how very good it is to see you. Do sit down and let me take care of these. Would you like a drink? Tea?"

"Tea," he said, "would be nice." Then he turned to Jeff, confidential, man-to-man. "Extraordinary woman, your aunt, just extraordinary."

"She's very special."

Jeff had little practice in hiding his emotions. The idea of taking tea in Felix Dupre's library with Felix Dupre's murderer was so far removed from anything in his experience, it might have been happening on Mars. In another world, with other standards. And Jeff was trapped in this strange other world. They all were. Neville, in the meantime, seemed to be enjoying himself greatly. The feeling, maybe, of pulling the strings.

Luckily for the conversation, Minnie was back in a minute, bearing a small crystal vase containing Neville's flowers. "How sweet of you to remember I adore this shade of yellow."

"Minnie, my dear, I am so grieved I couldn't be here for the funeral."

Jeff looked at him in wonderment.

Minnie sat down and composed herself. "It was just a little memorial service, Neville. I didn't even want that, but something had to be done, you see. He had so many friends, so many people who admired him. But tell us about you. Jeffy says you were a wonderful host at Berwick. He also said you and Bess are thinking of leaving. Is that true?"

The duke sighed, a short, considered, theatrical sigh. "I'm afraid it is. The old place has just gotten to be too much. For a time I thought, with selling everything off, it might just be possible to keep it up without, you know, turning it into a circus. We're skipping to get away from the taxes, Minnie, it's as simple as that. Bess, bless her, doesn't mind at all. And the boy, naturally, doesn't know. But I care. Deeply. Yet there's nothing for it, you see. If we stay, they'll just take everything."

"Poor Neville."

She actually said it. Jeff looked at her. Minnie's face was a study in warm sympathy. Jeff had always admired his aunt. Now he admired her even more. She did it so very well. She would not let Neville Fleet suspect even for an instant that he wasn't quite getting away with his deceptions.

Hastings came in then, with a message for the duke. "The telephone, your Grace: it is Mr. St. James."

Neville got up to answer the phone in the drawing room. Jeff looked at his aunt. Her eyebrows elevated just a bit. It was signal enough. So Morgan knew where the duke had been going. They dared not speak. Jeff's head was churning with a dozen conflicting thoughts. Where the hell was Ted Kavanaugh? Jeff knew the answer to that one, knew it well, but the sense of abandonment was looming dark and scary.

Clever of Neville to seek them out. To test the waters. To try to find out what they knew, if they knew anything.

Maybe they could put him at ease.

Maybe. And maybe that would buy a little time. Maybe.

He came back quickly. "I am so sorry, but Morgan has some stupid papers that have to be signed, and it seems they have to be signed today. Will you forgive me, dear Minnie, dear Jeff?"

They would forgive him. He left, kissing his hostess, shaking Jeff's hand. The duke assured them they would meet soon again. The only place Jeff wanted to meet Neville Fleet was from the other side of a witness stand.

Then he was gone. Minnie came to Jeff and hugged him. "Do you think it worked?" she asked, trembling.

"You were great, just great. I don't know him well enough, Minnie. I can't tell. Surely he must have been snooping."

She sat down just as Hastings appeared with the tea.

"It was," she said, pouring, "a plain case of kiss him or kill him. I think it would have been easier to kill him, Jeffy, but there's been enough killing. And we don't know one hundred percent, do we?"

She looked up, pleading.

"No," said Jeff, "not a hundred percent."

56

The Credit Suisse gold ingot was warm in Ted's hand. He looked at it, hefted it, stroked it. It was smooth and a bit rough at the same time. The corners rounded off, the surface slightly pitted. Four ounces of very portable wealth. Serially numbered and therefore traceable.

Someone was getting careless.

The Winchcombe Chalice, if Ted remembered it correctly, weighed just about two pounds. Somewhere around ten thousand dollars' worth of raw gold, depending on the crazy gold market. Plus, of course, the rubies. Ted had no idea what rubies went for.

But he knew the estimates on the chalice.

And he knew he was in the workshop of a very talented forger, who had very likely been fooling Dupre's best experts for some time.

It seemed just incredible enough to be true.

Ted turned to Nipper Muir. "With the appropriate receipts and all," he said, "would there be any objection to my taking one of these back to New York?"

Muir looked at him. "None at all. You really think that . . ."

"I think," said Ted, pocketing the ingot, "that we ought to consider the possibility. If they have been fooling around with the chalice, and this is what they used, it will be useful to have a sample in New York. With you, of course, as witness to where and how we found it."

"There are," said Nipper, "tests."

"That match up the mineral content?"

"Exactly. Very good tests. Irrefutable tests."

"They'll be made, Nipper."

"Excellent."

The two men walked out of the cottage and closed the door behind them. For a moment then they walked in silence in the timeless hush of Berwick Forest.

"We'll have to find the silversmith, of course," said Nipper finally. "Dead or alive."

"He could have simply skipped out." Ted said this without really believing it.

"Yes, he could have. But you don't think so, and I don't think so." Nipper Muir chuckled. "It's a terrible thing, Kavanaugh, what this line of work can do to a man, makes us all suspicious-like."

Ted told him Jeff's story of Berwick dungeon, of the death pit, the sudden scare.

"Charming," said Nipper. "Death pits. Charming. I'd have a look down there. But not, I think, today, Ted. I think we should be getting you back to town, to the airport if there's a flight still today, tomorrow first thing anyhow. Then I'll come back with helpers. Especially Nijinsky."

"Who's he?"

Again Nipper's chuckle came crinkling on the warm afternoon air. "Not the dancer, mind you. We call him Nijinsky because he's forever in midair, all enthusiasm. Our best bloodhound, is Nijinsky. Track anything anywhere, he would, through bog or fen. One sniff of the poor bugger's wardrobe and he's off. An hour of Nijinsky's time is worth all the logical deduction ten men could do in a month. We'll know for sure, then, if the silver feller skipped."

The trip back to London was even faster than the drive down. They phoned from Ted's hotel and discovered that there was an evening jet to New York. Ted booked it. He packed in five minutes, paid his bill, and let Nipper drive him to Heathrow in the rented MG. They had a drink there, killing the hour before Ted's flight boarded.

Ted could feel the weight of the gold ingot pulling down his jacket pocket. At least that was real, solid, a thing you could touch and measure. Unlike everything else in this case. It was a step, a false alarm maybe. And maybe not. At least the trip hadn't been a total waste of the Dupres' money. Ted didn't want to be in Jeff's debt for anything.

"Well, then," said Nipper Muir, lifting his glass, "down the hatch."

Ted grinned. "To your good health, sir. And, thanks."

"I thank you, Kavanaugh. We're not home yet, but the path is growing clearer. You'll have the tests made quickly?"

"The quickest. It could be I'm imagining all this, but . . . well, would you leave a bunch of gold sitting unattended in a little cottage like that?"

"Not bloody likely, nor would any sane man."

Ted's flight was announced just then. He finished off his

drink, shook hands with Muir. "Thanks for everything," said Ted.

"Happy hunting, Kavanaugh. Let us know."

"You bet."

He walked to the gate, fingering the gold bar as though it were a talisman. And maybe it was.

Polly felt like an intruder in the Dupre house, as though someone might question her right to be there. She sat in the library with Jeff and Minnie, listening raptly to Father Devlin.

The priest had appeared on the Dupres' doorstep at eleven that morning. Jeff had been home. He immediately welcomed the slightly bewildered old man, invited him to stay.

It would never do for the duke to discover that his tame priest was not so tame anymore.

So now they sat, fascinated, hearing his story and waiting for Ted.

It seemed to Jeff that they were always waiting for Ted now.

The priest told his strange story briefly and well. "So," he said, finishing, "I am afraid the authorities will think these the wanderings of a senile old man. They are not."

"No," said Minnie quickly and with some force, "no one will think that, Father Devlin. You shall be our guest, and tomorrow at the latest the police officer on the case will be back. How sad you missed each other at Berwick."

"I flew," said the priest, "without thinking, or really planning. It seemed urgent that I do . . . something."

"You did the right thing, Father," said Jeff, "coming to us."

"I didn't know where his grace might be staying."

Jeff knew The duke put up at the Carlyle these days, and damn the British revenue officers. But it would be better if the priest didn't find that out. Having been this bold, he might grow bolder. And that could be fatal to him, as it had been to others.

"There are," said Jeff reassuringly, "simple tests that will be made on the chalice, Father. They'll prove once and for all whether we have the real thing."

"The chalice on my altar was not real."

Jeff turned to Polly. "You've done your homework on the testing?"

She nodded. "Cavior of the Met is the best man on ancient

321

gold. He'll be in your office at Dupre's tomorrow at ten. The trick will be to snaffle the chalice for an hour or so then."

"Done."

"Well," said Minnie, smiling, "I do get the feeling that you children are really doing something . . . positive about all this."

"At last," said Jeff, who had been seething too long.

Father Devlin sipped his sherry, blinking. The world seemed to be moving faster and faster every minute.

"I daresay," he said. "How lovely to have real proof."

"Yes," said Jeff, grinning, "it would be lovely."

He felt a warm glow starting up somewhere deep inside him. It was happening—beginning to happen. The first steps had been taken. He could feel it. And it was a good feeling.

The Pan Am 747 made strange noises as it descended through the humid sky over Costa Rica. Neville Fleet smiled. It would be a very quick trip, but essential. Paving the way.

In his wallet was a certified check from a New York bank for the sum of six million, eight hundred thousand, and forty-three dollars, and seventy-two cents. That cleared out the account but for a hundred dollars. And as soon as the Berwick sale was concluded, there would be more. Much more. Enough to live handsomely, beyond extradition, forever.

The landing was announced. They touched down lightly at San José. The Banco Nacional de Costa Rica was expecting him. He would be treated well, very well. He would be one of the leading citizens. There would be no fuss about taxes, only gratitude that so distinguished a personage was bringing so much prosperity into the republic. The account would be established, connections would be made, and then, after the sale, he would begin his permanent residence here. Bess would soon join him, bringing the Berwick heir and her daughter with her. And they would be beyond the reach of Smythe-Davies forever. Costa Rica did not recognize international extradition agreements. Let them find what they would in Berwick Forest. Let the chalice be proven false. By next week the real chalice would repose in the vault at the Banco Nacional.

Neville thought of the crypt at Berwick.

He wondered if the eyes of those old Fleets were on him now. How proud they'd be, to see such a bold coup being brought off, and so cleverly, too. It was a very Fleet thing to do, Neville decided. He smiled as the jet touched down on Costa Rican soil.

It was a smile that would have fitted in beautifully in the long portrait gallery at Berwick Castle.

The young man at the Banco Nacional de Costa Rica was named Rivera. He treated Neville like a king. It was almost embarrassing, the bowing and fawning.

Neville loved it.

The account was established, Neville was given a passbook, the young man took him for a drink afterward and insisted on escorting him back to the airport.

They shook hands formally. Rivera bowed, the complete diplomat.

"You will enjoy it here, your Grace," he said smoothly, "and we shall enjoy having you."

Neville smiled and boarded the plane.

First class, naturally.

It was all going to be first class from now on, and Inland Revenue be damned!

Jeff stood in the foyer, close to Polly, wanting her, needing her.

He wanted her with a depth and an urgency beyond reason, past analysis. He wanted her so much he was afraid to speak, or to touch her. Minnie had gone upstairs with Father Devlin. For a brief blazing moment Jeff considered taking her up to his room now, and to hell with conventions. But he knew he couldn't do that. As much as Minnie urged him to consider this house his home, he'd never taken a girl to bed here. So he stood there trapped in his good manners. It seemed like an hour. It was less than a minute. Finally he spoke, slowly, feeling about ten years old. "I wish . . ."

She grinned, and quickly leaned forward and kissed his cheek, and took his hand in hers. "I know, Jeff," she said softly, "and so do I." The dark eyes seemed to be throwing sparks. "It'll be over soon, Jeff, in a few days."

"It'll have to be." He could feel things crumbling inside him. Only her hand, warm and strong and gentle all at the same time, seemed entirely real.

"You'll come to Dupre's tomorrow?"

"Of course. Ten, is it?"

"Ten."

He smiled. Here they stood like strangers, mumbling banalities about time and place. And the ashes of Felix Dupre lay unavenged in their ugly urn. And the reputation of the firm

Felix had worked all his life to build was threatened by a gold cup that might or might not be the real Winchcombe Chalice.

"I'll be there," he said quickly, and kissed her.

And then she was gone.

57

The security systems for Dupre's had been designed, in the 1930s, by the same team of engineers who did Tiffany's, Cartier's, and Fort Knox. Every year the systems were examined, evaluated, and if necessary, updated. There were seven separate alarm systems, both silent and audible. There were electric eyes and heat sensors accurate to within one-ten-thousandth of a Fahrenheit degree above or below the average room temperature. These would detect fire as well as intrusion by any warm-blooded creature, mouse or man. There were pressure plates countersunk into the floors of all the main galleries and storage areas.

These systems were monitored around the clock at the nearest police station and also at a central security console in Dupre's basement, where, twenty-four hours a day, one member of Dupre's security force watched a panel of lights programmed to flash a stunning variety of warnings as to the precise location and nature of any irregularity. The high priest of vigilance at Dupre's was a sixty-year-old black ex-FBI man, incorrigibly alert, named Marcus Aurelius Jones.

The electric bills for Dupre's alarm system would have gladdened the heart of any Con Ed stockholder.

Not content with his sophisticated electronics, Marcus Jones drilled his troops to patrol, in pairs, all the main hallways and fire stairs of the building from six in the evening until nine in the morning. The security corps also guarded the exhibition galleries and attended the sales. Small, readily pocketable items were kept in locked vitrines, and the guards would open these upon request for prospective buyers. And while it was impossible to preclude all pilferage, there had never been a major loss in all the years the House of Dupre had been in its present location.

The heart of this many-layered security operation was the vault.

This was a strong room in the best nineteenth-century counting-house tradition, framed in concrete, plated with steel panels and closed by a bank-style laminated steel door eighteen inches thick.

Only three men knew the combination to the vault, and one of these was dead. Felix, of course, had known, and Morgan, and Marcus Aurelius Jones.

The vault was fifteen feet square and its ceiling, plated in the same welded-steel panels that covered the walls and the floor, was nine feet high.

The walls were lined with shelves, and the shelves were lined with felt, rather like the inside of a silver chest, to prevent uncased jewelry or silver from scratching.

Only the most valuable pieces were kept in the vault.

Paintings and furniture and big sculptures had their own storage facilities on the third floor, solid and lockable but not quite so awesomely secure as the vault itself.

Jeff had known Marcus Jones since that summer, twelve years ago, when Felix had induced him to help out at Dupre's. Jones was a quiet man, reflective, a man who said very little, who knew much and acted swiftly. Jeff looked at him now and smiled. A flicker of a smile crossed Jones's lips. That was about as much as anyone got.

"How are you, Marcus?"

"I've been worse, I've been better. We are all sorry about your uncle, Mr. Jeffrey."

There was no hint of servility in his tone. Marcus Jones had been calling Jeff Mr. Jeffrey since Mr. Jeffrey was twelve years old. Jeff had phoned him immediately after Polly left. It would be necessary to retrieve the chalice from the vault before the exhibition opened. And Jeff was not at all eager to have Morgan discover its absence.

Morgan might or might not inspect the exhibition first thing in the morning. Jeff was betting that he wouldn't. Not, of course, that Morgan could in any way stop the test from being made. But the less he knew, the better.

Jeff watched Marcus's strong fingers manipulate the lock. The vault swung open and a light inside went on automatically.

The air was stale in there, faintly musty.

Once someone had found a dead mouse inside the vault, and ever since, the legend had arisen that the place was airtight. Sniffing the unfresh air, Jeff could believe that.

The felt on the shelves was a depressing brown. There were a few mysteriously draped objects on the shelves, all tagged with the familiar Dupre numbered stickers, red-bordered ovals of white paper. Even the chalice was tagged and numbered 103. That would bring it one hundred and three minutes into the sale, if Morgan's average timing held true. He imagined the audience waiting. And he wondered if they'd be waiting for the real thing.

There would be no way to cancel the auction, or to remove the chalice from the sale without causing an uproar that would be heard from Kyoto to Kuwait. Still, Jeff was prepared to do just that. Even if the House of Dupre went down with it.

Quickly he picked up the cup and left the vault.

The place was creepy, no doubt about it. Marcus locked the vault and accompanied Jeff to the elevator. There Jeff hesitated, then said, "I'd appreciate it, Marcus, if you'd come with me."

Again the faint ripple of a smile appeared and left the man's lips.

Marcus said nothing, but followed Jeff into the elevator. Jeff felt better for having him there. He was so unused to fear that it was necessary to keep reminding himself. Somewhere, right this minute, and in Manhattan, too, there was a man with the motive and the means to kill him. Jeff doubted that Fleet would pursue him into Dupre's.

But you never knew.

The elevator went swiftly up to the fourth floor.

Marcus walked at Jeff's side down the deeply carpeted hallway. Morgan's office was empty. Jeff walked into his uncle's office and quickly hid the chalice in one of the desk drawers. He closed the drawer and turned.

Marcus Jones was watching him closely.

"Would you like some coffee or anything, Marcus?"

"No, thanks, Mr. Jeff, I'd best be getting back."

"Thanks. When we're through with the chalice, I'll call you."

"Don't mention it," said Marcus, turning. "Anytime."

It all seemed so routine.

There was nothing routine about it. And it could all be a wild-goose chase. Maybe the priest was senile, having fantasies. They often did, old men who lived alone. Maybe Father Devlin harbored some kind of grudge, a resentment at having the chalice sold out from under him. A perverted kind of faith.

But the fake deLamerie teapot wasn't imaginary, nor Felix's car crash. And the death of Carla di Cavolfiore was much more than a bad, bad dream.

Jeff looked at the desk drawer as though it bore a stenciled warning: "DANGER, HIGH EXPLOSIVE."

He heard Polly's laugh before she came in.

"You look," she said, "as though you've lost your last friend."

"Or my last battle." He kissed her. "You smell good."

"Thanks. Gardenia."

"Want coffee?"

He could hear the ever-efficient Miss Winn bustling about at her desk just outside the door.

"Thanks."

He went to the door and asked for two cups. It would appear, he knew, on a silver tray, maybe with cookies. Felix's way.

Jeff walked up to Polly and touched her cheek. It was just as soft and silky as he remembered. She reached up and caught his hand and kissed it.

"I missed you," he said.

"Me too."

Jeff stood there for a moment, holding on to Polly's hand as though his life depended on it. He had missed her. Somehow, when he was with her, all the doubts and fears and anger and impatience seemed to fade away.

He had missed her very much.

He kissed her again.

Miss Winn appeared, magically quick, with fragrant coffee in a silver pot on a silver tray. There were cookies. She set the tray on the coffee table between the two settees by the fireplace.

They sat down. Polly poured.

"He'll be here soon," Jeff said unnecessarily.

"What," she asked very softly, "do we do now? If the tests prove your . . . houseguest right?"

"That," said Jeff in equally low tones, conspiratorially, "is a matter for Lieutenant Kavanaugh."

And at that moment Ted Kavanaugh walked in the door, grinning and humming, off-key, a fractured version of "Rule, Britannia." "The prodigal," he said, shaking Jeff's hand, "has returned."

"Hi," said Jeff. "We were just taking your name in vain. How did it go, Ted?"

Ted told them how it went.

At the end of his story he reached into his jacket pocket and produced the gold ingot.

"Wow," said Polly, "I've never seen one of those before."

Nor had Jeff. He picked it up, hefted it, examined it, squinting. "Found at the scene of the crime?"

"In a thatched hut in the forest. Elves, most likely." Ted Kavanaugh smiled as he said that, but his eyes weren't smiling.

Polly looked at Ted, at Jeff, at the ingot.

Jeff got up and closed the office door. "Want some coffee, Ted?"

"Thanks, I've just had some."

"This," said Jeff, picking up the ingot once more, "is really incredible."

"No," said Ted, "credible. Too credible. And someone's getting careless."

There was a knock on the door then, and Miss Winn opened it. "Dr. Cavior, Mr. Dupre," she said, "from the museum."

Jeff stood up and walked to greet the Metropolitan's expert on ancient goldwork. Cavior was tall and thin as a reed. He had a quick smile and a reputation for wit. And he knew more about ancient gold than anyone else in New York, maybe more than anyone else in the world.

"Sit down, Dr. Cavior," said Jeff after introducing him to Polly, whom he had met before, and to Ted. "Would you like some coffee or tea?"

"Tea, please."

Jeff asked Miss Winn for the tea, and told her not to disturb the meeting under any circumstances. Her eyebrows rose just enough to convey a mild astonishment. Jeff was imagining Morgan popping in on them. Morgan had only to see Cavior, to ask him what was happening.

Satisfied that he'd done as much in the way of security as he reasonably could do, Jeff went over to Felix's desk and retrieved the Winchcombe Chalice. He set the cup on Felix Dupre's mantelpiece.

Cavior moved easily through the sudden silence, walked up to the mantel, and stared at the chalice. He looked at it for a long moment before speaking. "I've seen it only once before, at Berwick, some fifteen years ago. It's remarkable."

"If real."

Jeff spoke very quietly. Cavior looked at him, then at the chalice. He picked it up, squinting, and examined it very closely. Then he set the cup gently on the mantelshelf and fished in the pocket of his crisply tailored seersucker suit. Out came a small black jeweler's loupe. He fitted this magnifying eyepiece into his left eye and picked up the chalice once more. Saying nothing.

The air was dense with expectation. They all watched him closely, anticipating magic.

The silence stretched thin in the big room.

Dr. Cavior now carried the chalice to Felix's desk, set it down, and sat in the desk chair. Then he turned the cup slowly in his hands, around and around. The loupe seemed to be growing from his eye socket. He turned the cup upside down. He peered deep into the bowl and examined the rubies one by one.

Finally he spoke.

"Astonishing," said Cavior, half to himself, "absolutely amazing."

He stood up quite suddenly and walked to the little group by the fireplace. Halfway across the room Cavior remembered the loupe, grinned shyly, and removed it. "If," he went on, "you hadn't planted the mischievous seeds of doubt in my mind, I daresay I'd have taken the thing for granted. Its authenticity, that is. And I am not at all convinced, even now, that this isn't the same cup I saw years ago at Berwick Castle. The tests, of course, will help us a great deal. But if this is a replica, the workmanship is just extraordinary. It is the work of a master, whenever it was made."

The ingot from Credit Suisse lay on the coffee table. Jeff picked it up and handed it to Dr. Cavior.

"This," said Jeff, "was found in a silversmith's workshop at the castle. We thought it might be part of a lot they used to make the replica."

"If," said Cavior quickly, "it is in fact a replica."

"What," asked Kavanaugh, "would convince you absolutely? I mean, evidence that could stand up in court, not just opinion."

Cavior's smile was bland. "Well," he said smoothly, "having the original to compare it with would be helpful. Failing that, there are several reliable tests that may tell us whether this gold could be Roman. I say 'could' advisedly. That's because a bracelet you bought yesterday at Tiffany's could contain traces of Roman gold: there's only a finite amount of gold, you see, and for centuries we've been melting and remelting and remelting again. After the Renaissance, it got all mixed up. In terms of technique, whoever made this cup followed the old methods exactly. The basic form has been cast with a lost-wax technique, and the vines and the bezel that holds the stones have been brazed by hand, fusing gold to gold. Which is how the Romans would have done it. There's no evidence of modern machining. The wear signs could have been induced by a tremendous amount of buffing with, let's say, a sheepskin on a rotary polisher. But they're most artfully done. If in fact they aren't authentic."

"How," asked Jeff, "do you go about testing the cup? We'd like to keep it on the premises if we can."

"That's no problem, if you'll allow me to take a very small shaving. Nothing that will be noticeable at all."

"Shave away," said Jeff almost under his breath. "Technically, Dupre's owns at least part of the thing anyway. We've given him a big deposit against the sale."

Cavior produced a small silver pocketknife and a little glassine envelope of the type favored by stamp collectors and heroin dealers. He moved back to Felix's desk again, sat down, and inserted the loupe in his eye. He held the cup tightly against his chest, cradling it in his left hand as though it were a newborn baby. He shaved off a tiny curl of gold from the inside edge of the foot. The scar was undetectable to the naked eye. Using the point of his knife as a spatula, Cavior deftly lifted the tiny curl of gold into the envelope, sealed it, and put it inside another, larger envelope of plain white paper.

"You'll do a spectrum analysis, doctor?" Polly asked almost casually, as though the detection of multimillion-dollar forgeries was an everyday thing with her.

"Exactly. Charged-particle irradiation, I imagine. It's quick and it's getting wonderfully accurate. But it is, we must realize, a test for content, not specific age. The organic boys have done quite well there, but we have not. Yet."

"How long will it take, doctor?"

Jeff had a sense of entrapment. He could hear the ticking of nonexistent clocks. He could feel the sands running out. And he felt it all the more intensely because there seemed to be so very little he could do.

"Maybe two days. Is that a problem?"

"The sale's in a week." Jeff resisted the urge to shout, to rage, to break things. His voice was calm. His heart was churning. "But the sooner we know, the better."

"Of course." Cavior smiled and seemed ready to go. "I'll tell the lab to give this top priority."

Jeff walked to the desk, took a piece of notepaper from a drawer, and wrote two telephone numbers on it.

"Here's the office number, and home," he said. "Call me anytime."

"Or me," said Kavanaugh, adding his number at the precinct house.

"I'll do everything I can," said Cavior. "You can count on that."

"Thank you, Dr. Cavior," said Jeff. "We'd appreciate it if you keep this very, very quiet. You understand."

Cavior smiled. "I certainly do."

They shook hands all around, and the man left them.

Jeff remained standing. "I feel," he said to no one in particular, "like a time bomb."

Kavanaugh stood up and moved close to Jeff and, briefly, touched his hand to Jeff's shoulder. "If it helps any," said Kavanaugh, "that's probably just how you should feel."

Polly watched this in silence. Then she stood up and walked to the door. "My desk," she said, "looks like the day after Waterloo. Call me, will you, Jeff, when you hear?"

He looked at her and smiled. "You bet." Inadequate words, not the right words at all. Jeff watched her leave, and wondered what the right words were. Then he turned to Ted Kavanaugh. "The waiting game stinks," he said.

There was confidence in Kavanaugh's grin. Jeff wondered where in the world it came from. "I thought," said Ted, "that you archaeologist types had nothing but patience. Thousands and thousands of years' worth."

Jeff smiled, and realized it had been days since he'd even thought of the dig at Veii. The Grove of Voltumna was waiting out there, someplace. He wanted, and wanted very badly, to be the man who found it. Patience. Voltumna was waiting, secret androgynous god of the Etruscans. Source of love and death, of bounty and famine. No one really knew much about Voltumna except that he/she had been a very big item in the spiritual lives of the entire region three-thousand-some years ago. The undiscovered shrine of Voltumna might be the richest source of Etruscan material yet uncovered. If it existed. Patience.

"It isn't," Jeff said, smiling, at last, "exactly the same thing. They very seldom come gunning for you on digs."

"The glamorous life of a cop," said Ted, sitting down again, "is about ninety-three percent waiting. My calendar's so damn crowded, there isn't a week I'm not waiting on about two dozen cases. Yours is a big priority, not only because of what it is, but because of who you are. But right now I'm waiting, talking to informers, tracking down

331

witnesses, filling out forms on at least sixteen other cases. Of the sixteen, if I get four convictions, that'll be a red hot record. Fifty percent would set the whole world on fire. Of the four convictions, two will get off scot-free due to some damned technicality or other. Of the other two, one will get a suspended sentence and be right out on the street again. One will go to jail and come back worse. It's swell. It's really swell."

"Why do you stick with it?"

Ted stood up suddenly, made a fist, and slammed it into the palm of his other hand. "I told you that once, Jeff. You weren't listening. I do it for Hamlet Bendito."

"I was listening."

"We are—believe it or not—doing everything we can. We are making all the right moves. I could pull the duke in now, but all that would make is a big legal mess, and a lot of publicity Dupre's doesn't want, and the chances are excellent he'd get off. We can't prove your uncle was murdered and it is going to be just about impossible to pin the shooting from the park on him without some kind of witness."

"What about your man in England?"

Jeff knew he was being unreasonable. He wanted to turn the crank a little faster, get it all over with, get back to the real world. The two-thousand-and-some-year-old world. Where everything made sense.

"Nipper," said Ted evenly, "is first-rate. Grade A. Right now . . ."—he glanced at his watch, grinned, imagining Muir's raid on the castle—"he's down at Berwick with bloodhounds. If we find the silversmith, and he talks, there's our case. It is happening, Jeff, trust me."

"I trust you."

Jeff did trust him. Whatever that was worth.

Jeff trusted him and resented him at the same time. Resented being patronized. Resented Ted's old affair with Polly. And especially Jeff resented being so completely in Ted's power. Hell, he couldn't even walk out of his own house without police permission. The fact that such precautions might be saving his life didn't make them any easier to put up with.

He looked at the closed office door.

At least they'd gotten Cavior out of there without interference from Morgan.

Morgan. Jeff had to force himself to think that Morgan might be involved.

"Tell me," Jeff said to Kavanaugh, "where you put Morgan St. James in all this."

"He's something of an old family friend, isn't he?"

"Something like that. He was always very good to me, as a kid. But . . ."

"But someone on the inside has to be helping."

"Someone."

"It could," said Ted quietly, "be anyone. Anyone at all."

Jeff looked at him, not believing what he'd heard.

"You don't mean that. That it could be Polly?"

"I mean we can't take anything for granted."

"That's pretty rotten, Ted."

"Look, nobody said it was going to be pleasant. Or even nice. You've been pretty sheltered in that marble palace, Jeff. A surgeon's got to cut. I've got to be suspicious. It isn't something I necessarily like."

"I hope not. And I'm sorry if I jumped on you. This whole damn thing's making me jumpier every minute."

Kavanaugh stood up and smiled. Jeff tried to smile back at him. He only made it about halfway.

"All in a day's work, Jeff. Keep your eyes open, especially around the . . . gentleman we were talking about. Cavior will get to you—or me—maybe tomorrow. It's happening, it really is."

"It can't happen fast enough."

Jeff got up too, and showed Kavanaugh to the door.

And he thought of Polly Kunimara.

58

Frederik von Kronholtz hadn't felt this cheerful since the glorious day some years ago when his appointment had been announced: the curatorship of the most important Roman collection in America!

Dorothy Dutton had played her part superbly.

The trustees were in agreement now. The romance of the Winchcombe Chalice had reached even that rather ponderous group. The sale had made headlines for weeks. Dorothy had charmed, cajoled, lectured them on their duty.

Dear Dorothy!

He must think up some special reward for her. How do you reward a woman who has, literally, everything?

Maybe something to do with her newfound faith in Roman Catholicism. He ran down a mental list of church dignitaries who might amuse Dorothy. Well, there would be time enough after the auction to think about that.

Her name on a plaque, perhaps.

But Dorothy's name was on so many plaques.

No matter. He'd think of the perfect gesture. He always did.

The guard at the entrance to Dupre's main gallery smiled at von Kronholtz. All the guards in all the auction houses knew him. He made his rounds regularly, whenever really fine antiquities were coming up for sale.

Not for Frederik von Kronholtz the coy anonymity of a semi-recluse like Oswald Webster. The curator didn't seek the limelight, but no more did he avoid it.

The right sort of publicity could be highly useful in one's career.

The capture of the Winchcombe Chalice for the Met would definitely be the right sort of publicity.

He made his way across the crowded gallery, past a set of magnificent hunting tapestries, past eight Queen Anne chairs of haunting elegance, past a vitrine filled with silver, all the way to the far end of the room, where the chalice stood in its specially constructed Lexan case, illuminated from above.

There was no one in the gallery whom von Kronholtz recognized. He wondered if any of them recognized him. Six people and a guard stood reverently by the case that held the chalice.

His chalice. Already he thought of it as his.

The glory of his collection, of the whole Metropolitan Museum. The chalice seemed to strike its viewers dumb with awe. They stood transfixed or moved like people in a dream, slowly, almost floating, around and around the case, viewing the cup from every possible angle.

Von Kronholtz found himself joining in this odd ritual, circling the cup as if he were some exotic wild animal in mating season.

He smiled.

There was an element of courtship, seduction even.

Surely the chalice had seduced him, even as he and Dorothy had seduced the board of trustees.

Well. It wouldn't be long now. One week was little enough time to wait, for he who had waited so long.

Leonard Muir was all business when he returned to Berwick. He brought two assistants and the famous hound Nijinsky. The duchess was not at home. Nipper Muir presented his warrant to the astonished maid and embarked upon a thorough search of the castle.

This took four hours of the morning.

They went into the village and had a quick lunch at the pub.

By two in the afternoon they were in Berwick's dungeons. The first tier of the dungeons contained an immense wine cellar, dozens of irregularly shaped honeycomb rooms, and a large cedar-lined storage vault that had been used, the housemaid told Muir, during the Second World War to protect some of the more valuable art objects in the castle. Other than a notable collection of fine wines, there was nothing of interest in the dungeon.

Other than the grinning skeleton of Mortimer, there was nothing to be found in all the many chambers of the lower tier of Berwick dungeon, either. When they reached the top of the stairs again, they went directly out into the bright late-afternoon sunshine. For a moment they simply stood in the courtyard, breathing the pure country air. There was a hint of roses. Nipper retrieved the dog from their car and headed toward the cottage in the forest.

The hound was happy in his work. His leash was long and flexible, and the dog pressed forward with eager, bounding movements. It was all Muir could do to keep up with him.

The cottage was untouched since Muir's last visit. There was, perhaps, a bit more dust. The same half-eaten cheese in the refrigerator, a pint of cream going sour.

The clothes in the bedroom closet were few in number and stout in quality, well-cared-for. And they made up a complete wardrobe.

If the silversmith had skipped out, he must be traveling lightly.

Muir gave the dog a good sniff of the closet, and they were off. The scent would be well-established between the castle and the cottage.

But the bloodhound headed immediately in the other direction, deeper into the forest. Sniff, leap, leap, pause, sniff, leap. Nipper came bounding behind. They had gone perhaps two hundred yards into the forest when Nijinsky paused.

The dog seemed puzzled. He paused, sniffed, scampered to one side of the trail and then to the other. There was a huge old beech tree by the path, and others equally as large in the distance. Muir guessed they must be hundreds of years old. The dog went poking around the backside of the nearest beech and gave a yelp. Then another yelp. Muir followed. He came around the tree, bent, and patted the dog's head.

The bloodhound looked up at him with enormous wet eyes. The damned dog was laughing at him! *You think you're so smart*, the dog seemed to be saying, *yet look who's gone and done your bloody job for you.*

At first the detective failed to see what had excited the dog. Muir stood, the tree at his back now, and surveyed the ground. The silversmith must have passed this way. Maybe he'd dropped something. His eyes moved slowly from one side of the little clearing to the other. It was only on the second sweep that the shallow, roughly rectangular depression in the earth became apparent. It was a slight variation, faint but definite, perhaps an inch of difference masked by the fallen leaves and mulchy detritus of the forest.

The silversmith, or someone, had passed this way indeed.

The poor gullible sod, thought Muir, to imagine he'd be allowed to walk away from it. Nipper Muir liked his work in general, but there were aspects of it that made him sad. And he was saddened now, sad for the man who must lie in this secret grave. And in spite of everything, Nipper Muir was sad for the duke.

It would be all over now for the duke.

A little hanky-panky among the antiquities was one thing. Sudden death—deaths—were quite something else. Kavanaugh would be pleased. But there was no sweetness, no triumph in it for Nipper Muir.

Only the bloodhound seemed thoroughly cheered by the discovery.

Muir patted the dog again and headed back through the forest, moving more slowly now. There wasn't anything to be in a rush for. The damage had all been done.

Berwick Castle rose shimmering in the heat of September, glorious and immutable. Muir passed through the little arched gate in the perimeter wall, crossed the courtyard, and hitched Nijinsky to the handle of his car. Then he went into the castle to collect his assistants. The duke, Muir knew, was in New York. The transatlantic telephone lines would be humming tonight. Wherever the duchess was, Muir assumed she knew nothing of her husband's activities. Why he assumed this, he would have been hard-pressed to say. Time would tell.

Just before he opened the great front door, Muir looked up, up at the weathered crest of the Fleets carved in Berwick stone, up past the mullioned windows, to the towers and beyond the towers to the pale blue infinity above. *Poor Berwick!*

Oswald Webster smiled at his host. Morgan smiled back.

In forty years of collecting rare art, Webster had never known a thrill like the thrill he got from handling the Winchcombe Chalice. It seemed to dance and glow as he held it.

One of Webster's representatives in New York had arranged a private viewing. Webster hated to appear in public, to have his photograph taken, to be recognized at all. He avoided any form of transportation, any entertainment that involved showing himself to the world. Webster traveled in private jets and helicopters which wafted him to chauffeured limousines which drove him to secret entrances of office buildings, hotels, and apartment buildings.

He knew that his presence in the public viewing rooms of Dupre's would cause gossip, and that the effect of that gossip would be to escalate the price of the Winchcombe Chalice in next week's auction.

He stroked the glittering cup and thought of the avocado ranch.

How many avocados equaled one such object?

Morgan St. James poured a 1928 *fino* sherry from Felix Dupre's private stock.

Oswald Webster was the man who would stop at nothing to possess what he desired. Be it a painting, a corporation, or a lovely woman. The women seldom lasted and the fate of his business empires varied. But the art collection grew and grew, and there wasn't a museum in America that didn't lust for it.

To Webster, as he grew older and felt his body crumbling bit by bit, only the art collection had any real significance.

He lived for it and through it.

If there was a chance of true immortality for Oswald Webster, it would come to him through the treasures of civilization.

His accountants and tax men might natter on about how broke he was, about cash-flow crises and double-digit credit rates and on and on.

But no man was poor who owned such a thing as the Winchcombe Chalice.

He accepted the sherry and set the chalice on Morgan's desk.

"Tchin-tchin," said Morgan smoothly.

"Tchin-tchin, yourself," replied his guest, sipping the pale golden wine. Superb. As one would expect of the House of Dupre.

His mind was in Santa Barbara, in the great living-room/gallery of his house high above the Pacific. He saw himself, who rarely drank anything stronger than mineral water, sipping old claret from the chalice.

It would have to be claret, to match the depth and fire of the rubies.

He saw the cup glittering—where?—in a dozen places, illuminating any space it filled.

You might own a Rembrandt, and Webster had five.

But there were other, perhaps finer Rembrandts irretrievably held by great museums.

There was and could be only one Winchcombe Chalice.

And it would be his. Webster promised himself that as the supple fragrant sherry glided down his aging throat.

The wine warmed him. But the thought of owning the chalice warmed him more.

Oswald Webster smiled graciously at his host. He hadn't forgotten how to do that, and he was grateful to the man. He could count the hours until the auction. Maybe he'd break his long-standing rule and actually attend. And damn-all what that might do to prices.

There was a certain grandeur, after all, in paying record-breaking amounts for a thing.

This was a feeling that Webster would be quite willing to forgo if there were some way of getting an object on the cheap, privately. That was out of the question with the chalice. He knew it and was prepared to face the consequences of a public sale.

How fine it felt, this girding for battle!

How very much finer it would be to have the thing for one's own.

He reached out with one hand and touched the cup. His long, dry fingers ran down the stem, passing over the leaves, the curling vine, the rubies that encircled the base.

He could almost taste it. One week. Seven days. A lifetime.

Oswald Webster smiled.

The Winchcombe Chalice was as good as his.

59

Neville Fleet stood in the drawing room of his suite at the Hotel Carlyle. On his face was a smile. In his hands was the Winchcombe Chalice.

The phone rang. It was Bess, calling from Berwick.

"Darling," he said, "what a nice surprise!"

"The police were here, Neville. A man from Scotland Yard. Muir's his name. I'm frightened. Father Devlin ran off to New York to see you. Has he come?"

Neville held the phone a bit away from his ear. It did not make her words any less real. Finally he spoke. "The man from Scotland Yard. What did he want?"

"Tauranac." The connection was a very good one. Too good. He could hear her sigh. "Neville, they found . . . something in the forest. They found a corpse."

This news hit Neville with the unexpected velocity of a bullet. "Are you sure? Whose?"

"They don't know. I didn't see it. I'm frightened, darling. What does this mean?"

He had to remind himself that Bess didn't know. Didn't know about any of it. And the less she knew, the better for both of them. Dear Bess! Loyal Bess. He'd make a proper Fleet of her yet. "You didn't ask me," he said quickly, "about Costa Rica. It's lovely down there. And I've set everything up quite nicely. Rooms are awaiting us at the Casa Jacaranda, darling—that's a charming little inn by the sea. How quickly can you pack?"

The hesitation in her voice was perceptible only if you strained to hear it there.

"Quickly," she said. "I can be there by the end of the week."

"You'll find me there already, I think, and I'll tell you all about it. Casa Jacaranda, take a cab from the airport. And, to put you at ease, darling, I've no idea at all about the man in the forest. It's just terrible, but someone must have gotten in somehow, perhaps a poacher. Poor sod."

"Yes," she said. "Poor sod."

"Well, darling, I must ring off. We'll meet in the sun."

"Good-bye, Neville. Remember that I love you."

"Good-bye, my darling."

He hung up, thinking: Through it all, she does love me. Bess was the best thing that had ever happened to him.

Neville hastily put the chalice in a bureau drawer, straightened his necktie, and left the suite. He walked briskly through the elegant lobby and out the Seventy-sixth Street entrance. A cab was waiting, and he took it.

In the lobby, unseen by Neville and barely noticed by the other guests, an old man sat reading the *New York Times*. Now he slowly lowered the paper, folded it, and tucked it under his arm as he rose.

Father Devlin's black clerical suit had been cut by Neville Fleet's own tailor, many years ago. But it endured, fine as ever. He was glad of the suit now as he approached the desk. Surely the duke's own personal confessor would be allowed to wait in the ducal suite.

He walked up to the small desk and smiled benignly at the beautifully dressed young man who stood in attendance. "My name," he said quietly, "is Father Devlin, of Berwick Castle. Has his grace arrived yet?"

Ted Kavanaugh felt as though he'd spent half his life in Minnie Dupre's elegant library. Now he sat there in the twilight, talking to Jeff and to Minnie. They drank tea. He'd down an ocean of tea before this damn case ended.

"You see," Ted said reasonably, trying to overcome his own frustration, "Muir's right. Everything we have on Fleet is circumstantial. It'll be a few days before they get an autopsy report. No one doubts the priest. As for the silversmith—if the body they found in the forest is his—we don't know anything about the man. Who else might have had a motive? Who, for example, ever saw him actually making a fake? Where was the duke when Tauranac died? And of course, after the man's been in the ground awhile—forgive me, Mrs. Dupre—it gets hard to tell, precisely. They begin giving you estimates, one week to ten days, let's say. These days you can be around the world twice in that time."

Jeff interrupted. "We do know Fleet was in New York—at least in the States—at the time Carla was killed. And Felix."

"Yes," said Ted. "We know that. So were a few hundred million other people. I know how frustrating this is. It might be even more frustrating for me, if you can believe that. But we need one solid, nonslippery hunk of evidence. We've got him surrounded, but a smart defense lawyer—here or over there—could pulverize us."

"Even with Felix's letter?"

These were almost the only words Minnie had spoken since Kavanaugh had arrived.

Ted hesitated. He wanted to choose his words. You never knew what funny emotions might be bounding and rebounding around the minds of recent widows. Even widows as smart and as classy as Minnie Dupre.

"The letter," he said evenly, "is going to be fine as corroboration Mrs. Dupre. But you couldn't build a whole case on it."

Jeff broke in. "If Felix had told us exactly *how* he knew, it might be different. But all he did say was that he knew. Or guessed. And that Fleet confessed."

"Which amounts," said Minnie softly, "to what they call heresay?"

"I'm afraid so," said Ted, "but the letter turned the whole case anyhow. Because we know."

"Somehow," said Minnie, "that seems a small, small consolation."

Father Devlin walked in then, bowing politely to his hostess, then to Jeff and Ted Kavanaugh. In his left hand was a rolled-up edition of *The New York Times*. A rather fat roll, it made.

The priest walked up to Jeff. In his old eyes was a boyish twinkle. He handed the paper to Jeff. "I have felt so very useless," said Father Devlin, "and so very guilty about that poor boy. About all the things I might have done to prevent this . . . horror. I thought, Mr. Dupre, that you should have this."

Jeff accepted the paper dumbly, smiling faintly. The roll of newspaper was quite heavy, heavier than just paper.

He unwrapped it. The roll of paper contained the Winchcombe Chalice.

For the space of a few thundering heartbeats they all looked at the golden cup in absolute silence. Of the four people in the room, only Father Devlin, perhaps, did not know that the Winchcombe Chalice was even this minute on display in a bulletproof vitrine in the main gallery of the House of Dupre.

Father Devlin sat down then, beaming. "Would it be possible," he asked, "for me to have some tea?"

Jeff felt the relief rush through him with the warming velocity of some addictive drug. Suddenly his cheeks glowed. He held up the chalice in an almost religious gesture.

"First," he said, "we get Dr. Cavior. Then Marcus Jones. And then the fun begins."

"I think," said Ted, "that we have our smoking pistol."

Minnie smiled a seraphic smile. "One lump, Father Devlin," she asked, "or two?"

60

Suddenly it all became very simple.

Minnie called Morgan St. James and asked him, urgently, to come at once.

That served to get Morgan out of Dupre's.

In the meantime, Jeff and Ted and Father Devlin went by patrol car to the auction house, where Marcus Jones was waiting. Jones, at Jeff's request, had asked one of the staff photographers to stay late.

Dr. Cavior arrived from the Metropolitan Museum, a little breathless. Polly came into Felix's office on his heels.

"You were right," he said to Jeff without looking at the others. "It's modern gold. I don't have the written report yet—that'll take a day—but you were dead-on the money."

Jeff merely smiled, and pointed toward the mantelpiece in Felix Dupre's office. There stood an almost perfectly matched pair of chalices.

"Good God," said Cavior. "If anyone had suggested, even a week ago . . ."

"We have Father Devlin here to thank," Jeff said happily. "He detected the switch first—back at Berwick—and he performed his own little caper this afternoon."

Father Devlin smiled shyly as he shook hands with the famous authority on ancient metalwork. "It was no more than my duty," said the priest modestly.

"It was no more than brilliant," said Ted. "And if we can impose on you, Father, I may ask you to perform still another switch."

Four pairs of eyes swiveled in Ted's direction.

"Switch it back?" asked Jeff incredulously.

Ted just smiled, the smile of a cat who has eaten an entire

cageful of canaries. Then he spoke. "We're all witnesses to the fact that two chalices exist. We'll photograph them in detail, side by side, for further corroboration. I'll ask you, Dr. Cavior, to take a sample of the real chalice—assuming it is real—and get that tested as you did the replica. In the meantime, the duke is going to be detained, on a minor but nevertheless urgent technicality about his passport, long enough for Father Devlin to visit his suite one more time."

"To replace the real chalice with the fake one? But why?" Jeff frowned as he spoke.

"To keep him from suspecting we're on to him."

"He suspects that already. Or else why is he so eager to kill me?"

"Suspects, sure," said Ted. "But suspecting is way different from knowing. And if we don't get the chalice—some chalice—back where Father Devlin found it, he'll know for sure, and skip. You see, this becomes a crime only when the fake is actually sold."

The tension in Polly's voice was palpable, and she did nothing to hide it. "Couldn't he just claim ignorance? I mean, he had a replica made—for, let's say, sentimental reasons—and switched them accidentally."

"Would you believe that? If you were a jury?" Ted smiled as he spoke. It was a slow smile. Jeff didn't like it at all.

"I don't know. Maybe. He is the Duke of Berwick."

The photographer came in then, and they all adjourned to the photographic studio on the floor below.

The picture-taking went quickly because the Dupre in-house studio was all set up for exactly this kind of work.

Both chalices were placed against a black velvet back cloth.

The original was labeled A and the replica B.

They were photographed round-the-clock, from above and from below, and at three angles.

When Ted had Father Devlin driven back to the Hotel Carlyle, less than two hours had passed from the time of the priest's arrival at Minnie's house.

Jeff and Polly and Ted all rode up Madison Avenue with the priest. It was a short ride, but the conflicting emotions in the unmarked dark blue Chevrolet made it seem endless. Jeff still wasn't sure they should be giving the replica back to Neville Fleet.

"If we want to be strictly legal," said Ted patiently, "it's his property."

343

"Fuck strictly legal," said Jeff instantly. Then: "Beg your pardon, Father."

Father Devlin laughed. His life, until now, had been remarkably free of adventures; even spiritual adventures seemed to elude him. Now he was in the thick of several conspiracies and taking positive action for the first time in his long, quiet life. He was beginning to enjoy himself thoroughly. "Legality," he said cheerfully, "does not seem to be one of the duke's primary concerns."

The car stopped in the middle of the block below the corner occupied by the Carlyle. Father Devlin got out and walked resolutely into the Seventy-sixth Street entrance of the famous hotel. The front desk was just inside that door. But there was, as Ted had explained to the old man, another entrance, on Madison Avenue, that would allow him to leave without attracting the attention of the manager. The duke, they knew, would not be in. Father Devlin once again would ask to wait for him. And once again, his request would be granted.

Fifteen minutes later the priest walked calmly out of the hotel and down the street toward the waiting car.

Ten minutes after that, they were back in Minnie Dupre's library having drinks.

She asked them all to dinner.

Ted had to decline. "After the auction," he said, "when we actually arrest the guy, we'll have a victory celebration. But right now I am unbelievably backed up on other cases. And on some parts of this one."

Jeff disliked himself for being relieved to see Ted go. Every time he was in the same room with Ted and Polly, Jeff found himself thinking about Ted and Polly together. Together in bed. Together anywhere. Jealousy was a new emotion to Jeff Dupre, and even though his head told him this was nonsense, his heart had a tendency to churn. He looked at Polly. She was being attentive to Father Devlin, who basked in it. As who wouldn't? thought Jeff, wanting her.

Jeff thought of the incredible afternoon, of Father Devlin's foray into enemy territory. *God does protect the innocent.* He thought of Cavior's odd request, and the bizarre logic of it. Toothpaste, indeed. The man had asked for toothpaste. They'd had to send one of the night guards around the corner.

"Small size, please." Cavior smiled, then turned to Jeff. "With your permission, I'll erase these little scratches."

And he pointed to the two tiny parallel scratches on the replica.

"And," said the eminent scholar, grinning like an urchin, "I'll just take my little penknife and make two very similar scratches in this."

Jeff had nodded, not really understanding. Cavior's knife flashed. Two tiny scratches appeared on the chalice.

"Now," said Cavior, "if my theory's cockeyed, there's no real harm done. But if someone—our old friends the person or persons unknown—were to be studying either chalice closely, they'd expect to see these little scratches on the cup in Dupre's vitrine. And the duke would expect *not* to have the same scratches on his version. The real version."

The guard arrived with a tube of toothpaste.

Cavior whipped out a linen handkerchief and applied a small amount of the paste and began rubbing the base of the replica chalice firmly with his left index finger.

The finger described tiny circles.

Cavior rubbed for five minutes, then wiped the cup's base clean. He looked at it very closely, squinting. Then he repeated the process.

On the third try he was satisfied. He looked at his efforts through the loupe. Then he handed the chalice to Jeff.

The scratches had disappeared entirely, and there was no trace at all of the rubbing.

"Toothpaste," said Cavior, "is a really fine abrasive. You can polish things like lucite with it, almost undetectably."

"I'm glad you thought of this," said Ted. "If it is is a code, or whatever you call it, he would have known immediately."

"It may not be," said Cavior, "but I'd bet quite a lot that it is."

"Why?" Polly asked.

"Because they look wrong. They look new and deliberate. Small as those scratches were, they weren't quite natural. Straight and fairly deep and nearly absolutely parallel. You have to look for them, even if you know what you're looking for, and they're undetectable to a lay person."

"As you said," said Jeff, "it can't hurt, and it could help enormously."

All of these thoughts were competing for Jeff's attention now as he sat in the seemingly impregnable comfort and security of the Dupre library. Polly chatted on with Father Devlin. Minnie had seen Ted to the door. Somewhere below, Emmalee would be stirring magical pots and caldrons and making simple ingredients into unforgettable fantasies of culinary artistry. *Then why do you feel like a condemned man?*

Because you are a condemned man.

Jeff forced himself to review all the positive things he knew about his predicament.

He knew that Neville was being followed, round the clock, and was therefore not likely to do him any immediate harm.

But he also knew that Neville had a pal, and that the pal was almost surely Morgan, and who knew where Morgan was, or what he might be up to?

Ted hadn't said anything about having St. James followed.

The real chalice was now in Dupre's vault.

No one suspected the switch.

As far as they knew.

The auction was the day after tomorrow.

The day after tomorrow might be fifty years away, feeling as Jeff felt right now.

He only noticed Polly's hand on his hand after it had been there awhile.

Her laughter came racing after her hand. "We hate to interrupt your reverie, Jeff," she said, "but dinner is served."

He looked at her, blinked, grinned. Sanity was a wonderful thing. He must try it sometime.

He held her hand as they went downstairs to the dining room.

Minnie sat Father Devlin on her right, Polly on her left.

Hastings poured a chilled Loire wine for Jeff to taste, a Sancerre. It was fruity and crisp. It tingled. It complemented the grilled prawns to perfection.

The priest from Berwick proved to have a well-developed if quiet sense of humor. Minnie kept the conversation dancing with all of her tact and charm. And Polly was splendid. Splendid to look at, splendid in the way she pitched right in to help make the day's many tensions go away, if only for a while. Even the food and the wines seemed to join happily into the conspiracy.

And none of it worked on Jeff Dupre.

Jeff smiled, even laughed, told a story.

And he felt his gut clenching like a giant fist.

He sipped the wine and thought it might be a good thing to get roaring drunk. But he didn't get even mildly high.

From time to time during the otherwise cheerful meal Jeff felt Polly's glance, saw the wary expression in her eyes and how quickly she turned away. Wondering, obviously. Wondering what?

How simple everything had been, in Veli.

How urgently he wanted it to be that simple again. Where most of the pieces fit the puzzle and the ones that didn't would, one day. Where you knew that for a fact, the way you knew your own name.

Dessert came, a magnificent frozen mousse of lemon and orange. It was a deep rich yellow in color, and the flavors sang.

Jeff looked at it, and as he looked, the yellow of the dessert turned into another yellow. The yellow of his father's sailboat. And now he could see the empty sailboat, as he had seen it in his head so many times these past few weeks. There was the little yellow boat, almost a toy boat, brashly, defiantly yellow. There was the boat bobbing empty in the friendly blue sea.

The frozen mousse melted in his mouth.

The fear did not melt. It lay thick and cold and heavy in Jeff's heart, alternately chilling him and making him hot with the raw, unappeasable rage of pure frustration.

The auction was the day after tomorrow.

The day after tomorrow it would all be over.

Jeff kept telling himself that.

61

The Duke of Berwick was not pleased.

To begin with, there was the nagging sense that something was not quite as it should be. The sense of being watched, perhaps followed. The disturbing news from Bess: what could have possessed old Father Devlin, anyway? And then this evening, just as he'd walked into the hotel, the man from Immigration. The long ride downtown. The long wait while his passport was examined, reexamined, and finally found to be in perfect order.

Outrage!

He paced the drawing room of his hotel suite.

He reviewed his plan, the orderly procession of bold maneuvers that would lead him—and Bess and the child—to a lifetime of security and wealth in Costa Rica.

The receipt from the Banco Nacional de Costa Rica lay in

his wallet like a magical shield. A shield that would protect him from any tricks the world could devise.

Then who was behind the investigation at Berwick?

And what else might the damnable police discover, if they looked long enough, hard enough?

Yet the replica chalice was sitting in Dupre's even now. He had seen it, seen the greed in the eyes of the hundreds and hundreds of people who came to inspect it. That had been a good feeling. That was a thing the old Fleets would relish. Even here, now, in the elegantly chilled air of the Carlyle Hotel, Neville could feel the tropic sun as it would be in Costa Rica. He could see the boy—heir!—growing strong and brown, running on the milk-white beaches, splashing in the aquamarine sea. As for Berwick, well, it wasn't so very long ago that a life outside those ancient walls had been beyond imagining. How quickly one could change, adapt, grow! With Bess, with enough money, what limitless pleasures would be his! Far from Berwick, true. Far from the unspeakable Smythe-Davies and his dunning letters. And far, far away from any possible retribution for the death of Felix Dupre or the silversmith.

Great rewards needed great deeds behind them.

And he, Neville Fleet, eighteenth Duke of Berwick, had risen to the challenge.

He could almost hear the hoofbeats of his armored ancestors, galloping down the ages, trailing legends, seizing what they needed.

The glory days weren't over, not yet!

Still, something was wrong.

Perhaps he was too new at the game, still a bit too apprehensive, still governed by the piddling fears and cautions that imprisoned ordinary men. Fears and cautions were not for the Fleets of Berwick. Hundreds and hundreds of years had proven this, gilded the bare bones of fact and certified them in the history books.

Fleets sometimes made laws. If a law must be bent or broken, it ill became a Fleet of Berwick to hesitate for an instant. And if Neville had hesitated once, that day was behind him now. The feeling of soaring freedom was a tonic for him now, and more than tonic.

Then why did he find himself looking over his shoulder on crowded streets in the broadest daylight?

And why did unexpected noises in the night alarm him?

And where was Morgan, who had been summoned and even now was fifteen minutes late? The strain was showing on Morgan, too. He hadn't been himself these last few days. The eyes, usually spilling over with confidence, seemed a little shifty now. He sweated more, and not from the heat. Morgan. Well, blackmailer he might be, but Morgan had been every bit as useful as he had promised to be. Had been! Would be.

For there was one final request—no, command!—that Neville must impose on Morgan St. James, and it would be done tonight.

Neville turned at the sound of St. James's knocking.

He opened the door.

Morgan smiled, a smile too quick, too eager. It was not the smile of a man for whom the universe was in perfect alignment.

"Come in, come in, dear Morgan," said the duke, twelve hundred years of noblesse gilding every word.

They chatted while room service rushed up a bottle of Dom Perignon 1959.

The wine, rarest of the postwar vintages, appeared with two slender flute glasses and a block of fresh foie gras with melba toast from the hotel's kitchen. Neville opened the wine with silent expertise. There was the faintest hiss as the cork eased out under the gentle, practiced pressure of his strong hands. Then the icy sizzle of the pouring.

They raised their glasses in a toast.

"To the highest bidder," said Neville, smiling, "whoever he may be."

"The highest bidder," said St. James quietly, "is death. The ultimate collector, inescapable."

"You're wonderfully cheery, old boy."

Morgan laughed. "Death and divorce, perhaps an occasional fluctuation of currency, a war now and then—these are the fruitful seeds of the entire auction business, Neville. Surely you know that by now."

The duke turned from his guest and looked out the window. The suite faced south and west. The lights of Manhattan were blinking themselves to life. The Hudson River wrapped the glittering town in a sweep of melted silver. The ugly scar that was New Jersey looked almost romantic, a plum-colored smudge in the afterglow of sunset.

For a moment Neville was silent.

He sipped the wine and wished that all perfection were so easily obtainable.

"I want insurance," he said, half to himself.

Then he turned to find Morgan St. James staring at him

349

with the astonished, almost paralyzed expression of a rabbit transfixed by the headlights of a speeding, heedless motorcar.

The smile that formed on Neville's lips was not a pleasant thing to see. "Does that surprise you, dear Morgan?"

Morgan blinked, shook his head slightly as if to clear it. When he spoke, it was slowly. He picked up each word gingerly, as though it might explode. "It would surprise me less, perhaps, if I knew what in the world you're driving at."

"Insurance. You know what insurance is. It's a guarantee that if something . . . untoward should happen, compensation will be made."

Morgan could feel himself sliding into some vast cold and probably bottomless abyss. "What do you mean, 'untoward'?"

"I simply mean that accidents can happen. The best-laid plans and all that rot. I mean that certain of our recent activities might not be viewed with, let us say, sympathy in some quarters. Were they to be discovered."

"They won't be discovered. I'd be the first to know, and they haven't been. Jeff Dupre moves in an archaeological fog. If he suspects that the sun is going to come up tomorrow, that would be a major act of creative thinking for the boy. Charming as he is."

The scorn in St. James's voice had a special resonance. The duke wondered what young Dupre had said—or done—to so antagonize St. James.

"It would be lovely to think so. Nevertheless, Felix knew. He may well have told the boy. In fact, as you know, Felix promised he would do just that."

"He never lived to make the promise good."

"We don't know that for sure."

Morgan flushed. The duke's arrogance reminded him of another man, another time.

"You're so very sure, Neville. Right now you sound like Felix Dupre. Felix was the most charming man in the world when he chose to be. But there was another Felix, a Felix who must be the boss, who must rule absolutely. For twenty years I suffered under that side of Felix Dupre and smiled, and studied the business, and waited."

Neville laughed. It was a harsh and desperate sound. "Tell me, Morgan: was I worth waiting for? I did you the service of killing the man. Not to mention making you rich."

"You kill too easily, Neville. Killing Felix was an unfortunate blunder. You complicated it by your clumsy efforts to get rid of Jeff. And whatever has become of the silversmith Tauranac?"

"Tauranac is resting comfortably, thank you."

"And you talk of insurance?"

Morgan was naturally cautious. Lately, his gut had known the first ragged nibblings of fear. And now, as he looked at Neville Fleet, Morgan knew he had gone too far. The fact was that Fleet did kill too easily. The insurance he was talking about might just include the death of the one man who knew everything. The death of Morgan St. James! Slowly, making a conscious effort not to let his hand tremble, Morgan raised the champagne glass to his lips. Lucky that he'd actually seen Fleet open the bottle. There could be no hanky-panky there. He sipped from the glass, a deep, crystal flute on a pencil-slender stem.

The glass! Maybe there'd been something in the glass. But no. It was a Carlyle room-service glass, he'd seen it come in. Morgan looked all around the room, so quickly it seemed to spin.

Everywhere there was danger.

There was danger in Neville's eyes, in his words, in the lethal capabilities of those strong overbred hands.

Morgan felt the dampness on his brow—clammy, uninvited sweat. Insurance. What insurance? "Tell me, Neville, please, exactly what you want of me."

As plain as that. As naked as death.

Neville smiled again. That lazy, menacing smile. "It isn't really all that difficult, dear Morgan," he said, "but events seem to be quickening. I won't be here for the sale, the way things are. So I need to be very sure that all goes as planned. That, whatever price the chalice brings, I get it. In full. And promptly."

"You already have a million-dollar advance."

"Piddling. The cup will bring three, maybe four million. Not to mention everything else in the sale. Another— what?—two million on top of that?"

"Perhaps. And it will be deposited, like the rest."

"I want the normal waiting period waived."

"Two weeks?"

"Why should I wait? I want it within the week. And I want guarantees that, no matter what the silly Dupres may do, or the police either, all goes forward. Forward to the Banco Nacional de Costa Rica."

"How can I possibly guarantee that? The law can do anything. Including putting the both of us in jail."

"Exactly. That's why I want insurance."

Morgan put down his glass and slumped into an over-stuffed armchair. "I simply don't see what you're getting at."

Neville sipped the wine, frowned slightly, poured some more. "Suppose," he said softly, "that there were a hostage. Someone the Dupres care about. Suppose this hostage were to be held in some secret, very secure place until after the auction, until after the money has been paid as specified?"

Morgan went deeper into his slump. To Neville's eye, he seemed to be melting. His hands thrust deep into the pockets of the immaculately tailored dark blue linen suit. Shoulders hunched as if against the cold. Neville thought of Costa Rica, of the sun, the sea air.

"What," asked Morgan after a pause that seemed eternal, "makes you imagine anything like that is necessary?"

"I'm being followed. Earlier today somebody claiming to be from Immigration took me on a wild-goose chase. And things are going just that tricky bit too smoothly, on the face of it."

"You're imagining things. To do anything like you suggest is the surest way to bring the whole house down on us."

"On you, dear Morgan. I'll be far, far away."

Morgan looked at him. At the sneer, at the smile. The man had killed twice, maybe more than twice. Morgan looked with hunted eyes at the landscape of fear. "Without me, Neville, none of this would have happened. Without me you'd be a penniless has-been sulking under the drafty roofs of Berwick Castle. And without me the chalice will not be sold, payments will not be made. Remember that, in your plans. Remember it well."

"You are a full-fledged partner in all of it."

"Don't count on proving that, Neville. Don't bet anything you can't afford to lose."

The insolence of the little bounder seared Neville to the soul. That such a man dared confront the Duke of Berwick! And more maddening than St. James's words was the sting of truth in them. The poisoned sting of inescapable fact.

"You really are dense this evening, dear Morgan," said Neville Fleet smoothly. "Have some wine and compose yourself. We're both on edge, and perhaps we should be. Perhaps it's a healthy sign."

"Perhaps."

The tone of Morgan's voice was dull now, drugged, despondent.

"We both have so much to lose. And so very much to gain."

"You seem," said Morgan very slowly, "to imagine it's lost already. Is it lost?"

"Don't be so bloody limp, man! This isn't some picnic threatened by a summer rainstorm. This is disgrace, Morgan, perhaps jail, losing everything. You'd never work in the art business again. Or any other, for all of that. What we're doing is a simple matter of self-preservation, can't you see that?"

"You phrase it charmingly. But I still don't see it. I don't see who, or how, or where. And I especially don't see how taking this hypothetical hostage could do anything—assuming someone is on to us—other than make them come down on us faster and harder. We could still plead ignorance. It may be foolish, Neville, and unprofessional, for an auctioneer to make a misjudgment in appraising a piece. But it's far from being a crime. When Dupre's sold your damned deLamerie teapot, and we were caught red-handed, no one went to jail. It might not have been the best thing to have happened, but the fact is, it happens quite regularly, and one survives. Perhaps your silversmith was making unauthorized copies and slipping them into the Berwick collection without your knowledge. How could you possibly be more expert than Felix Dupre? So you made a mistake—even a few mistakes. That's not a criminal action. They'd have to prove criminal intent. How could they do that?"

The duke sighed. "You can't possibly be as dim as you're sounding, Morgan. Two men are dead, and that damned Italian female. And there you sit blandly telling me about mistaken attributions. You are, needless to say, a great bloody accessory after the fact, or whatever they call it here. A partner in crime. Prosecutable. Hangable, perhaps. Can I make it more clear than that? Than conspiracy to murder?"

Morgan stood up as if propelled by rockets. "You wouldn't!"

"Dear, dear Morgan, what a sight you are. Wouldn't? Would I not! Would I not bring this filthy little house of cards all tumbling down? Ha. Ha, ha, ha. Let me show you, fool that you are, what I would not do."

He went to the desk drawer.

Morgan watched him, hypnotized, sure that a gun was inside the drawer, wondering if he could make a dash for the door, wondering if anything mattered.

The duke opened the drawer and pulled out the Winchcombe Chalice.

Morgan gaped. His jaw sagged open. He stopped breathing. His eyes blinked. "No."

"Did you really imagine I'd sell the Winchcombe Chalice?"

The duke enjoyed his triumph. The one forgery he hadn't mentioned was this. What a lovely feeling it was, to have so utterly and completely fooled this little blackmailer. For that's all he was, in the end, a blackmailer. There was nothing grand in him, no sense of his destiny. He was a small man, grubbing after the leavings of his betters.

If Morgan weren't so vital a link in the golden chain of Neville's plans, it would have given Neville some pleasure to eliminate him.

But such an indulgence could not be.

Not, in any event, at the moment.

"You are presiding, dear Morgan," said the duke smoothly, pouring the last of the Dom Perignon into the chalice and lifting it to his lips in a mocking salute, "over the art hoax of the century, maybe of all time. Surely it would be only prudent to make very sure no one else suspects that it is, in fact, a hoax?"

Suddenly Morgan felt himself smiling.

The smile turned into a laugh. The laugh started out as a kind of chuckling rumble deep inside him, out of some secret place. The laugh built and soared and became something close to shrill. Then it died down, but by that time the man was shaking, clutching himself as though he'd been shot in the gut.

It was so like a dream, a fantasy, entirely unreal.

Of course he was watching the Duke of Berwick sip vintage champagne from the Winchcombe Chalice while all the art world imagined the damned cup was resting comfortably in the steel-clad vault of Dupre's.

The mad logic of it was irresistible.

Morgan drifted with the current, not fighting anymore.

Why should he fight? What was worth fighting for, anyhow, other than one's freedom, one's hard-fought gains?

The vault. Dupre's vault.

He stopped laughing and composed himself as best he could. He considered what the duke had asked of him—a secret place to secure a hostage. "I think," said Morgan softly, "that I know just the place."

"And I think," said Neville smoothly, "that I'll just come along with you, Morgan, to make very sure the thing is done right."

62

The popular press was calling it the Auction of the Century. Even the conservative *New York Times* allowed that the Winchcombe sale at Dupre's would probably set all kinds of new records.

The House of Dupre fairly quivered with the excitement of it. Tension, expectation, and a sense of building drama filled the polished hallways, made the densely crowded exhibition galleries seethe and tremble with anticipation. The excitement had a life of its own. It stalked the elegant rooms, prowled through the little cubicles, made itself felt even in the paneled, carpeted executive office suites. The doormen and guards caught it. They seemed to stand a little taller, to smile more readily.

The glow and the grandeur of it were rubbing off, transforming everyone in every nook and cranny of the great auction house.

It would definitely not be just another sale day.

Crews of technicians fussed with cables for the closed-circuit television system that would relay the action from the main salesroom to the less-fortunate bidders packed in antechambers.

The sale was strictly by invitation only. In all, just eight hundred of the richest and most prominent dealers and art collectors would be admitted. Invitations were coveted, schemed for, counterfeited, left conspicuously on the marble mantelpieces of people so rich they should not have needed the social reassurance that seemed to be conveyed by the thick cream-colored card engraved simply in black.

Morgan was in charge of the invitation lists.

Felix had created the famous card file, cross-referenced with name after world-famous name. The index contained financial information of a scope and accuracy to make an IRS agent drool with envy. It cataloged people's tastes in art and in furniture, their several residences, and the style in which each was furnished. Felix Dupre had been quietly proud of his reference file. His pride was justified. At any moment, and at a glance, he could determine who owned what, who needed what to fill out some gap in a collection, who might be ready to sell, who was panting to buy.

Key prospects were cultivated like rare flowers.

Acquisitive millionaires were notified by personal note or phone or even by international cablegram when a choice item was coming up for sale.

Many of his best clients had given Felix carte blanche to buy, at his discretion, any first-rate example of this or that painter, of a certain type of furniture or silver, sometimes jewels.

There was a South American dowager who looked strikingly like a gila monster and had an incurable passion for rose-colored diamonds. For her, over the years, Felix Dupre had assembled one of the world's definitive collections. At any opening night of the Buenos Aires opera she could be seen waddling from her Bentley limousine, a gila monster decked in pink fire.

Morgan St. James was lord of the list now, and he played it like the sensitive instrument it was.

The secret, Felix had always said, was in the combinations of people rather than their net worth. Who might bid against whom, and thus send prices soaring heavenward on the golden wings of rivalry.

It was a high-stakes game, and nobody played it with quite the cool élan of Felix Dupre.

The art world was wondering how it would go now, with Felix dead.

Not that any of them doubted Morgan's knowledge or his skill in choreographing a big sale.

Still and all, this would be the first major sale since the death of Felix Dupre. The Winchcombe sale would be twice a landmark, then.

It might well decide the future of Dupre's.

If Dupre's had a future.

Jeff got out of the patrol car in front of the auction house on the afternoon before the sale. He felt faintly foolish. Hauled back and forth like an invalid. Like a political prisoner.

Like a target.

He could sense the excitement. The quick grin of the doorman, proud to be a part of it all. The subtle deference of the elevator operator, carrying an authentic Dupre.

Jeff went straight to the exhibition gallery.

The gallery would close early today, as the objects were marshaled for tomorrow's sale.

But now the place was crowded. It was a polite crowd, as you'd expect of Dupre's. But it simmered. There were people there, Jeff guessed, who had probably never set foot in an auction house before. Attracted by all the hoo-ha in the press, on TV. The chalice was the biggest thing to hit the pop-culture scene since King Tut's treasures, equally golden, had created mob scenes, at the Metropolitan Museum.

On any other day, Jeff would have been proud and happy.

Today he merely wanted it all to be over.

He wanted the fear to stop, and the killing, and the gnawing, grinding feeling in his gut. He wanted, most of all, to take Polly by the hand and walk out into the bright afternoon, free, together, laughing.

It seemed like forever since he'd really laughed.

He wondered when he'd feel like laughing again.

Jeff made his way through the crowd, unrecognized, and up to the specially built vitrine that held the cup. The real cup, thanks to Father Devlin. That was one good thing that had come out of all the horror: the old priest had come into his own that day, switching the fake chalice for the real one, cool as a field filled with cucumbers.

The Winchcombe Chalice sat in its bulletproof case, radiating magic. As it always had. As it always would, somewhere, for someone. Jeff, almost idly, found himself wondering where the golden cup would end its strange journey.

Then he saw Morgan.

Morgan did not see Jeff.

Morgan stood very near the case, staring at the chalice, an expression of anguish on his usually bland features.

Something was bothering Morgan St. James. Jeff decided. Something was bothering him a lot.

Jeff came up behind the man. "Hi, Morgan. What's happening?"

St. James nearly jumped. Jeff could see the shock of his voice jerking through the man. Morgan flinched, turned, managed a kind of smile. There was a slightly greenish tinge to his skin, Jeff thought. Maybe it was the light in the gallery.

"Oh," said Morgan too quickly, "jolly good."

It wasn't jolly. It wasn't good. Jeff decided, reluctantly, not to press the man. Let Kavanaugh do the pressing.

Jeff was forming his reply when Morgan was buttonholed by a plump and richly dressed lady. No doubt a good customer. Jeff smiled his thanks for this small miracle of fate, and walked out of the room.

Polly wasn't in her cubicle.

He went up to Felix's office and asked for tea, without really wanting it. Miss Winn produced her usual appetizing spread, China tea in old cups, cookies, a smile. No haunting fears for Miss Winn. Jeff sipped the steaming, fragrant tea. It was the color of pale amber. He bit into a cookie. Chocolate-chip. Crunchy. They always tasted home-baked, Miss Winn's cookies. He wondered if they were.

The phone rang.

Kavanaugh.

"Maybe," said the detective, "we got too cute. With the chalice."

"What do you mean, Ted?"

"Switching. Now we can't get him for selling a fake."

Jeff paused. None of them had thought about that part of it. Still, even if they couldn't pin that particular crime on Fleet, there were others. And now, at the very least, Dupre's wouldn't have to face the scandal of having sold a fake.

"Yeah," said Jeff at last, much less troubled than Kavanaugh obviously expected him to be, "maybe. But God knows there are worse things to hang on him. Carla, for instance." He couldn't say the name without trembling.

There was a pause.

"Have you seen his grace today?"

"No."

"Call me if you do, okay?" Kavanaugh then gave Jeff three numbers where he might be reached.

"Sure. Why?"

"Fleet just lost the tail I had on him. And he's gone from his hotel suite, but he left all his clothes there. And the chalice. So he's got to come back."

"It figures. Morgan looked pretty nervous a few minutes ago."

"We're checking the airports, shipping, but there are a million ways to skip out, if that's what he's doing."

"What do you hear from your man in London?"

"Nothing more, dammit. If Nipper finds anything tangible, we could really blow the whistle. Bring his grace in. Helping the police with their inquiries, it's called."

"Otherwise known as in the slammer?"

"Something like that."

Kavanaugh's voice was quick, urgent. He sounded tired. He had every reason to sound tired. He'd been working almost around the clock on the Dupre case and four others. With no more results than you could carve on the head of a pin.

"I'll keep my eyes open, Ted, but it looks like he has skipped out."

"Doesn't it, though. I sing a song of extradition."

"What about his wife?"

"What about her? My guess is, she doesn't know a thing. This scam has been going on longer than he's known the lady. Muir checked that out. And her reputation is a good one."

"Still," said Jeff, "the duke did talk very openly about their leaving, together with the little boy and her daughter. So at least she might be able to lead you to him."

"Maybe. I'll call Muir. That'll be the fastest thing."

"I'll call you if anything turns up here."

"Right. Thanks, Jeff."

The phone clicked off. Jeff sat at his uncle's desk for a moment after he'd hung up, staring at the phone as though he'd never seen one before.

Then he picked it up and dialed Polly's cubicle.

The phone rang and rang.

Just as Jeff was hanging up again, she walked into the office. "Good morning," she said solemnly.

He got up and went over to her and kissed her, hard. Not caring that the big door was open, that anyone might walk in.

"How do you feel?" he asked.

"Useless. I want to make time speed up—to have this whole damn thing all over, Jeff. It's the old watched-pot syndrome. Just won't boil."

He looked at her. There was no other girl like this, not anywhere. Never had been. Jeff felt lucky to be in the same room with her. With the dark and bottomless eyes. With the elegant body. With the ivory skin. He reached to touch her cheek.

Polly smiled. "I know," she said softly, "I know."

It seemed to Jeff in that moment that she knew everything, and that she was everything. Would be. He tried to say what he felt and couldn't find words. It was an enormous feeling, and elusive, too, all at the same time, a great cosmic whirlwind of a feeling, deep and exciting and more than a little scary, like falling suddenly from some high place, falling and falling and somehow knowing you'd land safe.

Some people might call it love.

"When this is over," Jeff began, going slowly, "just as soon—"

"Don't say it."

"Don't say what?"

Jeff hadn't been sure himself of just what words might come out next.

"Anything," she said softly. "Don't say anything at all, until you're absolutely sure."

Then, quick as lightning, she kissed him on the cheek and was gone.

Jeff stood in his uncle's office looking after her.

He wondered if, among all the mysteries of the universe, there could be a mystery more wonderful than the intuitive magic of women.

63

Polly felt their presence before she saw them.

She looked up from her desk just as Morgan knocked. There he stood, at the entrance to her cubicle, the Duke of Berwick behind him.

She managed a smile. It was the day before the auction. And here she was, being visited by the world's arch-forger of silver. Not to mention faking the chalice itself. She wondered what to say, whether Kavanaugh knew where the duke was, or Jeff, or if she should call them.

Morgan hoped the girl couldn't see the beads of sweat he felt forming on his upper lip. The gentle nudge at the base of his spine was the small automatic pistol the duke carried inside his jacket pocket.

"Polly, my dear," said Morgan quickly, "the duke has brought a few things for us to look at, things we missed in Berwick. Can you come for a minute? I hate to tear you away . . ."

Slowly, the smile fading, she stood up. *Don't let them know what you know, what you suspect. Not by a word, not by a gesture. Be casual. This is an everyday kind of request.*

"Of course," she said quietly, wishing the floor would open up and swallow her.

She followed them down the hall.

"They're a bit bulky, all in all," said Neville Fleet lightly. "So we just put them in the vault, don't you know?"

Marcus Aurelius Jones smiled as he gave the address to the taxi driver. The people who designed the Vigilance Laser Alarm system were going to have a tough sale. He tried to imagine the advantages of a laser alarm over the existing warning devices at the House of Dupre. Well, maybe.

And Morgan St. James had asked him to check out the Vigilance device. Friend of a friend, said Morgan, you know how that is. Marcus Jones hadn't been in the FBI twenty years without learning exactly how things like that worked. At least they'd be on record as having looked into the damn thing. And, who knew, there might be something to it after all.

If only it weren't this afternoon, day before the Berwick sale. Marcus liked to be on hand for all the big sales, and for the shows preceding them. Well, an hour or two couldn't hurt. The place was well covered, as always.

The Vigilance Laser Alarm Company had a weird address somewhere in darkest Brooklyn. Places like that usually did. The cab sped down the FDR Drive. The sun shone. The harbor sparkled as they wound their way through the traffic on the Brooklyn Bridge. Marcus could see the tall green lady of the harbor waving her torch at him. He smiled. It was good to get out of the auction house once in a while.

"Where," asked Polly as they stepped out of the elevator on the basement level, "did they come from?"

The duke beamed. He was enjoying himself thoroughly. He felt like a Fleet to his toes.

"Bess found them," he said, "and thinks they'll be quite salable. She does know her silver, does Bess."

It was creepy in Dupre's basement, for all the bright fluorescent lighting. Purely utilitarian, and looking it. Concrete walls painted an institutional tan. Scuffed linoleum floors in a particularly ugly gray. The steel-framed vault door gleamed with authority.

Polly stood aside, subdued, as Morgan twirled the knob that controlled the combination.

It was very quiet in the basement.

The door swung open with a hissing sound. The sound of well-oiled steel sliding on steel. The door, Polly guessed, was more than a foot thick.

Morgan reached in and switched on the light.

Then he stood graciously aside and motioned her in.

Polly was just crossing the slightly raised threshold of the vault when the blow came.

Morgan struck her on the back, very hard, with the flat of his hand. The force of it knocked her breath out, sent her reeling across the small room and crashing into the shelves on the opposite side.

Gasping, she turned, one arm raised across her face to ward off the next blow.

The next blow never came.

What Polly saw as she turned was the vault door closing.

She gasped for breath.

Disbelief mixed with horror. She felt knots in her throat, knots of cold fear. She formed a word and couldn't say it. The word was "Help!" She croaked. There was no one to hear. The door closed with an evil hiss.

Now she could hear the tumblers, faintly, clicking into place.

Polly felt her knees giving way. She reached out and gripped the nearest shelf to steady herself. The trembling slowed, stopped.

She took a very deep breath, then another.

"Help!" she screamed. "Help! Help!"

Her voice had power now. Too late. Her screams echoed off the steel-plated walls, off the floor, off the steel-clad ceiling.

Only Morgan and the duke knew where she was.

Only Morgan and Marcus Jones had the combination of the vault. She walked quickly across the vault and stopped at the door, listening. Very faintly, from the steel belly of the thick door, she could hear small metallic noises.

The bastard must be changing the combination.

The clicking stopped.

The silence was enormous, thick, heavy. She could feel it crushing her. *I will be calm*, she told herself through clenched teeth. *I won't panic. I won't give them the satisfaction.* Polly thought of how she had questioned Jeff's suspicions of Morgan. Give him the benefit of the doubt, she'd reasoned. Some benefit. Well, now she knew. And she was the only one who knew. And no one knew where she was. And no one could hear her. Polly looked at the walls, the shelves, the ceiling. There was no silver. A few small items, some gold-and-enamel snuffboxes, no weapon. A gun might make enough noise to be heard. Might. But there was no gun.

I will be calm. I will not panic.

She knew the story of the mouse—it was part of the Dupre mythology. The very dead, very dehydrated little mouse someone found in the vault. A mouse-mummy, weightless.

Suffocated, the legend had it. That place must be hermetic, airtight. No air in. No noise out.

Polly went to the door again, listening.

Nothing. No sound at all.

She began pounding on the door with clenched fists. She pounded and she pounded. Echoes. Could anyone hear, if there was anyone to hear?

Now she stopped, paced the little steel room, thinking.

She looked at every item on the shelves.

Gold snuffboxes, wonderfully wrought. Useless. A small roundel of Limoges enamel, too light, too fragile. She wanted something strong, something brutal, an iron crowbar, maybe. There was nothing. She wondered how much noise a gold snuffbox might make, pounding. She looked down, noticed her shoes. Damned sensible shoes. Soft, light, low-heeled. Six-inch spike-heeled numbers might make a dent in something. In spite of herself, Polly grinned. She owned nothing resembling six-inch spike-heeled shoes.

She paused, looked all around the vault one more time, then sat down on the floor. Cool, hard concrete. She drew up her knees, rested her arms on them, rested her head on her arms. She could still feel the spot between her shoulder blades where Morgan had shoved her. Lucky she hadn't been standing on the edge of somebody's skyscraper terrace.

At least she was alive.

For the time being.

She wondered just what Morgan and Neville Fleet had in mind. She could understand them wanting to kill Jeff. But this made no sense at all. Beyond reason. But maybe they had always been beyond reason. Jeff thought they'd killed Felix. The Italian woman. Maybe others. Why hadn't they just killed her?

Maybe they had.

Maybe no one would find out in time.

The vault was used regularly, Polly knew that. Marcus Jones had the combination. But Morgan had changed the combination. Or at least it had sounded like that, all the fiddling with the tumblers after he'd shoved her inside. When you closed the vault, normally you simply closed it, spun the dials, and that did it.

She was aware of every breath, the air coming in, going out.

The air in the vault had smelled stuffy from the first. That didn't mean she was suffocating. Yet. Maybe the story about the mouse wasn't true. Do people perform autopsies on mice?

Polly hadn't worn her wristwatch. That might be better. She imagined herself watching the hands of the watch, slowly, slowly. There was no sense of time now, just the terrible need of counting every breath. In, out, in, out. She had sometimes imagined what it must be like to drown, the choking, gasping, taking in water when you needed air. The silence. Suffocating wouldn't be like that. Suffocating would be slow, very slow. Probably you'd just drift off, like a child going to sleep. Peaceful, say your prayers, kiss Daddy good night.

Polly thought about that for a while. Then she stood up. She went to the door then.

And she began screaming.

64

Kavanaugh came into Felix Dupre's office, walking fast. He started talking as he came through the door, no greeting, all business. "She's not at home. None of 'em are around. Damned duke slipped past us. He may be gone."

Jeff looked at the cop, sensing his frustration, trying to sympathize, and failing. The New York City police were juggling with Jeff's life, maybe with Minnie's, too. They were juggling and they were dropping the ball.

"What," Jeff asked, "can I do?"

"What you've been doing. Sit tight. Keep a low profile. And try not to go too crazy with the waiting. It'll be over tomorrow, Jeff."

"Tomorrow," said Jeff, "is a long way away."

"It's getting to you, isn't it?"

"It's been there and back. And I probably am going crazy. But never mind, it'll hardly show."

"Look, Jeff. It may not help you, but this is how it is. How it always is. The waiting. The frustration. I'm going to check up on a couple of things. Search St. James's house one more time. Why don't you just go home and sit it out?"

Jeff stood up. "OK."

Kavanaugh looked at his watch. It was just after five. "I'll meet you there at eight, maybe sooner."

They walked to the elevator together. The patrol car Ted

had come in was waiting. But Jeff Dupre did not get into the waiting police car. He was seething with the thousand pressures of forced inaction. To get into the patrol car would be like going to jail. Completely on impulse, Jeff turned left and walked briskly up Madison Avenue toward the Carlyle.

The Carlyle lobby was its usual calm, elegant self. Nothing bad could happen to you here. Not among the deep carpets and old tapestries and the blue-haired ladies in silk and pearls. If Kavanaugh had people watching, they were undetectable.

The receptionist at the small registration desk didn't know whether his grace was in. He rang the suite and no one answered. Jeff said he'd be back, and left his name. Then he walked through the lobby toward the bar.

The lobby was L-shaped. Jeff walked past the marble fireplace and turned right. The receptionist couldn't see him now, had the receptionist been watching. Here were the elevators. The only elevators, so far as Jeff knew. Maybe there was a service elevator. And there must be fire stairs. The suite was on the sixteenth floor.

There was a sitting area near the bar, but not in it, where you could have tea, or a drink, or just sit. It was empty now, at the beginning of the cocktail hour, but for two elderly ladies sipping sherry from tall flute-shaped glasses. They conversed in whispers.

Jeff walked up the three steps to the bar and looked in. It was dark, many-angled, lined with deep banquettes. Not a room to be taken in at a glance. Jeff strolled through the place. There were two doors besides the one he had come in: a door leading directly onto Madison Avenue, and another leading to the Madison Avenue entrance foyer. There were a few people in the room, but no Duke of Berwick.

Jeff went back through the bar to the little door that led to the lobby. He opened it and stepped through just in time to see the elevator doors closing on Neville Fleet.

The man had killed Felix. Suddenly Jeff was as sure of that as he had ever been of anything. Neville Fleet had killed Felix, and Carla. And his own unborn child.

Jeff felt the anger bubbling up in him, hot and hard. That the man walked into his hotel cool as ice, a forger and a multiple murderer. Jeff knew he couldn't prove any of this in a court of law.

But in the court of his heart it was open and shut.

Jeff found a house phone, called Minnie, and told her where he'd be, should Ted check in early. Then he waited five minutes and walked to the elevators as though drawn by some irresistible magnetic force.

His hand went up and pressed the button.

He had been a target too long, been trapped too long, had worried and been frightened for much too long.

"Sixteen, please," he told the elevator attendant.

The doors slid silently shut. The car rose. For a moment Jeff felt suspended in time. He could still go back to the lobby and call the police. The car stopped. The doors opened. Jeff stepped out onto the soft carpet. The decision was made.

He was smiling as he pressed the discreet little ivory-colored bell-ringer set into the doorframe of suite 1632.

The duke opened it, looked at Jeff, hesitated.

"Tell me," said Jeff, pushing past him into the drawing room, "how you killed my uncle."

Polly looked at the bruise on her hand with some detachment. It wasn't the biggest bruise in the world, nor the most painful.

The painful part was inside her head.

And the hardest thing was admitting there didn't seem to be a single thing to do about her predicament. Screaming only hurt her lungs. Pounding her fists black and blue didn't work, not kicking at the heavy steel door. She had prayed, cursed, wept.

She tried to imagine why Morgan would do this, what might be in it for him. There was no doubt about it at all now: Morgan was in with the duke. So they were both killers. Maybe they'd killed Felix. Surely they'd tried to kill Jeff. Why not her? Of course, she might die anyway, if no one came.

It was possible to imagine Neville Fleet made desperate by the British tax laws, by being suddenly so poor after having been so very rich. Polly could understand that. But Morgan? Morgan of the gentle manner and elegant life? Morgan who stood at the top of his profession, with all the rewards that implied, both social and financial?

It would be all over now, for Morgan. Polly shuddered as the terrible knowledge came back to her that it might be all over for her, too.

Morgan must be planning on skipping out, too.

Jeff had said the duke was doing it, talked openly of leaving England. How far would they have to go, that the law couldn't reach them?

Polly thought of these things, of Morgan and the duke. She

tried not to think of the steel walls around her. It was so very like a crypt.

She thought of Jeff.

She thought about loving Jeff Dupre, of his smile, of the cool blue eyes that weren't cool really, the touch of him, the quiet intensity, the easy charm.

It was good to think about Jeff. It made the cold room seem warmer, and her situation a little less grim.

Jeff.

Where the hell was he? And Ted too, for that matter.

A girl could get very damned impatient, waiting for the hoofbeats of her knights in shining armor. A girl could just about die of impatience. Conserve oxygen. Rest. Sleep, maybe.

If she slept, she might die in her sleep. Lovely thought. Polly thought of family, her brothers, their sudden laughter. That was more painful than anything.

She examined the snuffboxes in minute detail. Before long she knew every ribbon on the enameled shepherdesses' gowns, every gadroon and swag, the makers' marks (French, pre-Napoleon). Precious little trifles. Here was a portrait box, a young man with huge eyes and not much chin. Someone's son, husband, lover. Elegant in his top-heavy Louis XVI wig and lace jabot. The young man's eyes were watchful, perhaps a bit alarmed. Maybe he heard the distant rumbling of the Terror.

Maybe it would be better with the light off. Maybe if she couldn't see the damned vault she wouldn't think about it so much. But she couldn't bring herself to switch off the light. It meant something, that light. It meant a connection to the world outside, even if that connection was one thin copper wire. Better that than nothing.

Slowly she lowered herself to the floor, sliding down the wall until she was sitting. Then Polly stretched out her legs and lay down on the clammy steel floor, cradling her head on one arm. She closed her eyes. Maybe it didn't matter if she slept. Maybe it would be better that way. She concentrated on breathing very slowly, counting each precious breath as though it were a pearl on a necklace, on a string of hope. A very thin string of hope.

The last thing she remembered thinking of was Jeff Dupre.

Ted Kavanaugh sighed. Back at the precinct house his pals thought he was optimistic to the point of stupidity. The

Dupre case was trying his optimism severely. Especially tonight.

In the hour since he'd left Jeff Dupe, Ted had checked out Polly's apartment and Morgan's town house. Nothing and no one. He'd made three phone calls to men who were checking airline-ticket sales, and one who was watching the Carlyle. Nothing. Not worth the trouble it took to find a working pay phone.

And if he had the Duke of Berwick what would he do?

Arrest him, most likely, evidence or no evidence.

Nipper Muir would have evidence. The body in the woods at Berwick, God knew, was evidence. Not just a body in the forest, but neatly wrapped, the definite result of premeditation.

Of course he'd arrest the duke. Maybe he should have done that sooner.

Now Ted stood outside Morgan St. James's house hoping against all odds that the man would show up. The futility of his waiting was pressing in on his head with the cruel efficiency of some medieval instrument of torture.

And where in hell was Polly?

He'd give it ten—make that fifteen—minutes more, then go back to Dupre's. By then it would be time to pick up Jeff. He looked at his watch and thought of all the leads that had come to nothing.

Morgan's house was clean as any surgical operating room. Not a note, not a hidden vault with the ill-gotten loot inside, not a bag full of forged silver. Nothing to point to Morgan St. James as being a part of the operation. And yet he almost certainly was a part of it.

Ted looked at his watch again. One minute had passed. Swell. At this rate they'd be carrying him screaming into Bellevue before the fifteen minutes had passed, and what good would that do the Dupres? What good would anything do the Dupres, for that matter?

He thought of Polly and how weird it was, coming full circle like this. He'd spent quite a few years trying not to think about her, and failing. Failing miserably. Maybe she'd gone back to Dupre's, to work late or something. He'd check that out when he went there. Search the damn place from top to bottom. His arm came up again, automatically swiveling the watch face into view. Ten more minutes. A lifetime. And for what?

The duke stepped back, propelled by the shock wave of his

own astonishment. Suddenly Jeff was in the room, his back to the fireplace, surprisingly controlled, and very threatening.

Neville's mind made quick, darting little excursions into the possibilities of the situation. They were few, and getting fewer. Here was a situation fit for a Fleet. Here was a chance to show this callow upstart not to meddle with a Fleet of Berwick! Here, at last, was a way out.

Neville smiled. "Jeff, dear boy, you seem upset. Sit down, have a drink. What's this about your uncle?"

Jeff looked at him, fighting the rage, wrestling with control. "He was your friend, Neville, and Minnie too. Didn't that mean anything to you? You had no reason to kill him. Or to try to kill me. Or to kill your tame forger and bury him in Berwick Forest. Felix wasn't going to prosecute. You didn't have to do any of it."

The smile on Neville's face hardened a little, but it remained a smile. Or something very like a smile. Jeff could see a new light in his eyes, a sort of metallic glint, sudden and probably dangerous. And Jeff could almost hear the adrenaline flowing, pumping in the sudden silence.

"Jeff," said Neville gently, as though he were explaining something to a very small child, "you must understand I have no idea at all what you're going on about. Did someone kill your uncle? Surely you can't imagine it was me!"

This was followed by a little tinkling laugh, a sound like ice breaking.

"It's no use, Neville. We know. Just as Felix knew. I know. The police know. It's all over for you, Neville. I only want to know why. So tell me. Why?"

"You are a fool," said the duke. "You're more stupid than I imagined."

His hand went to the pocket of his jacket, and the small automatic pistol came out, seemed to grow in his hand, a little steel toy of a gun, but deadly all the same.

Jeff looked at it, fascinated. "That won't work either," said Jeff, surprising himself with his own calm. It was a calm he definitely didn't feel inside. "As I said, they know. We all know. Even Minnie knows."

"You are wrong again, as usual," said Neville, his voice rising a little now, showing the strain. "Nothing can be proved. My departure is all arranged. And, where I am going, dear boy, no one will be able to reach me. Not your silly police, nor England's, not anyone. You ask me why. You should know why, but I forget you are stupid, and with the arrogance of stupid people everywhere. As the tax people in

Britain are stupid little crawling creatures, yes, and the people who buy what I sell—sold—the copies, lovely copies. All stupid little people, scarcely worth one's attention."

Jeff looked at him, holding Neville's eyes as best he could. It wasn't easy. The duke's eyes were burning with madness now, darting and shifting, becoming more and more the eyes of a trapped animal. Jeff was tensing for the leap he knew he must make, and soon. Wondering how big the bullets could be from such a little gun, how good a shot the duke might be.

"You asked me why." Neville paused, took a deep breath. "Why, indeed. Felix presumed, dear boy. Felix challenged the honor of a Fleet of Berwick. The graveyards of Europe are crowded with men who presumed to do that. And failed. As Felix failed, and as you have failed."

Jeff could sense the tension in Neville Fleet, could see the finger tightening on the trigger. "Honor!" he shouted suddenly, making it a battle cry as he leaped for the duke's gun hand.

The shots were loud in the quiet room.

Jeff could feel the burning in his chest, a burning and a throbbing. He fell, and it seemed to take hours, like falling through space forever, never going to land.

Jeff didn't feel the landing. It was getting dark in here. He did hear the distant laughter, Neville Fleet's laughter. It seemed to be coming from the far end of a long tunnel, a very long, dark tunnel.

"Good-bye dear boy," said the laughing voice. "We will not meet again in this world."

And a door closed, followed by utter darkness and a silence as deep as the grave.

65

Ted Kavanaugh raced up to the House of Dupre in a taxi, raised the night watchman, and asked for Marcus Jones. Jones wasn't there. The guard hadn't seen Miss Kunimara.

They called Jones at home, and no one answered. Ted told the guard to try the Jones number every half-hour until Jones answered. Then, in company with another guard, he commenced a fast but thorough search of Dupre's from top to bottom.

The futility grew more intense with every room that turned up nothing, with every closet and cubicle and hallway. There was no sign of the girl. Her cubicle was just the way it always looked: messy, crammed with paperwork, not enough space to organize things properly.

Finally they reached the basement level, the vault.

"What's in here?" Ted asked the guard.

"Jewelry, mostly, rare silver, gold things. Like that."

"Who's got the combination?"

The guard frowned. "Mr. Dupre, he had it. Mr. St. James got it. And Marcus Jones, he has it too. I think that's all."

Ted looked at the door. No way was he going to get in there, not without the combination or a team of safecrackers. He raised his left arm and made a fist and pounded on the door.

"Polly! Polly!"

Her name echoed in the empty hallway. The guard looked at him, puzzled. Finally Ted stopped. Even if by some chance she was in there, she probably couldn't hear. He looked at his watch for maybe the millionth time this evening. Nearly eight.

"Okay," he said, "just let me use a phone for a minute."

He called the precinct house. No sign of Fleet, or Polly, or St. James.

Ted left Dupre's then, with firm instructions to the head of the night guard shift to keep on trying Marcus Jones, and to let Ted know, through the precinct number, when they had reached the head of Dupre's secruity system. In five minutes Ted was at Minnie Dupre's house. Five minutes after that he was turning into the Carlyle.

There was no sign of Jeff Dupre in the Carlyle lobby, nor in the bar.

The receptionist was helpful. "Yes," he said, frowning slightly at Ted's police ID, "the duke left not half an hour ago. He went out this entrance." The man pointed to the Seventy-sixth Street door.

Ted asked for and got an assistant manager to go up to the ducal suite with him. The quiet elevator seemed to take forever.

Maybe Jeff simply got fed up with it all and walked home. Ted doubted that. He might have followed the duke when the duke left. But first, check out the rooms. The discreet, silent elevator seemed to take forever. The doors glided open. The carpet in the corridor absorbed every sound. It was like walking in a dream.

The assistant manager opened the door and stood back.

Ted swung the door open wide.

The carpet was pale ivory. Except where Jeff's blood had soaked into it in a burgundy-colored puddle.

Ted was at Jeff's side in seconds, crouching, feeling for the pulse. It was there, very faint. Already the assistant manager was on the phone for a doctor. And to Lenox Hill Hospital for an ambulance.

Jeff lay face down, his head cradled on one arm, the other arm flung out across the rug. Gently Ted rolled him over. Jeff was pale under the deep tan. His thin summer shirt adhered to the thick hotel carpet, caked with half-dried blood. Ted opened the shirt, took off the tie, got a towel and dampened it, and tried as best he could to clean up Jeff's chest. The two bullet holes were small ones and they had stopped bleeding. That didn't mean Dupre wasn't bleeding inside.

The doctor came then, quickly gave Jeff a shot of something, and then the ambulance men came and took him down the service elevator to the waiting ambulance. Ted went with them, riding in the back, the few blocks to Lenox Hill.

He waited while they rushed Jeff into surgery. No point in calling the aunt until he knew more about Jeff's condition.

Ted made more phone calls from the hospital. The guards at Dupre's still hadn't reached Marcus Jones. Polly was still missing. And there seemed to be no sign of Morgan St. James.

He put out an all-points alert for the duke. Planes, trains, buses, and even car-rental agencies would all be queried. It might be too late, but then again it might not be. It was a chance worth taking.

Jeff was on the operating table less than an hour. They'd given him blood, probed the wounds, found the bullets—.22 caliber—and sewed him up. Nothing important had been penetrated. One bullet grazed a lung, the other narrowly missed his heart. Pure luck. Jeff, the doctor said, would be fine in a few days.

It was only then that Ted called Minnie Dupre.

They were both at Jeff's bedside when he woke up out of a deeply anesthetized sleep.

"Good morning," said Jeff, smiling weakly.

"Darling," said his aunt gently, "you're going to be fine."

"No fault of my own," said Jeff in a kind of a croak, "that I'm not dead."

Ted grinned. "Listen," he said. "You did one thing right. Now we know. Now we really know for sure."

Jeff looked up at the big cop. "Right," said Jeff. "Now let's find Polly, Okay?"

Then, without meaning to, he closed his eyes and slept.

Neville Fleet smiled.

The Metroliner sped southward. Not the smoothest train in the world, for all its modern trappings. But it was comfortable, soft as clouds for the Duke of Berwick.

Because the Duke of Berwick carried his comfort with him. In his heart. In his suitcase. He could almost feel the chalice glowing, warming him. Like the Costa Rican sunshine. Like money in the bank. Like the love of his Bess.

Taking the train was a bit of instinct.

Plenty of jets left the New York airports for Latin America.

But the New York airports, Neville had suspected, might just be watched. It would be far less likely that they would be watching the Dulles International Airport in Virginia.

He got off the train in Baltimore. It was only about an hour's cab ride. The driver charged him fifty-three dollars. Neville tipped the man generously. The cab sped away. Neville lifted his lightweight suitcase.

There would be all the time in the world to buy new clothes now.

He wondered about the local tailors. Surely there must be some good ones. New clothes. A new life. He smiled.

The girl at Pan Am smiled too. "You have a reservation, sir?"

"Lapin," said Neville smoothly. "Pierre Lapin."

Half an hour later the Pan Am jet was climbing out of the Baltimore-Washington smog into a September sky of the purest blue. The gentleman in the first-class window seat leaned back and closed his eyes, feeling the power of the great 747 surging through the sky, through him, pulling him up into the bright unclouded future. The future glittered with possibilities.

The seat next to him was empty.

Neville put his case under the empty seat. As he did this, he could feel the faint, hard outline of the chalice, wrapped in a thick towel he had appropriated from the Carlyle.

Reassuring.

Let the hotel cry for their towel.

Let the police, the revenue people in Britain, let them all cry, shout, plead, rage.

The man who traveled under the name of Peter Rabbit, translated into half-forgotten schoolboy French, was immune to all their clamor.

The chalice would have a new and splendid home.

The future beckoned, warm and rich, seductive.

The Duke of Berwick smiled.

Ted got about four hours' sleep. Then he was up and off to the House of Dupre. The day of the big auction. The day it was all going to wind up, one way or the other. When they hadn't located Marcus Jones by three A.M., Ted called it a night. He couldn't authorize anyone's blasting into the vault at Dupre's without a lot more evidence than he had.

He thought of a million places Polly could have gone. Most of them were other men's apartments, and Ted had no way of knowing whose. She could have gone home, or to visit a sick friend, or to the moon in a rocket. Nowhere was it written that she had to give notice to Ted Kavanaugh, or Jeff, or any other damn person.

Ted hadn't a firm plan for handling Morgan St. James. They had the duke's involvement all wrapped up now. But still there was nothing to connect the two men. Nothing but Jeff's instinct and the sudden disappearance of Polly. Well, it was pretty sure Morgan would show himself for today's auction. The high point of his career.

Meanwhile, Ted had business with Marcus Jones.

The security officer appeared at eight-thirty sharp, offered no apologies when he was told they'd tried to reach him the night before, and led Ted straight to the vault. The vault door gleamed thick and intimidating. It had a small spoked wheel and knurled steel knobs, like something on a warship.

Marcus Jones twirled and fiddled. His face was calm, confident. He might have been flicking a light switch. Then, as Ted watched, the man's face changed. The beginning of a frown formed itself on Jones's broad brown forehead. He started to say something, then shook his head a little and thought better of it. He spun the dial again, back and forth, then stopped and frowned more deeply.

"Never forgot the damn thing before," he said. "Never."

Then Jones turned to Ted Kavanaugh.

"In Mr. Felix Dupre's office, on the middle bookshelf, is a Bible. Could you fetch it?"

"Sure. Why?"

"It has the combination in it. Maybe I did forget."

Ted was back in less than ten minutes, cursing the elevators for taking as long as they did. He handed the elegant leather-bound Bible to Jones.

"Page one-ninety-eight," said Marcus Jones. "Corinthians sixteen. Victory over death." He flipped the pages as he spoke, reached the page he'd mentioned, looked closely, frowned. "Yep. Thirteen, fourteen, seventy-eight. I knew I knew it."

He handed Ted the book and turned to the dials one more time. What Ted saw was an annotated column running down the center of the page between the two main columns of text. From the top, it read:

    aCt. Hos. 13. 14
    bCt. Ro. 7.8
    cRo. 8. 37.

And a similar string of concordance references continued down the page.

Ted closed the Bible and held it while Jones twirled the dials. He felt like some country preacher on a wedding day with a runaway bride.

Finally Jones stopped fiddling with the dials and stepped back, hands on hips in disgust. "Damn thing's been changed, lieutenant, I swear it has."

Ted looked at him. Then he attacked the vault door as though it had been coming at him with a knife.

"Polly!" he yelled. "Polly! Polly! Polly!"

There was no reply at all.

He turned to Jones.

"Okay," said Ted grimly, "we'll blast our way in."

Then they went off to phone the police demolition squad.

Oswald Webster was up before the sun rose.

He pulled on an old flannel robe against the air-conditioned chill of his huge bedroom and walked to the window. The hills of Santa Barbara rolled and billowed below him, all the way down to the Pacific two miles away. Far below, the ocean lay dull as lead, stretching out forever, surging and ebbing in the gathering light.

A small black ship trudged across the middle distance, a freighter of some sort. Webster smiled briefly, thinking it might well be loaded with Webco tomatoes. But his mind was three thousand miles away.

Today was the day of the big auction.

Today he would own the Winchcombe Chalice. For this day, he had sold the vast avocado ranch, taking a loss, collecting only sixty million dollars for a tract that was easily worth eighty, eighty-five. No matter. He wanted the chalice more than he had ever wanted anything else. And he would have it. Today.

In the vault at Dupre's, Polly Kunimara lay dreaming. Her breathing was shallow. The air was thinning, musty, nearly all used up. Polly's dream was a dark and restless one, but she did not wake up. Which was merciful.

For Frederik von Kronholtz, the day began with a most unpleasant surprise. He was sitting in his office, early as usual, sipping bad coffee and imagining ways to display the chalice. For the Metropolitan would get the chalice. There was no question about that. His reverie was disturbed by a knocking. He frowned.

"Come in."

Cavior poked his elegant head in the door.

"Got a minute, Frederik?"

"Of course. Come in."

"It's about the chalice."

Cavior told his story quickly and well, and when he was finished, von Kronholtz just sat there gaping.

"You saw all this?"

Von Kronholtz knew Cavior too well to suppose his colleague had imagined the forgery.

"More than that, we photographed it. Incredible, let me tell you."

"Dupre's wouldn't dare. It would—*will*—ruin them."

"Remember, Frederik, it was young Dupre who called me in. They knew nothing of it either, but there was a suspicion, somehow. They were merely trying to be sure."

"And they're going ahead with this madness."

"What they are selling is the real thing. But I would be very sure, nonetheless, before bidding. If you get the cup, we should check it again before paying one penny."

"Of course."

Von Kronholtz just sat there, stunned, hating his visitor. The implications were obvious. The Met's Roman curator had been duped! Gulled, deceived like any bumpkin at a fair! Intolerable!

He rose, frowning, trying to bury his outrage. "Thank you, Cavior. I wish I'd known this earlier."

"Well," said Cavior, "don't lose sight of the fact that what's being sold today *is* the real Winchcombe Chalice and it is a great masterpiece."

"Yes," said von Kronholtz, straightening his necktie as he headed for door, "I will surely keep that in mind."

He stormed out of the side entrance to the museum. It would be just as quick to walk the short distance to the House of Dupre. And with every step he advanced in that direction, von Kronholtz could sense the chalice getting smaller and smaller until it was almost invisible. His mind danced with possibilities. Whatever happened, Cavior would spread the word about his deception. His gullibility. A small but possibly fatal wedge in the armor of his scholarly reputation.

In the first wave of his indignation, the curator had decided to have nothing to do with the damned chalice.

Now he reconsidered. There might be a way to get the cup cheaply. All he had to do was strew a little suspicion—and not bid for the thing himself. Brilliant! The frown melted into a smile now. How very, very clever. Just a murmured doubt. Not so much as to cause the chalice to be withdrawn from the sale. There would always be some fools who'd bid on anything. He'd get to the bottom of this, and get the chalice too. The real chalice.

Frederik von Kronholtz was still smiling as he walked into the cool, elegant lobby of the House of Dupre.

Dawn came to Sutton Square. Dorothy Dutton stirred in the big canopied bed, stretched, yawned luxuriously, and looked at the young man beside her.

It was awkward, this being between husbands.

But the escort service was always reliable. Idly she wondered where they got them, all the fine strong young men. The recruiting, she decided, must be fun. The service was called simply the Escort Service. Its number, unlisted, was known to a very few, very discreet customers. The young men were always presentable. They were not given to violence or stealing things. And always they gave pleasure. It was a neat arrangement, no strings, one bill at the end of the month. Dorothy did tip them, of course. That was expected. All in all, it was cheap. Far cheaper, when you thought about it, than expensive divorce settlements.

He was sleeping. He'd earned his sleep.

Dorothy snuggled deeper into the eiderdown pillow. Today was going to be special. Today was the day of the auction. She thought of the chalice, of all it represented. Of what a fine thing it would be for the museum. How cleverly Frederik had played upon her religious sympathies, enlisting her help. Well, it was a good cause. Twice she'd been to Dupre's to see the exhibit. Frederik, as usual, was right. The cup was extraordinary. *The sacred,* she thought, looking at her sleeping companion, *and the profane.* Well, that was life, in all its richness, its lovely cornucopia of surprises. Maybe, she thought, smiling, she'd have a surprise or two for Frederik von Kronholtz. Lazily, confidently, she reached across the short distance that separated her from the young man. Such a beautiful young man.

Such a charming way to start the day of the Winchcombe Chalice sale. The young man murmured something unintelligible in his sleep. She stroked him gently. His eyes fluttered open. He smiled and moved toward her.

The day was showing more promise with every second.

Morgan dressed carefully. The suit was dark blue linen, more cobalt than navy. His shirt was cream-colored Egyptian cotton, finer than most handkerchiefs, the tie a Liberty silk foulard in shades of rust and dark blue and cream. The shoes, black, custom-made and gleaming, were built on the monk-strap pattern British cavalry officers had favored for more than a hundred years.

The small nick on his cheek didn't show.

But still, his hands had trembled, shaving. He had thought about the girl, about Neville Fleet, about the day that stretched out before him, long and dangerous, crowded with peril.

It had been almost a reflex action, shoving her in the vault. He should have killed her. But he had never killed anyone in his life. Leave the killing for Neville. Neville almost seemed to enjoy it.

But maybe he had killed her. Maybe she'd suffocated in the vault. It was possible. The thing must be nearly airtight. Or entirely airtight. It was a sickening feeling not to know. If she were alive, she'd be more dangerous than dead. Clever, though, to change the combination. That, at least, would give him some leverage.

Morgan finished tying the necktie and looked at his reflection in the mirror. Leverage. He was going to need leverage. He was going to need it badly. He looked at his watch.

Eight-forty-five. Just time for a cup of coffee. Then the bank. He'd packed yesterday, rather lightly. His passport was in his pocket even now. Actually, what was preventing him from going right out to the airport this minute and getting on the next jet to anywhere?

As Neville had done.

Mentally he asked this of the man in the mirror.

The man in the mirror was confident, elegant, charming. And very frightened. But the man in the mirror could bring it off. He'd go through with the auction because after he did that he'd be something like three million dollars richer. Dividing up with Neville.

Only, maybe he wouldn't divide anything with Neville.

Maybe he'd keep it all. All the profits of the chalice. All the profits of the silver, the furniture, the paintings.

Why should Neville have it? He had enough, and the real chalice, too.

Neville was very unlikely to come back and argue the point. The man in the mirror smiled. Of course. Pity it had taken this long to reach such an obvious decision.

Suddenly there was a sound in the quiet bedroom.

It was the sound of Morgan St. James laughing.

Polly woke to darkness. She blinked and moved a little. Then the hardness of the concrete floor reminded her where she was.

The darkness was total, deep, impenetrable.

The light had somehow gone out while she slept. Her first instinct was to scream. The noise died in her throat, a dry gurgle. She realized that the dryness was chronic. She'd had nothing to drink for . . . how long? Her stomach rumbled.

This was it, then. Darkness, thirst. When in the world would someone need to open the vault?

She tried to remember the sale date for the snuffboxes. They weren't even cataloged yet. Polly hadn't even seen them until yesterday.

Yesterday. One million years ago.

She thought of Morgan, and the scream formed itself one more time in her throat. And failed to come out.

Polly rubbed her eyes, hard, with both fists. It didn't help.

The blackness was just as black. The isolation was just as complete.

At least she wasn't dead. Not yet.

There must be a little air coming in, somehow. God but it was stuffy, musty. How long did it take to suffocate?

Maybe she was dead. Maybe this was what it was like: all alone in the darkness. No heaven, no hell.

No Jeff. And no Ted.

Whenever Polly had thought about death, which was seldom, she'd imagined terrible accidents, unspeakable illnesses. But never this. Never this slow, eternal, timeless waiting. Never the breath getting slower and slower, harder and harder to breathe at all, stuffier and stuffier, slow drowning in your own used air, breathing and rebreathing the same air. How many times can you do that before it isn't air anymore?

At first, when she heard the soft metallic noises, Polly thought she was imagining them.

Could it be? Somebody turning the combination lock?

She held herself very still.

Yes. There it came again, that faint, muted clicking. Tumblers tumbling. Slowly, in a kind of a trance, she got up. Painfully she stood and straightened herself. The concrete floor hadn't been kind to her. She groped, found a shelf, guided herself down the length of it. To the corner.

She had no sense of left or right, no way of knowing which direction she was moving. But it was a small room and square: she couldn't miss.

There. The shelves' end. The doorframe, cool and steel and much too efficient.

The noise had stopped.

No. There! There it was again. She hadn't been hallucinating.

Now the scream came for real. And the pounding of her fists.

No response.

The clicking stopped.

Polly stood there in the darkness, gasping, the breath dragging out of her, ragged, searing her dry throat. She panted like an animal. Caged animal. She reached out and touched the door, as though by touching it she could somehow make contact with whoever it was on the other side.

Suppose it was Morgan, come back to finish the job?

She kept her hands on the door. Somehow it was reassuring. For a long moment she simply stood there. Whoever had been clicking the lock must have gone away. Maybe forever. Or maybe she really had imagined the whole thing. She ran her hands down the door. There was a knob on the inside, fixed solid, incapable of being twisted.

The sound of her breathing echoed in the little vault. She

imagined a tall, iced glass of sparkling mineral water. With lime, please.

She imagined Jeff Dupre.

And when the tears finally came, they were dry as her throat, hopeless as wishes.

Polly slowly sank to the floor. She sat there, the door at her back, her head in her hands, sobbing. It was stupid to cry.

After a moment she stopped. A girl could get very angry, thinking about it. Angry and helpless and sad, and more angry because of being helpless. Damn Morgan anyway. Damn him and damn him.

She'd do more than damn him, if she ever got her hands on the man. On the man's throat.

She sat up very straight now and rested her head against the cool steel door. Self-pity never solved anything. She thought and thought, cataloging things she might do, should have done to get out of this damned steel box. But the answer was always the same: there was not one blessed thing to do, not for her, not without tools. Especially not in the dark.

Polly sat there trying to keep calm.

Then the metallic noise began again.

66

The demolition crew got there fast, but not fast enough for Ted Kavanaugh. There were three of them and a lot of equipment. They were prepared to blast, but when Ted told them there might be someone in there, the head of the crew wouldn't risk it.

"Hell, no, lieutenant, we'll drill, right quick, to get some air in there. Then we can get at the locks and hinges and all. It'll take a little longer, but this way there's much less risk."

"Do it, whatever's best."

He turned away, hating the feeling of impotence. Ted turned toward the entrance to the long hallway just as Jeff walked through the door.

Jeff walked slowly, very slowly. But he was up and walking, and Kavanaugh hardly believed it.

For a long moment the two men just looked at each other.

"You really don't take much advice, do you?" Ted grinned as he spoke.

"She's in there?"

Jeff smiled, winced, leaned against the wall. He felt weak. The doctor had warned him he would, had threatened, cajoled.

"We don't know, Jeff. But someone—has to be St. James—changed the combination."

"She's in there. And it's airtight."

Suddenly Jeff wished he'd stayed right in the hospital, just where everyone seemed to want him to be. If . . . Hell, he couldn't think about anymore ifs. The drill made a shrill whining sound, a dentist's drill multiplied by a thousand. And could she hear it? he wondered. Could Polly hear this, or anything, ever again?

"Tell me," said Ted quietly, "about last night."

Jeff told him. They went back to Marcus Jones's office and sat down and drank some coffee.

"Put sugar in it," said Ted, watching Jeff's stiffness, knowing how it feels when you're trying to hide the pain.

"Hate sugar."

"Put sugar in it, dummy, for energy."

"So he skipped. The duke."

Jeff picked up two little paper envelopes of sugar, tore them open in one quick motion, poured them into the coffee.

From out in the hallway came the shrill sound of drilling.

"So it seems," said Ted.

"If she's in there . . ."

"Don't say it," said Kavanaugh, "whatever it is."

And they sat there helpless as condemned men, while the drill bit deeper and deeper into the cold tempered steel of the vault.

The certified check from Knickerbocker Trust was in the amount of three million, seven hundred thousand dollars.

It represented every cent Morgan St. James owned in the world, his share of the profits from the Berwick forgeries.

He could almost feel the warmth of it glowing through its thick envelope, through the polished ostrich hide of his wallet.

A man could travel far and well on that amount of money.

A man could go where the Duke of Berwick could never find him, or anyone else, either.

A man could leave Dupre's and everything in it far, far behind. Especially, he could leave the Dupre vault behind.

The vault.

Damn the vault. He'd gone nearly half the morning without letting himself think about the vault.

Morgan walked out of the granite portico of the bank into a dazzle of sunlight. He thought of the auction. Two-thirty.

At two-thirty precisely he would step up into the Jacobean oak pulpit that was the auctioneer's platform in the House of Dupre. He would pick up the famous ivory-headed gavel, Felix's gavel, and begin. Morgan could see the crowds, sense the excitement. He could feel it in his veins like some wild tingle of electricity. All that drama, and himself in charge, in control, playing them like gamefish, building, building.

And now he must leave all that behind, maybe forever.

Suddenly he decided not to go directly back to Dupre's.

He must think, plan.

Leverage. He must calculate the best way to play out his advantage. For surely it was an advantage, a clever stroke really, sure to buy him time. No one could possibly know where she was, or guess.

He walked up Park Avenue, north from the bank.

As he walked, Morgan began to feel more confident. It had all gone so very smoothly until now. They had gotten away with so much. He smiled at the people on the avenue. In this part of town, on the day of the Berwick auction, the passersby seemed to fairly glow with prosperity. He'd have a quiet luncheon somewhere near Dupre's. A quiet, elegant luncheon. As becomes a man with nearly four million dollars in his pocket and a passport ready to take him . . . where?

Morgan walked briskly, smiling the smile of one who knows secrets.

Half a block behind him an unmarked dark blue Chevrolet sedan cruised slowly. Two men were inside. One spoke softly into a small microphone. "Subject proceeding north on the east side of Park Avenue, crossing Sixty-first . . ."

Morgan walked on.

He thought of the chalice. Who'd have thought old Neville Fleet had it in him? The sheer audacity of the maneuver had its own special magic. And this afternoon the magic would be brought to its inevitable climax, and he, Morgan, would do it.

Already he could feel the triumph of it. A coup worthy of Napoleon, of Alexander! To sell the chalice, and undoubtedly for the highest price ever paid for a gold Roman artifact, and to have the double pleasure of knowing it was all a glorious fraud!

There was a delicious irony in it, after all. He remembered

his incredulity when Fleet had first produced the real chalice in his rooms at the Carlyle.

He kept on up the avenue, considering and rejecting restaurants. Somehow, today he didn't want to go where he was known, where he might run into friends or people from Dupre's. He looked at his watch, slender, golden, and pleasing. Eleven-thirty. A bit too early for luncheon. He decided to take a stroll in Central Park, then. Perhaps to the zoo. That would be amusing. That would pass the time. And avoid the House of Dupre.

Somehow it seemed important to avoid the House of Dupre until just before the auction. For a moment a restless, uneasy sensation came over him. Then it went away. The sun shone brightly. Morgan turned left at the intersection of Seventieth Street, crossed the avenue, and headed toward Central Park.

The vault at Dupre's seemed very far away.

The drill was electric and very fast. It made a noise somewhere between a whir and a shriek, a shrill tormented noise that matched Jeff's frayed mood to perfection.

And for all its speed, it took forever and forever.

"Chrome steel," muttered the man using the drill, half in admiration and half in disgust.

Sparks flew. Tiny fragments of steel were thrown back from the spinning diamond-faced drill bit. The noise persisted. After a few minutes it seemed to be drilling into Jeff's mind, into his soul.

And he kept thinking about Polly.

Polly, trapped.

Polly, dead.

Polly.

Jeff stared at the door.

It was more than the door to a vault now. It was the entrance to the rest of his life. His whole future was inside it.

Maybe.

Suddenly the drill gave a shrill uncharacteristic screech. There was a blue flash, and an odd metallic odor filled the air. And smoke. The man working the drill cursed and dropped it. "Damn thing backfired on me," he said, shaking his fist.

"Are you all right?"

The urgency in Kavanaugh's voice was unmistakable.

"Yeah. A little shock, lieutenant," he said casually, rubbing his right hand with the left. "Nothing like the chair." He grinned, but he kept rubbing the hand. It was red. Another man in the little crew unplugged the drill, which was still smoking.

"Fused," he said disgustedly. "Shorted out and fused. Charlie, ya got a spare?"

"Sure," said Charlie, still rubbing. "I got a burned hand, too, wise guy."

Kavanaugh interrupted. "Look, guys," he said, "this is pretty urgent. Can one of you get the spare while someone else gets going with the torch?"

Three heads turned to Kavanaugh.

"Sure," said their leader, reaching for a welder's mask.

Jeff looked at his watch, dreading what he might find there. It was just after noon. The policeman with the mask reached for his acetylene torch and flicked it on.

Jeff stepped back involuntarily as a blinding blue-white light filled the corridor. The man wore heavy gloves. His battered mask was an arc of some special steel with a rectangular slit of a window set into it. The effect was medieval, monstrous.

The white-hot torch cut steel. He was attacking the thick hinges of the vault, steel encasing steel, more than a foot long and several inches thick, countersunk into the face of the vault door.

It had all been designed, very carefully, to prevent what was happening to it now, to resist any kind of intrusion or interference.

The hinges resisted well, too well.

But the man with the torch knew just what he was doing. He worked with almost surgical precision. It was a question, Jeff quickly saw, of digging a trench around the entire hinge, then excising it like a diseased tooth. No quick, simple cuts were possible. Jeff silently cursed the cleverness of the person who had designed the door.

The touch burned on, steadily, hot, white, creating its own pungent, acrid stench in the stuffy corridor.

Shortly after one o'clock, the other man came back with a new drill. He plugged it in and began drilling where he'd left off.

Jeff stood dumbly, staring at the workers.

There was a touch on his arm. He looked around. It was Kavanaugh. "Let's see if St. James showed," said Ted. "He'll have to, if he's going to run the auction."

Jeff was startled to discover he'd nearly forgotten about the auction. He simply nodded and led the way to the elevators.

Morgan had not returned.

They went into Felix's office.

"It doesn't do any good," said Kavanaugh, "our being there. It'll take them another hour at the least."

"In another hour," said Jeff quietly, forcing himself not to scream the rage that was threatening to consume him, "she may be dead."

"She may be dead already, Jeff. Face it."

Jeff closed his eyes tightly, as if that would make the ugly thought go away. Finally he spoke. "And Morgan? What about Morgan?"

"We need Polly for that, or the fact of his selling the chalice thinking it's phony, or both. For hard evidence. As it is—and we've got to face that, too, Jeff—we don't even know for sure that he did alter the combination of the vault. It's even conceivable—think of a jury trial now—that he altered it not knowing she's inside. If she is inside. Surely as a director of Dupre's he has the right to change the combination if he wants to?"

"I suppose so," said Jeff dully.

He looked at the antique French carriage clock that ticked quietly on Felix's desk. Nearly one-thirty. Jeff felt his gut sinking, felt the walls closing in, felt trapped and helpless. The two bullet holes in his chest burned and throbbed. The firm bandages itched. And it seemed that his whole life was going to be lived in the next hour.

Until they broke into the vault.

Until the Berwick sale began.

In the echoing salesrooms of the House of Dupre, extra folding chairs had been set up in precise rows. Closed-circuit-television sets flickered and blared as assistants tested them and tested again. Pencils were sharpened and microphones tuned.

The relay systems from the two auxiliary salesrooms to the principal auction gallery were checked and double-checked. The seating was as precisely ordered as any White House reception: only the three hundred customers who could best afford the treasures of Berwick Castle were allowed into the main gallery. But you never knew what might develop in the secondary rooms, or over the phone, or in the form of secret instructions to the house bidders. There could be no chance of mechanical failure in any of the electronic systems.

The rooms were nearly empty, yet they hummed with anticipation. Guards bustled. Assistants and departmental heads hurried importantly across the empty stage, making notes in well-thumbed catalogs, taking a final, farewell look at the rare objects huddled together backstage awaiting their quick glorious moment—usually no more than one minute—when they would be the focus of all eyes, the cynosure of desire among the richest and most avid art collectors in all the world.

A quarter to two.

Still there was no sign of Morgan St. James.

In chic little restaurants up and down the East Side of Manhattan, checks were being signed, a final demitasse sipped, ties straightened, lipsticks renewed, catalogs consulted one final time.

The sale of the season was about to begin, and nobody wanted to be late.

Limousines purred up the avenue.

The grand-luxe hotels disgorged a very special clientele, men and women who had flown in from Europe and the Far East, from the oil countries, and from every corner of America and Latin America to be on hand when the Winchcombe Chalice went to the block.

Out of the Carlyle they came, and the Regency, the Plaza, and the Waldorf Towers. Some had pieds-à-terre at more than a million dollars a throw in places like Olympic Towers or the Galleria on Fifty-seventh Street. There were even people on their way to the Berwick sale who actually made their home in Manhattan.

By a few minutes past two, invitations were being presented to the two guards who flanked the elevator doors in the street-floor lobby of Dupre's.

The room in which the invitation-holder was to be seated was indicated on the card. The seat itself was not. This produced a certain amount of discreet scrambling for the better seats in the main gallery.

By two-fifteen the galleries were half-filled.

There was a low buzz and ripple of conversation. Hands were waved, and, where distance permitted, cheeks were kissed, lips barely brushing, and the air itelf seemed to change.

Suddenly the air was thick with money. It smelled of Arpège and clipped coupons, of silk and Cuir de Russe, and it reverberated with "Darling, you're looking marvelous" and "Basil, how grand to see you," and all the other well-practiced passwords of politesse that help build up, plate by polished plate, the impregnable facades of the very rich.

Two-twenty came and went, and saw a final bustling as some few latecomers were ushered in. The galleries were packed. People stood at the back of the main salesroom, and there were no empty chairs at all in the secondary chambers.

At two-twenty-five there was a hush and a rustling of catalogs. A great drama was about to begin, and everyone in the House of Dupre knew it. And nobody wanted to miss a moment of it.

Here in this room were represented several of the world's greatest fortunes, and the air seemed to quiver and vibrate with the raw power of massed millions and millions.

Here were individuals, men and women who could, with the wave of a pen, possess almost anything, almost anyone.

And great institutions were present here too: the Metropolitan Museum personified by Frederik von Kronholtz, who stood alone and smiling near the door, having spent a most delightful lunch hour whispering doubts into the ears of several key prospects for the chalice. The bidding for the museum would be done, not by von Kronholtz himself, but by a paid agent, a discreet little man whose instructions were very clear: stop at nothing this side of six million dollars.

Frederik looked for Dorothy Dutton and didn't find her. He shrugged and took a seat near the front. Dorothy slipped in just before two-thirty, discreetly dressed in black silk and smiling an almost beatific smile.

"Dorothy," someone murmured, "has found God."

"Ah, yes," hissed his companion, "but has God found Dorothy?"

There was a ripple of anticipation in the crowd just then.

Morgan St. James stepped smiling onto the stage and climbed the three steps up into the pulpit.

He paused for a moment, surveyed the audience with satisfaction, picked up Felix Dupre's well-known ivory-headed gavel, and began the sale.

They were back in the basement corridor now. The safecracking team had cut through the hinges. All that remained was the lock itself, and they had started on that. The torch hissed and glowed white-hot. They waited, and prayed.

Kavanaugh had been getting telephone reports from the men tailing Morgan. Jeff had gone himself, at precisely two-thirty, and stood hidden at the back of the main salesroom for just long enough to see Morgan take his place on the platform.

It had been a strange and disconcerting moment.

Jeff wanted to run up to the stage and take the man by the throat and shake the combination out of him.

But they had gone too far for that now. Now it was a question of minutes.

The drill had finally penetrated the vault. They tried shouting through the tiny hole it made, and got no answer. But maybe, Jeff told himself, maybe the hole was too small, maybe a voice couldn't carry through such a space. And he wondered what he'd do if his worst fears were true.

The torch kept cutting. The corridor smelled like some kind of industrial furnace now, all fumes and glare.

"Five minutes," said the man with the torch.

It might as well have been five hours.

They had hooks and clamps to pull the great door out of its frame. Two guards and Marcus Jones stood by ready to help.

Finally the torch cut through the last bolt of the enormous steel lock. It clicked off. The silence was sudden and deafening. Jeff held his breath. The clamps and hooks were inserted in the ragged wounds of what had been the slick steel door. Six men pulled, heaved, strained at it.

"Goddamn thing," said someone, "must weigh three tons."

An ambulance was waiting. Ted went for the ambulance attendant now, and asked him to bring a stretcher and oxygen equipment.

They pulled once more. Jeff took one of the ropes, and Ted another. Even the man from the ambulance pulled.

"Together. Now. One . . . two . . ."

The door wrenched forward, jerked, teetered, and came toward them. Jeff leaped to the side, or he might have been crushed when it fell. It did fall, but slowly, lurching thunderously to the floor.

Suddenly Jeff was in the vault.

Polly lay at the far side of the little room, curled up like a small child, her head cushioned on her arm. He couldn't tell if she was alive or dead.

Then she was in his arms, his hand on her cheek. She was breathing. His life was not over.

"Polly!"

Nothing.

"Polly!"

Her breathing grew deeper. Her long dark eyelashes fluttered a little. Her eyes opened. For a moment she didn't focus at all. Then she saw Jeff.

Her face was blank, transfixed.

Then, slowly, the beginnings of a smile.

It was only a little smile, but for Jeff Dupre it held all the future he ever hoped to have.

"Jeff?"

It was a faint dry whisper, the ghost of her voice.

He said nothing, but just held her tight.

Then she was being lifted, placed on the stretcher. Polly was very pale, but obviously not injured in any way. The attendant put a portable oxygen mask over her mouth and nose. She breathed into that for a few minutes. The color came back quickly. Her eyes, which had been dull and unfocused, regained the sparkle Jeff remembered. Finally she reached up and removed the mask herself.

"Thank you . . . thank you," she whispered. "What I really need is some water."

Someone brought water, a tall glass and a pitcher.

Polly drank ravenously, gulping down three glasses before she spoke again. "Morgan," was all she said, or had to say. "Son of a bitch Morgan."

Jeff looked at Ted. It was a quarter to three.

Polly was still sitting up on the stretcher. The two ambulance attendants who held it looked restless.

Suddenly she laughed. Then she swung her long elegant legs off the stretcher and stood up. Jeff helped her.

"I could have died, the bastard," she said softly.

"I love you," said Jeff, not caring that seven strangers were there to hear it.

"Jeff . . ." was all she said, or could say.

His arms were around her then, and they were alone in the crowded corridor, and suddenly it didn't matter if the world ended.

Finally Jeff looked up to find everyone gone, with the exception of Ted Kavanaugh.

Kavanaugh grinned. "Okay, lovers," he said. "Shape up. There's work to be done."

Morgan abandoned himself to the rhythms of the auction. It was a feeling he knew well and cherished, the feeling of control, of mastery, of setting the pace. Gently, subtly, sometimes with a hint of irony, now with a pause for the sake of building drama, he swept the Berwick sale to record price after record price.

The last of the Berwick Holbeins went for eight hundred thousand dollars to a man Morgan had never seen before. A Louis XVI corner cabinet dripping with gilt bronze and supporting a huge and vulgar clock on its ornate top set a world furniture record at one-million-ten. The estimate had been three to four hundred thousand.

Something was in the air, a special reckless feeling. It was the kind of day auctioneers dream about, a day on which nothing can stand in the bidders' way.

The extreme politeness of the audience was a veneer that barely managed to cover deep and savage lusts after the treasures that were carried, one after the other, onto the auction platform of the House of Dupre.

The Janus easel swiveled, quick and smooth as a headwaiter's smile. And nearly every time it rotated, revealing some new object that had once graced Berwick Castle, the prices soared.

Morgan found himself thinking how very much Neville would have enjoyed being here.

The chalice was number 103. He was up to eighty-four now, averaging, as was traditional, about one minute per sale. Already he could feel the tension, deep as it was, growing.

In years to come, this auction would be a watershed in the business. It would be a great thing to point to an object—any object—and say, "Oh, yes, I picked it up at the Berwick sale."

Although every item in the sale was fine of its kind, the prices that were being paid transcended reality.

Legends were being bought and sold at Dupre's today. Morgan smiled and kept up the pace and thought: Today I am part of history. The check from Knickerbocker Trust crinkled softly under the thin material of Morgan's suit. Once or twice, not entirely by chance, he ran his hand over it, snug in his inner breast pocket. Yes. It was almost difficult to keep his mind on the sale, considering all the possibilities that were built into that beautiful piece of paper!

Ninety. Ninety-one. Ninety-one was an old silk hunting carpet that had once been a sultan's most prized possession.

It went to the Cleveland museum for one hundred and six thousand dollars. Swiftly, precisely, Morgan totaled the proceeds of the sale. More than three million dollars had changed hands so far, and the chalice was still to come.

And that would be the finest joke of all.

On the buyer.

On Neville.

On the entire auction business now and forever.

He went faster, pushing. He could hardly wait.

In the library of her house on Sixty-fourth Street, Minnie Dupre was having coffee with Father Devlin.

"It will be over soon," said Minnie, trying for casualness, glancing at a small gilt-bronze clock on the bookshelf, "and not a minute too soon for me."

"Yes," said her guest, stirring an astonishing amount of sugar into the little cup. "Yet in a way I've enjoyed it. The adventure. Your kindness."

Minnie smiled. He was a charming old man. Jeff had kept her informed, as much as Jeff knew, as much as he thought she should know. This sense of being protected from reality was new to her.

Felix had made his own realities, and she had shared them to the fullest.

Well, that was over, done.

Soon it would all be over.

"What will you do, Father Devlin? After it's over?"

"Ah, there are places for old priests. Homes for the sancti-monious, we call 'em. I suppose there'll be a place for me in one of them. I shall miss Berwick, though, for all the sadness that's come upon it lately."

"Yes," said Minnie, "I'm sure you will."

Jeff insisted. And to hell with the searing pain in his chest. He rode with Polly in the speeding patrol car, its siren wailing, all the way to her apartment.

"If I'm going to make an entrance, it won't be in rags."

Jeff had figured the timing to the minute.

After the water, Polly had consumed two thick malted milkshakes. She was resilient, had her color back, and all the bright efficiency he remembered. She even got her temper back, and that had to be a good sign.

"Try to keep me away. Just try!"

They didn't try.

In ten minutes she was out of the shower and drying her long silky black hair. Five minutes after that she was immac-ulately dressed in scarlet silk and they were back in the car, speeding again, the siren wailing again.

He kissed her.

She grinned and squirmed away. "Later," she said.

"You're mad at me."

"No, Jeff. No, darling. Not mad. Not mad at all."

Polly turned to him and smiled, and reached up and

392

touched his cheek with one finger, tracing the fine line of his cheekbone.

She never called me darling before.

For a moment he said nothing, only reached for her hand and held it.

Then they pulled screeching up to the front door of the House of Dupre.

"Number one hundred," said Morgan St. James, "a matched set of twelve Queen Anne dining chairs, two armchairs and ten side chairs in burled walnut with the original tapestry seats. I will start the bidding at eighty thousand dollars."

Two hands shot up, one program fluttered, and there was a signal to Morgan from the girl who operated the microphone from the secondary salesrooms.

In less than one minute the chairs were sold for two hundred and twelve thousand dollars. Morgan's face was calm, just as though a very similar set had not sold only six months ago, at Christie's, for half the price.

"One hundred and one," he said, "a miniature painting by Nicholas Hilliard, portrait of a lady, her name unknown, circa 1590–1595, probably a noblewoman at the court of Elizabeth. I open with twenty thousand dollars."

The miniature went for fifty thousand, an all-time record.

The tension in the crowded room was simmering and threatening to boil over.

Morgan had arranged the catalog himself, alternating high points and items of less dramatic interest, building, always building, toward the chalice. The chalice was number 103 out of 107 items in the sale. Make them stay till the bloody end. Maybe they'd bid on more objects than they'd intended to, just to keep the action going.

The strategy was working better than he'd dared to hope.

And no one seemed to have thought of the vault or the damned Kunimara girl, or any of it. Maybe he wouldn't need his leverage. Maybe he could just fly away this evening and leave the whole thing.

The silence in the salesroom was complete.

"One hundred and two," said Morgan matter-of-factly, "a pair of Ming polychrome hundred-deer vases, containing the six-character mark of Wan-li within a double circle, of the period. I will begin at two hundred thousand dollars." The bidding raced up to three-fifty, staggered a bit, then inched

393

past four. They were knocked down soon after that at four hundred and twenty-two thousand dollars.

Morgan had lost count of the total now. It must be stunning.

He paused, smiled, then gave the signal for the Janus easel to revolve.

It turned soundlessly.

Everyone in the audience had seen the Winchcombe Chalice before. Yet, as the easel turned, a sigh rippled through this gathering of the world's most sophisticated art collectors. It was a soft noise with a special deep resonance, a sound like a sudden breeze in a sacred grove.

It was the sound of pure awe.

Morgan loved it.

The chalice made the simple easel seem noble, made the room itself a special and sacred place. For one brief transcendent moment the salesroom at Dupre's was transformed from a temple of Mammon to a temple pure and simple and soaring with aspiration.

Oswald Webster had been plugged into the direct tie-line for fifteen minutes now. Once more, impatiently, he asked if the chalice's number had come up.

"Not yet," was the reply.

Morgan paused, let the audience settle down.

The audience did not settle down.

The sighing faded and stopped, the rustling quieted down, but no one in that big room was paying anything less than the fullest attention to the glittering object on the easel.

"Number one hundred and three," Morgan began smoothly, "the Winchcombe Chalice. Pure gold with twenty-six unfaceted rubies, Roman, circa . . ."

He paused. This time it was not for effect.

Something was very wrong in the room.

At first she had just been a flash of scarlet at the back, barely catching his eye. Then he looked, as the girl in scarlet walked slowly down the aisle, found the one empty seat in the room, and sat in it.

Polly Kunimara stared gravely ahead, not acknowledging Morgan, merely watching the chalice. Watching and waiting.

At the back of the room Morgan could see Jeff Dupre, and behind Jeff the tall red-haired policeman—whatever his name was, vulgar sod.

Morgan could feel the tiny beads of sweat breaking out on his forehead, his upper lip.

He cleared his throat, wondering how long he had paused.

No matter. They'd think it was because of the cup.

And no one could prove he'd put the girl in the vault. It would be his word against hers. A disgruntled employee. Happened all the time. He could detect a new flavor to the restlessness in the audience now. Now they wanted blood.

". . . circa A.D. 50–75," he said, as though nothing had happened, "discovered in Britain in the ninth century, treasure of Winchcombe Abbey, collection of his majesty King Henry Tudor, Mary Tudor, Philip II of Spain . . . and the dukes of Berwick."

Three thousand miles away, Oswald Webster paced the floor. "Has he started yet?"

"Not yet, Mr. Webster."

"Damn."

Morgan paused.

"I will open the bidding at two million dollars."

"Two million bid, Mr. Webster."

The little man who was the Metropolitan's agent in this sale lifted a finger to touch his sprightly bow tie. The bidding instantly jumped to two-million-five.

Frederik von Kronholtz smiled.

Elsewhere in the silent room, hands went up. Signals were made. Von Kronholtz's smile quickly faded. He had anticipated three, at most, five people bidding. There seemed to be seven, or even eight, and what was happening on that bloody telephone?

"Three million. Three-million-two. Three-million-four."

Morgan controlled his voice. The sweating persisted. He didn't dare reach for his handkerchief.

"Three-million-six."

He couldn't see damned Jeff Dupre anymore, or the policeman.

"Three-million-eight."

In Santa Barbara, Oswald Webster felt a strange fullness in his chest. He paced the floor, straining, barking prices into the receiver.

At the relayed bid of three-eight, Webster went to four.

The bid quickly came back to him: four-million-two.

They were flying now. They were well past the estimate. He smiled and looked at the hardbound edition of the Dupre catalog open before him.

The chalice gleamed, beckoned him.

"Four-million-four," said Webster.

"Four-million-six," came back the bid.

He paused, swallowing.

"Five million."

So be it. Shut the bastards out by the sheer drama of the leap. He had done the same tactic before. That'd make 'em think. He thought of his avocado ranch and smiled. He'd jump to more than five if he had to. Much more. His breath seemed to be coming in short spurts now.

"Five-million-two," said the girl's voice from New York.

Oswald Webster shifted on the phone from his left hand to his right. There was a darting pain down his left arm. Must have been holding the damned phone too tight. And no wonder.

"Five-million-four," said Webster.

Frederik von Kronholtz twisted on his seat. The six-million-dollar limit that the trustees of the museum had imposed on him had seemed like a very remote possibility.

But the possibility wasn't remote anymore.

It was breathing down his neck like a pack of wolves.

Damn! Why hadn't he thought to pick up Dorothy Dutton, and keep her at his side. Dorothy could bid the chalice up past six, if she wanted. Hell, Dorothy could bid sixty million if she wanted. And where was she? He strained and twisted and couldn't see her.

"Five-million-six," said Morgan St. James quietly.

He did not need to raise his voice. Every ear in the room was tuned in to him.

Oswald Webster heard the new bid. He opened his mouth to answer. No sound came out. The pain was sharper now, insistent.

And he was absolutely alone in the big house.

He had planned it that way giving the servants a holiday, the better to enjoy his triumph in the exquisite grandeur of solitude.

He gasped.

"What was that, Mr. Webster?"

There was concern in the girl's voice.

"Help me."

But it was only a whisper on the line.

"Mr. Webster?"

There was a soft clatter as the phone fell to the thickly carpeted floor. Webster staggered, clutching his arm, groping for the table. He fell, and the table came with him.

The Dupre catalog slid to the floor, still open to the beautiful four-color spread of the Winchcombe Chalice.

Oswald Webster died alone on his hilltop.

"He seems to have hung up," said the girl who was monitoring the Webster connection.

"I have five million, eight hundred thousand dollars," said Morgan, unconcerned, lost in the momentum of the sale. Five-million-eight! If he could manage to bring that off!

Only then did Morgan see that the detective, Kavanaugh, was not alone. There was another, uniformed policeman with him. Morgan sensed, without looking, that there would be others, on the opposite side, just behind Morgan's pulpit.

A signal came from his assistant.

"Six million dollars bid," said Morgan smoothly.

Don't let them know you have a worry in the world. Don't make their job one bit easier.

Frederik von Kronholtz was frantic now.

He stood up. Unprecedented. He didn't care. Where was the bitch Dorothy? He couldn't see her. Maybe she hadn't come. No. Dorothy would come. She'd be here someplace. Damn! All that work, lost, gone.

The chalice gone!

He sat down slowly, because von Kronholtz felt that if he didn't sit just then he might fall.

There was an empty feeling in the pit of his stomach.

"Six-million-two," came the voice from the stage.

Von Kronholtz couldn't see who was doing this outrageous bidding. The signals were so subtle. There were no raised hands now.

"Six million, two hundred thousand dollars," said Morgan. "I have six million, two hundred thousand dollars once . . . twice . . . six-million-three!"

There was a gasp. The bidding had just doubled the estimate.

Morgan paused. He risked looking over his left shoulder. Yes. There was another policeman in uniform. And there would be others, beyond doubt.

For a man unused to physical violence, Morgan felt oddly cool. He looked around him, thinking of ways out. How fine that the chalice was setting records, false as it was. The total of the sale must be up near twenty million now, and it wasn't through yet.

And neither was Morgan St. James!

His eyes roved through the audience, about the stage.

Guards.

The guards.

The fine, loyal, not-too-bright House of Dupre guards, in their well-cut uniforms. *With their loaded guns.*

397

"I have," he said evenly, "six-million-three."

There was dead silence in the big room.

"Six-million-three," said Morgan, sweating now, "six-million-three. Going . . . going . . . *sold* for six-million-three!"

There was a loud groan then. Heads turned.

Frederik von Kronholtz didn't even try to disguise the fact that the cry of despair had come from him. He leaped to his feet, mumbled excuses, stepped on some very elegant toes, and rushed up the center aisle of the salesroom. Luckily, the door was open. The curator of Roman antiquities of the Metropolitan Museum of New York had barely made his way through it when he was violently ill into a large Chinese urn.

Onstage, Morgan St. James continued, playing for time now. There were only four more items in the sale. All of the tension was gone now. There was shuffling and coughing and a general exodus. Perhaps a third of the audience left.

This had been anticipated: the remaining items were minor ones, three chests of drawers and a small Tang-dynasty urn.

Morgan got through the lot in exactly three minutes.

The police were waiting.

As the last item was lifted off the easel, Morgan smiled and stepped down from his pulpit. Easily, conversationally, he approached the nearest guard, a short black man who stood perhaps five feet from the pulpit. "Well, Roscoe," said Morgan easily, coming quite close, "I'll just be borrowing this for a while, if you please."

The guard blinked, not understanding.

Deftly Morgan slid the man's Police Standard .38 revolver out of its holster and cocked it. He shoved the barrel into the guard's spine and pressed hard.

"Now, Roscoe, you and I, we're going for a little walk, understand? A quiet little walk."

"Yes, sir."

Crablike, scuttling backward and sideways at the same time, the two men made their way into the wings behind the auction platform. The guard shivered. The gun was eating into his back.

Suddenly Jeff Dupre was there.

Blocking their way.

"It's all over, Morgan. All over."

"Out of my way."

"We've already got you on one count of attempted murder, Morgan, and conspiracy on a couple of others. Just don't try anything that'll make it worse for you."

"Dear boy, you force me to do most unpleasant things."
His tone was mocking. His eyes were hard, desperate.

"I'm going to take that gun, Morgan."

"You'll regret it if you try."

Jeff moved closer. Morgan gulped, inched backward. He
pressed the pistol even harder into the guard's back. The
guard's eyes bugged out with pure fright. "Please, Mr. Jeff,"
he said.

"It's all right, Roscoe," said Jeff quietly. "You know as
well as I do the thing isn't loaded."

Morgan stopped, blinked, reconsidered.

Jeff's hand sliced through the air faster than St. James
could see it, the hard edge of his palm down and cutting.

It caught Morgan on the forearm.

There was a dull metallic click as Morgan pulled the trigger.

The gun went off.

Then Jeff was on him, ignoring the searing pain in his
chest, driving his fists into Morgan's arrogant face. Two
punches landed, then Jeff felt the quick, firm grip of Ted
Kavanaugh's long arms pinning his own arms back.

The two punches had been enough.

Morgan St. James lay flat on his back and bleeding.

Ted's grip relaxed. "We wouldn't want to destroy the evidence, now, would we?"

Jeff looked at him, grinning.

It was going to be all right now.

Then Polly was there. She looked at Jeff, at Morgan, at
Ted.

Jeff took her in his arms and held her tightly.

For a moment they said nothing at all.

Somehow they both knew, in that moment, that now there
would be all the time in the world for them.

Epilogue

Jeff knelt in the trench, probing, gently scraping away the
crusted earth from the edges of a bronze implement. The
bronze was deeply green and pitted. It had a long shaft and
clusters of large bronze hooks, fishhook-shaped, protruding

from the central shaft. Probably, he figured, it was a free-standing rack designed to hold wine jugs by their handles. They were definitely on to someone's kitchen. A big, hard-working kitchen.

He could hear sounds from the next trench. Corky was digging late too. The afternoon sun was still strong, warming Jeff's back. The effort felt good. It was almost the same. But nothing would ever be the same again. He bent closer to the bronze shaft, probing and scooping with a small trowel, then with his fingers.

Then he heard her voice, and smiled.

"Jeff, you will rot in that damn ditch. Do you know what time it is?"

He looked up.

"Oh, God," he said, "a nagging wife."

Polly handed him a tall glass of iced tea. The amenities on Jeff's dig had taken a dramatic turn for the better since Polly had been coming along. The tea was delicious. Jeff drained it in two long swallows, then climbed out of the ditch. The bronze could wait. The light was going anyway: it was nearly seven o'clock. Hand in hand, they walked back to the farm-house. Jeff and Polly had taken over the whole house now. Corky and Fred were down the road a short distance, in an-other, similar house. Often they took their meals together. But tonight Jeff and Polly would dine alone. It was his birth-day. He showered the days' sweat away in the primitive semidetached bathroom, and by the time he had changed, the sun was nearly down.

They had a glass of wine on the little terrace, which wasn't really a formal terrace at all but only a flat space between the kitchen and the garden at the back of the house. Still, it was pleasant to stand there in the fading light, sipping the crisp white wine and listening to the sounds of the gathering night. It was very still in the little garden.

Polly had set the table at the edge of the garden, and somewhere she'd found a fine white cloth to cover it. There were flowers, and, at Jeff's place, a gaily wrapped package the size of a shoebox.

"Happy birthday, darling," she said, handing it to him.

Jeff sat down and opened it. There was a little card inside. *I love you*, it said. He just looked at her. Then the smile came, but no words. The card said it all.

Under the card was a beautiful camera, the newest model Nikon 35mm with a special attachment for extreme close-up work.

He grinned. "This really is just what I always wanted," he said, and leaned across the table to kiss her. "Thank you, Polly."

"The new managing director of Dupre's deserves the best," she said, squeezing lime on her prosciutto and melon.

"Managing figurehead, is more like it."

"Do you miss the teaching?"

"Not as much as I thought. And they've asked me to do two courses at Columbia this season."

"Greeks?"

"Etruscans. Even though we haven't found the Sacred Grove of Voltumna."

"You've never doubted it, have you? That it really existed."

"No. It's out there, somewhere. If we don't find it, someone else will. I guess I'm greedy. I want to be the one."

Polly rose and took their plates and walked into the kitchen.

A moth flirted with the candle flame.

The twilight was nearly over now, purple deepening into black.

Jeff heard the gentle bustle of Polly in the kitchen and thought about all the good things that had happened in the last two years.

He thought of the time, earlier in the season, before Polly had joined them in Veii, when he'd taken the Jeep for one last trip to Cavolfiore. It had seemed important to visit Carla's grave.

Jeff had had no communication from Beppo since the tragedy. The sales of his art objects had been accomplished, and at a handsome profit, and the proceeds duly forwarded.

The Jeep had roared up the hill, gears protesting, dust trailing. The big old *castello* squatted on it hill, ugly as ever, shimmering in the heat.

For one wild moment Jeff's heart raced as it had raced of old. For one moment he was sure she'd be there, waiting. He remembered her words that last night before he flew to Felix Dupre's funeral.

"I think you will not be coming back to Cavolfiore."

But I am, Carla: I'm here!

His hands were white, clenched on the wheel.

The old iron gate was shut, locked with a big chain and a new padlock. He could see through the gate to the inner courtyard where she had greeted him so often. The doors were boarded shut, crudely nailed. Jeff stopped the car at the gate and got out. There was no one to be seen. The silence was intense. Even the air itself seemed to be heavy with memories. He drove down to the little village and asked at the church. The contessa, he was told, had been buried at the *castello*, in the old family plot behind the chapel. So he would not mourn at her graveside. The town of Cavolfiore was at the bottom of the hill.

Jeff looked up at the castle. She would be there forever now, and his baby too.

"Something is wrong, *signor*? May I be of assistance?"

The little priest was kind.

Jeff turned to him and ran a hand over his eyes, as though by doing this he could erase memories. "Thank you," he said quietly. "I'll be all right."

Then he got back into the Jeep and made it fly across the dusty plain to Veii.

Polly came back with plates of her wonderful scallopini, and homemade green noodles on the side.

For a moment they ate in silence.

Then she spoke. "You have another present, Jeff, but you'll have to wait awhile to get it."

"Tell me."

She picked up the wineglass, sipped, and looked at him over the rim. "It's a baby," she said. "We're going to have a baby."

He put down his fork and reached for her hand. For a moment he said nothing, overwhelmed. "Darling," he said at last, "a baby. A baby!"

"I couldn't believe it. I wasn't sure, until just the other day, when I went into Rome. It's due in March, give or take a few days."

"Well," he said gently, "maybe there could be better news, or a better present, but I can't think what."

She laughed, a low and lovely sound. "Not even finding the sacred grove?"

He was still holding her hand. He squeezed it. "I've found it, Polly. It's anywhere you are, anytime."

"Happy birthday, darling."

"It's the happiest I've even had. Because of you."

They sat like that for a long time, as the warm Tuscan night grew deeper, fragrant with the flowers of late summer, alive with promise and gilded with love.

Between Playa Bonita and Puerto Cortes on the Pacific coast of Costa Rica, the little fishing village of Quepos lies baking in the sun. There is one public square, a small church, three cafés, and an all-purpose bodega that also serves as the post office. The pavement of the square is uneven. There is a stone fountain. No one can remember when last it flowed with water.

The endless sea laps at the edges of the town, and the air is forever sticky with the odor of yesterday's catch.

Every afternoon at about three o'clock, just after the long midday siesta, an old man comes shuffling across the square from his room on the third floor above the least expensive of the three cafés. He is very thin now, and his eyes are rimmed with the redness that comes from cheap brandy and self-pity. He goes to the bodega, to the counter that serves as the town's post office. He stands as tall as he can, clears his throat, and asks for his mail. Some days he manages a smile.

The proprietor of the bodega, Roberto, is very polite.

His answer is always the same.

"*No hay nada, Señor el duque, no hay nada.*"

And the old man nods and turns away. He walks back across the square to his little room above the café. And he pours himself a brandy. Just one. Well, until the next one.

By evening, he has poured so many brandies that he often forgets to eat. Sometimes, by the light of one cherished candle, he will rummage in his traveling case and produce the toothless wreck that was the Winchcombe Chalice. The rubies have all been torn out now, and sold in San José. Soon, quite soon, the gold itself will have to go. After that? Well, surely Bess will come by then, Bess and her daughter and the boy. It has been two years now, more than two. Fully a year since her last letter.

He has kept the letter. It is stained, frayed, and smells of damp and sweat. It is a brief, formal, heartbreaking little note.

The crest of the Fleets of Berwick is engraved proudly at the top of the thick ivory-colored paper.

My poor dear Neville,
    I have tried to understand what you've done, and to forgive you, and I will keep on trying for the sake of all that has been between us, and for the boy. But I cannot, you must understand, leave England—or Berwick—to join you in your exile. To have done what you have done is one thing. To have done all that and run away like a coward is quite something else. If ever you choose to return, to face your punishment, be assured that I will stand by you. You would be tried in Lords, my dear Neville, and while the publicity would surely be terrible,

the chances of the death penalty are slight, or so the solicitors tell me. But this is something you must decide, as you have made so many other decisions that affect us all. We are well, Neville, and the results of the sale in New York will suffice to keep us in some comfort for a good long time. Long enough, surely, to educate the boy and to let him take his proper place in the world.

We think of you often, dear Neville, and we will try to understand. Should you decide to return, you know where to find us.

Bess

The words seem to dance in the flickering candlelight. He pours some more brandy. It is terrible brandy, but it is all he can afford. Soon he may be reduced to the stinking local *pulque*, which tastes as though it is made of kerosene and spoiled fish guts—and well it may be. He sips the brandy. He thinks of how the bank betrayed him. How, when he came to claim his deposit, to discuss its investment, they blandly denied any knowledge of the man Rivera who had greeted him so charmingly on that first trip down. Rivera, it seems, had been some sort of confidence man, who simply took the money and fled. Fled where? No one knew or seemed to care. Investigations would be undertaken, of course. This was the official story, and Neville Fleet was absolutely helpless to do anything about it. Raging, he was on his way to the British consulate to demand justice when the truth of his situation came down on him with the swift and terrible impact of a lightning bolt. He had outrun British law, British justice. He had outrun everything but hope.

More brandy. The candle is guttering. Tomorrow he must buy a new candle. He thinks of the small reserve of *colones* in the local bank, and the other, smaller hoard hidden behind the sleazy chromolithograph of the Virgin that decorates the peeling wall of his room. Tomorrow. Tomorrow Bess will write, she'll have a change of heart, good old Bess, she will come with the boy, with money, the dream will come true after all. There is just an inch left in the bottom of the brandy bottle. Might as well finish it off. Then there will be three things to do tomorrow. Buy a candle. Buy more brandy. Visit the post office for the letter that will surely be there this time. Must be.

The bottleneck chatters against the chipped rim of the glass as he pours. Two cockroaches play out a kind of mating dance on the wall. The candle goes out, leaving a coil of waxy smoke in the room.

There is a wet, snuffling sound.

It is the sound of an old man weeping.

Frederik von Kronholtz was not yet fifty-five, but today he felt old. Old and defeated and more than a little bitter. The loss of the chalice rankled in his soul. He took it personally. All that work, planning, cajolery, and dreams had gone for nothing. His shame was deeper because of the terrible way he'd behaved at the auction. It had been purely physical: he couldn't help being sick. But being sick in the foyer of Dupre's main salesroom, into an old Chinese urn, before the eyes of half the art world! It was more than one could bear.

He had gone away the next day, and stayed away for two full weeks.

Nothing had been heard of the chalice. Dupre's would reveal nothing more to the press inquiries than that it had been purchased by a private collector who wished to remain anonymous.

Dupre's, Frederik was delighted to observe, had troubles of its own. Morgan St. James had been indicted for attempted murder on the evidence of Miss Kunimara. His plea was temporary insanity, and the plea did not convince the jury. St. James had been sentenced to six years of imprisonment. The charge of attempted murder was all that could be proven. If the duke were apprehended, he would be tried for the deaths of Felix Dupre, Carla di Cavolfiore, and the silversmith Tauranac. But the duke, it seemed, had fled beyond extradition. No hint of the faked chalice was allowed to reach the public. Dupre's claimed—and rightly, von Kronholtz was convinced—that the item they had sold for more than six million dollars was the original.

Von Kronholtz stood on a street corner in the rain, thinking of the chalice and cursing Dorothy Dutton.

Where had she been, bitch, when he needed her?

He had seen very little of Dorothy in the last two years. She traveled a great deal, as did he. And now, this very damnable afternoon in the rain and no taxicabs, she had summoned him. Make no mistake, when you are a curator of New York's greatest museum, an invitation from a collector like Dorothy Dutton is definitely a summons. Rain or no rain.

He was thoroughly damp by the time an ancient yellow Checker crept up to the curb. He thought of the chalice, of

Dorothy, of the limit imposed on him by the trustees. Six million had seemed a generous limit. No one thought it would go over five. Even four and a half might have seemed adequate. Von Kronholtz had not given up on the cup. It was someplace. He would find out where. He would do whatever seemed necessary to secure the chalice for his museum.

The cab pulled up to the curb. Von Kronholtz undertipped the driver and got out. The butler opened Dorothy's door and escorted Frederik upstairs to her boudoir, just as he had done on the last occasion. How much everything had changed since then! What hopes had been dashed. He tried to arrange a smile on his face. The butler knocked and opened the door.

The room was as he remembered it.

Dorothy Dutton stood in the center of the room, all in black. She wore no jewelry. Her hair was simply arranged, pulled back severely. She seemed to have no makeup on. She's either in mourning, thought von Kronholtz, or she has become some kind of a lay nun.

"Frederik," she said. It was a statement, not a greeting.

He came to kiss her. She turned away.

"My dear," he said, "is something wrong?"

"Ah, Frederik, I have failed you. Myself. I've failed us all."

She turned suddenly, dramatically, and with a sweeping gesture of her black-clad arm pointed toward the altar. He remembered the altar: a small dark oak Renaissance cabinet covered with old wine-colored silk velvet. On it were two candlesticks. And the Winchcombe Chalice.

Von Kronholtz simply stared at it, boggling. He wanted to kill Dorothy Dutton, to take her scrawny neck between his hands and twist it until the life went right out of her. He did not dare to speak for fear of what he might say. To have been put through two years of brutal suffering and humiliation on account of this crazy woman's whim was almost too much to contemplate. He felt her thin hand on his arm. He shuddered. It was like being touched by a snake.

"Please, Frederik," she said, suddenly a little girl again, "don't hate me. It's just that you did your job too well, describing the chalice, its history, the symbolism of it. You made me want it for myself, Frederik dear, and that was a most unworthy thing of me to do."

"But you . . ."

"Yes," she said from someplace far away, her voice a dim echo. "I had someone there bidding for me. Against you, against the others. Absolutely without reserve."

She left his side and walked to the altar and picked up the goblet. "Here," she said, "it is yours now. The museum's. A free gift from me."

"Dorothy!"

"You see," she went on. "once I had it, I thought . . . Oh, I thought very selfish things, Frederik—I thought that its grace would somehow become mine, that I would be the better for owning it."

He listened in a daze. Six million, three hundred thousand dollars' worth of spiritual experimentation with one of the world's greatest art objects. The woman was certifiable.

"Alas," she went on, "it was not to be."

"Dorothy," he said finally, fighting for control, "you are sure you want to do this—make this amazing gesture?"

"Oh, yes. Yes!"

He looked at her, holding tightly to the chalice. "Well, my dear, you will be remembered forever. We must, of course, execute the appropriate papers."

"Done, done, dear Frederik. I have them all here."

She went to her desk and produced a bulky manila envelope. He took it. She went to a closet and returned with an oblong leather box clasped in brass. It had a brass handle on its top. She opened the box. Inside was a fitted, velvet-lined recess that had been specially made to accommodate the Winchcombe Chalice. She set the case on the altar. Von Kronholtz gently put the chalice into its niche in the deep green velvet interior of the case. He closed the top, clicked the brass locks, and picked up the case by its finely wrought handle.

"Well, Dorothy," he said, exhausted from the emotional drain of his experience, "I hardly know what to say. 'Thank you' is scarcely adequate, is it?"

"No one," she said, "should own such a thing. It belongs to all of us, to the world. And to God."

"I must get this to the museum before it closes."

"Good-bye, then, dear Frederik. And I *am* sorry."

"You did what you had to, Dorothy. And you may be right. Perhaps no one should own the Winchcombe Chalice."

"Take care of it, Frederik."

"Of that, Dorothy, you may be very sure."

This time she let him kiss her, just a brush of his lips on her dry cheek. And then he was gone.

It was still raining. Dorothy's limousine was at the door. It took von Kronholtz swiftly uptown to the museum. He did not open the leather case in the big silent car. He carried it to his office, set it on his desk, and then slowly unclasped the twin locks.

He lifted out the chalice and stood it on his desk. The chase was over, then. The prize was won. He felt drained, empty, a little sad. Dorothy was right. No one could own it, any more than you could own a sunset, or the wind. Von Kronholtz ran his fingers over the intricately carved gold vines, leaves, and grapes, and the rubies in their ancient bezel.

Then he smiled, and reached for the telephone.

ABOUT THE AUTHOR

Tom Murphy is a vice-president
of the New York advertising company,
Bozell & Jacobs. His previous
novels are BALLET!,
ASPEN INCIDENT, and LILY CIGAR.